THE SAUCIER'S BONES

Bobo Blankson, MD

Illustrated by Debi Hammond
Cover Illustration by Tom Norris

www.thesauciersbones.com

This is a work of fiction. Names, characters, businesses, organiza-
tions, places, events, and incidents either are the product of the author's
imagination or are used fictitiously. Any resemblance to actual persons,
living or dead, events, or locales is entirely coincidental.

Layout by Tom Norris.

ISBN 978-0692539071

This book is dedicated to Amy, Christiana, Gabriella, and Kobi Lyn. But especially Ana. If she had never uttered the words, "Hairy Pasta", this project would have never been born.

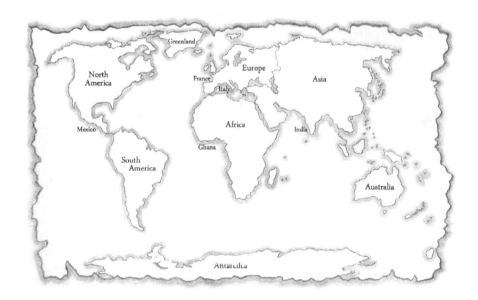

In days to come expect a change
Italian food will not be the same
More fat, more salt, vegetables few
Unhealthy choices, through and through

An evil lurks along our shores
A sickness rotten to the core
It slowly grows, disguised, a mole
To own your body, soon, your soul

But there will come from Italia's loin
A native son to cure those who dare join
This Master Chef with a bacchetta magica
His hair will be tutti tipi di pasta!

He could save us all from wicked food
Restore the kitchen to all that's good
An epic war over arteries and veins
Should he lose? Our world goes down in flames.

Della Morta, venerated Italian chef, on her deathbed

Table of Contents

TABLE OF RECIPES

Antipasto

(the Appetizer   the First Course)

Recipe #1
How to read a Jerry Pasta book

Read this book like you're eating a great meal. If people around you don't hear mmmms, and ooohs, and ahhhs as you read, they'll assume you're not enjoying it, that the flavor's not quite right, that it needs some salt, a little more spice. If that is the case, follow these easy steps:

Stop reading immediately, and put the book down.

Find the nearest ten- or eleven-year-old (boy or girl, doesn't matter)

Mimic their every word and deed for at least ten minutes.

Resume reading.

You should now find your pages freshly seasoned with just the right amount of zest. And, please, feel free to stop and burp at regular intervals; these pages may be tough to swallow at times. But I assure you that in the end, your hunger will be satisfied. Though if my instincts serve me right, you'll probably ask for seconds.

Chapter 1

Camp RSVP

The invitation to Presto Pesto's International School of Culinary Excellence was hand-delivered in an envelope fashioned like a cannoli, one of Jerry Pasta's favorite desserts. However, instead of creamy, white, mouth-watering filling inside a flaky pastry, Jerry found a neatly folded sheet of glossy stationary paper stuffed inside a beige, pockmarked scroll. He cradled the unwrapped invitation in his hands as he backed away from the front door, eagerly consuming the words on the off-white paper as quickly as he would a bowl of *cioccolato* gelato.

Jerry wasn't the only one who received a fancy invitation. Everyone offered a spot at Presto Pesto's received a gourmet invitation fashioned to represent his or her country of origin. Jerry later found out that his America friends received a rolled-up brown invitation that looked like a hot dog. Nothing screams "America!" like an all-beef Ballpark weiner in a foot-long paper bun...so the invitation designers thought.

With just his scrawny legs and peripheral vision to guide him, Jerry burst into the kitchen, startling his parents who were busy preparing dinner. "Mamma! Papa! I've been selected to go to Pesto's this summer! I didn't think I could go until I was twelve!" he cried, finally looking up from the invitation.

"Congratulations, Jerry!" Toni Pasta exclaimed, making an about-face from his cooking at the stovetop. Standing by the refridgerator, Olive Pasta raised her hands to her mouth, her brown eyes wide with surprise. Toni genuinely shared his son's excitement . . . but he knew the invitation was coming. In fact, only weeks prior, Toni and Olive Pasta had hesitantly agreed amongst themselves to allow Jerry to attend the prestigious cooking school that took only one hundred children from around the world each year.

But this was not the first time Jerry had been formally invited to culinary camp. The three previous years' invitations sat in an old size 10 shoebox at the back of Toni's closet.

For the unfamiliar, "culinary" is just a fancy word for "cooking." And for most teens, this combination of summer school and summer camp was a little bit weird. Summer camp is fun. Summer school? Not so much. You'd have to enjoy cooking more than a smidge to spend a whole month of summer halfway across the globe at culinary school/camp.

Jerry *enjoyed* cooking . . . like a cat enjoys catnip, like a teen enjoys texting. Though camp was still three months away, he did what any eleven-year-old would do: he abandoned the cannoli-styled invitation on the kitchen table and dashed to his computer to pore over the website. He only needed to type in the first few letters of the URL before the computer auto-completed "www.prestopestos.org"—he'd been to the site hundreds of times, so the computer knew his intentions as well as he did himself. He scanned through the "About Us" link first, relishing every morsel of basic information about the camp. The culinary school was located in the tiny coastal town of Monterubbiano, a mere eight miles from the Adriatic Sea. Jerry and his family lived in Rome, and his abbreviated life's travels had only taken him as far as other big cities in Italy (Bologna, Venice, Milan) for cooking competitions. So an opportunity to spend some time away from the hustle and bustle of city life sounded relaxing. And a summer on the Italian countryside was a runner's dream!

Eyes glued to the monitor, Jerry scrolled down to the bottom of the page. The posted minimum age requirement of twelve had always

seemed like an ETERNITY of time away. *They've made an exception for me!* Jerry exulted, unaware that a minimum age ensured the camp enrolled mature young adults, not thumb-sucking preteens who would cry the minute their parents dropped them off. Overnight summer camp is a big deal; it's the first time most adolescents spend extended time away from parents—much to the glee of parents who wouldn't otherwise know what do with them when school lets out for the summer. And much to the glee of teens who know *exactly* what to do with their parents after nine months of "do your homework!" and "do your chores!" and "stop, for the hundredth time, teasing your sister!"

But since, generally speaking, parents wouldn't let their kids fly by themselves before age thirteen, most first-year campers at Presto Pesto's were at least that age, some even fourteen.

Jerry could still hear his parents in the kitchen marveling at the ingenuity of the pastry invitation—living in a two-bedroom apartment meant you could hear everything from any room. Smiling to himself, Jerry clicked on the website's "Cost" tab. His eyes widened . . . his smile faded . . . and in an instant, the five-hundred square foot apartment felt even smaller. As many times as he had visited the website, this was the first time Jerry had actually considered how much camp would cost his parents. The invitation had made his dream to become a Master Chef a reality. But the reality was . . .

Olive Pasta hadn't worked consistently for a long time, given her struggles with her depression. Substitute teaching pay hardly covered the family expenses.

Toni was a completely different story.

Antonino "Toni" Pasta was one of the most infamous graduates of Presto Pesto's International School of Culinary Excellence. Being "infamous" might be a good thing for a criminal. Not so much for a Master Chef.

In Italy—heck, in most of Europe, being a Master Chef was like being a professional athlete in America. High-profile. Minimum six-digit salary. Who wouldn't want to be a Master Chef? "Infamous" Master Chef Toni Pasta graduated near the bottom of his class, his educational days at Pesto's marred by frequent cooking mishaps. But the incident that defined his career came after graduation. Toni Pasta's very high-profile job was that of chef for the Italian national football (soccer, to you American readers) team, which was like being the chef for the New York Yankees or the Los Angeles Lakers. It was a job he was lucky to get, considering his less-than-stellar standing at Presto Pesto's. But, hey—a Master Chef is a Master Chef. There were no bad jobs waiting for a Pesto's student upon graduating. All seemed well until the team came down with food poisoning before the 1994 World Cup final, Toni blamed for their stunning loss. Shamed by this outcome, he left Italy for a life of much desired anonymity in America, New York City being the perfect place to start anew. There he met and married Olivia Jackson, returning to Italy nearly a decade later only because of his desire to raise Jerry amongst Italian relatives. Toni still enjoyed cooking at home for family and close friends, but he especially loved teaching Jerry how to cook.

Toni had been content with his current far-from-glamorous job as cook for a local middle school—that is, until he was laid off when the struggles of the Italian economy forced budget cuts in every sector. So instead of warm, school-provided meals, parents were instructed to send their kids with sack lunches, leaving Toni out of a job until the school district's finances improved. "School-lunch man" wasn't the career he had envisioned for himself after graduating from one of the world's most prestigious culinary schools. But he needed to pay the bills, including Olive's costly medical prescriptions. And culinary camp was far from free.

Staring at the large number on the screen in front of him, Jerry gulped and knew what he had to do. He rose from his computer, his hand lingering on the mouse for a few precious seconds. He was midway down the hall when he heard his parents whispering in the kitchen, their voices anxious.

"It's an enormous amount of pressure to put on him, Toni. How many times a day do you think someone will remind him of the prophecy—or comment on his hair?"

"Olive, we can't baby him forever. People will likely tease him for the rest of his life about his hair. And only the fanatics out there believe in that prophecy. A 'savior-y' chef with hair 'like the finest pasta'? A food hero? I am not the only one who thought old Della Morta was a few links short of a sausage chain, if you know what I mean. *Dio accolga la sua anima*—God rest her soul."

Jerry had heard about "the prophecy" like he had heard about Bigfoot, the Lochness Monster—as far as he knew, it was more legend or myth than anything else. But that didn't stop adults from believing it. None of the kids at school had ever referenced the prophecy in Jerry's presence—though they had never missed an opportunity to make fun

7

of his hair. His hair that was made out of pasta. That bears repeating: Jerry's hair was actual, real pasta. Even Jerry didn't know what to think these days. Every once in a while, while walking in public, an adult would try to touch Jerry's hair as if it was some religious relic—inappropriate and freaky. Imagine little old ladies, pupils fixed, arms extended zombie-style, muttering in Italian under their breath as they reached for Jerry's pasta locks...yeah, *frrreaky*. Such weird behavior convinced Jerry to try to keep his hair covered in public. But this was the first time he had ever heard his own parents talk about the prophecy.

Olive's voice grew more frantic. "And do you think he'll be safe? I can't lose him, Toni, I can't. You Pasta males seem to be plagued with the accident curse. Jerry is lucky to be alive and not horribly disfigured. I mean, I left him alone in the kitchen for less than thirty seconds. *Less than thirty seconds!* And that was all the time it took for him to climb up onto the stove and pull that forty-pound wrought-iron pot full of piping-hot spaghetti onto his gorgeous head of curly black hair. I know he's not two-years-old anymore, but he's still my baby!"

Jerry could hear his dad consoling his mother over muffled sobs. Any little thing made her cry these days—smushed spiders, overcast skies, losing at board games; she was more sensitive than a sunburned back. But Jerry just chalked it up to her depression (her "unhappy days" she called them), something he'd known her to have his whole life, but he was pretty sure became a more regular occurrence after "the accident" that left him with pasta for hair. And whenever she got supersensitive like this, it meant one thing: *Mamma hadn't been taking her medicine.*

Toni grabbed Olive by the hands and leaned in. "Olive, I've said it a million times. It's more my fault than yours. It was *my* dinner party for old Presto Pesto's friends," he said, pulling their joined hands to his chest. "*I* should have been the one greeting new arrivals, but I was too busy socializing with the guests already there. And Jerry was too smart for his own good." Tony flashed a grim smile and shook his head. "He probably thought the pasta was overcooking, so he was just trying to help. Stop blaming yourself."

But Olivia had never forgiven herself. So she rarely let her Jeremiah out of her sight. It was a wonder he was even able to be as active as he was: volunteering at local food pantries, actively participating in his church youth group, successfully running on his school's track team (hence, his daily morning runs—and about the only time his mother *wasn't* with him).

"Jeremiah will be perfectly safe, Olive. You know Alberto Dente and I have been friends for a long time. Al's given me every assur—."

"But wh-wh-what about . . . M-M-M-Moldy Coeur?"

It was hard to hear Olive's whispers through the sobs; Jerry tiptoed closer to the kitchen to catch the words more easily.

"He's g-g-got his . . . fingers deep into the school's p-p-pockets, with all that m-m-money he's been reeling in w-w-with his fast-food chain. Every t-t-time I . . . hear that stupid 'Fasta Pasta' j-j-jingle, I want to throw up. And s-s-since the accident at the d-d-dinner party, I . . . don't w-w-want that man . . . anywhere n-n-near my son. I . . . don't want Jerry p-p-put in any . . . danger."

What could be dangerous at cooking camp? An icy chill ran down Jerry's spine. The name Moldy Coeur was new to him though. He couldn't understand why his mom would be so concerned with some school donor—and the crying made everything sound worse than it actually was. *Was this Coeur guy really such a bad person?*

"Olive, I promise you that I will personally bring Jerry home from camp if there's any hint of danger. I'll make him write home every week to keep us informed. I'll *telefonare* Al Dente daily if I have to. Frankly, I'm more worried that Jerry won't be able to handle the pressure of being around older kids."

He'd heard enough. Jerry took a deep cleansing breath and cleared his throat before striding into the kitchen, acting as if he hadn't heard a thing. His parents quickly rose from their hunched positions over the kitchen table—his father had a reassuring arm around his mother's shoulders—and broke into wide smiles. Olive discreetly backhanded the tears on her cheeks.

"There's our future Master Chef!" Toni exclaimed, his arms spread wide and inviting, the tinge of trepidation previously in his voice gone completely. "Have you packed yet? Camp is only two months away!" he quipped. Toni quickly dusted the flour off his apron before pulling Jerry in for a hug.

"Three months away, Papa," said Jerry, correcting his dad about the particulars.

In Toni's embrace, Jerry could sniff out exactly what the family was having for dinner: veal parmesan with homemade fettuccini. *Yummmm . . . one of my favorites.* Lifting his head away from his dad's chest, Jerry immediately remembered his original reason for making his way to the kitchen. Given his mother's reservations, Jerry felt his timing was perfect.

"Actually, Papa," Jerry began, taking a step away from his dad into the middle of the cramped kitchen, eyes to the floor, "I was thinking that maybe we should wait until you get your job back. Camp is so expen—"

"Jerry, didn't you see the back of the invitation? You've been granted an all-expenses paid scholarship from an anonymous donor!" Toni picked the invitation up from the table and flipped it over, proudly revealing the text Jerry had missed on the opposite side. "I wish we knew who to thank for this generosity. But thank you, Jerry, for being thoughtful as always. Your mother and I are hoping some temp jobs open up this summer so we can send you off to camp with a little extra spending *denaro.*"

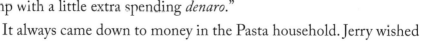

It always came down to money in the Pasta household. Jerry wished his parents could enjoy all the nice things he saw other kids' parents doing: extravagant vacations, fancy restaurant dinners, frequent movies nights. Jerry honestly believed that Presto Pesto's would be his ticket to a new life for himself *and* his parents. It was the opportunity of a lifetime; training over four years (the majority of classes in the summer) that would lead to "Master Chef" status *before* the age of eighteen! (If you're reading this thinking that four summers isn't enough time to become a Master Chef, think again. Some eight hours of cooking instruction a day, five days a week for four weeks, adding up to one hundred and sixty hours per summer times four summers… essentially totaling over six hundred hours of culinary education, not to mention the weekly competency exams, the online exams during the regular school year, and the cooking externships that proved you actually had legitimate skills! Culinary school is no joke.) Jerry's income from being a Master Chef would be enough to support the entire family. They could even take that long-desired trip to America to visit his mother's family.

"I had no idea about the scholarship Papa! That's great news! *Grande!*" Jerry forced a smile and tried to sound excited despite the turmoil brewing in his head. It felt like there was even more pressure now. *Did someone out there expect me to be some amazing chef from the get-go? Is that why I got a full scholarship?*

Let's be honest, though. Even at his tender age, Jerry Pasta was no slouch in the kitchen. When he made his first five-course meal at the age of six, his parents knew it was time to let him branch out and take his cooking skills on the road. He entered local cooking competitions, and in his first one (yes, at age six), he competed against adults and *won*. And in the subsequent years, he progressed regionally and nationally; it seemed like everything "The Boy with Pasta Hair" cooked at these amateur contests turned to gold: gold medals, gold ribbons, gold trophies. . . . But graduating from Pesto's was the only way to finally be taken seriously as a chef, not just a kid with goofy hair, a novelty. A Pesto's education would truly legitimize (and refine) his cooking skills; it would bring back to the Pasta name the honor it deserved—every hiccup from his dad's tarnished reputation would be forgotten. A fresh start.

"I just want to make you two proud," Jerry said. "What if I screw up?"

"Jerry, my angel, you're there to learn." Olive had quickly pulled herself together, though her reddened eyes matched the color of her blouse to perfection. "Don't worry about messing up. If you were already a Master Chef, there'd be no need to send you to camp. And, besides, you know we love you no matter what."

Jerry rolled his eyes; he hated it when his mom called him her angel. He knew it was a veiled reference to his hair. His mother often tried to soothe him by stroking his head gently and saying, "Your angel hair is perfect, my son, don't listen to those mean kids at school".

To which Jerry would reply, "But, Mamma, it's not angel hair, it's spaghetti. Or rigatoni or tortellini *per amor di Dio*."

In his toddler and elementary years, Jerry rarely paid attention to his pasta hair. When people pointed at him and exclaimed "how cute!", he just accepted the praise and kept picking his nose (or whatever five-year-olds do when they're deliberately not paying attention to adults). But then at age six, things changed. Jerry became more self-aware. His pasta hair might have still been cute, but it was drawing more and more attention. Jerry had grown quite tired of explaining to everyone why he had pasta for hair. You try telling someone that you poured boiling spaghetti on your head as a toddler and by some miracle your face didn't get horribly burned, but the pasta *did* burn the real hair off your scalp and from that point on became your actual hair—then watch for their reac-

*for God's sake

tion. Are they laughing because it sounds utterly ridiculous or because there's no better explanation for why you have pasta for hair?! Half the time, kids thought Jerry was pulling a fast one on them until they yanked his hair, followed by painful screaming, followed by a raised fist, followed by a furious chase, followed by more laughter . . . you get the picture.

So at the ripe age of six, Jerry decided he'd had enough. When he tried to shave the pasta hair off completely, the real comedy began. The good news is that his hair grew back. The bad news is that it always grew back as pasta! As *different* pastas—and it was completely unpredictable what kind of pasta would grow next or how long he would have that variety!

Clearly, this wasn't ordinary pasta.

Imagine the embarrassment the day before his seventh birthday party when he shaved his "hair" (without his mother's permission, of course), hoping to wake up the next day bald, or at least with a crewcut spaghetti hairdo (much easier to hide under a baseball cap), but instead Jerry woke up with a head full of bowtie pasta!

"*Ridicolo!* Farfalle pasta on my birthday with my three best friends coming over?! You have got to be kidding!!!!!"

For years, he devised ways of hiding his hair or at least making it less conspicuous. He tried wearing caps. He tried tying it in bows. He tried braids, dreadlocks, cornrows, you name it. Some hairdos looked more natural than others; you couldn't even tell it was pasta hair unless you were up close and personal. Sometimes, without even cutting it, Jerry's hair would change overnight. He'd go to bed rotini and wake up penne!

So in spite of her use of the pet name "Angel," Olivia Pasta was the best mom a boy could ever have—Jerry knew that she meant well, even if she was a bit smothering at times. He could sense his mother's anxiety but opted to press her no further about her concerns about camp. He knew he would be going to camp on a short leash, and it seemed as if his parents almost *expected* something bad to happen to him while at camp, whether by accident or at the hands of the older, bigger campers. *Best not to say or ask anything that might make them change their minds*, Jerry thought to himself.

So he hugged his parents and sat down in his usual seat at the kitchen roundtable. His dad placed a hearty helping of steaming veal and cheesy fettucini in front of him, sending Jerry's salivary glands into a frenzy. Jerry could hardly control himself as his father brought two more plates to the table then sat down. The three joined hands and Olive offered a simple grace, careful to mention gratefulness for the wonderful opportunity ahead for Jerry. Then the family engaged in an activity they had done *together* everyday of Jerry's life, as long as he could remember: they ate. And while they ate, they looked into each other's eyes, laughed at terrible jokes, shared stories about each other's day, made plans for the upcoming week. The bellowing worries of the day were drowned out completely, lost in the din of forks and knives scraping plates, and sounds of mmmms and ahhhhs from a meal thoroughly enjoyed.

After dinner and dishwashing, Jerry went back to his room, cannoli invitation in hand. He carefully taped the invitation over the headboard of his bed so that camp would be the first and last thing on his mind every day.

The time between receiving the pastry invitation and the start of camp went by quickly. Jerry had faithfully collected the short list of cooking supplies needed for a successful stay: a ladle, grater, whisk, measuring cups for both dry and wet ingredients, and appropriate headwear. (Nobody wanted hair in their food—though Jerry's hair didn't taste so bad; he'd tried it a couple of times, and it tasted like regular pasta to him).

Toni gifted Jerry with a ladle that had been passed down in the family for generations. It was brown, about a foot long, well-worn but sturdy. The handle was slightly weighted toward the bowl end but retained its lightness and was easily manipulated. It gave Jerry great pride to know he was using something that generations of Pastas had used to create culinary delights. The measuring cups were standard fare. But the headwear—oh, where to begin?

Due to Jerry's, um, condition, he had quite a collection of head accoutrements (accessories, to be clear). Berets, baseball caps, chef's hats—all had been used to tame the pasta locks. And Jerry was going to bring all of them because what he chose to wear (if anything at all) depended entirely on the pasta shape his hair decided to take on any given day.

Toni was a little concerned. "So are you really going to take that whole *valigia*... errrr ... suitcase ... of headwear?"

Jerry defiantly stared back at his dad, both index fingers pointed accusingly at his head. "*You* try accessorizing linguini on Monday, tortellini on Tuesday, and macaroni on Wednesday with one hat!"

That was the last time Toni questioned Jerry's hair-care plan.

Chapter 2

Father Like Son

The Pasta family's 1998 Fiat Multipla lumbered into the Presto Pesto's campground parking lot at 11:55 a.m. on Sunday morning, precisely five minutes before the noon arrival deadline. Why an arrival deadline for cooking school? you might wonder. The school's directors wanted to make a clear point: timeliness was a core principle in cooking. A minute could make the difference between perfect pasta and chewy pasta. Between over-easy eggs and overcooked eggs. Between a medium-rare steak and a slab of rubber. So while five minutes early was cutting it close, it was still good enough, though Jerry could have lived without the anxiety and extra perspiration—sweat made his noodle-hair glisten. *Gross!* The Fiat's ineffective air-conditioning, combined with the humid weather, left Jerry feeling like an oven-baked casserole—and from the neck up like undrained linguini. Jerry wiped the sweat off of his brow with the sleeve of his red and blue striped t-shirt. He looked down at his white cargo shorts and silently cursed at his mother. She'd insisted he wear white shorts to complete his "Italian-favored" appearance, and Jerry was sure these shorts guaranteed two things: 1) every camper would be able to see-through to his LEGO® print underwear and 2) the shorts would be brown by the end of the day because what 11-year-old boy (or boy of any age) can keep white shorts clean for an ENTIRE day?

Most of the other ninety-nine campers had already arrived and were completing registration. While Jerry's father got the gear out of the car (terrible with good-byes, Olive had declined coming), Jerry walked briskly to the back of the registration line, standing behind a stocky dark-skinned boy wearing a crimson T-shirt, khaki shorts, and a backward-facing red baseball cap emblazoned with a cursive, white *A*.

Stepping out of his comfort zone, Jerry timidly tapped the boy on the shoulder and announced, "Hi, I'm Jeremiah Pasta. What's your name?"

The kid beneath the red cap slowly turned around, caught sight of Jerry's hair, and did little to hide his surprise as noted by the first words out of his mouth.

"Nice wig! You have *got* to tell me where you bought that! Geez, is that *real* spaghetti?!"

Before Jerry could reply, the kid continued with another outpouring of words.

"Oh, hey," he continued, right hand extended, "I'm Kwabena Louis Gyan, but my friends call me Louie G. Are you from Italy? I grew up in the States. United States. Alabama, actually. But you could tell from my hat, right? My family is from Ghana, a tiny country in West Africa; hence the peculiar first and last name, and hence the nickname 'Louie G.'" He paused to give a big grin, then continued without taking any apparent breath. "Where are you from, Jeremy? Or is it Jerry?—like the curls? Your hair is off the hook . . . it's awesome! Ready to start camp?"

This kid is talking so fast, Jerry had to remind himself to breathe . . . and to let go of the hand he was shaking. This "Louie G" was quite the character. *Maybe a good person to be friends with: quirky enough to distract others away from my pasta hair,* Jerry told himself. *Though my hair was the first thing he noticed, no surprise there.*

"Ummm . . . *molto lieto*—nice to meet you, Louie G," Jerry began. "It's Jerry—short for Jeremiah, not Jeremy—and I'm from Roma—Rome—so I didn't have to travel nearly as far as you to get here. And, yes, I am excited about camp but a little nervous about what to expect today. Do you have any idea?"

Louie G grinned back at Jerry. "First, let me say that I love how you say my name—with that 'Italian rhythm and flavor.' Gives me goose-bumps! And your English is really good—you sound kinda American, like you grew up on the East Coast or something. Second, I—"

"*Next!*" A loud, deep-pitched voice interrupted Louie G midsentence.

"Let's talk after registration," Louie G said quickly as he turned around to face the booming voice.

Jerry looked at the man who had spoken. He was portly, seated in a metal folding chair entirely too small for him at the center of a long table. The man was surrounded by aides scurrying around to file paperwork, review medical records, and generally assist with every aspect of the check-in process. Jerry looked up to find his father was now standing beside him.

Toni nudged him and whispered, "That's Alberto Dente, head culinary administrator at the school. Al was one of my campmates here years ago! He'll take good care of you, I promise."

Great! Papa has an extra set of eyes here at camp! The sarcastic thought briefly ran through Jerry's head and then tripped as if its shoelaces were tied together as his mind quickly changed gears. Jerry suddenly remembered his parents' hushed kitchen conversation a few months before. Aside from his father's brief mention of the name Al Dente, Toni had never really talked about his own experiences at camp at all. Everything Jerry knew about his father's time at Presto Pesto's had come from his grandparents or other relatives who often used stories of Toni's camp mishaps to brighten dull conversations. Boring Pasta family gatherings were only a Toni story away from turning into a barrel of laughs at Toni's—and, by extension, Jerry's—expense, unfortunately. (The cousins in particular found the stories about Uncle Toni especially amusing and teased Jerry to no end about his inept father.)

While Jerry was lost in thought, Louie G had completed registration and headed to the edge of the pavilion, where the other campers were gathering.

"See you in a few," Louie G yelled over his shoulder as he strode across the lawn.

Jerry nodded in reply, then took a few steps forward and found himself face-to-face with the man he now knew as Alberto Dente. Al Dente's yellow double-breasted suit, red vest, and white ruffled shirt did little to distract from his large frame. But his graying hair gave him an air of respectability, and his large smiling brown eyes and rosy cheeks were quite welcoming. To Jerry, appreciating all the layers of clothing, personality and, uh, plumpness, Al Dente was like a walking, talking lasagna. Jerry guessed that if appearance meant anything, Al Dente had probably *eaten* his fair share of lasagna over the years.

"Jerry Pasta! Eet is both a privilege and an honor to-ah finally meet-ah you," he said with an Italian lilt and rhythm, with many of the words in his sentences ending with a tacked-on *ah*. Dente even turned some one-syllable words into two. "Your father has done an excellent job-ah of keeping you out of my reach-ah . . . for better or worse, I suppose. But I knew you'd do the right thing-ah, Toni," he said with a wink at Jerry's father while wagging his sausage-shaped right index finger, "I knew you would-ah. I'll try not to fill-ah the boy's mind with too many crazy ideas, OK? Relax-ah, you've been een the same shoes as-ah your boy . . . take a deep-ah breath-ah."

Toni's face was beet red—though embarrassment, not anger stoked the coloration. He hadn't expected Al Dente to be so upfront or honest, considering the two classmates hadn't spoken for over three years. Three years ago, Al Dente was one of the most vocal critics of the fast-food expansion phenomenon in Italy. With obesity and heart disease on the rise in Italy along with the rest of the world, Al believed Della Morta's thirty-year-old prophecy that someone would "restore balance to the kitchen." Like many others, Al truly believed that Jeremiah Pasta was destined to be this balancing force, and it was he who had pressed Toni to let a mere eight-year-old Jerry attend Pesto's. Toni had found this idea ludicrous and in no uncertain terms chastised Al for trying to push his young child into an endeavor over his head. (Hmmmm . . . pun not intended but c'mon? It's nearly impossible to write about a kid with pasta for hair without accidentally cracking a joke—or three.)

Nonetheless, the camp's invitations were sent year after year, though no further response—verbal or otherwise—came from Al Dente's old friend. Until this year. So it was hard for him to hide his enthusiasm that Jeremiah Pasta had actually arrived for camp at the ripe age of eleven.

Toni reminded Al of his earlier promise to keep Jerry safe. "Jerry's barely old enough to be away from home for four weeks, so I expect you to keep an eye on him. Older children can be cruel, Al, and I want Jerry to have a positive camp experience."

"No need-ah to worry, Toni. The faculty and I will take good-ah care of your son. And I'll personally make sure that a, um, *certain powerful-ah food critic* has nothing to do with Jerry."

The two men exchanged knowing glances while Jerry looked on curiously. But nothing more was said.

Once Jerry's registration paperwork was completed, Al Dente pointed out that the first camp activity had already begun. "Campers are participating een a cheese-ah tasting activity. As I'm sure you know, Jerry, cheese-ah can be an essential element-ah of the culinary experience-ah, and we want all of our campers to appreciate various cheeses from the word *andare!* From the go! So *andare!* Go! Get-ah grating!"

Al Dente chuckled to himself as Jerry hurried toward the edge of the pavilion where other new campers had congregated. Jerry was halfway there when he realized his father was still right behind him. He stopped and wheeled around to face Toni.

"Papa, you can go now. I'll be fine."

Toni let out a resigned sigh. "I don't have to remind you to be careful, Jeremiah," he said sternly. "Remember everything we talked about during our drive here. I expect a letter from you every week, and if there's any trouble, I'll be back to pick you up before you can say *precipitevolissi-mevolmente.*"

"But I can't even say *'precipite*-whatever-you-said.*"

"My point exactly. That means 'as fast as possible,' and I promise to be here as fast as I can if anything goes wrong. *Anything.* But try to have some fun and make some friends, *capisce?*"

"*Capisce,* Papa, I understand. But do you understand that embarrassing me is not going to help me make friends?" He glanced around. "You see anybody else's parents hovering?"

Toni offered up a brief, awkward hug and then began slowly shuffling back to the parking lot, shoulders slumped, head drooped.

Uh-oh, Jerry thought, *I think I've been a bit hard on him.* After all, Jerry was about to follow in his father's footsteps, beginning the journey to becoming a Master Chef. Jerry knew instinctively that in Toni Pasta's mind, this was an opportunity for his son to become everything he wasn't.

Toni was nearing the car when Jerry caught up with him.

"Papa, sorry for being so mean back there."

Toni turned to face his son, an expression of delight replacing the forlorn one.

"I think I'm just worried about embarrassing myself," Jerry admitted.

Toni placed a hand on his son's shoulder, making purposeful eye contact. "Jerry, you will learn so much while you're here. About cooking. About yourself. Just remember to be true to who you are." Poking Jerry gently in the chest with his free hand, Toni added, "Cooking is in your bones. Be original, not an everyday chef."

This time the father-son hug was much more genuine.

Toni Pasta drove away with a huge smile on his face.

Chapter 3

A Grate Beginning

Jerry hurried back to the pavilion, feeling somewhat wistful about his father's departure. But as he drew closer to the cheese-tasting event, any lingering pensive feelings were quickly erased: His nostrils were assailed by *formaggio* . . . yes, the aroma of cheese.

Stepping into the pavilion, he found tables stacked with various cheeses divided by country. The Italian table overflowed with mozzarella, Gorgonzola, Parmesan, ricotta, Asiago, provolone, and pecorino. The "tableau de France" had a cornucopia of that country's bests: Camembert, Roquefort, Brie, Boursin, Munster, Chèvre. Not to be outdone, the United Kingdom table presented an assortment of cheddars and blue cheeses, emitting a fragrance that left Jerry dizzy and drooling. And there were cheeses from other countries featured at smaller tables (Mexican Queso Fresco and Cotija, German Limburger and Butterkase, Spanish Manchego and Garrotxa, to name a few). A brassy voice (part-French, part-Italian, part-British?) broke the silence of this happy cheesy dream.

"OK, everyone! Let the taste testing begin. Points to the student with the most discerning tongue. Grab a blindfold and put it on as you approach the tables. The instructors will then grate or slice a little cheese onto your plates. Since this is a cheese-tasting contest, not a finger-tasting one, we feel it would be poor form to bloody the cheese on the table by slicing it yourselves while unable to see what you're doing—

and, besides, our nurse cannot sew back fingertips."

This morbid humor elicited subdued chuckles from the campers.

"You will then report your guesses to the instructors who will be standing by." How could Jerry not be excited by this contest! Cheeses were one of his specialties . . . somewhat embarrassingly. Cheese had been one of the first things Jerry had tinkered with as "hair gel." He'd tried dozens of cheeses (melted, of course), eventually abandoning the experiment after being made fun of at school for smelling like, as one classmate so succinctly put it, "funky feet." Nicknames such as "Dirty Hairy" and "Stinkaroni" hadn't exactly done wonders for Jerry's self-esteem.

He meandered between tables tasting various cheeses—and not surprisingly answering correctly on each one. At one point at the French table, a lengthy monologue began in Jerry's head: *Hmmm . . . yes . . . this distinct smell, with a hint of ammonia, can only belong to the soft cheese Brie. I remember last year trying to impress Gabriella Sabbatini, a cute girl in my class, who we all called Gabrie, or Brie for short. I thought she might have a thing for her namesake cheese, so I tried using Brie in my hair (which kept my spaghetti bangs out of my eyes really well), hoping to see her at school Monday morning—but she got sick over the weekend and didn't show up at school until Wednesday. I didn't want to wash my hair and lose all that good Brie (it's expensive cheese!), so I left it in until Wednesday. Big mistake. . . . Gabrie was not impressed, and I smelled like Brie for weeks. Everyone thought it was some old cheese I had left in my lunchbox until they noticed the smell was following me around. Don't think Gabrie spoke to me for the rest of the year . . . and come to find out, her favorite cheese was Camembert. Who'd have guessed?* Jerry finished reliving the humiliating moment and of course correctly identified the Brie solely by smell.

At one table, Chef Imran Khan was particularly impressed when Jerry correctly identified paneer, a South Asian cheese made by curdling heated milk with lemon juice or another acidic liquid. A much younger voice standing beside Chef Khan whispered astonishment at Jerry's paneer identification.

"How on earth did you know that? I thought I would be one of the only campers who knew what paneer was. There are only a handful of us from India," the feminine voice with an adorably proper British accent remarked incredulously.

Jerry lifted up his blindfold to behold a beautiful brown-skinned girl with flowing black hair falling gently across her shoulders and a red dot in the middle of her forehead (which he later learned was called a *bindi*). She wore a colorful bejeweled gown (which he later learned was called a sari) and cloth slippers. Jerry guessed she was no more than two years older than he.

"Well, if you're done staring, I'm Marirajah Nera."

"Hello, Marirajah, I'm Jerry Pasta. *Mi scusi* —I mean, I'm sorry—for staring. It's just that I've been so excited meeting new people. And I love the texture of paneer. It's almost like cheesy tofu." Jerry felt his cheeks flush with warmth.

Mari returned the staring favor by blatantly scrutinizing his hair. Looking quizzically at Jerry, hands poised on her hips, she declared, "So, you're Jeremi—", catching herself, "you're forgiven," abruptly completing her sentence before slowly lowering her hands to her sides. "And you appreciate paneer, so I guess we can be friends." Smiling, she added, "And my friends drop the 'rajah.'"

Jerry took that as an invitation to claim a friend, a true victory on the first day of camp. Plus, with his blatant display of exotic hair, how many friends was he really going to make today? He had consciously decided not to wear a hat to registration. He figured it was better to let the *bucatini* out of the bag (ugh, really bad pasta joke) early; sooner or later people would find out he had pasta for hair. What was the point in hiding it? But he appreciated the offer of friendship despite his physical … uh … imperfection? "Thank you, Mari" was Jerry's heartfelt response.

"Why are the stinkiest cheeses the *tastiest* cheeses?" Louie G remarked as he sidled up to Jerry and Mari, licking aged Stilton crumbs off of his fingers. "What other foods smell so bad but taste oh-so-good?"

"Ever had roasted goat shank?"

A large crumb of Stilton fell from Louie G's mouth and landed at Mari's feet. It was his turn to stare. "Yeah, I have! West African-style. But from your exotic looks"—Louie G was giving Mari a good onceover, sly grin on his face—"I'm guessing you're talkin' Indian-style. Allow me to introduce myself. I'm Lou—."

"Attention campers!" yet again, the brassy voice grabbed the campers' attention, "we have a winner in the cheese competition. The highest point scorer was Jerry Pasta. In fact, he scored more points than any first year has ever scored in the Blindfolded Cheese Tasting competition! While this is remarkable, we encourage fair play in all cooking competitions; the instructors will be watching carefully."

Jerry felt his face flush yet again—only this time it was over the insulting implication that he had cheated. Insinuating that Jerry had cheated while congratulating him on winning was both disrespectful and rude. It'd be like telling your older sister on prom night that she looked awesome—for someone headed to a funeral. Now all the students might think Jerry was a cheater. And the fact that they announced that he had the highest score EVER put even more attention on him. Limelight was the last thing Jerry wanted at school or *anywhere* in life, for that matter. Sure, he wanted to be great at cooking. But he also just wanted to fit in with everyone else. It was obvious his hair already made this nearly impossible, and now Captain Brassy Voice had made matters worse.

Jerry felt as if the energy in the room had built up like static on a rubbed balloon; it seemed like a thousand eyes were staring at him at that very moment. If his pasta hair could have stood on end, it would have. Instead, it lay limp, barely swaying.

Suddenly Jerry felt someone slip something between the fingers of his right hand. He swiveled his head to his right but just saw several of his new classmates talking amongst themselves, not even looking his way. Jerry discreetly opened his hand and found a small crimson envelope with no addressee. He turned it over, noting the wax seal on its back. *Very official,* Jerry observed. He waited a few seconds, hoping attention on him had waned, and then delicately broke the seal. The text was simple:

> The Mufia requests a meeting before
> dinner tonight. Meet us at the open pavilion.
> We'll make you an offer you can't refuse.

Confused, Jerry quickly hid the letter behind his back as Louie G and Mari Nera turned to him.

"Nice job in the cheese competition. I hope we get assigned to the same kitchen!" Louie G exclaimed, slapping Jerry playfully on the shoulder. "So you prefer Jerry, not Jeremy, right?" He grinned. "Can't blame you. 'Jeremy' almost always ends up sounding like 'Germy', and unless you're not into hand washing, that nickname kinda sucks. I mean it sucks for someone trying to be a chef at an elite cooking camp. *I'd* think twice about eating food cooked by a kid named 'Germy'. Ok, I-I-I've said enough. And, um, sorry about the wig comment. I, uh, sort of heard from some of the other campers that . . . ." Louie G's voice trailed off.

"No offense taken," Jerry replied. Jerry thought this was the perfect time to explain how he got the name Jeremiah. Olivia Pasta's grandmother, who raised Olivia when her mother unexpectedly died when she was a teenager, had been a deaconess at her church for over forty years. Grandma Ruth was adamant that Olivia's first-born child have a good Biblical name like her mother, Esther. Her suggestions were Habbakuk, Zephaniah, Nahum, Malachi, and Samson. Olivia balked. She loved her granny but found those names completely unpalatable—to use a culinary term. Toni wisely stayed out of the family spat. Until the due date. As the nameless baby crowned, laboring Olivia Pasta screamed to Toni from her St. Vincent's Hospital birthing room bed, "Bring me a Bible!!" Luckily for Toni he found a worn Gideon's in the bottom drawer of the bedside dresser. Olivia, a mop of sweaty black hair covering her clenched eyes, yanked open the book and jabbed her right index finger onto a wafer-thin page. She opened her eyes, honing onto the spot her finger had landed, and stared. When she looked up, a peaceful calm had washed over her.

"His name is Jeremiah."

Jeremiah Pasta, with a head full of curly, ebony hair, arrived seconds later.

"*Mio figlio** . . . Jerry!" Toni squealed, ecstatic.

Jerry was just beginning to explain how his dad was from Italy and his mom was from America when the piercing, brassy voice stopped all conversation for yet a third time.

"We will now hand out the kitchen assignments. These assignments are based on multiple factors: essay responses to questions we sent you after selection, country of origin, the entrance exam score, and faculty discretion. Please take your kitchen assignment seriously. You will belong to this kitchen for the next four summers. We hope you grow to love and respect the tradition from which your kitchen was named. Kitchen assignments are final—no discussion, no exceptions."

The "kitchen" was much more than a place where a camper would cook during the summer. The kitchens were the actual cabins where campers would *live* with each other for the duration of their time at

---

*   My son

summer camp. The kitchens were named after the five "mother" sauces, the basic sauces from which all others are made:

Béchamel (pronounced Beh-kah-mell), a white sauce, whose base is butter and flour cooked in milk

Velouté (pronounced Veh-loo-tay), another white sauce like Béchamel but with the addition of a chicken or fish stock

Espagnole (pronounced Ess-pan-yole), a brown sauce with meat stock as its base

Tomato, a tomato-based red sauce

Mayon-daise (pronounced May-yun-dez), based on combined mayonnaise and hollandaise sauces

Each kitchen took pride in its "mother sauce," even though they were taught about all five mother sauces and were expected to know how to cook each of them by camp's completion.

Every kitchen at Pesto's yearned to win The Toque, an award in the form of a chef's hat given each summer to the highest-performing kitchen. Various cooking competitions were sprinkled throughout the four weeks of camp that pitted the kitchens against each other. The school faculty critiqued meals, and points were awarded to each kitchen accordingly. Occasionally a kitchen might be assigned cooking duties for all the campers and staff, but this never happened during the first week of camp—faculty were terrified of the idea of having to consume meals prepared by rookie chefs. They were more confident that first-year campers would know the difference between rosemary and thyme by the second week of camp.

Annoyed by the frequent interruptions to his conversation, Jerry turned to Mari and whispered, "Who does that obnoxious voice belong to, anyway?"

Mari's face soured as she nodded towards a man standing at a podium at the front of the pavilion. "That's Moldy Coeur," she began with obvious disgust in her voice, "he's a school trustee—one of the people who gives Pesto's a lot of money. The top money givers are designated 'Wards of the School,' so he's known as Ward Moldy Coeur. In return for all the money they give, wards are allowed to participate in many of the school's activities such as registration, kitchen assignments, club sponsorship . . ."

Jerry turned toward the voice and appraised the speaker. Ward Moldy Coeur was a hulking, pot-bellied man with piercing green eyes and jet-black hair that accentuated his pale skin. His face seemed to be stuck in a permanent frown. He gripped the microphone with long yet pudgy fingers. His ankle-length black cloak was fastened at the neck with a silver clasp—perhaps too tightly, contributing to the coarseness of his voice, Jerry theorized. Jerry's visual assessment ended with a shudder, and he was struck by a slight chill in the air that oozed fear mixed with a whiff of familiarity. *So this is who Mamma was talking about.*

"Huh . . . Sounds like you're not a fan of this guy," Jerry whispered to Mari.

"That would be an understatement," she shot back. "I'll tell you more later. He's about to announce the assignments."

Coeur cracked his knuckles loudly and cleared his throat. "Before I read off the kitchen assignments, I would like to announce a special award that will be bestowed at the end of the season." He paused for dramatic effect. "In the past, The Toque has been the pride and desire of every kitchen. Every kitchen has relished the opportunity to claim that they were the best during a given summer. But now there is added motivation. Every member of the winning kitchen will receive a fifty-percent discount in camp fees for next year—needless to say, a sizable monetary saving."

Gasps erupted from the campers.

"Wow! Fifty percent?!" Louis G exclaimed. "Do you know how excited my parents would be if I told them that camp was half price next year? They'd buy me a Playstation *and* an Xbox!" He gazed dreamily off into the distance.

Jerry was speechless. He knew he couldn't expect an anonymous donor to cover his entire summer fee every year (and he couldn't let anyone here know that was the case *this* year), but a discount of that size would make camp much more affordable next year. *Papa might not even have to work weekends.* If he and the rest of his kitchen cooked well this summer, they'd be celebrating a Toque victory (including bragging rights for a year!) *and* winning a sizable monetary prize.

"I wonder if this is just some gimmick to get us to come back next year," Mari scoffed, crossing her arms defiantly. "Imagine all the kids who *aren't* here because they couldn't afford the huge fees. My parents took out a rather large loan to get me here. I'm sure Presto Pesto's is having the same financial woes the rest of the world is having. If campers drop out or don't come back next year, the school loses money."

"Don't be such a cynic, Mari Nera," Louie G countered. "Anyway, my philosophy is, 'Take the money and run.' Who cares why the school is doing it?"

"Well, you might want to rethink your philosophy: Nothing comes free," Mari panned, a look of gloom on her face. "I bet the cost will be made up somewhere else—higher fees next year for everyone else."

"All the more reason to win The Toque, then," Louie G quipped matter-of-factly.

Before the exchange could escalate further (and make Jerry feel any more awkward about his free ride), Ward Moldy Coeur quieted the audience and began methodically reading the kitchen-assignment names in alphabetical order. Despite their quibbling, Jerry was pleased that Louie G and Mari were assigned together to the Mayon-daise Kitchen and hoped he would end up in the same cabin as his two new friends. As Moldy Coeur finished with the "O" names, Jerry took a deep breath in anticipation.

Moldy Coeur appeared to do the same. Whereas the other announcements had been straightforward—"Olumena Abaka, Velouté Kitchen; Suzette Crepe, Béchamel Kitchen; Lumina Foyle, Tomato Kitchen" and so on—Moldy Coeur seemed to pause dramatically for a few extra seconds before reading Jerry's name.

"Jerry Pasta . . . Yes, this was quite a difficult decision. Very high scores on the entrance exam, outstanding essays. Appropriately, he has been assigned to Tomato Kitchen." For such a straight-faced character, Moldy Coeur's face was now unusually expressive, a mixture of elation and utter satisfaction.

At least for a moment.

Because behind him, a throat noisily cleared. "Eh . . . Ward Coeur, there's been a slight-ah change." Al Dente beckoned Coeur over to his side, where they began a private but very animated conversation, Coeur gesturing wildly while Al Dente shook his head and held up his hands disapprovingly, palms outward as if fending off an attack. The conversation abruptly ended, with Dente turning his back to Coeur, who then stormed back to the podium.

Coeur took a moment to regain his composure, pointedly adjusting his cloak and smoothing his unnaturally black hair. The frown had returned.

"There has been a change," Coeur growled. "Regrettably, Jerry Pasta has been reassigned to Mayon-daise Kitchen."

Jerry's heart leaped with excitement that he'd be paired with his new friends. But it quickly dropped as he recycled Moldy Coeur's comment through his head. *"Regrettably?" What could he have meant by that? Were some kitchens better or more desirable than others? And why would Moldy Coeur show kitchen bias? And what happened to "no exceptions" to kitchen assignments? One minute I'm in Tomato, the next I'm in Mayon-daise?*

The rest of the list was read without incident. Jerry couldn't help but wonder what the other campers thought about Coeur's minor meltdown over Jerry's new kitchen assignment. *More limelight . . . heavy on the lime. Could this day be any* more *sour?*

Afterward, there were quiet greetings amongst new kitchen/cab-inmates, and a natural separation by kitchen seemed to immediately occur. Camp aides ushered the campers towards a large table near the pavilion to pick up their official camp gear. No camp T-shirts, shorts and logo-emblazoned water bottles for these eager teenagers. Instead, standard-issue white chef's toques (made from poly/cotton fabric, Velcro back closure), white chef's coats (double-breasted with cloth-covered buttons that matched the color of your kitchen's mother sauce), and cookbooks (individual names embossed in gold on the front). Campers happily thumbed through their cookbook's pages, noting the various basic recipes and margin space for notes.

Louie G held his cookbook high in the air and gazed at his new friends. "Well Mayon-daise crew, thanks to Jerry Pasta, we are already winning the best kitchen competition. Here's to a grate beginning. And that's g-r-a-t-e."

The pun was lost on a few of the campers, but Mari and Jerry giggled quietly—Jerry appreciated the for-once positive attention. For the most part, Jerry thought, aside from a few bitter moments, this *was* a great—and that's g-r-e-a-t—beginning.

Meanwhile, behind the Tomato Kitchen cabin . . .

"Did you deliver the package?" the shadowy figure asked.

"Yeah, I did," the rotund boy answered back curtly. "Didn't see if he opened it though. Why do ya care so much about that kid?"

"Because he's the key to everything."

"That little runt is a key to something? Really, Mister—"

"*Silence!* Your only job is to get him to accept the offer."

"OK, OK. Can I beat him to a pulp if he says no?"

"No! It would be better if he came willingly. He would be unsuspecting—it would make it easier to destroy him. We will turn to physical violence only as a last resort. So, go! Do not try to contact me—it would draw unnecessary attention. I will come to you. Tell no one of our plans."

"What about your promise?"

"Tsk, tsk, young man. First things first. Get me Pasta!"

Chapter 4

Camp Sweet Camp

Toting their cookbooks and chef apparel, Jerry and his new friends headed to the Mayon-daise Kitchen's cabin, where they'd be staying for the next several summers to come. Camp attendance was staggered each summer so that there was no overlap between the various levels of trainees. In fact, after attending for three summers, fourth-year students usually did a three- to six-month externship off-campus, often in another country—but graduation was always held at Pesto's. From the outside, the lodging didn't look like much, resembling a cross between a log cabin and a gingerbread house with a brick chimney visible on the rear wall. Though rustic, simple, the cabin was garnished with colorful flowerbeds, making the hued browns of the exterior wood appear darker and highlighting the bold colors of each petal on every flower.

Jerry's face lit up in surprise as he entered the front door of the cabin; the outside clearly did not do the inside justice. Before him lay the most beautiful kitchen he had ever seen in his life. A large rectangular oak table (seating twenty) dominated the center of the kitchen. To the left of the table was a state-of-the-art stainless-steel stovetop with multiple burners and two side-by-side conventional ovens, also stainless. A large brick oven was carved into the chimney that Jerry had previously noticed. To the right of the table was a stainless-steel refrigerator that was more armoire than fridge, and spacious oak cabinets lined the walls. Copper Calphalon pots and pans hung from racks anchored to the low ceiling.

Mayondaise Cabin

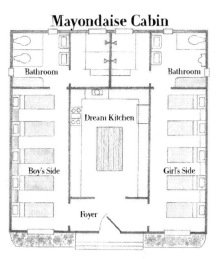

The other campers were as awestruck as Jerry. Everyone had immediately dropped their bags at their feet. "Do all of the other cabins look like this?" one incredulous camper asked. Slowly, some of the campers began to explore, opening the cabinets to find them fully stocked with nonperishables, spices of every variety, and fine dishware. The fridge was filled with fresh vegetables, fruits, and meats—almost anything you could think of. The kitchen was mesmerizing, and it was fittingly constructed to be the centerpiece of the cabin. In fact, they were all so mesmerized by the kitchen facilities that they hadn't yet bothered to look for their sleeping quarters.

A voice crackled over an intercom, interrupting the sounds of elated laughter and cupboard doors opening and closing:

"Campers, this is Alberto Dente, and let me once again welcome you to culinary camp-ah. By now you should have found-ah your cabins.

I suspect that most of you are still-ah standing in the kitchen. There is more to the cabin, I assure you. Please find-ah the male dorm room off-ah to the left of the kitchen, and the female dorm off-ah to the right. Each dorm contains bunk-ah beds, a bathroom, and a shower room."

"Does this guy always sound like this?" Louie G whispered to Jerry. "This is-ah gonna get a little old-ah after a few days! Sheesh."

Jerry quietly chuckled as Al Dente continued. "Linens are in the large closet in each dorm-ah, and some toiletries are also provided—though hopefully you thought to bring-ah your own-ah. This cabin belongs to you. Should you survive this first-ah year of culinary camp-ah, you will return-ah to this same cabin every year until your fourth year, providing a sense of ownership and continuity. But know too that at the end of your camp-ah session, the second-year campers belonging to your respective kitchens will be moving in to begin their own four-week residency. With this in mind-ah, understand-ah that you are responsible for the upkeep of your cabin. The cleanliness of the sleeping areas and bathrooms, the stocking of the refrigerator and pantry—these are all your responsibility. We will provide you with any supplies you request-ah, but the day-to-day affairs will be your own doing. We task-ah you to assign one camper to be the 'Head Chef' of your kitchen, and we recommend various roles be delegated. How you rotate these roles is completely up-ah to you. But your success as chefs will largely depend on how well you organize yourselves and keep-ah your cabins in good order. Good luck-ah. Oh, and dinner will-ah be served promptly every night-ah at six o'clock. So that gives you three hours to get-ah settled in. We will announce the first-ah formal kitchen cooking competition at dinner. Do not-ah be late. Points will be deducted for tardiness."

The next three hours were chaotic. Bunks were quickly claimed. Belongings were put away. Job assignments resulted in bickering and grandstanding. Someone in the cacophony of voices suggested that since Jerry

Pasta had already won points for Mayon-daise Kitchen in the cheese competition that he be given the role of Head Chef.

"He clearly knows about cooking—or at least cheese," one camper affirmed.

"But he's one of the youngest campers here," another camper retorted.

Jerry hated that people could tell he was younger just by looking at him. Who knew there was such a difference between eleven-year-olds and thirteen-year-olds? *Haha, maybe this is all a big prank,* Jerry thought. *Elect the eleven-year-old to do what a thirteen-year-old should be doing, and watch how bad he screws it up.*

A vote was called, and thirty seconds later Jerry found himself Head Chef of the Mayon-daise Kitchen. Louie G and Mari were the first to congratulate him.

"You're going to do great, Jerry!" Mari exclaimed, patting him on his shoulder.

"Eh, I don't know . . . glad one of us is confident," replied Jerry, a pained look on his face. In Jerry's neighborhood, eleven-year-olds that told thirteen-year-olds what to do usually got beaten like cake batter, but it looked like he had no say in the matter. "I guess I'll just have to do my best."

"Hey, you could be the camper cleaning the toilets. Instead you get to delegate that role. Your cup is half full, Jerry. It's all in your point of view."

"Yeah, uh, good point Louie G."

"Only making the point so you *don't* assign me to clean toilets. Pretty please? Tee, hee, hee?" Louie G nervously laughed.

During the thirty minutes before dinnertime, Jerry was prodded into spearheading the rest of the job-distribution effort—everyone had a job to do, including bathroom cleaning (Louie G's wish was granted), sweeping, and dishwashing duty. It soon dawned on Jerry that his job might be the hardest—he would be responsible for arranging any meals the campers didn't have in the main dining hall, which on average was one to two a week. Jerry paused to think about his unemployed father. *Wouldn't Papa have had a better attitude than me? "Be thankful for your job—hard work builds character," he would say.*

At ten minutes to the hour, Jerry feebly announced, "We should be heading to the dining hall for dinner, campers." Only a handful of his cabinmates responded.

He didn't like this feeling of being in charge. He'd never really been in charge of *anything,* except for some meals at home. His father and mother often let him cook for the family, which was more than other eleven-year-olds were probably doing for their families. Jerry knew that it would be tough work convincing himself—more than anyone else—that he was qualified to do the job, but imagining a pep-talk from his dad was helping. Being in charge was character building and would make him stronger—and not the cartoon-kind of strength, where the hero has powers that are always saving others from certain disaster. "Mutant" pasta hair wasn't exactly a superpower. "More like a super annoying power," Jerry whispered to himself. He sure couldn't imagine his weird mane ever coming to anyone's rescue.

"I can do this," he told himself confidently, brushing the spaghetti hair out of his eyes and looking up to the ceiling as if he could see into the heavens. "This is no different than some of the cooking competitions I've been in and won."

He said a quick prayer and mustered the campers more forcefully this time; he knew almost everyone by name now. If he was going to be a successful head kitchen chef, he needed to be the most knowledgeable one in the cabin. While the others were assembling in the cabin's foyer, Jerry scoped out the kitchen in detail, familiarizing himself with the layout and supplies, even beginning to think about the menu he'd serve during the week. He almost felt like a parent. To that end, he was determined to make the Mayon-daise Kitchen home, sweet home—at least for the next four weeks.

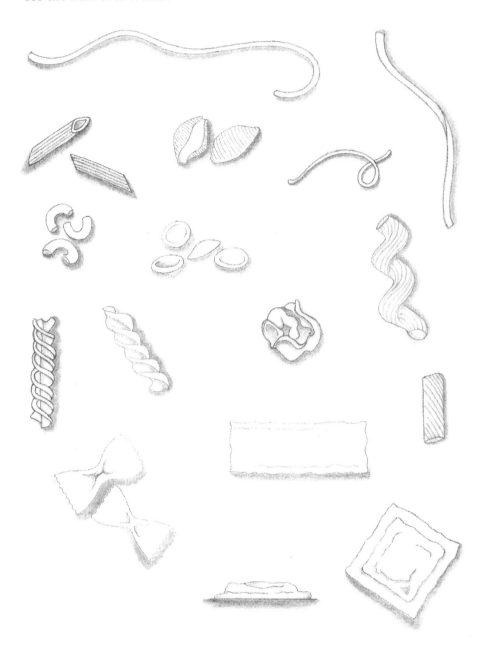

Chapter 5

Missing Ingredients

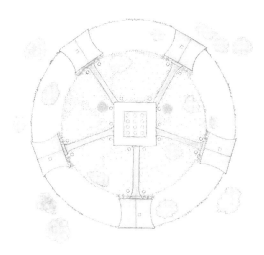

So with their reluctant leader in front, the Mayon-daise Kitcheners left the cabin and made their way to Apley Court, the main campus building, which was in the center of campus. Campus resembled a large wheel, with Apley Court being the hub and paved pathways like spokes leading from the central building to the cabins positioned circularly around the perimeter. The grounds were sparsely wooded, with carefully manicured wedges of green grass separating the cabins from each other. Stately and bountiful, olive and fig trees lined the pathways, lending their sweet scents and fragrances to the pedestrian's journey. In the distance, one could see the jagged and uneven terrain of the rocky coast, but the swirling, cool sea breeze it created provided pleasant relief from the sun's oppressive summer heat.

Unlike the rustic cabins, Apley Court itself was a palatial building modeled after the Palazzo Farnese of the Renaissance era. Its grandiosity seemed to clash with the simplicity of the residential cabins, but the sharp contrast added to the magic of the entire campground. Apley Court included the main dining hall, the classrooms where the campers would learn the culinary arts, *and* the kitchens where the cooking competitions would take place.

As with the cabins, the dining area was the centerpiece of Apley Court. Eaditt Hall was a grand dining space with Calacatta marble flooring, frescoed walls and multiple round oak tables scattered throughout the room. The design of the tables was strategic: campers were to feel like equals, and round tables offered no head position. The tables allowed each camper to make eye contact with every other seated camper—something the faculty believed was an important aspect of eating etiquette.

The Mayon-daise campers arrived two minutes before the appointed hour and distractedly (to Jerry's chagrin) congregated around three tables on the west side of the dining hall, their eyes drawn to the elaborately painted walls that now surrounded them. A deep voice with a distinct English accent issued a terse statement via intercom:

"This is Chef Brit Favreau. Campers, we highly discourage sequestering yourselves based on kitchen. No more than three campers from the same kitchen at one table, please. You need to mingle with other kitchens and get to know each other. And please do not sit in the one chair at each table labeled *I*, which are reserved for your *instructeurs*."

It was tradition to always have at least one instructor seated at each table. The teaching faculty hoped that this strategic inclusion might lead to greater camaraderie between the staff and students, encourage the students to ask questions about cooking, and cut down on rowdy behavior. (Before the instructor-at-the-table tradition was instituted at Presto Pesto's, food fights were quite common at mealtimes. But that shouldn't have surprised the faculty. It's a cooking camp full of hormone-driven, consequence-flaunting teenagers, for crying out loud!)

Jerry, Louie G, and Mari found seats for themselves at a table with five other students and an instructor who nervously stroked the arms of his horn-rimmed spectacles before quickly rising to introduce himself, narrowly missing whacking the edge of the table with his plump belly.

"*Bonsoir* . . . good evening! I am zeh sauce teacher, and I have been doing zis for a few years now. Do not believe any of zeh rumors you have heard about me. My sauces are easy to learn, and I expect you all to be experts by the end of the camp. Oh . . . *pardonnez-moi*, forgive me, I did not introduce myself. My name ees Jo-Guy (pronounced Zho-Gee) Beurre. I will take exception to those of you who insist on calling me 'Yogi Bear.' I yam obviously NOT a character from a silly American cartoon from the 1960s," Beurre stressed in his thick French accent, pushing his glasses farther up the bridge of his nose. "But I yam one of the key ingredients to any sauce worth its salt."

A few of the students giggled, including Jerry, who, drawing from his French-language training at school, gathered that Chef Beurre was referring to his last name, which was French for "butter."

"Furthermore," Chef Beurre raised his chin and continued, "the proper pronunciation of my last name ees more like 'burr' than 'bear.'"

One student boldly emitted a quiet growl.

Another whispered, "He's clearly eaten his fair share of *Butterfingers*."

"*Not funny!*" Chef Beurre roared, slamming a fist on the table and just as quickly recoiling in pain.

The hearty guffaws were quickly followed by muffled coughs and then silence. Jerry wasn't sure why Chef Beurre had taken on such a defensive tone. Maybe he didn't like his name being mocked—Jerry could certainly identify with that.

Dinner was served exactly at six o'clock. The meal—much like those in restaurants—consisted of multiple courses: appetizer (antipasto), salad, entrée, *plat principal* (main course), and dessert. The main course was a lightly sauced baked chicken fricassee with broccoli florets and roasted red peppers on the side. Jerry deemed the chicken rather unspectacular after a few bites, which was more than a little surprising considering this was the preeminent cooking institution in the world; "unspectacular" and "chicken" should never be used in the same sentence at a venue like this. *How could the food be just OK?*

That's when Jerry noticed a nondescript sauceboat in the middle of the table (he glanced around and saw that every table had one, and it seemed that most of the other students hadn't noticed the sauceboats, either). Each of the sauceboats looked rather old and plain, except for some random, letters etched on the sides: UMZOW.

UMZOW? Jerry had never heard of that brand of dishware. He shrugged and reached for the sauceboat, thinking anything would be an improvement on the evening's meal. He poured a liberal helping of this supplemental  cream sauce onto the fowl in front of him and shoveled a forkful into his mouth and . . .

His tastebuds erupted with flavors he had never imagined in combination! Lemon . . . and lime? Pepper . . . thyme . . . tarragon . . . wild mushrooms . . .

Meatballs! (This was Jerry's favorite all-purpose exclamation to himself. There weren't actually meatballs in the sauce.) He felt he'd hit the jackpot! Halfway through devouring his chicken breast, Jerry paused to ask Chef Beurre who had made the sauce.

"Oh, yours truly. Not only do I teach sauces, but I also oversee the making of every sauce in zeh main kitchen. Zeh sauceboat in your hand ees one of dozens that were donated to zeh school over fifty years ago by one of its founders, a true saucier, Karim de la Carème."

Everyone else at the table likewise poured on the sauce, then nodded in happy unison, finishing the chicken on their plates within minutes.

"Great find, Jerry," Louie G muttered, mouth half full. Then he smiled at the instructor. "Chef Beurre, will you teach us how to make sauces this tasty by summer's end?"

Beurre merely smiled enigmatically in response.

The eight campers at the table polished off their meal to the last morsel, continuing to rave about the sauce even as dessert was brought out. Five flavors of gelato were offered: straicciatella, tiramisu, dulce de leche, mascarpone, amaretto. Gelato, for the uninitiated, is an Italian iced dessert much like ice cream but . . . better. You'll just have to try it and see for yourself.

Louie G had never had gelato before, and his reaction was memorable. "This stuff is amazing! It's . . . it's smoother than ice cream. It's beautiful, soft, creamy, and . . . *arrrrgh-hhhh!*"

"You OK?" Jerry was alarmed by Louie G's contorted grimace.

"Brain freeze, Jerry . . . and totally worth it!" Louie G's eyes were now wide with excitement and satisfaction as a toothy grin broke across his face. "Somebody pass the mascar-whatever-you-call-it. It'd be rude to not try each flavor at least once!" he declared.

Everyone at the table laughed and continued savoring, all the while making conversation about where they were from, how old they were— typical meeting-you-for-the-first-time stuff. Jerry was happy to see people enjoying the Italian treat he'd grown up with. He was also eager to learn more about the favorite foods the other campers—especially his new friends Louie G and Mari—relished in their respective countries. A few announcements were made during dessert—schedules would be found back at their cabin kitchens, lights out was at nine o'clock, and other camp logistics—and Chef Beurre announced that he was looking forward to seeing each of the campers in his classroom. It was precisely at this point that Jerry remembered he had forgotten about his pre-dinner meeting invitation.

Meatballs!

Jerry anxiously pulled the now-crumpled cryptic summons from the back pocket of his browning (*sigh*) shorts and reread the ominous text. *An offer I can't refuse, and I forget to show up?!* Jerry grunted in frustration and shoved the letter back into his pocket, trying to refocus on every-thing that had gone well during the day. He wouldn't worry about the "offer" now. He needed to get back to the cabin, find his schedule, and get organized for the next day.

From the front of the dining hall, Al Dente made the last announce-ment of the evening. "The first-ah individual cooking competition is tomorrow morning. The winning recipe will be served as the following day's breakfast, and significant points will be awarded to that camper's kitchen. The remaining top-ah ten recipes will be awarded fewer points in a graded fashion. Study the 'Breakfast' section in your cookbooks, and be prepared-ah to make a complete meal. Report-ah to Apley Court no later than 8:37 a.m. to find your assigned cooking hall. More details when you arrive-ah in the morning."

A general buzz of excitement permeated the room. Students filed out of the dining hall with a sense of urgency, eager to return to their cabins and study their cookbooks. Jerry, Mari, and Louie G caught up to their Mayon-daise Kitchenmates and followed them out of the dining hall down the well-lit path back to their cabin.

"Why do you think the competition starts at 8:37?" Mari wondered aloud.

"Because the instructors are ridiculous?" Louie G was not amused. "Why not 8:37 and 43 seconds?"

"It probably has something to do with teaching us about timing and how important it is for cooking, just like the 'no later than noon' camp arrival deadline or the 'dinner at exactly six o'clock,'" Jerry surmised, as Louie G continued to mutter under his breath.

They entered the cabin, said good-night, and headed to their respective sleeping areas. Jerry brushed his teeth, tied his spaghetti hair into a bun (grateful as always that as weird and annoying as his hair was, at least it had properties that also made it tolerable—like being able to be tied back without breaking) and put on his sleeping cap just in case his hair grew during the night. There's nothing quite like waking up choking on noodles that you snorted through your nostrils—that was a "fun" experience he'd had once and *never* wanted to repeat.

As Jerry left the bathroom and walked to his bunk bed, he abruptly realized that for the most part, no one had really bothered him about his hair. He wondered if the general anxiety that probably most of the campers were feeling had been a sufficient distraction. Then he realized, as he saw the whispering and not-so-subtle pointing as he made his way to his bed, that his *own* anxiety and new responsibilities had distracted *him*. The other campers had probably been talking about his hair all day behind his back, but he just hadn't noticed. *Hopefully the novelty of it will wear off in a few days, and nobody will care about my pasta hair—except adults who care about the stupid prophecy.*

Jerry wanted to stay motivated for his goals, both for that summer and the future: Complete camp session #1, the first step toward becoming a Master Chef. Limit embarrassing moments. Make Mamma and Papa proud. Open my own restaurant someday.

So it begins, Jerry thought to himself. He climbed into his comfy bottom bunk and flipped the switch on the reading light attached to the upper bunk's bottom rungs. (The ceiling lights in the cabin had already automatically turned off—a function set up to enforce the "lights out" time). Jerry reached into his satchel for his cookbook to study up for tomorrow morning's first competition, but . . . his cookbook was gone!

Chapter 6

Scramble Gamble

After the initial panic wore off—and a second look in the bag confirmed that his cookbook was indeed missing—Jerry took a deep breath and decided to concentrate on what he had control over. It was too late to disturb any of the other campers, asking if they had seen his cookbook or even temporarily borrow theirs. So he pulled out his class schedule and perused it:

Morning Session M-W-F: Culinary History
Afternoon Session M-W-F: Sauces
Morning Session T-Th: Starches and Grains
Afternoon Session T-Th: Cooking Study Hall/Community Gardening

Weekends were generally class free, though often a speaker was brought in to enlighten and entertain the students—a culinary school graduate or a famous chef, for example.

Jerry placed the schedule back in his satchel and turned off the light. Lying on his back, he concentrated on waking up early, finding his cookbook, and making sure the kitchen was otherwise in good order. As he began making a mental list of all the things he needed to do in the morning (*brush my teeth, take a shower, do something with my hair, pack my cooking supplies, find my cookbook*), Jerry drifted off to sleep . . .

In his dream, Jerry was sitting at the kitchen table at home, eating lunch with his parents. Midmeal, droplets of water started falling from the ceiling onto the table. Strangely, his parents didn't even look up from their food. Then again, they didn't seem to be getting wet, either. The droplets began falling faster, scalding Jerry's arms and hands in the process. Suddenly the ceiling caved in, followed by a deluge of boiling water!

Screaming, Jerry awoke with a start.

Nightmares. Night sweats. Again. He looked at his wristwatch: 8:15.

"*Meatballs!* I forgot to set my alarm!"

No one seemed to have heard Jerry except for Louie G, who was on his top bunk, arranging his backpack.

"You OK down there, Jerry? Having a nightmare about this morning's competition?"

You have no idea, Louie G! Jerry said to himself.

The other campers were milling about the cabin, some getting dressed, others packing their schoolbags, and still others furiously reading their cookbooks.

My cookbook! Jerry's memory flooded into focus. Not wanting to seem irresponsible after being elected kitchen head chef, Jerry discreetly asked around, desperately trying to find his cookbook.

"You wouldn't happen to have seen an extra cookbook lying around?" he casually asked his nearest bunkmates.

No one had seen his cookbook, including Louie G. "Honestly, Jerry, there's a lot to cover in the breakfast section . . . it may not even be worth cramming this morning. Why don't you just look on with me during the competition?"

"*Grazie*, Louie G," Jerry replied. "Thank you. As long as the teachers allow it." Jerry hurriedly shoved his left arm through a sleeve and pulled his shirt down. It was on backward.

Louie G stifled a laugh. "We'll need to leave here in about fifteen minutes to make it to class on time. So relax, playa, you have time for a shower—which hopefully will clear your head."

Jerry knew that he had made a true friend in Louie G. He thanked him again for being thoughtful and scampered to the bathroom, taking his shirt off on the way. Jerry chose the shower stall closest to the door. He turned on the water and adjusted the temperature until it was luke-warm, almost cold. Much to his chagrin, Jerry realized he had left his shower cap in his luggage. He *hated* getting his hair wet—he'd been this way as long as he could remember. Probably some subconscious fear left over from the boiling water accident that left him with pasta for hair, instead of hair like his dad's: black, curly, delicate but thick. Jerry angled the showerhead as low as he could and then took a quick (but awkward) shower, holding his chin high the entire time and washing most of his body without looking down to ensure that his hair stayed dry.

He dressed himself quickly (nothing on backward this time) and grabbed a cap at random from his duffel bag, which contained a four-week supply of headwear. Before leaving the cabin, Jerry double-checked his satchel to make sure his cooking utensils were there. He gave a sigh of relief seeing that the family ladle was in the bag. It was just the con-fidence booster he needed.

Jerry and Louie G barely made it to Apley on time. A quick glance at the entryway bulletin board revealed that nearly half of Mayon-daise Kitchen had been assigned to Tuscany Hall, one of four large cooking classrooms within the main building. Tuscany Hall—like each of the other three halls: Marche, Abruzzo, Lazio—contained twenty-five in-dividualized cooking stations or ICSs. A technological wonder, the ICS was a fully functional kitchen for a single chef contained within a space no larger than two side-by-side kitchen sinks. It consisted of two burners, a conventional oven, and a grilling surface; a galley-sized sink;

a complete ventilation system; plus a pantry and mini-refrigerator.

Pesto graduate Kobilyn Bryan (class of 1996) had developed the ICS in 2002 and donated a generous number of them to the school pos-pro-duction. The ICSs were well-spaced within the hall, allowing teachers to stroll comfortably between them, grading cooking technique, taste testing, or putting out fires—literal ones as well as problem solving—if need be. And the self-contained ventilation system meant that you didn't have to smell someone else's overcooked steak while your medium-rare filet mignon was cooling.

ICS (Individualized Cooking Station

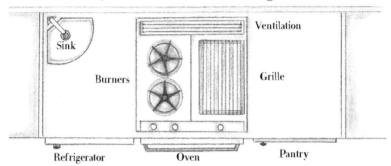

Jerry and Louie G took their places at two ICSs near the back of the room. They spotted Mari Nera a few rows ahead, pacing nervously and biting her nails. A deep British voice (Chef Brit Favreau again?) began to outline instructions over the intercom:

"Good morning, mates, and welcome to your first official cook-off. We hope you've studied the breakfast section well. You will be making a breakfast entrée based on page ten of your cookbooks; should be easy peasy. You are welcome to augment the recipe as you please. Anything within your ICS refrigerator and pantry is at your disposable, and you may borrow from your classmates. You may ask the teachers for assistance, but if you ask *me*, I'll call you a namby-pamby to your face. Have some courage and do it yourself! You have fifteen minutes to complete your meal. We recommend that you create something not just edible but something you would enjoy. After all, you are making your own breakfast—and you don't want to be hungry for the rest of the morn'! Be sure to prepare enough food for interested faculty to sample. We will roam from room to room throughout the fifteen minutes. Our only guideline is that this breakfast entrée be savory and not too heavy; no pub grub. So chop-chop!" he staccato-clapped his hands together twice, for effect. "Time is ticking!"

Pandemonium broke loose. Campers from the various kitchens began frantically flipping through their cookbooks, and the hall rang with the din of clanging pans hitting the range—and the floor. Natalia Marta Catarina Paoladinho (thank God she went by Paoladinho for short, and even that was a mouthful), a Brazilian girl from Béchamel Kitchen two ICSs down from Jerry, dramatically fainted, barely avoiding smashing her forehead on the countertop. Chef Favreau entered the room and sternly reminded the novice chefs that every aspect of the cooking experience would be graded, including their composure. Things seem to quiet down a bit after that—but not by much. Jerry imagined the exact same scene was occurring in Marche, Abruzzo, and Lazio Halls.

Jerry, trying to hide his own fear though he knew the sweat stains forming on his underarms would eventually give him away, coolly walked over to Louie G's ICS and whispered, "So . . . what is page ten of the cookbook? What do they want us to make?"

Jerry couldn't quite tell if the look on Louie's face was confusion or mockery.

"It's . . . it's eggs. They want us to make *eggs?!*"

Jerry looked over Louie G's shoulder. Sure enough, page ten had basic recipes for eggs: scrambled or fried or poached or whatever else you can do to eggs. Throwing wasn't on the list.

Louie smirked. "Good luck, Jerry. I can cook eggs in my sleep!"

Walking back to his ICS, Jerry wished he had Louie G's confidence.

He scratched the tortellini hair underneath his tri-color, Italian flag–decorated cap. Thankfully the pasta was not tri-color, just tightly wound and a bit itchy on the scalp. He wished he had grown something a little looser, longer, something he could twirl with his fingers—like fusilli. That usually got the creative juices flowing.

He opened his fridge and the pantry, surveying the meager contents. Jerry wondered if he had managed to choose the most barren ICS in the entire room. *What can I do with this? Deli ham?!* He glanced around and noticed other students pulling out foods much more "exotic" than deli ham. One student had *prosciutto crudo* (a salty Italian ham); another had aged cheddar in one hand and chives in the other. Jerry glanced at his watch: 8:51. He only had nine minutes left to complete his entrée. So he employed his own patented recipe for success prior to a competition: he closed his eyes, said a quick prayer, and took a deep cleansing breath. And then he knew exactly what he needed to make.

Within about five minutes Jerry was nearly done. Chef Michel Jardin (pronounced "Zhar-dan"), a tall, lanky gentleman wearing a red chef's jacket with jet black buttons and an white toque, abruptly stopped while walking past Jerry's ICS. His eyes grew wide. Jerry feared the worse. "What eez that smell?!" Chef Jardin exclaimed in a heavy French accent. His thin lips broke into a coy smile. "May I have a taste?"

Jerry nodded vigorously.

"I taste . . . basil, mozzarella, tempered with a salty meat flavor over a creamy egg base. Perfection! And I see you have garnished the plate with tomatoes: green basil, white mozzarella, red tomatoes. A veritable Italian flag! Extra points for creativity!" The eccentric Jardin did a little dance, spinning in a circle and clapping merrily.

"Are you totally off your trolley? What's all the fuss about here?"

By now Jerry knew that the deep voice, cheery British accent, and funny phrases could only belong to Brit Favreau, who had stopped to see what had caught Jardin's attention. Chef Favreau sniffed his way toward Jerry's skillet and then quickly scooped a spoonful of eggs into his mouth. His eyes widened. "Talk about . . . taking the biscuit," he exclaimed with his mouth full. "I think we have an ace here!"

Jerry gave his Italian flag hat a playful pat, thanking it for the inspiration. (He'd pulled out this cap in a rush, forgetting to bring his white toque—none of the teachers seemed to mind, maybe cutting him some slack given his "unique" hair situation.)

Really, he should have been thanking his hair.

Without his hair, he wouldn't have worn the hat. Without the hat, the moment of originality would have been lost. "You should be grateful I didn't cut you off this morning," Jerry muttered as if his hair could understand.

Jerry Pasta's
ITALIAN EGGS
(EGGS WITH SPINACH, BASIL, MOZZARELLA, AND TOMATOES)

Feeds 1 to 2

Preparation time: 3 to 5 minutes

Cooking time: 4 to 5 minutes

INGREDIENTS AND SUPPLIES

Ingredients

2 eggs (or approximately ½ cup egg whites or egg substitute)

⅛ teaspoon seasoning salt

Dash black pepper

Dash onion powder

⅛ cup low-fat milk or light cream

¼ tablespoon unsalted butter

1 cup fresh baby spinach leaves

1 slice deli meat cut or torn into bite-sized pieces

   (ham or prosciutto is recommended)

½ plum tomato

   (diced if to be added to eggs or sliced if to be served separately on plate)

4 fresh basil leaves, torn into tiny shreds

¼ cup fresh mozzarella (or ½ stick low-fat string cheese)

Supplies
Medium-sized bowl

Spatula

Small skillet

DIRECTIONS

1. Crack eggs into a medium-sized bowl. Season with salt, pepper, and onion powder; then add the milk.
2. Beat the eggs until spices and milk are well blended. Set aside.
3. Grease a small skillet with butter, and bring to medium heat. Add the spinach and meat and stir. The spinach will shrivel. Cook for one to two minutes, or until the meat is lightly browned. Add the diced tomato if that's your preference, or save and serve the slices separately.
5. Beat the eggs again briefly as they have probably settled, and add to the skillet, increasing the heat to high.
6. After 30 seconds, stir in the basil and cheese. Use a spatula to scrape the bottom of the skillet frequently to prevent burning and to repeatedly fold the eggs, breaking large chunks into smaller ones.
7. Scramble to desired firmness (usually 2 to 3 minutes). When ready, serve and eat immediately!

Soon other faculty made their way to Jerry's ICS—first Chef Beurre and Al Dente, then others he didn't recognize. Before he knew it, his eggs were nearly gone. They had left two spoonfuls at best. Jerry scanned the room for his new friends. Mari had enough eggs in her skillet to feed ten people! Either the faculty hadn't sampled her offering, or Mari had made sure she had plenty to eat for herself. *Why didn't I think of that?!* Others, Louie G among them, were busy scraping their pans, heads down. A timer sounded, signaling the end of the session.

Ten minutes later, Al Dente's voice announced over the PA system, "We have a unanimous winner. We have sampled the offerings in all four halls, and it appears that-ah Jerry Pasta of the Mayon-daise Kitchen has created quite the breakfast dish-ah. You will all be enjoying Signore Pasta's creation at tomorrow's breakfast. You now have ten minutes to eat-ah what you have made, clean-ah your ICS as best as you can, and get to your scheduled morning class. The secondary winners will be posted on the wall in the dining hall-ah. Kitchen staff-ah will be coming by to help you clean up."

Jerry turned around just in time to see Louie G and Mari running at him, hands held high in jubilation.

"Two for two, Head Chef! You're keeping Mayon-daise on a roll! Or maybe a croissant…Ha!" Louie G exclaimed.

"I'm glad *one* of us wasn't too nervous to cook," Mari lamented, her white chef's coat covered with a pollenlike dust. "I spent five minutes just trying to get the burner on, my hands were shaking!"

The friends shared pleasantries for a few moments before realizing they would be late for class if they didn't hurry. They were happy to see that they all had the exact same class schedule. Mari and Louie returned to their ICSs to eat their breakfasts, clean, and gather their belongings. Jerry turned around just in time to see a pair of scarred, leathery hands wiping his countertop. The ICS was spotless! Jerry didn't know how to thank the old man who stood in front him, hunched over a bucket of soapy water.

"*Grazie!* Thank you so much! I was just getting to that—though I guess I've been running my mouth for the last few minutes. I'd have been late for class if you hadn't helped," he admitted.

The old man smiled, turned around, and began shuffling out of Tuscany Hall. Almost out of earshot, the old man cocked his head to the side and quipped, "*Merci pour les oeufs.*"

Jerry squinted quizzically, trying to remember the French he'd learned during the last school year to translate the old man's words. A quick glance at his now-empty skillet, and Jerry suddenly realized the price he had paid for a clean cooking station. He inwardly groaned. His stomach wouldn't let him forget.

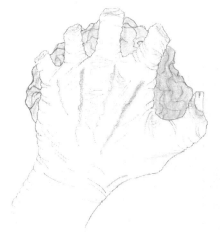

Chapter 7

Repast, Present, and Future

It was difficult to focus during Culinary History class. *"Merci pour les oeufs,* thanks for the eggs" played on a continual loop in Jerry's head, and his stomach rumbles seemed to be competing with those coming from his teacher, André La Gasse. Chef La Gasse didn't offer his students much to listen to other than those rumbles—the first hour of class was a review of the school origins, the founders, and some of the early graduates who went on to be successful chefs—and the egg-y odor of the room seemed to suggest that the teacher lived up to his name all too well.

Chef La Gasse was one of those people who clearly liked the sound of his own voice—though anyone having to listen to him wasn't nearly as enthralled. In a high-pitched nasal Italian accent, he stated, "Founded nearly fifty years ago, Presto Pesto's School of Culinary Excellence ees world-renowned in more ways than one. Students from all over the world are selected to attend. Many of the greatest chefs from around the globe, such as myself, serve as instructors."

Nice to see La Gasse is humble too, Jerry thought to himself.

"A clear Franco-Italian influence will be evident throughout the school. The founders were a French chef, Karim de la Carème, and an Italian chef, Presto Pesto II. Their collective love of cooking and a desire to share its joys with children eager to learn the culinary arts led to the school's creation. Both friends and rivals, these two men fought over everything: the best chef status, the best recipes, the school name— Pesto won that last battle—the names of the school divisions or 'kitchens'— Karim won that one."

Laboriously squatting to pat the floor, Chef La Gasse reverently informed the class that the founders were in fact buried directly beneath the main hall—essentially below where he stood.

"These great sauciers—saucemakers, if you will—requested that their bones remain with the school that they loved and created."

"Kinda creepy," Louie G whispered into Jerry's ear. Jerry, eyes wide, nodded slowly.

Mari overheard Louie G and piped in. "Local legend is that the ghosts of the founders roam the campgrounds at night, looking for victims. Apparently, a handful of campers every year get mysteriously sick and are sent home."

"You really believe that?" Louie G whispered back at Mari. "That's crazy talk. But now I'm a little freaked out. Thanks Mari."

Jerry quietly wondered if this new information would factor into his nightly terrors. *Skeletons and ghosts chasing me with boiling pots of water? It's less scary if I think up the plot of my own nightmares before I fall asleep.*

The second hour of class was an outline of what to expect for the rest of the summer: a review of the key players in culinary history, important dates to remember, and, of course, a final exam.

The afternoon session was marginally better, but only

because Chef Beurre was such a cartoonish personality, for lack of a better description. Jerry wasn't sure how at the dinner table yesterday evening he'd missed noticing the caricature that stood before him now. Beurre's brown corduroy pants strained over his rounded belly and were belted nearly up to his sternum, and the high-water effect exposed his pale, sun-deprived hairy ankles. His spectacles looked like two magnifying glasses glued together. Calling him "four-eyes" would have been kind considering the way the whites of his eyes creepily filled his lenses to capacity and then some. How could you *not* make eye contact?

Jerry forced himself to listen as Chef Beurre impressed on the class, "*Sauces* may be the most important class you take your entire time here at Presto Pesto's. Eet would behoove you to pay close attention."

There was no actual cooking during this first class; rather, like Chef La Gasse's morning class, just an outline of things to come. As the students rose to leave, Chef Beurre handed each an optional reading list, pointing out, "If you pay sufficient attention een class, you won't need to heavily rely on this reading list." With a wave of his hand, he drew the class's attention to a crammed bookshelf. "But avail yourself as you please."

Despite Beurre's hypnotic, owllike stare, Jerry knew he would have trouble focusing in the coming afternoon classes—especially after lunch when he usually got a bad case of the sleepies. Jerry looked at the first book on the reading list and decided that this would be a good place to start his sauce education, assuming he would miss a bit when dozing off. *Sauce for the Saucier*, by Karim de la Carème—one of the school's founders, Jerry reminded himself.

Jerry found a good-as-new copy on the top shelf. In fact, the pages still had that "new book" smell when Jerry rifled through them for the first time. The dust on the shelf suggested that very few students had actually availed themselves of these books, maybe intimidated by Beurre's directive to simply pay attention.

Jerry groaned under the weight of the heavy book in his satchel as he made his way through the door. He almost stumbled over the person waxing the floor directly outside the room.

"Pardon me," Jerry apologized as he walked gingerly across the floor.

"Find anything good to read in there?" queried the man. Jerry spun around and immediately recognized the gray mustache, cracked-pepper beard, and steely hazel eyes in a shroud of gentle wrinkles. It was the same old man who had helped clean his ICS. And his skillet. Jerry decided against asking the old man how he liked his eggs. And apparently the janitor spoke fine English, albeit with a hint of a French accent.

"Oh, just a book on sauces. Something to read at bedtime," said Jerry, trying to politely engage in conversation yet contain his frustration toward this breakfast thief.

The old man stared back at Jerry. There was a hint of something in those deep-set eyes—Jerry wasn't sure what—that made him uncomfortable. He almost expected the old man to apologize for eating his breakfast. The janitor broke the silence.

"Reading is important to cooking. There's an old saying: Respect repast, mistrust the present, save the future. Enjoy the book—and *bonne journee*."

The old man went back to waxing the floors as Jerry turned to walk away. He wasn't sure why this janitor was giving him advice. And he certainly didn't know how to make sense of it. *Did he say "repast"?* Jerry considered the meaning of the word repast: a meal or feast. *So what was the old man trying to say? Maybe the play on the words "the past" and "repast" was a reminder to give proper attention to the great chefs of the past. And maybe the ominous "mistrust the present" was a warning of sorts. Warning of what? Present-day fast-food shortcuts instead of homemade meals? So maybe tapping into the wisdom of cooking's past heroes could save the future of cooking . . . or maybe I'm just reading too much into this old man's words. For the love of meatballs, he's just a janitor!*

Jerry shook these thoughts away as he walked back to the cabin. About midway down the path, he bumped into Mari. After exchanging hellos, Jerry wanted to hear Mari's reaction to the first day of class.

"Overall, it was quite boring. I hope tomorrow is more entertaining," she mused. "I think I was distracted by this morning's competition. I was terribly nervous; when I added garam masala, one of my favorite Indian spices, to my eggs, I knew I had made a terrible mistake. Then I kept adding more eggs to dilute the overwhelming flavor. Just because you like a spice doesn't mean it needs to go into every dish you make— so at least I learned one important cooking lesson today. Congrats again, by the way, on your winning recipe. Looking forward to sampling it at breakfast tomorrow."

That "pollen" on her blouse earlier must have been curry or garam-whatever, Jerry thought. He wanted to say something that would make Mari feel better, but it seemed she had already made her own inner peace. He thanked her for acknowledging his accomplishment, and they continued to walk toward their cabin.

Thirty yards from their cabin door, three figures—one male, two female—emerged from the shade of a bordering fig tree to obstruct their path. The tallest of the three was a portly young man who was profusely sweating, likely due to the black three-piece suit he was wearing in the seventy-five degree heat. With three practiced strokes he combed his jet-black hair straight back, his perspiration serving as hair gel.

"You tryin' to ignore me, Pasta?"

Jerry had no idea what this big kid with the funny accent was talking about.

"Ummm . . . do I know you?"

"No," the fat boy shot back. "But we know you. I'm Robert De-

Journo, and I come from a long line of successful Italian chefs in the United States. This here on my right is Cello,—yeah, like the instrument—Feigni . . . my cousin from my fadda's side. And this here on my right is Lumina Foyle, my cousin on my mudda's side. We're part of the Mufia, and we wancha to join us. All of us are assigned to Tomato Kitchen—like you were supposed to be—but we're lookin' to make an exception for you."

Lumina Foyle looked like a backup dancer for Lady Gaga. Her silver-colored hair fell down over her heavily mascaraed eyes, and her sleeveless blouse revealed thin, toned arms. Cello Feigni, on the other hand, was more like a former bodybuilder turned nightclub bouncer . . . without the tattoos. Her all black jogging suit fit snugly around what Jerry assumed were muscular biceps and quads. And her face seemed welded into a permanent . . . a permanent . . . try as he might, Jerry couldn't really find the proper description. She had a freaky strained but totally expressionless look on her face, like she was standing in front of the world's most powerful fan set on HIGH. Not just that her face wasn't friendly; you couldn't tell if she wanted to punch you in the face or just pull your eyelashes out, one by one. You. Just. Couldn't. Tell!

The Mufia members collectively took two aggressive steps toward

Jerry; DeJourno was so close to him now that all Jerry could smell was a nauseating mix of pepperoni, Parmesan, and sweat. Surprisingly, before Jerry could say anything, Mari jumped in.

"Jerry's not interested in joining your cooking clique, thank you very much," she said, sounding very much like a mom rejecting a telemarketer's advances. "Have a nice day."

She yanked Jerry's arm to maneuver him past the trio. But Jerry's slight hesitation (out of fear? confusion?) gave DeJourno an opening to poke Jerry in the chest and make one final remark.

"You're makin' a big mistake, Pasta," he said, in what Jerry now recognized as a classic New York City Italian-American accent. "No one turns down the Mufia without consequences. And maybe you should watch where ya leave ya stuff."

Lumina Foyle reached into her backpack and threw something on the ground at Jerry's feet as the three Mufia members turned and walked away. Jerry stared at it, stunned. The gold lettering on the object said it all.

It was his missing cookbook.

Chapter 8

Hard Feelings

"*No capisco* . . . I don't understand what just happened here," he said to Mari. "What do you know about the Mufia? You clearly know more than I do, and I at least have a right to know everything you know, now that you made them mad at me." Though a little indignant and quick to pass blame, Jerry was mad at himself because he knew *he* was the cause of the Mufia's wrath because *he* forgot the predinner meeting he'd been invited to. Which now seemed more like a demand than an invite. But he wished Mari had let him speak for himself. *Does everyone here know that I'm only eleven?*

Mari, on the other hand, seemed quite happy with herself.

"Listen, Pasta," putting on a deep voice to mock Robert DeJourno's tough-guy act, "I did you a solid just now." Mari cleared her throat and returned to her sweet, elegant accent. "The Mufia are made up of mostly Italian students from some of cooking's most prestigious families. 'Mufia' is short for 'Muffuletta,' a characteristic Sicilian-bread-and-olives salad combination. Terribly salty but quite tasty, actually. Anyway, the Mufia's stated purpose is to 'prove the superiority of Italian cooking.' This is all on their Wikipedia page; I'm not making this up. The worse part of the Mufia is that someone associated with the school in a position of authority sponsors their shenanigans. And who might that be? you ask. None other than Ward Moldy Coeur."

Jerry bristled at the mention of the name. He suddenly remembered his mom's muffled words months ago and Mari's earlier expressed profound disdain for Moldy Coeur. And Jerry didn't like him much either, actually, for the way he brought attention to him and made a nasty insinuation about him during the kitchen assignment ceremony. He replayed the moment briefly in his mind to ferret out the details: Moldy Coeur had a lot of money, was a ward of the school by virtue of his donations, and seemingly regretted that Jerry was placed in Mayon-daise Kitchen and not Tomato Kitchen—a fact basically confirmed by Robert DeJourno.

"So what's your beef with him?" Jerry asked, the question transforming Mari's demeanor from serious to REALLY serious.

"Moldy Coeur is a terrible, terrible man," she began. "His name perfectly describes him: he has a rotten heart. When I was growing up in India, some of my best times were going to my parents' restaurant to learn the secrets of Indian cuisine. My parents taught me not to take food for granted—not just that we had food in abundance but especially because of the hard work that went into making it. For them, cooking was a form of art. People stood in line for hours waiting for a table at their restaurant, knowing that the food would be of the highest taste and quality.

"Then something terrible happened. A young Indian man named Tikka Masala who had recently graduated from Presto Pesto's returned to our region. Within a few months, Tikka had opened his own Indian restaurant—if you could even call what he served Indian food. People began flocking to *his* place, forsaking my parents' establishment, as he promised shorter waits and cheaper prices. My parents and I even went once, to see why so many people had left our business. What we found was Indian fast food. Variety but no flavor. Clearly frozen and thawed sauces, plastic-tasting bread, the cheapest cuts of meat. It was disgusting. Tikka opened up three more restaurants in the region, and his *Hurry, It's Curry* food chain effectively put my parents out of business. We later learned that while here at Presto's, Tikka had become one of Moldy Coeur's protégés. One of the reasons I came to this camp was to become everything that Tikka isn't: a real chef. And to go back to India to save Indian cuisine from frauds like him."

Mari was fighting back tears but continued.

"And you know Moldy Coeur's doing the same thing in Italy, Jerry." At that, Jerry raised an eyebrow, his hands nervously fumbling with the binding of his newly found cookbook. "As an influential food critic, he's been shutting down restaurants across Italy with his scathing reviews. Restaurants that don't conform to Moldy Coeur's way get negative reviews, while restaurant owners who fear displeasing him change their menus to his liking or simply become part of his Fasta Pasta franchise. The result? Italian fast food: little flavor, high fat and calorie contents, few vegetable options. Really, the name should be changed from Fasta Pasta to Fatter Faster. And making matters even worse, too often for it to be coincidence, patrons of restaurants that have received his negative reviews mysteriously get severe food poisoning."

Listening to Mari's simmering voice, Jerry felt his own blood begin to boil, and he now understood her hatred of Moldy Coeur and, by extension, the Mufia. She had clearly investigated the man responsible for so much sorrow in her life—Mari had certainly done her homework before coming to camp, and Jerry made a mental note to ask her later how she got to be so knowledgeable—and it seemed as if she was using this knowledge as motivation.

"Thanks for telling me all this, Mari. I guess you did do me a huge favor. I might have felt pressured into joining the Mufia if you hadn't been there."

Mari had unintentionally ignited a passion in Jerry concerning what Coeur was doing to Italian cuisine. He had seen the Fasta Pasta signs springing up not just in his neighborhood but in all the cities he had traveled to, and he'd had no idea who was behind the change. He also hadn't realized the gravity of the situation. Authentic restaurants and home-cooked meals would soon become a thing of the past if Moldy Coeur had his way.

"No thanks needed, Jerry," Mari said graciously. "Though I don't know you very well, I'm pretty sure you would have been smart enough to make the right decision by yourself—though doing a little reading on your own in the library might help. Plus, I'm just trying to keep 'the chosen one' informed . . . oh, that slipped out! Sorry, Jerry!" Mari quickly averted her eyes, suddenly finding intense interest in some fallen figs that had become insect food.

Mari's declaration felt like an open-handed slap; indeed, the blood rushed to Jerry's cheeks as if he *had* been slapped. His parents had been afraid of interactions like this.

"*The chosen one?!* Why would you call me that?" He maneuvered himself in front of Mari to force her to look him in the eye.

Mari nervously tapped her fingers together, stalling to cover her verbal blunder. "Well, Jerry, um . . . everyone kind of knows about you and . . . um . . . the, uh, the whole prophecy thing. You're actually quite famous in the culinary world. Especially with, um . . . your, um, hair," she stammered.

Mari's anxious words and pained smile didn't make Jerry feel any better. And if she already knew who Jerry was, that meant she had lied to him when she acted so oblivious when she first met him at the cheese-tasting contest.

"But I don't *want* to be famous! I just want to cook, start my own restaurant, help my family. And why has nobody ever explained this prophecy thing to me since I'm apparently the subject?"

"Wait! Not even your parents, Jerry?"

Jerry stared down at his shoes and shook his head. He hated feeling left out—though it was something he had grown accustomed to over the years; it was easy to get left out when you were different. Attempts to hide things from him only made him feel even more different. For years after "the accident" his parents pretended as if nothing had changed, as if Jerry's hair was perfectly normal. So having your first-grade teacher explain to you why the other kids are pulling your hair and calling you "Hairy Pasta" is NOT the way to find out that your hair really is made out of pasta. And maybe little Jerry knew all along his hair was different; but it was just easier pretending he was a *normal* six-year-old.

Feeling a bit of remorse, Mari was the first to break the tense silence. "You're right. It's only fair that I tell you everything I know, Jerry. I am a bit of a cooking-history nerd, so I may be giving you more detail than you'd like. Stop me at any point." Mari took a breath, then explained, "On her deathbed, Della Morta, one of the most venerated chefs in modern Italian culinary history, predicted a historic conflict. Forgive my perhaps overly dramatic paraphrasing of her words, but she said something to the effect: 'Italian cuisine will be challenged. It will be diluted, its integrity threatened. It will be made cheaper, faster. One boy, however, can save our cuisine—he will be a culinary genius who will live and breathe pasta. So much so, he will have hair like the finest pasta!'

Jerry felt his stomach lurch.

"Many have debated whether the 'pasta hair' she spoke of is literal or figurative. You may not realize it, Jerry, but *many* parents in Italy hope their child is the one spoken of. Why do you think every Italian parent wants their kid to come to this camp?"

For the first time, Jerry was now painfully aware of his reality. All those eyes staring at him everywhere he went, looking at his hair . . . apparently there was more to it than he realized—maybe even envy. *What if I am the chosen one?*

"I've got to also warn you about one other thing, Jerry. Something that I assumed you knew, but now I realize you're clearly unaware of, given the blank look on your face."

Jerry braced himself for the worst.

"You have enemies, Jerry—but one in particular worth noting. Rumor has it that Moldy Coeur believed every word Della Morta prophesied. For years he has looked eagerly for this boy of the prediction, often jokingly referred to as the 'Saviory Chef.' Get it? Savior plus savory?"

Jerry glared back at Mari, unamused. Her forced grin crumbled like feta cheese.

She awkwardly continued. "So, um, Moldy Coeur is quite paranoid—he investigates almost every claim of Saviory Chef identity. Some allege he attempts to preemptively thwart the prophecy by targeting the children of rival Master Chefs, whom he suspects would be most likely to fulfill the prophecy. You did know that Moldy Coeur is a Pesto's graduate, right? Anyway, the children of these other Master Chefs suffer mysterious food-related accidents and ailments—burning hands on a hot stove, developing profound allergies to tomatoes or cheese, completely losing taste buds—that render them useless for a career in cooking." Mari paused five seconds for dramatic effect. "No one has ever proven that Moldy Coeur is responsible, but the parents of the injured children suspect foul play at his hands because he is always conveniently in the vicinity. Watch your back, Jerry. I'll keep my eyes open too."

Hollow. That was the feeling in Jerry's stomach. Much different from the feeling of being hungry, he felt empty, angry, scared. *So maybe that's what Mamma and Papa were talking about in the kitchen that day my invitation arrived; it's all beginning to make sense. Yet they still sent me to camp, knowing this Coeur guy might be around. Maybe Mari is sensationalizing this a bit?*

Though if Jerry *was* to believe everything Mari had just told him, he had an enemy he didn't even know about—until now. But now Jerry had the advantage of knowing who his greatest adversary was, even if he had never personally met the man. And there was at least one person he could totally count on to have his back at camp, and it happened to be the brainy Indian girl standing next to him.

Mari and Jerry spent a good portion of the rest of the afternoon talking about their families, their cooking experiences, and their goals for the summer. At dinnertime, they linked up with Louie G and told him about their run-in with the Mufia. Louie G had his own story about a group of French campers calling themselves "The Sauciers" (pronounced *saw-see-ays*) who had tried to recruit him that same afternoon. The group educated Louie G that a saucier is a chef who specializes in making sauces. He was a little confused about why "The Sauciers" had come after him.

"They must have seen my last name, Gyan, on a roster and thought it was French or something. Plus people think that Ghana is a French-speaking country because it's so close to Cote D'Ivoire, the Ivory Coast. But Ghana, like the United States, had lots of British influence before its independence, so the official language is English. Anyway, I turned the Saucy Posse down. They didn't seem too happy." Louie G paused and stared at his friends incredulously. "Seriously? Nobody has a sense of humor these days. . . . Saucy Posse? C'mon that's funny! I came up with that on the fly!" He shrugged. "So I guess we're all making enemies already, huh?"

"But I guess that makes *us* all friends, right? How does the saying go? 'The enemy of my enemy is my friend,'" Mari noted.

The threesome chatted and cracked jokes throughout the rest of dinner—instant fast friends—and returned to their cabin that night feeling quite lighthearted. Jerry went to bed believing that with friends like this, camp wouldn't be so bad after all. Still, the hollow feeling in his stomach had no thought of leaving. At least not for that night.

Chapter 9

What? The EFF?

By breakfast the next morning, Jerry had already forgotten about his encounter with the Mufia. The day had started out well. Remembering to set his alarm the night before, he woke up at six a.m. for his usual two-mile run, showered, made his bed, said his morning prayers, and verified that the Mayon-daise Kitchen's kitchen was in good order. He was determined to take the responsibility of "Head Chef" seriously.

Jerry sat between Mari and Louie G as breakfast was served in Ea-ditt Hall. (Although the newly minted best friends knew they were supposed to get to know campers from other kitchens, they enjoyed one another's company so much that they pretty much stuck together like dried out spaghetti.) Out came his spinach, basil, and mozzarella eggs. The kitchen chefs had actually done a pretty good job replicating his recipe, though he thought the eggs could have used a little less cheese. Jerry was given an unusually large helping compared to his peers; he assumed this was a reward for winning the competition. He wasn't going to complain.

"Why are the portions at this camp so small? Are they trying to starve us?" Louie G lamented as he looked jealously at Jerry's plate.

"I haven't noticed the servings being . . . that small. What were you expecting?" Jerry managed to say with his mouth full of eggs.

"Guess I'm just used to the larger portions served back home. Everything's supersized. You never have to worry about running out of food."

Mari leaned over to Louie G. "Maybe those large portions are why so many Americans are themselves supersized!"

Louie G slowly twirled his fork in his eggs before responding. "You're probably right, Mari. We've got some large people in America, no question. From young kids on up. I'm one to talk," he added, playfully pinching his less-than-svelte waistline. "It's normal to see people pile food on their plates and stuff their faces like there's no tomorrow—and still manage to throw a lot in the garbage. Or if you're like me, your parents guilt-trip you about not eating all your food at restaurants, so you eat the whole huge plate of food even if you were full half a plate ago." Louie G stared at the last bite of eggs delicately balanced on his fork. "I guess there's a lesson in there somewhere: only eat the amount of food you need, not the amount you want. Plus I guess I could always take leftovers home."

"And always value quality over quantity," Jerry added. He looked at his plate and decided he didn't need the extra serving of eggs that had been doled out to him. As he pushed the plate away, Jerry noticed a sheet of paper inconspicuously sticking out from underneath the dish. He lifted up the front edge, revealing an envelope labeled FOR JARRY PASTA taped to the bottom.

If you're trying to recruit someone, at least spell their name correctly, Jerry huffed silently as he opened what he expected to be another Mufia threat/invitation.

The letter was sloppily handwritten, with a large food stain on the lower-left corner. The text itself was simple and straightforward:

FOR JARRY PASTA

AAS HEAD CHEF OF YOUR
KITCHEN, YOU ARE CAPTAIN
OF YOUR KITCHEN'S EFF TEAM.

YOUR FIRST GAME WILL BE
TOMORROW AT DUSK

DETAILS TO COME.

"Tomorrow at dusk?" Fear gripped Jerry; his palms were suddenly sweaty, his breathing shallow. He was team captain, and the first game was tomorrow at nightfall?! Fear turned to terror as Jerry realized he didn't even know what game they would be participating in. *What on earth is EFF? And when are these details coming? Hopefully before tomorrow!* When he was self-aware again, Jerry realized Mari and Louie G were gazing over his shoulder, looking equally bewildered.

Louie G's bewilderment quickly turned to excitement when Jerry showed him the mysterious note.

"I think EFF will be sweet! What kind of game begins by sending a cryptic message taped to the bottom of your plate? And you get to be the captain, you lucky dog! Pick me for the crew, Jerry!" Louie G squealed.

"Well, as soon as I know what the game is, I'll be sure to put you on the team. You could even be the captain. I have enough on my plate already—without worrying about what's *underneath* my plate—and we've been at camp for less than forty-eight hours." Jerry put his head in his hands and let out a loud sigh.

Mari seemed to be the only one thinking logically.

"Clearly, Jerry, the four other Head Chefs have also been contacted, and my guess is they have no idea what EFF is, either." A quick scan around the dining hall confirmed Mari's hunch. A few other tables had campers looking over one another's shoulders staring at pieces of paper similar to the one in Jerry's hand. The faculty didn't seem to be paying

any attention. In fact, only four chairs away, Chef La Gasse seemed thoroughly engrossed with his eggs and juice—perhaps imagining himself participating in an epic banquet with history's greatest chefs, himself included.

"Let's wait for more details, Jerry," Mari suggested. "I'm sure there's nothing to worry about."

Yet, Jerry quietly pondered. He feared it would be difficult to focus during the morning lecture, but fortunately, "Starches and Grains" class proved to be stimulating. Chef Pei Lei was extremely animated (understatement alert!). The spunky chef from mainland China promised to teach the students about grains from all cultures, stressing that it was imperative to start from square one.

"You must be able to make white rice—*NOT TOO STICKY, NOT*

TOO CHEWY! You will learn to make it in *POT! NO RICE COOKER SHORTCUT!*" Maybe it was the yelling that made her seem larger than her diminutive 4'10" frame. Her distinct Chinese accent was attention-grabbing, and her chopstick-turned-pointer looked deadly. No one could sleep through this class; you'd be afraid of waking up on a bed of rice, covered in soy sauce, on a plate in front of Chef Lei. A proper punishment for dozing off.

In the short break before lunch, Jerry jogged back to the May-on-daise cabin to grab new headgear; his angel hair was spilling out of his bandana, and he needed something more snug, like a beret, to contain it. As he walked by his bunk bed, Jerry noticed the bedclothes had been disturbed. He pulled the blanket back and found a worn, paper-thin manual with a stained cover titled: *EFF Rules and Regulations.* Jerry picked it up and without even bringing it close to his nose, he could smell the overwhelming aroma of nutmeg rolling off the cover. He turned to the first page and couldn't believe that this was the game he and his team—yet to be chosen!—were scheduled to play in less than thirty-six hours.

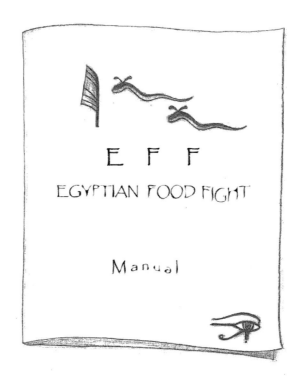

EGYPTIAN FOOD FIGHT (EFF)

Origins
Why Egyptian?

The food fight is structured around foods from the food pyramid: Grains, Fruits, Vegetables, Meat and Beans, Dairy

The game is a combination of Capture the Flag, Dodgeball, and Freeze Tag.

Objective
The first team to score 1,000 points wins. If this score is not reached, the team with highest score at the end of 60 minutes is declared the victor. The game is split into two 30-minute halves. The first half ends at the 30-minute mark or when one team reaches 500 points.

Playing Field, Personnel, and Players
The game is played at night on a lighted 100-yard field divided in half at the 50-yard line.

5 kitchen staff and janitors referee the games (2 on each side of the field, 1 head referee)

8 players per side, 4 males and 4 females

Each team consists of:
5 Jackals
2 Sphinxes
1 Pharaoh (+ wooden stool/throne)

1 soul/egg (+ copper bowl)

Players must maintain their roles throughout the entire game.

Twenty throwable food items are arranged along the center line in the middle of the field. The kitchen staff provides these items (various nonedible—moldy, rotten, out-of-date—leftovers. Should these items fall apart or crumble, their individual pieces, chunks, and hunks can be used as throwable items at the referees' discretion. "Fresh" items replace the used ones at halftime. (Note: A rotten tomato can only be thrown so many times before falling apart completely).

Rules of Play

The Pharaoh for each team sits on a stool (throne) in the middle of his/her side of the field, surrounded by a large circle that is 10 yards in diameter. The Pharaoh must remain on the throne at all times unless surrendering or forced off.

The Pharaoh's soul is a fresh egg that is hidden at the beginning of the game by each team's Pharaoh anywhere on their own side of the field—except inside the Pharaoh's circle. This soul is covered by a copper bowl to prevent accidental breakage. Once the game begins, the egg cannot be touched by bare hands. It can only be touched with a Sphinx's ladle.

Jackals are both attackers and defenders. They attack an opponent's Pharaoh and defend their own Pharaoh. When hit by a piece of food, they arc "mummified," signified by lying on the ground, unmoving, arms crossed. They can only be mummified on the opposition's half of the field.

Sphinxes are both saviors and thieves. They cannot be pelted or mummified—with one exception: They can "resurrect" (reanimate) their team's Jackals by tapping them on the head. Sphinxes also try to score a large point bonus by finding and stealing the rival Pharaoh's soul and crossing midfield. When carrying the soul with their ladle, Sphinxes can be pelted but not mummified, and the attacking Jackal must be at least 5 yards (15 feet) away. If the soul falls off the ladle, a sphinx can pick it up and continue toward midfield as long as the egg hasn't cracked open.

At the beginning of the game, all Jackals and Sphinxes line up at their own back line. When the whistle blows, they are to run to the middle of the field and pick up as many pelting items as they can.

Scoring

500 points for finding the soul and conveying it across the 50-yard line on the ladle

500 points are awarded to the opposing team if a thieving Sphinx drops the soul and breaks it.

50 points per direct food hit on a Pharaoh by an opposing Jackal while outside the 10-yard circle. Jackals defend their team's Pharaoh by "mummifying" any Jackals on the rival team—that is, hitting them with food items if they have crossed over the 50-yard line. No points are awarded for mummifying another player.

500 points for a Pharaoh's surrender: if he/she accidentally vacates the throne--gets off the stool--in trying to avoid being hit by food, or if

he/she voluntarily leaves the throne due to fear of being hit/exhaustion. Note that this is a very rare occurrence.

At halftime, a new soul is hidden by each team's Pharaoh.

Jerry had unconsciously wrapped a fistful of angel hair in each hand—he didn't even know where to begin with his questions. He was terrified of turning to the appendix. He glanced at his watch—
Meatballs!

Though he'd been reading the manual for over twenty minutes, he still was unclear how to play the game and was now two minutes late for lunch. Cramming the booklet into his pocket, Jerry sprinted to the dining hall, hoping Louie G and Mari had saved him a seat.

"You're late, Monsieur Pasta," Chef La Gasse curtly pointed out before emitting a loud, sustained belch.

Is it just bad luck that I keep ending up at La Gasse's table?

Chef La Gasse filled the "I" chair to capacity, his love handles spilling out beyond the confines of the armrests. "Tardiness does not become a chef. You have cost Mayon-daise Kitchen twenty points."

Twenty points? No big deal. Gasse's nasal voice makes everything sound worse than it really is, Jerry silently bemoaned. *And why are all of the instructors overweight? Are they having seconds at every meal? Or are they sneaking out to Fasta Pasta every night to raid the €1* menu?* He mentally shook his head. *Be respectful Jerry,* he reminded himself.

"*Mi dispiace, signore.* I'm sorry. It won't happen again," Jerry told the chef as humbly as he could. Meanwhile, the EFF booklet was burning a hole in his pocket. He could barely think about anything else.

As soon as he was no longer the center of attention at the table, he passed the manual first to Mari (who gave it a cursory onceover) and then Louie G, who flipped through the pages for about three minutes

---

** 1 euro, for you American readers

before shrugging and handing it back.

"So that's all there is to it?" the brash American asked. "I guess I was expecting the game to be a little more complicated. A combination of dodgeball, capture the flag, and freeze tag? Geez, I could play those games with my eyes closed! When's practice?"

Jerry and Mari exchanged excited looks. Clearly, their eager friend would be a vital asset if Mayon-daise Kitchen was to win its first Egyptian Food Fight the following night.

EFFruit and Salad

(the Second Course)

Chapter 10

EFFerything you need to know

Since no assignments were given during classes that day, Jerry devoted the afternoon's Cooking Study Hall to learning the rules of EFF, with Louie G as the primary interpreter and Mari another eager student. The camp library was relatively empty, so they could talk without worrying about disturbing anyone.

"Look, guys, American kids grow up playing these games all the time. You've probably played some version of them too. That's why I think Egyptian Food Fight is easy to understand. It's just three familiar games in one."

Jerry still felt confused. He needed the overly talkative big-brother Louie G to explain to him *exactly* how EFF worked, not the overly confident know-it-all Louie G. "OK," Jerry said, "just pretend I know nothing and tell me how to play—like you were explaining the game to your six-year-old sister for the very first time."

Mari grinned. "Pretend you have *twin* six-year-old sisters," she said with a giggle, bewildered herself.

Louie G sighed deeply, as if it would take every ounce of his energy to teach his friends the game. Then he smiled and began, "OK, here's the version for six-year-olds. As I said, Egyptian Food Fight is three games rolled into one. One part is like what we Americans call Freeze Tag. The five Jackals per team throw food objects at each other. If you're hit, you're mummified . . . or frozen"—Louie G pinned his arms to his sides and his eyes rolled back—"until you get tapped on the head by one of the two Sphinxes on your team, who have the power to resurrect you. Got it so far?"

Jerry and Mari nodded.

Louie G continued, "Jackals score points in the game by hitting the other team's Pharaoh. *This* part of EFF is like Dodgeball. The Pharaoh sits on a stool in the middle of a large circle, and Jackals can't cross the outline of the circle. Each time your team hits the other team's Pharaoh with food, your team scores 50 points. The Pharaoh can defend himself by catching the food or dodging it—but if the Pharaoh leaves his stool, it's an automatic 500 points for the other team." Louie G made a disparaging face. "Only a total wuss would leave the stool," he scoffed.

"I see . . . Building a winning team is like creating a great recipe," Jerry said, almost to himself. "You need just the right ingredients if you want to taste victory."

Mari patted Jerry on the shoulder. "That's a perfect analogy!"

So Jerry made his ingredient list: The Jackals would need to have fairly strong arms and good aim to be effective. The Pharaoh would need to be someone with good balance who could duck and dart well plus good hands to catch food thrown at him. And most of all the Pharaoh would have to be tough—someone willing to take a lot of food abuse without quitting. *Five or six oranges to the chest could leave a pretty good bruise. One between the legs could be devastating*, thought Jerry, subconsciously squeezing his thighs together.

"You still with me, Jerry?" Louie G prodded.

Jerry nodded. "Yep, I think it's finally coming together. Though I still don't quite get the Sphinx and egg thing."

"Well," Louie G continued, "that part of Egyptian Food Fight is like Capture the Flag—only in EFF the flag is an egg, which, as the rulebook said, represents the Pharaoh's soul. Each team hides their Pharaoh's soul discreetly on the field, protected by a copper bowl so no one steps on it by accident. The Sphinxes don't just resurrect mummified Jackals—they also search for the copper bowl on their opponent's side of the field.

Once they locate the copper bowl, they can pick the egg off the ground with their ladles—no hands!—and try to carry it back to their side of the field intact, all the while having food thrown at them. If the Sphinx reaches the other side with the egg, his team gets 500 points, which is virtually a guaranteed win, a real game-changer. But if the Sphinx drops the egg and it breaks, the other side gets 500 points. High risk, high reward; that's the name of the game."

Mari had been quietly listening as Louie G explained the rules. "Well thank you for explaining the game so well. It actually sounds kind of fun . . . ." She grimaced before adding, "Except the part about getting hit by food repeatedly. That sounds kind of dangerous. But I'll volunteer to play whatever role you need me to play, Jerry. I know there's not a lot of time to select the team."

"Thanks, Mari. I appreciate it. And Louie G, you're a lifesaver!"

They pushed back their chairs and were about to head out of the library to return to the cabin when two ominous-looking men entered the building and walked directly toward the three friends. One was bald and burly, with thick, hairy arms protruding from a filthy (blood-stained?) apron, a butcher's knife clutched tightly in his left hand. The other was short and pudgy, with flour splotches all over his face and clothes, as if he had been interrupted in the middle of baking a cake.

The two characters stopped directly in front of the trio. Jerry leaned back against the table, his eyes growing wide while his heart started to pound. *What do they want with us? Did the Mufia send them to intimidate me some more? What are the chances that these two just suddenly felt the need for a dictionary?* One part of his brain tried to process the threat of the gleaming cleaver in the hand of the giant in front of him, while the other part of his brain desperately tried to think of 1) anything he and his friends had done to ask for trouble and 2) a way to escape! He opened his mouth to protest, but the pudgy character spoke first—rather surprisingly in what Louie G recognized instantly as an American southern drawl.

"Hi, kids. I'm one of the kitchen staff," he said in a friendly near-whisper. "I work mostly with flours and starches. They call me Potatoes—Taters for short. This here is Meat. He's the kitchen muscle: meat tenderizer, butcher, you name it. If it takes brawn, Meat's your man. He doesn't talk much."

Meat smiled and grunted what sounded like *Hello*.

"I told you not to bring that psycho-lookin' blade! You freak the kids out every time! Put it away!!!" Potatoes growled.

Meat sheepishly placed his hands behind his back.

Hairy felt relief surge through him, though he hoped it would soon become clear what the heck was going on.

Potatoes nodded at Jerry. "I know from seein' you in Eaditt Hall that you're Jerry Pasta. Congrats on being picked Head Chef and captain of the Mayon-daise EFF squad. I see you got the instruction manual."

Jerry waved the booklet as confirmation, his eyebrows shot high and betraying how crazy he found his present predicament.

"Meat and I are here to tell you a little more about the game. You see, the kitchen staff has been running EFF for over twenty years. It's our job to referee the games plus make sure each head chef knows the rules so we have a successful EFF season. Got any questions?"

Jerry looked incredulously from Meat to Potatoes then back to Meat. *Was that some kind of joke?* How could he *not* have questions? Louie G's explanation was thorough, but it didn't resolve the turmoil in Jerry's mind.

"Aren't they precious, Meat?" Potatoes quietly reveled in Jerry's obvious helplessness. "First-year campers are like fresh meat; so raw, so innocent. Just need a little tenderizing here and there."

Meat chuckled, though his laugh sounded more wild boar than human. (The "tenderizer" comment would have been much funnier had there *not* been a shiny meat cleaver within a three-foot radius.)

"So what's with the whispering?" Jerry blurted out, not even vaguely attempting to control the volume of his voice. "Except for the librarian, nobody is here but us."

"*Shhhhhhh!* Keep your voice low, Pasta!" Potatoes looked over his shoulder cautiously. "The reason EFF has successfully existed for so long is because it operates under secrecy. Well, sort of secrecy. The faculty can't *officially* allow EFF to be played on school grounds on account of liability issues. So they turn a blind eye and let the tradition carry on. That way they can't be held legally responsible when . . . um, *if* anyone gets hurt."

Potatoes settled into a chair at the table as Meat stood by mutely.

"As you've probably seen from the manual," Potatoes continued, "it's basically a food fight. About twenty years ago we had food fights at Pesto's all the time in the main dining hall. Then when the faculty squelched the fighting, a few students, some kitchen staff, and a couple of the more adventurous faculty banded together to keep food fights alive as a part of healthy competition here. But the agreement was made that the fights could never be made public—how could any responsible parent send their child to a prestigious cooking school knowin' that their kid would be throwin' rotten food at other kids with faculty support? It'd kill the school's rep—reputation. Plus, well, people sometimes get hurt. Lips get busted. Noses get . . . rearranged. We've had a few broken arms. The school can't officially sanction an activity where campers can get injured. So EFF stays officially off the books."

This is getting stranger by the moment, Jerry thought. And a glance at Louie G and Mari told him that they were thinking the same thing. "So all of the faculty 'unofficially' know about EFF? Is that why they were acting so weird when we got our letters in the dining hall?" Jerry asked.

Potatoes shook his head. "I'm guessin' that only three or four of the faculty and several of the wards will actually admit to knowin' that EFF still exists—and they're likely recent grads who participated in EFF themselves. I bet they watch from a distance sometimes to relive the good ol' days. Some of the faculty are probably suspicious that the students are up to sumptin', and some of them think EFF is just a silly rumor. A handful pretend not to notice but secretly disapprove and would bring the game to a halt if they had the chance. My guess is most of them see the flood-lights come on at night and think we're out there kickin' around a soccer ball." Potatoes sniggered. "Suckers."

Would this explain Chef La Gasse's peculiar behavior at breakfast? Jerry wondered. He also wondered why his father never mentioned EFF to him during all those times they talked about camp—but then he realized what the first rule of EFF must be: *NEVER TALK ABOUT EFF. Would Mamma have ever let me come to camp had she known about this game? I should probably thank Papa later.* Knowing about the game's background, he definitely had a newfound respect for EFF and the tra-dition that had been preserved for almost twenty years.

Jerry felt part of something old but cool; yet he still couldn't shake the feeling that he was in over his head. How could he ever have a team ready by tomorrow night—*and* still have some meals to organize for his kitchen?!

While Jerry got lost in his anxious thoughts, Louie G had questions of his own. He began by asking about the Egyptian theme and the use of the pyramid.

"Great question, kid. The Egyptian theme comes from the fact that the game is spun off the American food pyramid. One of the game's creators was an American kitchen staff member, my Uncle Joe Blank-stone. He was a nutritionist by trade, and he wanted the food fight to have some structure; so he used the American food pyramid. As you undoubtedly know, son, the food pyramid was a tool created by the U.S. Department of Agriculture designed to help people eat a balanced diet every day. What you probably *don't* know is that the USDA first started doling out this advice waaaaay back in the day—1916—though the use of an actual pyramid didn't start until 1992.

"There are four main food groups in a food pyramid: Grains, Dairy, Meat and Beans, and Fruits and Vegetables. In EFF we choose to sepa-rate fruits and veggies, so there are *five* different rounds of food fights over the next four weeks, each highlighting a different food group. You can expect to be throwing week-old bagels and rolls during Grain Fight Day. Meat and Beans Fight Day can be treacherous: unfinished ham hocks, bags of rotten beans, an occasional fish head. The Fruit and Vegetable Fight Days are the best because there are always nice, rounded objects to throw. And not to worry, nothing edible is used; the kitchen staff picks the food out of the kitchen waste. We don't intentionally pick out food that will cause injury, but shoot, it's part of the game."

Louie G nodded. "We talked about the food pyramid once in my health class back in the States." And then a lightbulb went off in his head. "Duh! That's why there are five Jackals, two Sphinxes, one Pharaoh, and an egg. Because of the five-two-one-zero lifestyle initiative." Louie G smacked his forehead. Noting the blank looks on Jerry's and Mari's faces, he explained, "In health class we learned that kids are supposed to eat five servings of fruits and vegetables daily, watch TV or be on the computer for two hours or less, spend one hour exercising, and drink zero sugary drinks. Five-two-one-zero."

"Smart kid," Potatoes said approvingly while Meat tacked on his kudos with a supportive grunt. "I reckon the creators of the game wanted to remind the campers that being healthy could be fun, so they created the game with all of these subtle and not-so-subtle reminders. Granted, getting hit in the ribs with a cucumber ain't the most subtle of reminders to eat your veggies, but . . . ." Potatoes shrugged and his belly bobbed up and down as he snickered.

"And what about all the waste left on the field? Doesn't that get disgusting after a few days?" Mari challenged, arms folded across her chest.

"I knew one of you was gonna ask. EFF is a green game; we recycle. After the game, y'all collect up the appropriate waste—everything but meat, bones, and dairy, essentially—and place it into bins near the field to make compost. That compost gets placed directly into the community garden. The circle of life. It's beautiful, ain't it kids?"

Mari dropped her hostile stance and nodded. The kids thanked Potatoes and Meat for their time, saying that they had a much better appreciation and understanding of the game.

Potatoes had one last thing to say before leaving.

"As referees, Meat and I aren't allowed to bet on the games. We're supposed to be objective and everything. But rumor has it that in the main kitchen, most bets are on you, Jerry Pasta. That's saying a lot since the Tomato Kitchen has won more consecutive EFF championships than I can remember. Don't disappoint. Or you'll never be sure if that shiny stuff served on your chicken is grease or something else." Potatoes painstakingly cleared his throat in a "something is stuck deep down" sort of way, then paused and winked. "If you know what I mean."

Jerry frowned. *Yuck! I knew exactly what you meant without the sound effects and theatrics.*

"And one more piece of advice: Don't take these games lightly. Wins on the EFF field buy you street cred here at Pesto's—though I guess 'kitchen cred' would be more accurate. A win on the Field of Greens might help a little guy like you stand out, earn you some r-e-s-p-e-c-t amongst your peers." He stood to leave, then added, "The two kitchens that perform the best in the first three fights will meet up for a winner-takes-all championship played during the last week of school. Winner gets the Golden Pyramid—and bragging rights for a year. See you on the field tomorrow at dusk!"

With that, they headed out of the library. The three campers stared after them, with Jerry now more nervous than ever. *People are betting on me to win? Why? This game has nothing to do with cooking! Why all this pressure?* Nonetheless, earning a little noncooking-related respect was pretty good motivation—as was not having his food spat on. May-on-daise Kitchen might lose their game tomorrow night, but they certainly wouldn't go down without a good fight. Make that a good *food* fight . . .

Chapter 11

Knowledge is dour...and sour

Jerry suddenly had a huge headache. As he shoved the EFF manual back into his satchel, he realized thoughts other than the EFF games were contributing to his headache, including lingering questions about the prophecy that he and Mari had talked about the previous day. And then Jerry remembered Mari's suggestion of checking the library for answers. *How often will I find myself in the camp library?* he thought. *Well, since I'm already here . . .*

He made up an excuse to buy himself a few extra minutes alone, saying he wanted to see if he could come up with some interesting recipes, telling Louie G and Mari to go on ahead to the cabin and begin scoping out potential EFF teammates.

"OK, Jerry. Catch up with you later," Louie G said, as he and Mari picked up their bags, then headed out of the library.

Jerry began wandering up and down the rows of books, not really knowing where to begin his search, not really knowing what questions he was even looking to answer. He decided to start with the ones burning the biggest hole in his brain: *Who was Della Morta? And what did she really prophesy? Maybe everybody had it all wrong. Maybe the actual prophecy never even mentioned pasta hair; maybe everyone had mistaken an R for a P.* To Jerry, it made much more sense (and would be much more convenient) that someone with "Rasta" hair might save cuisine rather

97

than someone with "pasta" hair. There were hundreds, maybe thousands of people with Rasta hair (most of them probably in Jamaica, Jerry figured), but he only knew one person with pasta hair, and that was himself.

Jerry was lost in thought when he tripped over a stack of books in the middle of the floor and—*BAM!*—landed flat on his face.

"Mamma mia!" Jerry rubbed his nose gingerly as he glared at the scattered hardbacks. "I thought books were supposed to be on the *shelves* in a library . . ."

Suddenly two strong hands were lifting him from behind, followed by a female voice saying, "I so sorry! I really should not have so many book lying around, but I always get so excite reading in the aisles."

Jerry turned around to find himself looking at a woman whom he figured was an instructor.

"Hi, my name is Margarita Grodita. What's jour name?" she said with a Spanish accent that turned her *Y*s into *J*s.

Jerry did a double-take followed by a reassessment of his assumption that she was an instructor. Margarita Grodita had the body (and strength) of a grown woman but the voice and face of a thirteen-year old girl. *She even has boobies,* Jerry timidly observed, then quickly refocused his eyes on her bronze face and shoulder-length black hair (though it was difficult since she had about six inches of height on him).

"Buon . . . buon giorno. Mi chiamo Jerry Pasta. Nice, uh, to meet you . . ." The more nervous Jerry got, the more he forgot to use English.

"I tink jou just said jour name is Herry Pasta. My friends call me Rita. The mean kids call me 'Large Marge' or 'Rita GORDita.' If jou did not know, *gordo* means *fat* in Spanish." Rita blushed and looked down at her feet.

Rita had some serious curves. But Jerry steered clear from making any references to her size, hoping instead to find some common ground. Which he thought would be easy. Since as soon as Rita pronounced his name with the 'H' sound (she made *J*s sound like *H*s), he was reminded of a familiar taunt.

"People call me mean names all the time too, especially because of my hair. 'Scary Hairy.' 'Bad Hairy Day.' Stupid stuff like that." Jerry realized that Rita probably hadn't even realized what she had done, making "Jerry" sound like "Hairy," just like she would have pronounced the names "Jose" and "Juan."

And Rita didn't seem bothered at all by Jerry's hair. In fact, she was actually reaching toward it as if to fondle it. "Jour hair, it's . . . it's so beautiful and unique. Tell me how jou got it."

Jerry backed away before Rita could touch him. She immediately blushed, embarrassed by her own boldness.

"I'm sorry, Rita, I'm just a little sensitive about—" Jerry paused mid-sentence, realizing an important opportunity had been presented to him. Maybe Rita was the only other person aside from himself who didn't know about the prophecy. Maybe he'd found the perfect person, a neutral observer, to help him find the answers he was looking for. Jerry backtracked from his defensive stance and gave Rita the abbreviated version of how he got his pasta hair, then explained to her how he was looking for information about Della Morta and her prophecy.

"Well, Herry—"

Jerry winced a little.

"—I tink the easiest place to start is the computer terminal. We can just do online search by subject. And we could always ask *el bibliotecario*—um, the librarian, Chef Jo Moi-Erreur."

Jerry suddenly felt stupid. Just because this was cooking camp didn't mean it'd be low tech.

Rita and Jerry were able to quickly find information about Della Morta. She had been a Pesto's instructor around the time Jerry's father was a student. In her old age, Morta had been forced to live at a mental institution, which struck a chord with Jerry: his mother had frequented a similar place earlier in his childhood when her behavior had become unstable. Some thought Della Morta was just senile, chalking her behavior up to just the crazy things that old people almost seem bound to say. But the fact was, no one could really discount the things she said because she'd been such a well-respected chef in her heyday.

After about ten minutes of reading about Della Morta in a cooking encyclopedia (you know you've made it when you're in the encyclopedia), Rita stumbled across the prophecy.

"I tink this is it, Herry! Come take a look."

Jerry felt his stomach lurch. Sort of the same feeling he had after the kitchen assignments. And his Mufia encounter. And the EFF invitation. (You know, that feeling you get with the first *huuuuuuge* drop on a rollercoaster? Jerry wasn't sure he liked that feeling *everyday*, multiple times a day!) He was really praying for a typo, something that could easily be explained away as a simple case of mistaken identity. Something he could point to definitively as proof that the "Saviory Chef" was still out there, and everyone was just looking in the wrong place. *I'm not the hero you're looking for. Try Jamaica*, he'd say.

Jerry looked over Rita's shoulder, reading each word carefully.

```
    In days to come expect a change,
Italian food will not be the same
More fat, more salt, vegetables few,
Unhealthy choices through and through

    An evil lurks along our shores,
A sickness rotten to the core.
It slowly grows, disguised, a mole,
To own your body, soon your soul.

    But there will come from Italia's loin,
A native son to cure those who dare to join.
This Master Chef with a bachetta magica,
His hair will be tutti tipi di pasta

    He could save us all from wicked food,
Restore the kitchen to all that's good.
An epic war over arteries and veins,
Should he lose? Our world goes down in
flames!
                    -Della Morta, circa 1991
```

Jerry's hands were shaking. Mari's earlier dramatic paraphrasing wasn't that far off. Much to Jerry's chagrin, there were no typos in this version of the prophecy.

Rita looked puzzled. "Could jou—how do jou say—translate?"

Jerry assumed Rita was referring to the Italian words in the third stanza. "Sure, uh, a *bacchetta magica* is a magic wand, and *tutti tipi di pasta* means 'all forms of pasta.'"

She nodded thoughtfully. "I could see how this might be about jou," Rita intoned, her finger gently tapping the third stanza of the prophecy. "In Mexico"—she pronounced it *Meh-hee-co*—"where my family is from, people strongly believe in prophecy. And they look for miraculous signs *everywhere*. Jesus' ("Hay-soose'es") face appeared on ten tie-dyed shirts last week, I tink." She smiled.

Jerry considered Rita's point: People in Italy probably weren't too different from people in Mexico or anywhere else in the world. They look for confirmation of whatever they believe wherever they can find it.

And there were the other perplexing parts of the prophecy. First of all, Jerry was no Master Chef—at least not yet. And he certainly was no magician.

And then there was the last stanza. That was no victor's prophecy, the kind that might inspire greatness. No, this suggested, "He *could* save us," not he *would* or *will*. There were no guarantees here. Oh, and by the way, failure means the end of the world!

Jerry slammed the book shut, almost nipping Rita's fingers in the process.

"Did I say something to make jou angry, Herry?"

Jerry winced at his name pronunciation (again) and shook his head.

"It's not you, Rita," he said as reassuringly as he could. "It's the words on that page. It's what I've been hearing over the past few days. What if this 'hero' everyone's looking for *isn't* me? What if he's already come and failed, and we're all doomed?"

Rita shrugged. "Maybe it's *not* about jou, Herry . . ."

Yes, finally, the wisest thing anybody had said to me since I got to camp, Jerry mused.

"But a lot of us here feel like we have to be heroes back in our own countries. Especially those of us not from Europe. Jou think I don't feel the weight of my country on my shoulder? I am only the third person from Mexico to come to Pesto's in the last fie years." Rita made the *V* in "five" disappear.

Jerry paused. He hadn't really stopped to think about the fact that he wasn't the only one at Pesto's under high expectations. Come to think of it, maybe he wasn't the only one who'd had his summer fees paid for. This *was* one of the most prestigious cooking schools in the world. Admission was highly competitive, selective, *and* expensive. Maybe everyone here felt a little of the pressure he was feeling. . . . He inwardly sighed. *But I bet none of them had been told, "Go to camp, save the world."*

"I think I just need a moment to process all this, Rita. Thanks again for your help. I really appreciate it."

Rita leaned into Jerry and planted a quick kiss on his cheek. "Anytime jou need it, I'll be here to help." She giggled. "I mean that literally. The library is my home away from home. *Adios,* Herry." She picked up her books, gave him a brief wave, and left.

Jerry's cheek felt warm and tingly for the next five minutes. That was the first female kiss he had received from someone other than his mother in recent memory. Jerry quickly convinced himself that the kiss must have been a cultural thing and not a romantic gesture. He certainly didn't need any more complications in his life at this point. Though if he stayed friends with Rita this summer, he was going to have to teach her how to make his name sound more like 'Jerry' and less like 'Hairy'.

Feeling both angry and confused, Jerry continued to wander around the library to clear his thoughts. Near the librarian's desk he noticed what looked like a stack of old yearbooks. Jerry scanned them and pulled out the one from 1991, his father's first year at Pesto's. It only took him a few minutes to find his papa's photo. In those days Pesto's was a year-round school, and it took three years to graduate as Master Chef. The classes were even smaller than they were now, made up of mostly European kids. Toni's face hadn't changed much since his days at Pesto's—though he certainly looked happier and better rested in this old photo.

But then another photo several rows above his dad's picture caught Jerry's eye. The person was somehow very familiar yet at the same time quite changed. The face was thinner but he had the same jet-black hair and piercing green eyes. . . . No, it *couldn't* be! Jerry's gaze raced to the end of the column of pictures to match the face to a name.

Moldavi Ernesto Coeur.

So *that* was his real name! Jerry wondered how the unflattering nickname "Moldy" stuck. And he was even more surprised that Moldy Coeur had been in Papa's class—and Papa had never mentioned it! What a tale of two worlds! One Pesto graduate ends up as laid-off school lunch man while the other owns a burgeoning, successful fast-food franchise and donates tons of money to his alma mater.

Jerry quickly found the 1992 and 1993 yearbooks. He was eager to see how the two had changed over the next couple of years (or if he recognized anyone else from their classes). In the 1992 yearbook—which had changed to color—Jerry spotted Al Dente, noticeably thinner than his present-day embodiment, as a young student a year behind his dad. Toni looked slightly more haggard but still happy. Moldy Coeur had clearly gained a little weight in those two years. The color photos also picked up another oddity. Coeur's previously jet-black hair now had noticeable streaks of . . . green. Mostly at the roots. Jerry hadn't seen any green in Moldy Coeur's hair at the pavilion on Day One. Maybe he was dyeing his hair now? And in addition to the hair, Moldy Coeur had gained a substantial amount of weight. He had the beginnings of a double chin and the cheeks of a well-fed chipmunk. Plus there was no hint of a smile on his face. *Had something happened to Coeur during his time at Pesto's? Or was it after he'd left that he changed into the sour man he was today?*

Fascinated by his findings, Jerry turned the yearbook pages to see what else he could learn. A faded yellow parchment had stuck to one page. Jerry peeled it off carefully without creating a tear. It appeared to be a clipping from a Presto Pesto's newsletter. *What's it doing in this yearbook? Looks like a student publication. . . .* Jerry brought the page closer to better read the fading ink.

Pesto's Premier Newsletter   January 1993

January 13, 1993

School Founder Acquitted of Wrongdoing, But Ousted

As many of you know, at a New Year's Eve banquet two weeks ago, former beloved chef and teacher Jodie Macchio died after a severe bout of food poisoning. Others fell ill, with a few still recovering at a local intensive care unit. The meal, exquisitely prepared by school founder Karim de la Carème, was found to have deadly quantities of a toxin rumored to have been extracted from the organs of a deadly blowfish. (Police reports have not yet corroborated this claim). Chef de la Carème spent the last several days in court defending his innocence. Some have speculated his old age has led to more careless mistakes in his cooking.

The evidence presented by the prosecution was unable to secure a conviction for murder. To avoid their client getting stuck with a charge of involuntary manslaughter, the defense negotiated a plea deal. Carème accepted a mandatory probation: for a fifteen year period, he is forbidden from cooking at Presto Pesto's or at restaurants, only cooking meals for himself and perhaps small family gatherings. If caught violating the terms of his probation, Carème will be sentenced to death.

The defense cited a "lack of hard evidence," vehemently claiming their client was framed.

But why would a beloved founder of the school be framed?

This is the same question the wards and trustees of the school asked themselves. So after great deliberation, though Carème was not found guilty in a court of law, a jury of his peers, yes, the wards and trustees of Presto Pesto's, voted to have him removed from his *teaching duties*. This move by the wards and trustees was vital to preserving the school's reputation as the pinnacle of cooking instruction. How could the school's students continue to learn cooking from a convicted (almost convicted) felon?

I have gathered word through his lawyer that Karim de la Carème has quietly retired to the French countryside.

While this incident is tragic, we hope it does not mar what has otherwise been a stellar year for our senior class, Presto Pesto's Class of 1993.

By Moldavi E. Coeur

106

Jerry's jaw went slack. He wondered if any other students through the years knew about this. It would have made for great gossip seventeen years ago, which is probably why the article was slipped into the yearbook. And the author of the article was not overlooked by Jerry. The tone of the entire piece was quite negative. Jerry got the sense that Coeur believed Carème was guilty as charged. But Jerry was as confused as Carème's lawyers. *Why would the founder of the school poison former students and faculty at the very school he had founded and loved? That's the question the wards and trustees should have been asking!* Jerry was now even more interested in reading the Carème textbook he had picked up from Sauce class, curious to see what this notorious and banished figure in school history could teach him about cooking.

He closed the yearbook with a *thump*. His research had certainly provided Jerry with a lot more information than he'd had—maybe more than he wanted to know. The sour taste from Day One had returned to Jerry's mouth. And the camp rollercoaster car he was strapped in plummeted about 300 feet.

Again.

He gathered his belongings and headed out of the library. All the answers had only led to more questions—and a tummy ache—and he still had an EFF match to plan for.

Chapter 12

Grade "A" for "EFF"ort

Jerry wasted no time organizing his EFF team when he got back to the cabin; thanks to Mari and Louie G's advance scouting, the prospective squad was basically at the ready. And his first executive order was a no-brainer: he officially appointed Louie G as his co-captain since the young American clearly had a grasp of the rules and gameplay. At this point Jerry did too—but not to the extent Louie G did. Which is why the next thing out of Jerry's mouth initially shocked Louie G.

"Louie G, you're going to be the Pharaoh for this *gioco primo*, this first game."

"*What?!* The *Pharaoh?* And not use these amazing athletic skills—this cannon of an arm, these fleet feet?" Louie G punched the air and ran in place like a boxer prebout. If there was one thing Louie G wasn't, it was humble.

"Louie G, we've spent the last two hours discussing strategy. You yourself said that strategy is everything. And since we won't know our opponent until the game starts, I need someone on the field who can call the shots." He grinned. "You should be in the military; you've got this battle strategy thing down to a science."

Initially disappointed, Louie G now beamed at the encouragement and praise. Clearly Jerry had struck the right chord. "So you're calling me your field general?"

"Exactly!" Jerry replied. "You can tell Jackals where to position themselves, when to attack. You can analyze the other team's patterns and tell our Sphinxes where you think the opposing Pharaoh's soul is hidden. And you still get to use those athletic skills dodging the food thrown at you. Plus, you might be toughest guy in our kitchen."

Louie G's face looked as if it might get stuck in a permanent toothy grin.

Mari tried to bring Louie G back down to earth. "Some tough guy you are. Lefsa Stovon basically bullied you and the boys into cleaning our bathroom weekly as your camp job." *(Girls 1, Boys 0. Nice one, Mari.)*

"Hey, I was the best player on my Pop Warner football team back home. And the whole bathroom thing? I was just being a gentleman. Lefsa was only holding me up by my shirt because she wanted me to . . . uh . . . fix a lightbulb. . . . " Louie G's voice trailed off. Then he shrugged. "Forget the past. Let's look toward the future! Consider the EFF game won, Jerry Pasta. Choosing me proves you really are wise beyond your years."

By dinnertime, Jerry and Louie G had picked out the whole team. Jerry and Mari would be the Sphinxes. The Jackals would consist of Brad Vurst, a stout German kid with a big arm; Manny Cotti, a gangly Italian boy who'd shown great skill with a soccer ball during the free time before meals; Guinness Fishenship, a half-Irish, half-British girl who towered over everyone else; Lefsa Stovon, a brawny (just ask Louie G) Norwegian girl with the blondest of hair and bluest of eyes; and Sushimi Sashimi (who everyone called Susie Sash for short), a diminutive Japanese camper with sure hands and shifty feet; you'd want her on your dodgeball team because she'd probably always be the toughest out!

"I'm *pleased* with my role Jerry," Mari said, not exhibiting a shred of enthusiasm. "Though 'pleased' is clearly an exaggeration. *Satisfied*, maybe? This game is disgusting. Touching moldy food? Yuck!" Mari grimaced and shuddered at the thought. "But I'd rather *dodge* nasty food than run around fondling it for sixty minutes. Poor Jackals."

After dinner, Louie G taught the five new members the rules, and the team practiced some elementary tactics on the small field adjacent to the Mayon-daise cabin. When Jerry noticed campers from the other kitchens spying on them, Mayon-daise EFF training moved indoors, into the cabin. With limited space to practice, maneuvering was difficult, so Jerry emphasized the Jackals' need to heed Louie G because as Pharaoh, he would have the best view of the entire playing field.

Jerry did worry about the fitness of his Jackals. He had selected the most athletic-looking campers, but pickings were slim; this was *not* your normal summer camp. No one would mistake Presto Pesto's for a sports camp or boot camp. Fitness was going to be an issue. Regardless of this first game's outcome, this team was going to need to do some aerobic training to include distance running and sprinting. Jerry discussed this with Louie G as they lay in their bunks at lights out.

"Louie G, I think our team is, uh, to put it nicely, a little . . . athletically challenged. After five minutes of running, Lefsa looked like she was about to have a heart attack, and Brad kept saying his feet hurt. How can they last through an entire game? We're going to lose because our players' *mouths* move more efficiently than their *legs*!"

From his top bunk, Louie G gave a deep-bellied laugh. "That's where you're wrong Jerry. Well, OK, maybe you're not wrong, but it isn't going to matter. For this first match, we're going to take fitness out of the equation."

Irritated, Jerry inquired, "And how are you going to do that? By pushing everyone around in wheelchairs? And what if we don't score any points?"

"Whoa, JP! Relax." Louie G leaned over the edge of his bed and peered down at his anxious friend.

"Back home, scoring zero points is called 'laying a goose egg'—and I guarantee that we won't lay a goose egg tomorrow. And definitely not an egg the other team's Sphinxes will find, either. Have a little faith, Jerry Pasta; watch and learn. Besides, if I tell you all my tricks, you might decide you don't need me anymore. I'm sort of liking the view from up here on my Pharaoh's throne." Louie G placed his hands behind his head and fell back on his pillow, eyes closed.

Louis G's confidence had a calming effect, and Jerry soon drifted off to sleep. His last conscious thought wasn't about EFF, though. It was about what he had learned earlier that day in the library about Moldavi E. Coeur; Karim de la Carème the school's disgraced founder; and Della Morta's prophecy that had created more questions than answers.

Jerry woke less than refreshed: another night, another nightmare. This time he was being chased by giant vegetables and fruits, including a cluster of oversized bananas throwing water balloons filled with scalding water at him. He was sorry that he kept waking up Louie G with his dreams but thankful that Louie G rarely asked for details.

"How long have I known you—like, three days? Your dreams are your business, Jerry. They're personal. You can tell me about them if it'll help you sleep better, but something tells me it won't make a difference."

After showering, the two boys met up with Mari to walk to breakfast, discussing EFF strategy on the way. During Sauce class, Chef Beurre snapped at Jerry twice for whispering to Louie G.

"Pasta, just because you've won a few camp cooking competitions doesn't mean you don't have much to learn about zeh art of sauce making. Try setting an example for your peers and paying attention for a change."

Well, that *was a low blow,* Jerry fumed inwardly. He hated being called out. So, somewhat defiantly, he pulled out his *Sauce for the Saucier* book and opened it with a flourish; Chef Beurre couldn't yell at him if he was busy paging through a course textbook. The first page was typical, listing the publisher, the editor, the edition number (2nd), and the copyright date (2001). On the facing page was a picture of the author, a smiling, young Karim de la Carème, resting his chin in his hands. The backs of his hands were notably scarred. *Probably from kitchen accidents*, Jerry guessed. *Those are marks of true dedication to his cooking. At least Karim still had his real hair*, thought Jerry, mulling his own experience. Jerry did actually start reading the book that day, combing through the first twenty pages. It was surprisingly interesting and easy to read.

The rest of the day sped by fairly quickly. Jerry reminded the EFF team to eat a light, mixed carbohydrate/protein dinner so that they would 1) have energy during the EFF match and 2) not puke within the first five minutes of the game starting. The team fairly drooled over the delicious *sauce duxelles* (brown mushroom sauce) made for the rib-eye steak and au gratin potatoes but limited themselves to one helping each.

After dinner the team dressed in athletic shorts plus either gold or yellow T-shirts, per Louie G's instruction, so they could recognize each other on the field. Jerry picked out a tight-fitting cap that would rein in his macaroni hair; the feeling of his hair jiggling as he ran could be quite distracting.

Since at least two hours would pass between dinner and the start of the EFF game, Jerry designed a high-energy snack to carry the team over.

Jerry Pasta's
FIVE BY FIVE ENERGY SNACK MIX

Feeds 1
Preparation Time: 3 minutes

INGREDIENTS AND SUPPLIES

Ingredients

1 cup raisins

1 cup dried cranberries

1 cup cheerios

1 cup M&Ms

1 cup roasted peanuts

Supplies

1 large Ziploc bag

DIRECTIONS

1. Mix all ingredients in a Ziploc bag. Shake, shake, shake.

2. Eat!

The five cups of snack mix should last several days and will stay fresh as long the bag is well-sealed after opening.

Jerry gathered the team at 7:45 and led them toward the field, following the map at the back of the EFF manual. Three-quarters of a mile later, the WELCOME TO THE FIELD OF GREENS sign was a dead giveaway that they had arrived at the right place. Jerry noted that the thick, ankle-high fescue grass would be good for running, cozy for lying down in "mummy position," and perfect for hiding an egg under a copper bowl. The sun was beginning to set, and large floodlights were primed to shine as soon as darkness fell. The conditions were windy, leading Louie G to announce, "The Food Gods have smiled on us tonight. My game plan should work to perfection."

Jerry could only hope that Louie G knew what the heck he was talking about.

Chapter 13

Super Mari! Oh brother...

The referees were already on the field, marking the lines and placing the wooden stools (aka "thrones") in their appropriate circles. Someone on a bullhorn announced that the first matchup would be Mayon-daise Kitchen versus Velouté Kitchen. Butterflies flitted in Jerry's stomach. "At least we'll get it out the way quic

Louie G was much more confi-
dent. "Let's send a message with this
first bout, Jerry. Stick to the game
plan and make the other kitchens respect us after this match."

It was clear from looking at
the other teams that Mayon-daise
Kitchen by no means had the largest
or most-athletic looking campers on their team. Tomato Kitchen, headed by Robert DeJourno, was stacked with fourteen-year-olds, their shortest player seemingly a head taller than Mayon-daise's tallest. One remarkable feature of all of the EFF teams: The girls were noticeably taller than the boys. This is pretty universal at around the age of twelve. Most boys haven't quite hit their growth spurts, and most girls are much more . . . physically developed (like Rita Grodita). The EFF girls made some of the boys look like, well, little boys. Jerry was smart enough to take note of this immediately after his library encounter with Rita Grodita—and he made sure to take advantage of the "girl power" within the Mayon-daise Kitchen when assembling the team. The boys who thought that they were going to kick butt in EFF would be sorely disappointed; the girls had a monopoly on brawn.

"Welcome to the Field of Greens," charged the man with the bull-horn. "Mayon-daise, Velouté, take your positions. . . ."

Jerry was surprised to see that the person on the bullhorn was the aging janitor who had cleaned his ICS and eaten his leftover eggs. It seemed as if this guy would also be serving as the play-by-play announcer because he was positioned in a tall chair—like the kind a life-guard would occupy—on the sideline at centerfield. Meat and Potatoes were two of the five referees for the first game. 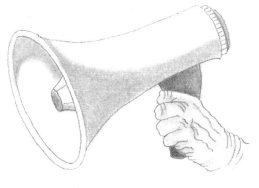 The head referee introduced himself as Brock Lee.

Mari had learned a little bit about each referee before the game and was prepared to give her report—she had her sources.

"Brock Lee is a martial artist turned chef's assistant. He was apparently a knives expert but had an unfortunate mishap that led to him being banished from the world of competitive martial arts. So he took up his second love, cooking, and is now one of the most senior kitchen staff at Pesto's. I guess it's good to have a referee who can stay sharp." Mari chuckled at her own joke amidst a sea of moans and rolling eyes.

Brock Lee gathered all the players at midfield for some pregame in-structions. "All referee decisions are final and not open for debate. I will keep the official score in my notebook while the sideline judge will update the manual scoreboard." A large chalkboard stood to the right of the tall beach chair. "The first half will last thirty minutes or until one team scores 500 points. Any points scored this half will carry over into the second half. The first team to score 1000 points or the team with the highest score when time expires wins. Begin on the sideline judge's mark!"

Suddenly a loud rattling sound echoed across the playing field, fol-lowed by a lone feminine voice yelling, "Go, Herry! *Vamanos!*"

Jerry and the rest of the Mayon-daise team looked in unison at the sideline to see Rita Grodita, wearing a flowery red dress with a yellow blouse, rhythmically shaking a pair of wooden maracas: Jerry's unofficial cheerleader.

"Isn't she in the Espagnole Kitchen?" Mari innocently asked, nudging Jerry playfully in the ribs. "It looks like you've made a fan."

Jerry tried to stay focused though his body betrayed him, blood rushing to his cheeks in embarrassment.

The old janitor raised the bullhorn to his mouth. "Ready on the left?"

Louie G nodded.

"Ready on the right?"

Robèrt Jammonde, the opposing team's Pharaoh, nodded.

"Then let's begin Egyptian Food Fight. GO!!!!"

The players began sprinting toward the middle of the field. From the sidelines, it looked like the players would collide at midfield, suffering more than minor concussions. Luckily, body contact was avoided as the players reached the centerline at different times. Jerry was the first to reach the middle; his daily run had really paid off! Surprised to find himself a little winded after the 50-yard dash, he grabbed all the food items he could hold and immediately retreated to the middle of the May-on-daise side of the field, near the Pharaoh's circle. Glancing around, he saw that only two other members of his team had grabbed food items: Mari, the other Sphinx, and Susie Sashimi, one of the Jackals. Jerry took stock of his inventory: two-week-old bagels, a rock-hard dinner roll (maybe from last year's camp? *Ouch!*), and a half loaf of pumpernickel about the size of both his fists. It took him a few seconds to tear the loaf in half, creating two projectiles. Mari and Susie had only grabbed two food items each, bringing the team total to nine. Which meant Velouté Jackals and Sphinxes had as many as eleven food items—maybe more if they were able to split any of their "ammunition" into multiple pieces.

About one minute had passed, and boos began to rain down from the stands; no food had been thrown! It was clear the two teams were playing it safe, trying to feel out the game. The crowd was growing more restless by the second, with some loudly chanting, "Food fight! Food fight!" in hopes of sparking something . . . *anything*. The Mayon-daise team huddled as close as they could to Louie G's stool in the middle of their side of the field. He had to give his instructions fairly loudly since the obnoxious cheers drowned out his voice, and no one could stand within fifteen feet of his stool (the boundary neatly outlined with a circle of white spray paint).

"Remember the plan, guys. Let them get impatient and strike first. They can't stun us on our side of the field, but we can stun them. They'll have to wait for their Sphinxes to resurrect them, then return to their own side before coming to attack again." Louie G snuck a glance at how the Velouté side was organizing themselves. "As soon as I have a sense of where their egg is hidden, I'll tell Jerry and Mari, and we'll put the plan in play."

Brad Vurst, one of the Mayon-daise Jackals, interjected. "Vhere is our soul hidden? You hid it before ze game when everyvone's backs vere turned to ze field. Ve can protect it better if you tell us vhere it is."

"Can't tell you that, Brad," Louie G replied, shaking his head. "I haven't told anyone—and that's exactly why, I hope, we're going to win. I don't want anyone inadvertently glancing over at the location of our egg to make sure it's safe or hovering by it; the other team could see that and take advantage of us. Which is how I'm banking on Velouté to screw up. Our egg's best protection is that I'm the only one who knows where it is." Louie G was keeping his cards close to his chest, but this window into his strategy gave Jerry and the rest of the team a huge surge of confidence.

Velouté finally prepared to make their move. Three of their Jackals stood poised at the 50 yard line, ready to cross over and begin their assault on Pharaoh Louie G. One Jackal hovered as a defender near the Velouté Pharaoh, a French kid named Robèrt Jammonde whom

Jerry recognized from Sauce class, and the Velouté Sphinxes were split between their attacking Jackals and the defending Jackal. One other Velouté Jackal stood about twenty yards to the left of his Pharaoh's circle and an additional twenty yards away from midfield.

"Aha!" Louie G cried, gesturing to Jerry and Mari and looking like he'd won the lottery. "Velouté's given away their egg's location! Jerry, Mari, stand at midfield and head toward that lone Velouté Jackal, in the back right corner of their field, when I give you the signal. That's gotta be where there egg is hidden. Remember the plan. Jackals, prepare to defend your Pharaoh!" he laughed. "I kinda like the sound of that!"

The game was suddenly afoot. The Velouté Jackals crossed the midfield line, arms cocked and ready to attack. Louie G had instructed his Jackals Brad, Guinness, and Lefsa to stand at the front of his circle as defenders, while Jackals Susie and Manny were to stand at the midfield line, thirty yards apart, poised to attack the Velouté Pharaoh. The attacking Velouté Jackals were good, deftly dodging the first few volleys of bread thrown at them. But Lefsa had a cannon for an arm. She caught one of the Velouté Jackals, Olumena Abaka—a tall, husky Nigerian kid who had once shared Jerry's breakfast table—squarely in the chest with a dinner roll. Abaka, who clutched his chest and tried to rub out the sting, was quickly prodded by Referee Potatoes to drop to the ground and assume "the mummy" position until resurrected by a Sphinx teammate.

It remained to be seen if Louie G's plan would work. He had accurately guessed that Velouté would go with a power strategy, given their size and strength: attack the Mayon-daise Pharaoh aggressively, find the egg if possible, get back on defense if Mayon-daise found the Velouté egg first. But Louie G's defense-first strategy was about to turn the game on its head. Jerry and Mari stood side by side right at the center of midfield, awaiting the signal. As two Velouté Jackals closed in on the Mayon-daise Pharaoh's circle, Louie G rose up, stood on the seat of his stool, raised his arms in the air and yelled, "Now!!"

The signal had its desired effect. The Velouté Jackals clearly couldn't believe their luck and launched brick-hard bagels and moldy rolls at the exposed Louie G. At the same instant, Susie and Manny, who had been poised at midfield to attack Velouté Pharaoh Jammonde, suddenly pivoted 180 degrees to become defenders and rushed the distracted Velouté attackers, pelting two of them in the back! Harry and Mari responded to the signal by sprinting to the back right corner of the Velouté field, frantically looking for the copper bowl that would reveal the Velouté egg. Meanwhile, Louis G was easily dodging everything thrown at him. The Mayon-daise and Velouté campers not playing in the game cheered their respective sides. The other kitchens watched and yelled encouragement too. Most of the kids just wanted to see some good direct food hits. The devious ones chanted for blood.

On the Mayon-daise side of the field, Louie G was expecting food to be thrown at him when he stood up, so it was easy for him to catch the first two bagels, then drop deftly back into a sitting position to avoid a pumpernickel roll to the chest. It also helped that the wind had picked up quite a bit, making many of the on-target throws suddenly wayward. One of the Velouté Sphinxes was doing her best to resurrect her fallen Jackals, who'd been "mummified" by Susie and Manny, and get them back into the action, while the other Sphinx was fruitlessly looking for the Mayon-daise egg.

Meanwhile, on the Velouté side of the field, Jerry had finally located the copper bowl. Actually, he tripped over it and almost landed flat on his face. The Velouté Jackal who had been monitoring that area of play was now occupied by a lone Mayon-daise Jackal, Sushimi Sashimi, who was pretending to attack Pharaoh Jammonde, but she was really just running interference, dodging food to keep the Velouté Jackal distracted from the Mayon-daise Sphinxes.

While the Velouté Jackal was otherwise occupied, Jerry caught Mari's attention, twenty-five yards away on the opposite side of the field, and gave her the signal that he'd located the egg almost exactly where Louis G had predicted it would be.

Nodding, Mari reached to the ground with her ladle in her right hand and then was up in an instant, running down the Velouté right sideline, yelling, "I found it!" Mari's left hand protectively shielded the bowl of her ladle.

Robèrt Jammonde was furiously barking at his now resurrected Velouté Jackals to turn their attention to Mari, who was now only thirty yards from midfield. If Mari crossed midfield with the egg, Mayon-daise would score 500 points, and the first half of the game would be over. But if she dropped the egg, it could break, giving Velouté 500 points, or at least cost her precious seconds to pick it back up and put it on her ladle.

The Velouté Jackals were throwing every food item in their arsenal at Mari, hoping to knock her off course. She dodged two bagels, then another one. A dinner roll glanced off her chin—but no penalty was called despite it being a shot to the head. She briefly stumbled but remained on her feet, to the amazement of the crowd.

Mari was haphazardly running fully erect with long, faltering strides—kind of like she'd eaten an elephant-sized rum cake. The five Velouté Jackals closed in on her as she was ten yards from the midfield line, pelting her with half-loaves from all directions. But when they were within the allowed distance of five yards (as they were constantly being reminded by Refs Meat and Potatoes), Mari dropped to her knees, eyes to the ground.

Mena Abaka, the closest Velouté Jackal, eagerly yelled, "She dropped it!"

The rest of the Velouté Jackals gathered around Mari in anticipation of victory . . . then their faces contorted into looks of confusion.

There was no egg to be seen.

No shards of shell. No sticky yoke. Mari, eyes squinted, looked up at the befuddled Velouté Jackals and asked in her clearest British accent, "Can you guys help me find my contact lens? It fell out while I was looking for your egg—I was carrying it in this ladle until you all started throwing food at me."

The Velouté Jackals immediately knew they had been duped! Instantly, they all turned to where they knew the egg had been hidden, but it was too late. Jerry Pasta was calmly walking up the left sideline, egg on ladle, and in only a few steps he crossed the midfield line.

Whssstttt! A whistle blew. From his chair, the janitor referee announced, "Five hundred points to Mayon-daise Kitchen. It is now half-time. The second half will begin in ten minutes."

The Mayon-daise campers on the sidelines were on their feet, loudly cheering and clapping. The agape mouths of the Velouté EFF team said it all; even the spectators gazed in stunned silence. Head referee Brock Lee turned to the other referees and exclaimed, "The last time a team retrieved the egg that quickly was 1999, more than ten years ago. Less than five minutes?! Unbelievable!"

The Mayon-daise EFF team gathered inside their Pharaoh's circle, exchanging hi-fives and back slaps. Louie G yelled out, "You were super, Mari!"

Only Mari still seemed concern about something. Her left eye was noticeably red, and her right eye was closed shut. "Excuse me, can I have everyone's attention? I really did lose my contact while looking for the egg. Can a few of you come help me find it?"

Louie G's praise of "Super, Mari" was replaced by an incredulously whispered, "Oh, brother. . . ."

Chapter 14

MVE: Most Valuable EFFer

The second half of the game was more conventional but still lasted only twelve minutes. Mayon-daise Kitchen methodically hit Velouté Pharaoh Robèrt Jammonde eight times for a total of 400 points (50 points per hit), and Mari (with Jerry's help) located the egg and brought it across midfield for an additional 500 points. The Velouté team was dejected after being shut out 500 to 0 in the first half, and it showed in their second-half performance. Their uninspired effort left them with only 50 points. They couldn't find the Mayon-daise egg (ably hid by Louie G right outside of the Pharaoh's circle—they never suspected it'd be that close by), and they hit Louie G only once. Arguably. The one food item that hit Louie G was a piece of bread that broke when he caught it, and the free end gently hit him in the stomach. He was still sulking after the game.

"I ruined the shutout. Sorry, guys. Aren't the referees supposed to set out new food at halftime? I recognized that onion bagel from the first half—and it was definitely already falling apart then."

Louie G would later explain to Jerry that his competitive drive was bred while growing up in Alabama. The fierce intrastate college football rivalry between Alabama and Auburn cultivated a culture of competition—with battle lines drawn as early as kindergarten. If Alabama lost to Auburn, Louie G was miserable (like "my puppy died" miserable) for several months—until the two teams played again the following year. Alabama winning was the equivalent of that dead puppy coming back to life *and* getting three weeks of spring break!

Simply put, Louie G hated losing. Generally that would have even included breakfast competitions to his good buddy Jerry. But at camp he and Jerry were on the same team, so even if Louie G lost and Jerry won, it was all good. And that's kind of why cooking camp worked for Louie G: competitive cooking and outdoor food fights felt like second nature given the cutthroat sports culture he'd grown up in.

The rest of the Mayon-daise team was excited that the EFF season had started so well, and they continued to exchange high-fives on their way to the bleachers. Mari touted having both contact lenses as the reason for finding the egg in the second half (good thing she had brought a spare set down to the field with her); she was quite proud of herself—and deservedly so. The one element of the winning game that wasn't entirely pleasant to Jerry had nothing to do with the game itself. Rather, it was Rita Grodita, who was by far the team's loudest cheerleader. To say that Jerry was a little embarrassed would be an understatement. He tried his best to avoid Rita during the postgame bustle, but she cornered him along the sidelines and gave him a big hug.

"*Felicidades!* Congratulations, Herry! Jou were *magnifico!*"

"Uh, *grazie*, thanks, Rita," Jerry replied sheepishly.

His entire team was watching him in breathless anticipation of what might happen next. Jerry had a not-at-all-secret admirer!

"I hope Espagnole wins today . . . are you playing?" he asked, and as soon as the words left his mouth, Jerry knew he had just asked the dumbest question in the world: *Are you playing?* Would Rita *really* run out onto the field in a long, billowing, floral skirt and throw pieces of food at other campers? Unlikely. No, impossible.

"Well, the captain deedn't pick me; he said I was too . . . he said I was in not-too-good shape. But I would like to play. Maybe I can train with jour team in case they pick me later?" Rita shrugged and looked away from Jerry.

Jerry was himself trying hard to not make eye contact. *Is she wearing makeup? I can't believe how* awkward *this is!!!* What next popped out of his mouth shocked him more than the ill-advised question he had posed seconds earlier. "Sure, come by the cabin any-time!"

Truth be told, Jerry had just wanted the conversation to be over. But in ending the conversation as he did, he had clearly made Rita's day—heck, maybe her entire camp experience. He got another hug before Rita bounded off to sit with her cabinmates to watch the next EFF match.

Louie G could barely contain himself. "Jerry Pasta! And I thought *I* was your number one fan! I think she may want more than EFF lessons from you, Jerry...."

Jerry's teammates teased him relentlessly as they made their way back to the bleachers. Mayon-daise watched the Tomato EFF team led by Robert DeJourno crush the Espagnole team. Béchamel Kitchen had a "bye," meaning they didn't have to play a game this round. Every EFF team except for one unlucky kitchen would get a least one bye during the season.

The Tomato-Espagnole match was aggressive and sloppy, and it lasted almost forty minutes. Multiple fouls were called on the Tomato team but they won, nonetheless. Rita didn't have much to cheer about during that game; the Espagnole squad looked lackluster and disorganized. The most notable aspect of the match was the uniforms. The Tomato players sported glossy, professional-looking tops, complete with names and numbers. They even had tomato-red socks to match the red stripes of their jerseys.

"Whoa! Where'd those fancy threads come from?" asked Louie G, clearly impressed. "Those look like professional soccer jerseys."

Mari quickly answered, "If I had to make a guess, I'd say that the Tomato EFF team is sponsored by Ward Moldy Coeur. Who else would have had prior knowledge of the Tomato camper names to have had jerseys made with their names on the back? And, look: most of the team is made up of Mufia members, Coeur's favorite club."

With the games completed for the night, the kitchens left the Field of Greens and headed back to their cabins. Jerry was talking animatedly with Louie G and Mari when he felt a heavy tap on his shoulder and turned around. Red-faced and drenched with sweat, Robert DeJourno stood before him, flanked by his two cousins.

"Not bad out there, Pasta. Coulda used someone like you on our squad. Too bad you have to play for the 'Con-diments' crew. You could be wearin' one of our swanky uniforms instead of a pajama top," he sniped, referring to the worn, mustard-colored shirts of the Mayon-daise Kitchen EFF team members. Jerry's was a wee bit . . . uh . . . large. In his left hand, DeJourno held up a clean Tomato jersey with the name PASTA emblazoned on the back. Jerry was confused. Lumina Foil and Cello Feigni emitted a few forced giggles in support of their athletically-challenged captain.

"Well, I'm happy with my kitchen, Robert." Jerry tried to sound congenial while trying to figure out why a Tomato jersey would have his name on it! *If these uniforms were made before camp even started . . .*

Jerry knew continuing along this thought path would just lead to more questions, and this was not the right time for another confrontation. He smiled insincerely. "Listen, I'd love to chat but I have meals to prepare for my campers."

"You're just now preparin' meals, Pasta?" he scoffed. "I knew I'd be Head Chef of Tomato before I even got to camp, so on day one I was already makin' pizzas and Momma DeJourno's homemade lasagna. I've got three or four days' worth waitin' in the freezer. I can thaw 'em anytime to feed everyone. You gotta lot to learn, Pasta." DeJourno looked happier now than he had looked after winning the EFF match, clearly believing he had shown Jerry up.

For the second time in the last hour, Jerry said the first thing that came to his mind—to his detriment. "My campers are always going to eat the freshest of foods. The pizza I serve will be made with toppings right out of the camp's garden, cooked fresh that day. I hope you enjoy your freezer-burned meals."

DeJourno's face abruptly matched his jersey. "You got one smart mouth, Jerry Pasta. Good thing you got your posse around. Otherwise I'd be havin' that hair of yours for dinner. Macaroni and SQUEEZE sounds pretty good right now," DeJourno snarled, balling his right hand into a fist and shaking it at Jerry. He turned to his cousins and ordered, "Let's get outta here." Then he stormed off toward his cabin.

Mari and Louie G linked their arms around Jerry's shoulders and steered him in the other direction. Jerry was happy his friends were there for support; but he was happier that they'd let him fight this battle on his own. It made him feel tough. And a little confidence goes a loooong way when you're eleven years old.

Back in the cabin, Jerry gathered everyone into the kitchen area. He felt like he needed to say or do something to celebrate the night. "Great win tonight, Mayon-daise! We played as a team and looked good doing it. I loved the energy both on the field and on the sidelines. The Jackals played brilliantly, Mari was a terrific decoy, but, especially, Louie G was an amazing field general."

Louie beamed.

"So," Jerry stood up on the dining table for effect, "I'd like to present the first Mayon-daise MVE award—Most Valuable EFFer—to Louie G!"

Jerry reached into his pocket and threw something in Louie's direction. Louie G caught the object in midair, his face breaking into an incredulous grin as he looked into his hands.

It was the captured egg from the first half of the game!

"You've kept that in your pocket this whole time without breaking it? Gutsy, Jerry, and stupid. Thanks for the gentle toss. I'd prefer not to have egg on my face after a big win," Louie G quipped, turning the egg slowly in his fingers.

"Well, I was hoping not to crack it in your hands, Louie G," Jerry shot back. "I prefer to do the cracking directly into a skillet! The award is an egg *reward*. Bring it over to the kitchen so I can make you a fried egg you won't forget."

It was one of the best fried eggs Louie G had ever eaten.

Jerry Pasta's
TWO-MINUTE EGG

Feeds 1

Preparation time: 2 to 3 minutes

Cook time: 2 minutes

INGREDIENTS AND SUPPLIES

Ingredients
1 egg (or 2 egg whites)

Dash garlic salt

Dash onion powder

2 tablespoons low-fat milk

Sliver unsalted butter

1 slice whole-wheat toast (optional)

Supplies
Small bowl

Small skillet

Spatula

DIRECTIONS
1. Crack egg (or pour egg whites) into a small bowl.
2. Season with garlic salt and onion powder. Add the milk.
3. Beat the egg until the spices and milk are well blended. Set aside.
4. Grease the skillet with the butter, and bring to medium heat. Add the egg mixture. Do not stir!
5. Let cook for about 45 seconds. Then flip the egg carefully with a spatula. Cook for an additional 45 seconds
6. Serve and eat—with a slice of whole-wheat toast if preferred.

Soon it was bedtime and lights out. Before the girls and boys retired to their respective sides of the cabin, Jerry reminded everyone to keep any conversation about EFF to a minimum (and at a whisper!) when around faculty the next day.

Jerry's body ached as he crawled under his sheets, and he decided he would sleep in and not go for his usual morning run. It'd been a long and productive day. He kissed the Pasta family ladle before tucking it back in his bag. It had served him well, carrying the Velouté egg safely across midline. "MVL: Most Valuable Ladle," Jerry whispered. He needed to practice getting faster at balancing an egg with the ladle—but that was for another day. Right now all Jerry wanted to think about was how soft his pillow was—and how good it felt to be a winner.

EFF TEAM	STANDINGS
Bechamel	0 - 0
Espagnole	0 - 1
Mayon-daise	1 - 0
Tomato	1 - 0
Veloute	0 - 1

Chapter 15

Swim with the fishes

The end of the first week was busy for Jerry, what with cooking meals for his kitchen, training for the next EFF match, and completing schoolwork.

The cooking meals part wasn't so bad. All the time he'd spent cooking for his parents at home was paying off. No one had complained about his meals, which were always fresh, made with seasonal produce and fresh herbs from Presto Pesto's community garden. Jerry even made good on his promise to make fresh pizza (in contrast to DeJourno's frozen creation), and it was a cabin favorite.

Jerry Pasta's
MINI-MARGHERITA PIZZAS

Feeds 1
Preparation time: 4 minutes
Cooking time: 8 to 12 minutes

INGREDIENTS AND SUPPLIES
Ingredients

1 tablespoon olive oil

½ teaspoon salt

1 multigrain English muffin

1/2 cup low-fat shredded mozzarella

4 basil leaves, torn into tiny pieces

1 plum tomato, thinly sliced

Supplies

Measuring cup or small bowl

Baking sheet

DIRECTIONS

1. Preheat oven (or toaster oven) to 400 degrees.
2. In a measuring cup or other small bowl, mix the olive oil and salt.
3. Split the English muffin in half. Then lightly brush both open halves with the olive oil/salt mixture.
4. Sprinkle a handful of the mozzarella on both halves. Top with basil and sliced tomato. Then add the rest of the mozzarella.
5. Place the mini pizzas on the baking sheet, and bake for 8 to 12 minutes or until the cheese is melted and bubbly.

(Note: For a meaty version, you could add a pepperoni to each half, or a thin slice of prosciutto.)

The Mayon-daise campers took notice of how healthy Jerry's meals were compared to the ones in the camp dining hall. On Friday night, the last weekday of camp's first week, Mari wasn't shy about carrying the analysis further.

"Well, just look at the instructors! Any of them strike you as particularly slender? If you ate the food served at this camp all summer, every year, you'd have a pot belly too!"

"Yeah, but this ain't health camp, Mari," Louie G countered, passing her a cutting board covered with chopped apples and strawberries. "We're here to learn cooking, not to play *The Biggest Loser*. Though I have to say, Jerry, my shorts are a little looser now than when I first got here," Louie G noted, looking down at his trimmer waistline.

Mari added the fruit to the salad bowl and continued to plead her case. "But there's nothing wrong with learning to cook healthy. Shouldn't one of the world's greatest cooking schools teach that?"

Jerry didn't want to get into the middle of the argument but really had no choice. "But why not just more *equilibrio,* more balance? I don't really see any problem in occasionally eating 'less healthy' foods, but there are ways of cooking healthier. And I think that's where good exercise comes in too; it helps balance out some of the poor food choices we're bound to make. We're kids!"

Mari and Louie G nodded approvingly.

"Good point, Jerry. Spoken like a true eleven-year-old going on twenty-five. How old are you? Honestly?" Jerry's wisdom and cooking skills had obviously impressed Louie G.

"I really am eleven—but I'll be twelve in a couple of weeks. I guess I learned a lot of this stuff from my dad. Did I tell you guys one of his first jobs after graduating Pesto's was with the Italian national football, I mean *soccer,* team? I think working with a bunch of young athletes changed his cooking a lot. He had to feed them wholesome meals so they stayed fit and in tip-top shape."

"So is that what you're doing, Jerry?" Mari inquired. "Feeding us healthy stuff so we'll be better at EFF?"

He laughed. "That's part of it! Though maybe I'm also feeding you so that you don't end up looking like Chefs Beurre and La Gasse by the end of camp."

Jerry Pasta's
FRUIT SALAD

Feeds 4

Preparation time: 5 to 7 minutes

INGREDIENTS AND SUPPLIES

<u>Ingredients</u>

1 bag (10 to 12 ounces) baby spinach leaves

1 apple, cut into cubes

8 to 10 large strawberries, chopped

2 tablespoons olive oil

1 tablespoon Balsamic vinegar

Pinch of salt

½ teaspoon sugar

Supplies

Large bowl

Measuring cup or small bowl

DIRECTIONS

1. Mix the spinach, apple, and strawberries in a large bowl.

2. In a measuring cup or small bowl, combine the olive oil, vinegar, salt and sugar.

3. Drizzle this salad dressing over the spinach and fruit, and toss well.

During the meal preparation, Louie G couldn't help but ask, "Why are we making a salad *before* the salad?"

"Because the first salad is the *antipasto*—almost like what you would call the appetizer. Back home, we usually serve *antipasto* as an assortment of cured meats and cheeses. Salad is usually served with the main course. So I'm trying something a little different tonight," Jerry replied.

"Um, let me get this straight," Louie G said, looking perplexed. "Is *antipasto* some magic spell that makes 'sick' meat better?"

Now Jerry's face mirrored Louie G's—until he finally understood what Louie G was asking. "*No, mi amico*—my friend— 'cured' meats are what we call pepperoni, proscuitto, pancetta, salami . . . meats that are salted, smoked, air-dried so they can be preserved for a long time."

"Ah, OK." Louie G sighed in relief. "I was just afraid you were talking about some Italian voodoo I've never heard of; I was feeling rather *anti*-antipasto, if you know what I mean."

Mari shook her head in disbelief. "Boys," she muttered.

Jerry's Pasta's
PASTA SALAD

Feeds 6-8

Preparation time: 20 to 30 minutes

INGREDIENTS AND SUPPLIES

Ingredients

1 box pasta (rotini, rotelle, fusilli, ziti—short shapes, not noodles)

1 green pepper, chopped

1 cucumber, chopped

1 bunch scallions, chopped

⅓ cup chopped cilantro

1 carrot, chopped

1 celery stalk, chopped

1 small container cherry tomatoes

1 cup pitted olives

4 to 6 grilled chicken breasts (optional; see note)

1 teaspoon garlic salt

4 to 8 ounce block of cheese (white cheddar or pepper jack or both), cubed

1 teaspoon black pepper

¼ cup olive oil

¼ cup red-wine vinegar

Supplies

Large saucepan

Large bowl

DIRECTIONS

1. In a large saucepan, boil the pasta until done. Drain, and set aside. (Boiling time depends on type of pasta you use. Don't overcook it! It should be a little chewy.)
2. In a large bowl, combine all the remaining ingredients except the olive oil and vinegar. Add additional salt and pepper to taste.
3. Mix in the drained pasta until all the ingredients are well blended.
4. Add the olive oil and red-wine vinegar, stirring to combine. Increase oil and vinegar to taste.
5. Serve at room temperature or chilled.

Note: Adding grilled chicken provides protein and turns this salad from a side dish into a main course.

Forks and spoons clanked loudly on empty plates at the end of dinner; none of the Mayon-daise campers were complaining about the salad-only meal. (And what better way to show their acceptance of the head chef than by cleaning their plates and asking for seconds?)

After lights out, the campers stayed up late sitting around the kitchen table with their flashlights to play card games, tell scary stories, and raid the fridge for "snacks" (only Jerry considered leftover fruit salad a "fun" midnight snack). Since the weekend meant no classes, the campers figured they could get by with a little less sleep. And if they were a bit bleary eyed all day, well, no big deal.

Saturday was the first day of camp with no instruction. In fact, campers were generally free to do as they pleased the entire weekend since only a couple of formal camp activities were planned: a *Meet the Chefs!* open house at nine on Saturday morning at Eaditt Hall and a camp seminar entitled "Cooking Over Open Flames" on Sunday evening at a to-be-determined outdoor location.

After an uneventful morning of meeting most of the cooking instructors, Jerry, Mari, and Louie G decided to spend Saturday afternoon going for a long hike, eager for an adventure and a welcome escape from cooking. About a mile and a half from the main campus, adventure came in the form of a four-foot tall wooden fence; one of the planks bore a wooden sign clearly labeled in black paint:

"I guess our hike ends here, guys," said Jerry reluctantly.

But Louie G was already scaling the fence.

"Louie G, what are you doing? We're not supposed to leave camp property!" Jerry knew this was the type of behavior that would get him sent home quickly. He couldn't risk it.

But before Jerry could blink, Louie G was on the other side and looking at a dilapidated sign nailed to a nearby oak tree indicating that a lake was 1.5 km to the east.

"Hey, a lake! Not even a mile away if I've got my metrics right! Looks like the adventure is just beginning. Come on, guys, it'll be fun!"

Jerry turned to Mari for support. Surely *she* would see the folly of breaking camp rules. Instead, she was already hiking up her *salwar* pant legs, and Louie G was helping her over the fence! What choice did Jerry have? He could hike back to camp by himself, but since campers were told to buddy-up before going into the woods, going back by himself would get him in trouble, anyway—and then he'd have to explain where Louie G and Mari were. Or just lie, and he was terrible at telling lies. Or . . . he could join his friends in this rule-breaking endeavor and hope that the camp staff (and his parents) never found out. Option Two seemed the path of least resistance.

Sigh. "OK, I'm coming. But we have to be back before dinner."

Jerry agilely climbed over the fence and caught up with his two friends. He was mad at himself that he hadn't been able to convince them to turn around. Maybe it was the age thing. *How many eleven-year-olds have ever talked thirteen-year-olds out of something they're bent on doing?* But Jerry was determined to make the best of it. He imagined himself skipping rocks across the water, wading in the shallows—that'd be as much as he'd venture into the water what with his hair—maybe even taking a quick nap along the shore.

The further away the three got from camp, the more heavily forested the grounds were. But the broken twigs and matted crab grass suggested that the trail had been used recently, otherwise getting lost would have been easy.

"Isn't it amazing that we're only about two miles from our cabin?" Louie G said as he negotiated around a gnarled oak tree with low-hanging branches.

Fifteen minutes passed. "Are we there, yet? I think I'm ready for a swim," Mari panted, perhaps not realizing the time it would take to cover the hilly terrain to the lake. Mari clearly wasn't the outdoors type—she didn't see a problem in wearing sandals and billowy pants on a nature hike—but she was game enough to give anything a try. First EFF, now trekking in an off-limits forest with two boys she only met for first time a few days ago.

"Look, I think I see it!" Louie G shouted exultantly, pointing slightly to his right. As the three navigated carefully down the slope, the forest slowly melted away and revealed a glistening lake nestled between the hill they just descended and another hill on the far side. The sun's reflection off of the water was nearly blinding.

"Are those herons over there, Jerry?" Louie G, eyes squinted, gestured at the far shore. He directed the question to Jerry, expecting Jerry would know since Italy was where he'd grown up.

"Io penso di si. . . . ."

"Translation, please?"

"Oh, sorry . . . yes, I think so." He wasn't much of a bird watcher, especially birds that liked to hang out in water.

Jerry had showed his insecurity by reverting back to Italian. Even though both English and Italian came easy to him, he often deferred to the Italian since it was what most of his peers spoke back in his neighborhood. But at his international school, and especially at home with his American mom, Jerry almost exclusively spoke English. Jerry and his mom watched American TV shows together (on the Internet, of course) and listened to American music; to the untrained ear, he sounded like a typical American kid. Here at camp, though, responding in Italian often bought him more time to think before translating his words to English. He didn't even have to really translate accurately—he could always say one thing in Italian and then something else in English; no one would know. While that ploy worked with non-Italian speaking strangers and acquaintances, Jerry made a mental note to never do that with his friends here at camp, mostly out of respect.

"Is that a kayak?" Mari was angling up the west side of the lake, toward a patch of short grass.

"No, it's a canoe!" Louie G exclaimed. "Sweet! Let's take it out!" Louie G was off and running toward the long birch canoe. He dragged it into the shallow water and then rolled himself inside. Settling onto the rearmost seat, he held up oars in each hand and yelled back, "Who's coming with me?"

Jerry stood frozen in place, his feet anchored to the rocky shoreline.

"What's wrong, JP? Never canoed before?"

"No, I haven't," Jerry responded timidly, linking his hands behind his neck, his legs locked and stiff like uncooked penne.

"It's easy. I'll help you. And you too, Mari. This'll be fun!"

Mari was already holding her pants high and wading into the water, then climbing into the canoe and settling into the bow seat. She grabbed one of the paddles from Louie G and was obviously capable of pitching in. Though Jerry was more than reluctant to join, he found it hard to resist the passionate pleading of his two friends. For the second time in thirty minutes, Jerry fell victim to peer pressure.

"You promise this won't tip over? I'd, um, prefer not to get wet." He warily eyed the canoe.

"You'll be fine, Jerry. I've canoed a lot back at home. Nothing's going to tip us over—unless there are sharks in the lake . . . Kidding! Breathe, man; just sit in the middle and relax. Mari and I will paddle."

Jerry glanced along the shore as if he'd lost something.

"Looking for . . . ?"

"Life jackets," Jerry replied. "Aren't you supposed to wear one in a boat? I'm, um, not the best swimmer."

"Relax, JP, you'll be fine. Just get in already."

Surrendering, Jerry wiped the sweat off his brow with the back of his forearm and waded into the water. He settled into the middle seat without too much difficulty, a reluctant spectator while his two friends provided the paddle power. The lake was larger than it looked from shore; this wasn't obvious until they had rowed out into the middle.

Louie G pointed out a fish jumping out of the water. "See those places where the water bubbles up? That's where I'd cast my fishing rod if I had one." He briefly stopped paddling to cast an imaginary line into the water to the right of the canoe. Seconds later he struggled mightily to reel in an equally imaginary fish, sending Jerry and Mari into a fit of giggles.

As the canoe gently drifted around the corner of the inlet, they spotted another canoe about 300 feet away.

"Do you think they're locals?" asked Jerry, hoping that he and his two pals wouldn't be identified as rogue campers who'd stolen a canoe and be reported to Al Dente.

"We might as well find out," Louie G said. "Maybe they can tell us if there are cool parts of the lake that we should know about!" He and Mari steered toward the other canoe. It looked like the other canoe had the same idea as it suddenly shifted direction and headed toward them. Jerry prepared himself for the worst. *Maybe we'll be arrested for trespassing! Maybe we'll be arrested for stealing this canoe!* It didn't help his sense of well-being (or lack thereof!) that they were sitting in the middle of the lake now, life jacketless. Jerry felt his heart racing.

And then when it was close enough, he recognized the people in the other canoe. His heart found an extra gear while sinking down into his stomach. His linguini hair grew heavy under the burden of sweat he was generating. *The moment has just gone from bad to . . . very bad.*

Robert DeJourno. Lumina Foyle. Cello Feigni.

The heads of the Mufia.

Jerry had a bad feeling about what would happen next.

"Well, well, well. What do we have here?" DeJourno stood confidently in the middle of the canoe, Lumina and Cello having stopped paddling to let their canoe peacefully glide toward the newcomers. Unlike Jerry and his friends, all three Mufia members were wearing life-jackets. "I thought we was the only people that knew about this lake," said Robert with a smirk.

"Well, I guess you *'was'* wrong," Mari sniped.

Don't antagonize them—not now Mari, Jerry begged silently, trying to avoid eye contact with his adversary.

"Well, *grammar queenie*, I guess I *would* be wrong if I considered losers like you actual people," DeJourno shot back. "Didn't think Jerry Pasta, or should I say *The Chosen One*, had the balls to break camp rules," he derisively added. The canoes were now only about twenty feet apart, passively drifting closer. "You know, Jerry, my Mufia offer the other day still stands. I think me and the girls might even sneak into town tonight to grab some Fasta Pasta. You're welcome to join us if you wanna. Whaddya say?"

Jerry wondered if this encounter could possibly have been more awkward: first Robert DeJourno insults Jerry and his friends, and then he invites him yet again to join the Mufia and go out for fast food?! DeJourno would have failed miserably at any job that required hospitality. *Clearly taking his cues from Moldy Coeur,* Jerry thought, remembering Coeur's less than hospitable words on registration day. Jerry's nervous mind wandered, finding no words to speak. Ironically, out in the middle of the lake, Jerry felt like a fish out of water—and like a fish out of water, he could barely breathe.

What am I thinking? That'd I'd breathe better in the water?

He wasn't a fish. And he hated water.

Swimming to shore was NOT an option.

"I, um, I . . . I think I'm going to, um, pass on joining the Mufia. No hard feelings?" asked Jerry, with an innocent shrug.

That was apparently the wrong answer.

"Bad choice, Pasta," DeJourno snarled, shaking his head in angry disappointment. "I hope your friends like wet noodles."

Jerry was puzzling over DeJourno's words when he felt the canoe lurch. Louie G and Mari were paddling furiously toward shore, away from the Mufia canoe. Robert DeJourno's eyes were wild with rage as he directed Lumina and Cello to paddle in pursuit. Suddenly Jerry understood.

His hair would be the wet noodles because DeJourno meant to flip their canoe!

We're never going to make it! Jerry internally moaned. He gripped the rough sides of the wood canoe as tightly as he could, nearly rubbing his palms raw. Mari wasn't very good at emergency paddling, and despite being weighed down by their cousin's two-hundred-pound frame, Lumina and Cello were closing the gap quickly. Fifty yards from the shoreline, the Mufia canoe pulled up alongside Jerry's. Louie G had given up on paddling and was using his oar to try to push the Mufia canoe away. Robert DeJourno reached over and pushed down hard on the edge of Jerry's canoe closest to him. Jerry, straddling his bench now, reflexively slid backward away from DeJourno, trying to stay out of arm's reach.

Jerry's reactive blunder played right into DeJourno's hands—if not literally. By shifting his weight to the canoe's other side, Jerry created a reverse tilt. He desperately threw his arms out behind him, hoping to balance himself on wood—but all he got was handfuls of water.

Uh-oh. . . .

As he fell backward, face to the sky, Jerry could only see fluffy clouds and hear Louie G and Mari's frantic splashing and muffled screams.

Chapter 16

Warned and Warmed

When Jerry had told his friends that he was not the best swimmer, he was being generous. Really generous. In fact, he had flat out lied. Jerry was not a swimmer at all—something his violent splashing undoubtedly now gave away. Despite his frantic efforts, Jerry felt himself sinking. He craned his head backward, mouth barely above the surface of the water. And as much as he hated getting his hair wet, survival was more important at this point.

But it was no use. Although it had probably only been seconds, he felt as if he'd been struggling for hours. Jerry took one last deep breath, then went under.

Underwater, he continued flailing, which was getting him nowhere fast. He was tiring.

And still sinking.

To say he was terrified would be an understatement—Jerry was sure he was going to die. He cursed his hair, hating that the fear of getting it wet had led him to shun swimming lessons for as long as he could remember. Not even a tight-fitting swim cap could convince him to submerge himself completely in water—making his current situation extremely ironic. So Jerry stopped struggling . . . and he realized he felt weightless, like he was floating in air—or water for that matter. In what he assumed to be his final moments, he took a couple of those moments to imagine the letter his parents would receive in the mail. *We are so sorry to inform you, Mr. and Mrs. Pasta, that your son drowned in a lake after leaving the campgrounds without permission. We're especially sorry because the world is doomed now. Jerry was our only hope.*

And for a second, Jerry thought it might not be so bad to disappear.

No more pressure, no more great expectations. A large marble trout lazily swam by Jerry's head, prompting him to take one last look up. Sunlight trickled delicately through the clear lake water. And then it suddenly grew very dark above him. *This must be the end,* Jerry thought. The burning in his chest from oxygen deprivation was reaching its peak. He closed his eyes, anticipating the moment of complete surrender when he'd exhale one last time before letting the water rush into his mouth, his lungs. . . .

But the moment didn't come.

Instead, Jerry felt himself being pulled vigorously upward, and Louie G's muffled voice instructed, "A little help, Jerry? You could kick your feet, you know!"

Jerry burst through the surface of the water, gasping for air.

Over his own wheezing, Jerry heard Louie G's voice again, strangely echoing, repeatedly saying "Jerry! Jerry!"

Jerry knew he was alive—*but where?* He was completely disoriented. It was really dark, wherever he was.

"Jerry! Grab on to this, we're safe here." Louie G pulled Jerry's hand up to something hard and wet. The cobwebs were finally clearing. Jerry's chest was no longer heaving for air. His eyes were slowly adjusting to the darkness, and he looked up to see what he was holding onto: the wooden bench of the canoe.

The canoe is upside down, and we're underneath it. That's why it's so dark—and I'm definitely not dead!

The words sputtered out of Jerry's mouth. "Wh . . . wh . . . where's Mari?"

"Right behind you, Jerry!"

Jerry swiveled his head to see a water-soaked Mari, her long black hair matted against her face.

"Louie G saved us! He told me to grab the canoe bench as we were flipping over. You had already flipped into the water. He dove down to find you once we realized you weren't under the canoe with us."

Jerry wasn't sure if he should be embarrassed or angry at himself. Sure, he had overstated his swimming skills. He didn't really want his friends to know he couldn't swim at all or that he was deathly afraid of water—as if that hadn't become painfully obvious. But he shouldn't have been in this situation in the first place. *They* had goaded him into jumping the fence. *They* had prodded him into boarding the canoe without a life-jacket. And *they* had rowed the canoe toward the Mufia canoe—albeit unknowingly. This predicament was *their* fault, not his . . . mostly.

(Yes, he could have told his pals about the whole fear of water thing, but would *you* have?)

"So I guess I should thank you for putting my life in danger and *then* saving it. Thanks a lot!" Jerry wrapped his words in sarcasm like bacon around a scallop.

Louie G retorted in kind. "Something tells me 'You're welcome' isn't the appropriate response here. Possibly the tone of your voice. I can't be sure."

The three silently kicked toward shore until they found themselves in water shallow enough to stand. Flipping the canoe over, they walked the remainder of the way, guiding the boat. While Mari squeezed the water out of her hair, Louie G and Jerry pulled the canoe onto the grass alongside the abandoned Mufia canoe with four lifejackets lying on the inside.

"Sure could have used those," Jerry quipped sarcastically.

Louie G turned to him. "SORRY, Jerry. I messed up. I just thought it'd be fun. And if we hadn't run into those creeps, we'd *still* be having fun. We'll get them back, OK? It's water under the, uh, canoe now, right?" Louie G's outstretched hand sought forgiveness.

Jerry nodded. "Apology accepted. But we don't need to get them back. That will just make things worse." He suddenly began shivering. "I'm freezing. Let's just get back to camp."

The hike back seemed interminable—first the long, exhausting hike back to the fence, then the trek through the forest to the campground. There wasn't a whole lot of conversation along the way, either. They were already late for dinner and needed to stop in the cabin to change out of their still-dripping clothes. Louie G put his hand on Jerry's shoulder before they walked into the cabin, pulling him aside. Mari continued on.

"Hey, Jerry, something I need to tell you." Louie G looked down at his wet shoes for a moment. "Uh . . . so I didn't really save you from drowning in the lake. I mean, I *did,* but I actually had help."

"What do you mean? If you're saying Mari helped you, I already thanked her."

"No, that's not what I mean. You should be thanking . . . well, your hair. After the canoe tipped over and I realized you were underwater, I looked down and thought I saw you about eight feet below me. But when I dove down to that depth, you had completely disappeared! I immediately knew the lake was a lot deeper than I realized. I freaked out . . . I thought you were gone. I was out of breath, so I swam back to the top to get more air—and there you were, only about two feet from the surface."

"You mean I was that close to the surface of the water? How is that possible? And what does my hair have to do with any of this?" Jerry asked, bewildered.

"Well, that's just it. As I swam back up toward the surface, I saw your body drop again, headed down—but then I saw that your hair . . . it had somehow gotten snagged on the canoe's wooden bench, I guess as the canoe tipped over and you fell backward. Your linguini hair was super-stretchy; you kinda looked like a big yo-yo in the water . . . you sank, then came back up, then sank again, then came back up . . . ."

Louie G started to giggle a little at the ridiculousness of the memory but stopped abruptly with one look at Jerry's blank face. "Ha ha, yeah, so . . . anyway, your hair is really what saved you from sinking to the bottom of the lake. Just thought I'd let you know." Louie G turned and opened the cabin door, Jerry following close behind, still pondering what he had just learned.

Al Dente was waiting in the Mayon-daise Kitchen as they sauntered in, a scowl darkening his usually sunny face. "I would like-ah to know where you have-ah been all this-ah time," the headmaster demanded, tapping his foot impatiently. Mari rocked nervously beside him.

Jerry was about to blurt out the whole truth when Louie G yelled out, "We got lost on our hike and ended up at this lake where we found a canoe . . . and it tipped over. It's all my fault! I take full responsibility."

Would Al Dente accept Louie G's half-truth version of the events? Jerry figured from the petrified look on her face that Mari hadn't said anything.

"This is a very serious matter. You could-ah all be sent-ah home. Consider this strike-ah one, as they say in America. Next-ah strike and you are out-ah. Understand-ah?"

Glancing at the pained looked on Louie G's face, Jerry feared that his friend's love of America's pastime would compel him to point out the obvious: that it took three strikes to be out. Jerry was relieved that Louie G no doubt realized this was *not* an appropriate time to correct the headmaster of the school—even if they could use that extra strike.

"Yes, Chef Dente," they replied in unison.

"Jerry, I need to talk-ah to you privately." He shooed Louie G and Mari off. "You two should-ah go to your rooms—no point in heading to the dining hall-ah. Dinner is already finishing up-ah."

Heads bowed, Louie G and Mari, shuffled to their respective sides of the Mayon-daise cabin. Jerry nervously sat down at the kitchen table at Al Dente's instruction.

"This-ah was a very foolish mistake, Jerry. You need-ah to be wiser, more careful. A lotta of people want-ah you to succeed, Jerry. But a lotta people want-ah you to fail, *capisci?* Remember why you came to Pesto's, OK? Do not make me have to call-ah your parents."

Al Dente's sharp gaze brought Jerry almost to tears. But the head-master suddenly winked, handed Jerry an envelope, then turned and walked out of the cabin.

Jerry wasn't sure what the wink meant. He only knew that he had barely missed getting kicked out of camp. He opened the envelope without looking to see who the sender was. He assumed it was another invitation to some camp club, maybe one sponsored by Al Dente. His stomach dropped as he instantly recognized the handwriting:

Hi Jerry,

Hope you are having a great time at camp! Papa and I are so proud of you. Are you staying out of trouble? Are the other kids being nice to you?

I miss you so much, my Angel. I expect a letter this week. Let us know if ANYTHING happens.

Love,
Mamma

P.S. Papa found some temporary work doing some construction near the post office. Then in true Pasta fashion he dropped a cinder block on his right hand. Guess who's doing all the cooking now at home? Can't wait 'til you get back! And be careful at camp no accidents!

P.S.S. And here's a picture of the two of us cooking together making your favorite fish dish!

A picture fell out of the folded letter onto the floor. Jerry quickly picked it up and dusted it off. There was Papa with his casted right hand, holding up a fish in his left. Mamma was playfully holding a skillet above Papa's head as if she was going to knock him out.

Their faces went suddenly blurry as tears welled up in Jerry's eyes.

Papa broke his hand? How was he supposed to earn money with a broken hand? There were no job offers out there for one-armed chefs.

But that wasn't all Jerry was anxious about. His parents could never know about the lake incident. They'd take him out of camp in a heartbeat. Jerry hoped Al Dente really would keep the incident to himself. *Maybe that's what the wink meant?*

But looking on the bright side, he was alive. And he had his hair to thank. Again. Jerry playfully tousled his wet linguini hair. "I still hate you even though you saved me. When I wake up tomorrow morning, can you just be normal? That's probably too much to ask; I've been asking for years now, and what good has it done me?"

His hair did not reply.

Jerry left the kitchen and walked to the bunkroom. Louie G wasn't there. *Probably in the shower,* Jerry figured. He taped the photo of his parents to the side of his bunk bed, both to keep them in mind and a reminder to heed Al Dente's words. *I need to remember why I am here at cooking camp,* he thought to himself as bent over to unlace his soggy sneakers. Tears sprang into his eyes again.

"Is that your dad and a family friend?"

Louie G, towel-wrapped around his waist, had entered the bunkroom without Jerry noticing. Jerry quickly wiped away his tears before turning around to face his friend, who was pointing to the photo taped to the bed frame.

"*Si,* yes, you could say that. If by 'family friend' you mean my mother."

Louie G stepped closer to get a better look at the picture. "Um, Jerry . . . the lady in this picture is dark enough to be *my* mother." Louie G looked from the photo to Jerry then back to the photo. His face broke into a huge grin. "Well, *duh!* I can totally see the resemblance now! And I always figured you were just tanned from all that running you do. My bad for making assumptions. I guess we have a lot more in common than I realized."

Talking about his parents for a few minutes surprisingly put Jerry in a good mood, maybe because it helped him forget about the unfortunate events of the afternoon. Jerry was glad that Louie G could appreciate that though they looked different, Jerry's parents had found love—and Jerry was a perfect blend of the two of them. "Our finest recipe," his parents would lovingly tell him.

Now aware of Jerry's mixed heritage, Louie G vowed to "Americanize" Jerry even more before camp ended. "I gotta get the 'America' in you to come out a little more. Your mom will love me for it!"

"And I promise to bring out the 'Italian' in you. Every great chef has a little Italy in them," Jerry playfully retorted.

After another minute of playful banter, Jerry hit the showers then changed into fresh clothes. When he returned to the bunkroom, he was in much better spirits, refreshed by time, talk, and the hot shower. And he felt a new bond with Louie G, a closeness that he hadn't felt before. It was similar to the feeling he had with some of the American cousins who had come to visit him during the summers over the years. It felt good.

Having missed dinner, Jerry asked Louie G if he was hungry (though he already knew the answer to the question) and said he would throw something together for the three of them—including Mari in the repast, of course. They walked into the kitchen virtually at the same time as Mari to find three steaming bowls of vegetable soup, filled to the brim. Though it wouldn't be enough to completely satisfy their hunger, the friends were grateful for whoever was  looking out for them. Halfway through his bowl of soup, Jerry had the sense that he was being watched and looked up at one of the kitchen windows. He thought he saw the old janitor peering in; the old man was smiling, a look of satisfaction on his face. Jerry nudged Louie G to share his observation, but by the time their heads swiveled back, the window was empty. They shared a glance, then shrugged and kept eating.

After finishing the soup, Jerry scanned the contents of the refrigerator, looking for inspiration. After a few moments he knew exactly what to make to commemorate the day's events. His near-death experience coupled with his parents' photo had provided the inspiration he needed.

Jerry Pasta's
FISH AND SEAWEED
(a.k.a. fish and sautéed spinach)

Feeds 3-6

Preparation time: 30 to 45 minutes

Cooking time: 15 minutes

INGREDIENTS/SUPPLIES FOR THE FISH

Ingredients

3 to 6 orange roughy fillets

(if orange roughy isn't available, substitute trout or flounder)

1 ½ cups orange juice

2 tablespoons sugar

1 tablespoon balsamic vinegar or vinaigrette

2 teaspoons garlic salt

½ teaspoon black pepper

¼ cup vegetable oil

¼ cup lime juice

Supplies

1 large Ziploc bag

Medium-sized bowl

Casserole dish

TO PREPARE THE FISH

1. Place the fillets in the Ziploc bag.
2. In a medium-sized bowl, mix all the remaining ingredients to make a marinade. Then pour the marinade into the Ziploc bag with the fillets. Make sure the bag is sealed well, and refrigerate for 30 minutes.
3. Preheat oven to 350 degrees.

4. Remove the fillets from the bag and place them side by side in an uncovered casserole dish. 5. Bake for 7 minutes, flip them over, and then bake the other side for an additional 7 minutes.

INGREDIENTS/SUPPLIES FOR THE SEAWEED ... ERRRR, SPINACH!

Ingredients

10 ounce bag baby spinach leaves

2 tablespoons olive oil

1 shallot, finely chopped

¼ cup balsamic vinegar

Salt and pepper to taste

Supplies

Medium-sized saucepan

Wooden spatula

TO PREPARE THE SPINACH

1. Wash the spinach well under cold water, and dry on a paper towel or kitchen cloth.
2. Heat the olive oil in a saucepan over medium heat until sizzling.
3. Stir in the shallot, and cook them for 6 to 8 minutes, or until tender. Add the spinach, mixing well with your spatula for about 2 minutes, until wilted.

   Remove the saucepan from heat.
4. Sprinkle on the balsamic vinegar and toss well. Season to taste with salt and pepper. Serve immediately.

Though it took about an hour to prepare, the three friends enjoyed the late-night meal. Until the rest of their kitchenmates returned from dinner and began questioning where the three had been. To avoid embarrassment (and frequent interruptions of their meal), they simply admitted they had gotten in trouble and weren't at liberty to share the details.

That night, at bedtime, Jerry spent a few minutes writing to his parents.

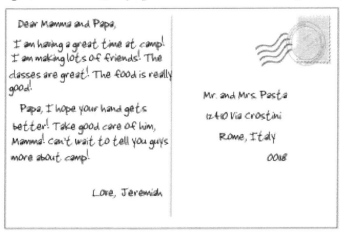

Jerry prayed his parents wouldn't see through his fake enthusiasm. Maybe one too many exclamation points? But Jerry couldn't risk his parents suspecting that anything bad had happened at Pesto's or that he was really worried about Papa's injury (which he was). He hoped this note was the perfect disguise. Lots of energy, not a lot of detail. He stamped the postcard and put it on top of his bag, where'd he see it in the morning and remember to put it in the mail. By the time Jerry closed his eyes to go to sleep, he had nicely warmed up not just on the outside but on the inside too. He reflected on his day, his conversation with Louie G, his letter from his parents. His nighttime prayers included gratefulness for being alive, and as he fell asleep, he might have even mumbled a word or two about his pasta-hair rescue.

After the lights went out at the scheduled time in all the cabins, a secret meeting took place near Apley Court between two hooded figures standing in the shadows.

"I sense failure from the look on your face."

"I tried as hard as I could. I asked him nicely. He didn't wanna join. What was I supposed to do?"

"Try harder! Maybe you're just the wrong person for this task."

"But—"

"*NO BUTS!* I think it's time to move to Plan B. Wooing has not been a success. Unfortunately that only leaves brute force."

"Yes! Somethin' I'm good at!"

"Not *your* type of brute force. I heard about the lake! Had the boy drowned, things would have been quite messy. Imagine the negative press, you IDIOT! We will have to be a bit more, hmmmmm, subtle." He handed over a piece of paper. "Get these supplies; I'll take care of the rest."

The younger figure scanned the list. "A dozen green tomatoes and two dozen rotten ones? A gasoline can? One— I can't read your handwritin'. Does that say 'blue fish'? Medical records . . . Why do you want these medical records? Can't you get them yourself?"

The older man sighed in frustration. "I've already told you; I cannot have any direct involvement. You haven't told anyone, have you?"

"Uh . . . no . . . I mean, not exactly. I, um, I did tell the only two people here who are fam—"

"*FOOL!* I clearly made a mistake to involve you! You must tell no one else!" The older man paused to shake his head. "I hope this next task will be easy enough for you to accomplish. To get the records, fake an injury to get into the nurse's office. The other supplies might take a bit more creativity on your part—I will help out where I can."

"I still don't see whatcha plan to do with all this stuff."

"The details of this plan are too complicated for your puny brain to understand. I will contact you on a limited need-to-know basis. Let's just say that one way to Signore Pasta may be through those two friends he spends all his time with. I hadn't anticipated they would be so influential. If you had been successful earlier, I would not be in this predicament. Can I depend on you this time?"

"Of course, M—"

"Shhhhhh! I hear someone coming. I will leave detailed instructions for you. This time, do not fail!

Entrée

(the Third Course)

Chapter 17

Everyone Loves the Substitute Teacher

Sunday came and went without incident. Unless you count Louie G almost burning off all of his arm hair when he got too close to the bonfire during the outdoor cooking seminar. (Louie G swore that someone pushed him from behind—and if it hadn't been for his "amazing balance," he would have face-planted into the flames.) Jerry skipped that seminar and spent most of the day resting and refocusing on why he was at camp.

To cook.

So when Monday rolled around, marking the beginning of Week Two, Jerry already had a menu of meals planned out. During Week One, he had only cooked a handful of meals, all dishes he was really comfortable and familiar with. He hadn't really branched out at all. But nothing at camp had really "wowed" him yet to be moved to experiment. Jerry was willing to take what he learned in class and apply it to his kitchen meals; he was just waiting for the right spark. It didn't take long for inspiration to be provided. At breakfast that morning Chef Beurre announced to all the campers gathered in Eaditt Hall what would be the third official cooking competition of the summer.

"Tomorrow you will be asked to complete a simple recipe. The successfully completed recipe wins. And by 'successfully completed' I mean zeh most delicious," Beurre articulated with a smile. "But this competition will be hardeur than it appears because one crucial ingredient will be missing from each recipe. But don't worry, we are not setting you up for *complete* failure: your ICSs will of course be stocked with supplies— but not necessarily zeh supplies on your ingredients list—hahahaha."

His evil chuckle echoed throughout the dining hall. "This contest will be a test of your ability to cook on zeh fly, to improvise. There is at least one way to prepare for zis competition, but you'll have to figure that out yourselves. *Bonne chance!* Good luck!"

Chef Beurre seemed to relish the fact that this was going to be a difficult competition. The groans around the cafeteria only fed his glee.

Jerry mulled over Beurre's clue, that there was *at least one way* to prepare for the competition. Thinking back to cooking at home with his father, Jerry had an idea. He shared it with Mari and Louie G after the morning classes.

"So I think I know one way to prepare for tomorrow's competition," said Jerry eagerly as they walked back to their cabin.

"If it involves memorizing the entire camp cookbook Jerry, I think I'll pass," replied Louie G, nonchalantly jumping up to tap a low-hanging tree branch in front of him.

"No, it's much easier than that. In fact, Mari is part of the inspiration behind this idea."

"Me? Well, pray tell, what do you have in mind?" Mari was blushing. She loved getting praise for a good idea.

"The library."

Louie G had leaped up to touch another tree branch. Landing, he spun around to face Jerry.

"You can't be serious. The library *again?*"

"Remember our earlier conversation, *mio amico:* 'value quality over quantity.' We don't have to read a ton—we just have to read the *right* stuff. I've learned a lot from cooking with my dad at home. And since we're not the wealthiest family, we sometimes have to, you know, cut corners. So my dad showed me all these substitutes, things to use if you don't have what the recipe calls for. And he showed me that in the back of some recipe books, an entire section is dedicated to common substitutes. So I figure we just go to the library and page through a few cookbooks . . . just skimming the substitutions lists. That should be a good start—no matter what the recipes actually are. If we have a good idea of what we can substitute for missing ingredients, we'll be ahead of the game."

"Brilliant, Jerry!" said Mari. "We can go between our afternoon classes and dinner."

"OK, I guess I'll come along too," Louie G grumbled, unable to hide his scowl. "But I don't want to spend hours in the library on a gorgeous day like this. This 'skimming' better be quick."

When their classes were finished, Jerry, Mari, and Louie G combed the library shelves, diligently studying an array of cookbooks and picking up hints on common substitutions.

"Honey instead of sugar, one-percent milk instead of heavy cream . . . You can *do* that? Doesn't the food taste funny?" Louie G asked incredulously.

"Sometimes you might sacrifice a little flavor, but you often come out with a healthier dish that still tastes pretty spectacular. Plus it's even a little cheaper sometimes," replied Jerry. "We cook like this all the time at my house."

"And that's why you're all skin and bones, Jerry Pasta. Come visit me in America; we'll fatten you up a little bit," joked Louie G.

"No thanks—on the fatten-up part. But can I still come visit?"

"Of course, JP! My family would love to meet you!"

They ended up spending only about forty-five minutes in the library, which was good since Louie G wouldn't have lasted a minute longer. (Especially when Thom Goleek from the Velouté Kitchen and Antoine Burden from the Béchamel Kitchen poked their heads through the library door with Frisbee in hand, which literally propelled Louie G out of his chair.) Jerry hoped the information they had gleaned was enough to spell success. While he didn't exhibit the kind of competitive behavior

Louie G did, deep down Jerry really wanted to win every cooking competition. His reputation depended on it.

Tuesday came quickly.

It was a routine morning for Jerry: run with the EFF team, shower, get dressed (including a hat for pasta hair control), pack satchel with books, chef's coat, toque, and cooking supplies, especially his trusty ladle. The competition would take place during breakfast, which had prompted a chorus of universal groans from the campers when that information had been announced at lights-out the previous night. The teaching faculty really wanted the campers to feel the pressure to perform well, knowing that whatever they made, good or bad, would be their breakfast. *I'll make sure to eat while I cook so no janitor can eat my leftovers this time*, Jerry said to himself.

8:45. Each camper was stationed at an ICS in their assigned halls. The recipes were handed out: all breakfast recipes. Only about ten different recipes were distributed, but as Beurre had warned, the novice chefs would discover a crucial ingredient would be missing from their provisions to complete the recipe as written. The competition began. Jerry looked at the recipe he had been given.

Blueberry pancakes.

The recipe didn't seem all that complicated. He began preparing the batter— measuring the flour, cracking the eggs—and then he checked the small fridge for . . . for the . . . Jerry realized what his ICS was missing.

Butter.

I'll just have to use oil instead. Jerry opened his ICS cupboard.

No oil. No shortening.

OK, think, Jerry, think. Jerry's mind drew a blank.

"Five minutes left. Make it snappy, you slow coaches!" Chef Brit Favreau announced (as only he could) over the PA system.

Jerry was beginning to sweat. His hair wasn't going to save him this time unless he could cut it off and somehow melt it down into butter-flavored pasta. *Thoughts like that are going to make me even more sick to my stomach!*

But then the solution came to him, in the form of another memory-seared, hair-loathing moment.

Jerry remembered making cupcakes with his mom before his eighth birthday, one of the many birthdays when he'd cut off his hair before going to sleep hoping to wake up with normal hair—or at least be bald. Of course, the hair grew back as pasta, anyway. But that's not the important part of the story. The Pasta family had endured a month of tight penny-pinching, and Papa's next paycheck wouldn't come for another five days. Jerry's mom was out of butter and almost everything else. Jerry was miserable because he wasn't going to be able to have cupcakes for his birthday—oh, sure, he could have stupid regenerating pasta hair but NOT cupcakes—and then Papa, like a knight in shining apron, briefly scanned the pantry and pulled out an ingredient that saved the day. And it turned out that those were the best cupcakes Jerry ever had. He smiled at the memory and smiled even more when he found the very same ingredient in his ICS supplies and added it to his batter.

Time was up. The faculty made their rounds through the various halls. Lazio Hall, where the Mayon-daise campers were set up, was the last to be judged.

Jerry felt confident. He had to admit, his pancakes smelled and tasted pretty good. They were a bit spongier than usual but very moist and extremely yummy. He hadn't paid attention to anyone else around him while cooking, but now he scanned the other ICSs visible from his station and could see the crumbled remnants of muffins, pancakes, breads, crepes, biscuits. The faculty was sampling, though it was apparent from their expressions that the results were underwhelming. But Mari and Louie G, situated only a few ICSs away from Jerry, had wide smiles on their faces. *I guess things went well for them too!*

Ten minutes later Chef Beurre's voice crackled through the speakers. "Today's competition was zeh most difficult to date. As I warned you yesterday, an ingredient would be missing to create your recipes. As dramatic as I made zeh competition sound, everyone had zeh same missing ingredient. *Moi. Beurre.* Translation? Butter!" Beurre couldn't have sounded smugger. "No one had butter in their ICSs. The successful chefs adapted." He paused for dramatic effect. "The winners of this morning's competition were three Mayon-daise campers. Jerry Pasta, Mari Nera, and Louie Gyan. Your uses of applesauce, yogurt, and sour cream as substitutes for butter led to zeh successful creation of, respectively, your blueberry pancakes, banana-blueberry muffins, and banana-oatmeal bread. FÉLICITATIONS!"

Jerry Pasta's
BUTTERLESS BLUEBERRY PANCAKES

Feeds 4 to 6

(makes 12 to 16 standard-size 4-inch pancakes)

Preparation time: 10 minutes

Cooking time: 7-10 minutes

INGREDIENTS AND SUPPLIES

Ingredients

1 ½ cups all-purpose flour (or substitute ¾ cup whole-wheat flour and ¾ cup buckwheat flour)

1 ½ teaspoons baking powder

1 tablespoon sugar

½ teaspoon salt

1 ½ cups 1-percent or low-fat milk

3 tablespoons unsweetened applesauce (can substitute yogurt, light sour
     cream, melted butter)

2 large eggs

½ teaspoon vanilla

½ to 1 cup fresh blueberries, rinsed well (see note)

Supplies

1 Large mixing bowl

1 Medium mixing bowl

Whisk

Large skillet

Wooden spatula

DIRECTIONS

1. In the large mixing bowl, combine the flour, baking powder, sugar, and salt.
   Blend well with a whisk.

2. In the medium mixing bowl, combine the milk, applesauce, eggs, and
   vanilla. Whisk well.

3. Pour the wet ingredients over the dry ingredients, and gently whisk them
   together just until they are well combined. Fold in the blueberries. 4. Heat
   a nonstick skillet to medium heat. (Grease lightly with butter if you wish.)
   Spoon about ¼ cup of the batter onto the skillet for each pancake. When
   many bubbles begin to form at the top (about 1 to 2 minutes) and the edges
   appear dry, flip the pancakes over with the spatula. Cook for an additional 1
   to 2 minutes, or until the underside is lightly browned. Remove the pan
   cakes from the skillet and serve.

4. Enjoy with honey or light syrup!

Note: Other fruit such as raspberries or bananas can be substituted—or added!

LOUIE G AND MARI NERA'S

BANANA-OATMEAL BREAD/ BANANA-BLUEBERRY MUFFINS

Makes 10 to 12 muffins or 1 loaf

Preparation time: 10 minutes

Cooking time: 20 minutes

INGREDIENTS AND SUPPLIES

Ingredients

1 ⅓ cups all-purpose flour

   (or ⅔ cup whole-wheat flour and ⅔ cup buckwheat flour)

¾ cup rolled oats

1 ½ teaspoon baking powder

⅓ cup sugar

¼ teaspoon salt

¾ cup ripe bananas, mashed

1 large egg, beaten

½ cup 1-percent or low-fat milk

¼ cup unsweetened applesauce

   (can substitute yogurt, light sour cream, or melted butter)

1 cup fresh blueberries, rinsed well

Supplies

1 Large mixing bowl

1 Medium mixing bowl

Cooking spray

Muffin pan or bread pan

DIRECTIONS

1. Preheat oven to 400 degrees.
2. In a large mixing bowl, combine all dry ingredients: flour, oats, baking powder, sugar, salt.
3. In the medium bowl, combine the mashed bananas, egg, milk, and applesauce.
4. Add the wet mixture to the dry mixture, stirring gently until well combined. The batter will be lumpy, not smooth. (Fold in blueberries at this step to make banana-blueberry muffins!)
5. Lightly spray a muffin pan or a bread pan, and spoon the batter into the greased muffin cups or pour into the bread pan.
6. Bake at 400 degrees for 20 minutes, or until golden brown on top. Use a toothpick inserted into the center to check for doneness. (The toothpick will come out clean when the muffins or bread are done.)

The three friends jubilantly exchanged high fives. After they had finished congratulating each other, they eagerly shared their leftovers with their fellow May-on-daise Kitchenmates in Lazio Hall, who gratefully accepted—especially since many of them hadn't managed to complete their assigned recipes. Twin brothers Paul and Marco Gagasol devoured two muffins each. Jerry was placing the last of his pancakes on Lefsa Stovon's plate when Rita Grodita came into the hall and ran up to Jerry, planting a big kiss on his cheek. She was accompanied by two giggly girls from Espagnole kitchen.

"Congratulations Herry! Jou are so great at cookeen!"

Jerry felt the blood rushing to his cheeks. *Ahhh!!!! Library kiss . . . ok. Public kiss? Not OK!!!* Jerry didn't need to look around to know that everyone was looking at him. (He'd developed an extra pair of eyeballs—

you know, the ones on the back of your head— when he first sprouted pasta for hair.) Once Jerry resigned himself to the fact that this extremely public encounter with Rita was unavoidable, he reluctantly kept his primary set of eyeballs focused on her, hoping that by giving her attention, the moment would pass quickly. And then he noticed . . . something different about her. For the past four or five days, Rita had been working out with the Mayon-daise Kitchen, participating in morning runs and EFF drills, and . . . *she looks . . . more fit . . . more alive . . . more . . . wow. She's . . . she's beau—*

"Jerry, clean up your ICS so we can get to class," said Louie G, rousing Jerry from his, um, noodling. Jerry was beginning to have feelings for Rita, feelings he didn't want to acknowledge because of the painful memories they stirred up. *Last time I felt this way, I smelled like Brie cheese for weeks.*

The rest of us generally call this feeling "attraction"—it makes the air smell sweeter, colors more vibrant, sounds more soothing. But attraction is also like that kick jalapeños give to fresh salsa: if you're not careful, it'll burn you.

Louie G tapped his foot loudly on the floor and sighed dramatically.

Jerry stared at Louie G, who had an annoyed, impatient look on his face. *Was Louie G jealous?* Jerry had to admit, it was nice to be the eleven-year-old boy who older girls saw as cute and innocent. He didn't have to worry about teenage boy issues like acne, musty body odor, and a cracking voice—yet. So at that instant, Jerry consciously chose to bask in the moment a little bit (take a bite out of the jalapeño, if you will) to see how far this feeling of "attraction" could take him without getting his feelings hurt.

"Actually, Louie G, why don't you and Mari head on to class without me. I'm going to chat with the *signorine*—the ladies—for a minute."

Stunned would be putting Louie G's facial expression mildly, and

Mari was speechless—though the look they exchanged as they headed off to class was as loud as a primal scream.

Unfazed, or maybe just unaware, Jerry shared with Rita and her friends the inspiration for his butter substitute. They stared at him, seemingly entranced; Jerry thought they were hanging on his every word until one of the girls, an American named Christiana Latte, reached out to Jerry and asked, "Can I touch your hair?"

And just like that, the spicy jalapeño evaporated. Apparently Jerry was just a novelty to them. A freak with pasta hair.

He backed away from Christiana. He wasn't a creature to be petted! Sure, he had almost let Rita touch his hair in the library a few days ago, but those were different circumstances. And right now Rita's face was chili red from embarrassment at her friend's behavior, but before she could say anything, Jerry grabbed his satchel and trudged off to class without even a good-bye. Had he looked back he would have seen a flustered Rita jab Christiana in the shoulder.

When he got to class, his usual seat between Louie G and Mari was already occupied by Manny Cotti. His pals hadn't saved it for him. And after class, Louie G and Mari still seemed to be giving him the silent treatment. Jerry caught up with them at the lunch table, sitting between them before anyone else could.

"Hey, guys!"

"Well, if it isn't the great Jerry Pasta! All the single ladies put your hands up!" Louie G sarcastically mimed a few of Beyoncé's choreographed moves, waving his hands in front of him. "Can I have your autograph?" He shoved a napkin toward Jerry.

"Jerry Pasta is sitting next to me! I feel sooooo special," Mari continued to pile on. "Do you think he knows my name?" She playfully batted her eyes.

Jerry grimaced. "OK, OK. I apologize if I hurt your feelings. I shouldn't have dissed you guys to schmooze with the Espagnole girls."

Smiling sheepishly he added, "I guess I just got caught up in the moment—truthfully, it was fun being a hero for a minute."

Mari let out an exasperated sigh. "But you *are* a hero, Jerry. All the time—especially to us. We would not have won that competition without you teaching us about substitutions."

Louie G nodded vigorously. "You see us hangin' out with any other eleven-year-olds here at camp?" He gestured dramatically at the other tables in the dining hall, knowing full well that Jerry was the *only* eleven-year old at Presto Pesto's. "Besides, every hero needs friends. So don't forget about us when you're famous and saving the world." Grinning, he added, "And the least you could have done was introduce me to that Christiana girl. She was pretty cute, and since you already seem to have something going with Rita, I think you could share the love a little."

Jerry pondered Mari's and Louie G's words. Their friendship was more important to him than winning cooking competitions and garnering fame and glory. *Maybe reputation isn't everything.*

"I promise to be a better friend. I'll make sure we share all of our successes from now on. And as ticked off as I am at Christiana, I'll try to put a good word in for you next time I see her, Louie G. I'll get over it." He grinned. "So, guys . . . how should we celebrate our win?"

Louie G replied, "Well you can start by passing the UMZOW sauce-boat this way!" It was a delicious *sauce verte* that complemented the pork tenderloin extremely well. Jerry made a mental note to ask Chef Beurre about the recipe later. More importantly, like the meal in front of them, Jerry felt his friends complemented him well and that through their brief conflict, their friendship had actually grown stronger.

Back at the cabin that evening, after completing their homework, Mari and Louie G played several rounds of checkers while Jerry worked on some meal recipes. The Gagasol twins stared at each other intensely across the kitchen table, engaged in a fierce game of chess, while Nigel, Brad, Guinness, and Lefsa battled on the bocce court outside of the cabin. The sheer number and ever-increasing volume of Nigel's whines floating through the open window could only mean one thing: the girls were winning. When it was time to turn in, Louie G challenged Mari to a checkers rematch the following night. She reminded him they'd be busy playing EFF tomorrow.

"Tomorrow's Wednesday?!" exclaimed Jerry. He was being slightly overly dramatic. It wasn't as if the Mayon-daise team hadn't been preparing. In fact, their EFF training had been insanely rigorous. Jerry had convinced them to wake up early with him to exercise, though instead of running every morning—since not everybody was in love with two miles of cross-country jogging—Jerry mixed things up. One morning they played soccer, with Manny Cotti teaching everyone the rules and trying not to get too upset when they were broken (Louie G had a really bad habit of catching balls in the air instead of using his head). Another morning they played football (the American version but no tackling), courtesy of Louie G, who tried to not get upset when Manny wanted to kick the football after catching it. ("I know it's called *football*, Manny, but don't be fooled by the name. Just catch the ball and run!") The EFF team definitely liked the variety—it made exercising more desirable, more fun, and even some non-EFF team members—including a few from other kitchens like Rita—joined in. The results were visible after only a week. Louie G was able to do a lot more with game strategy now that he had a bunch of budding athletes at his disposal. So Jerry really had nothing to worry about.

"Well, I guess we better get a good night's sleep," said Mari.

"Especially lover boy here. How will he ever throw food at his beloved Rita?" Louie G teased.

Meatballs! Could tomorrow's match really be against the Espagnole Kitchen?

EFF matchups weren't announced until the day of, when all the teams were assembled on the field. But Louie G's suggestion was enough to make Jerry anxious—hadn't there already been enough drama for one week?

Chapter 18

Attack of the Rotten Tomatoes

Jerry had trouble falling asleep that night. Partly because he was fretting over the EFF match tomorrow (he dreaded having another food-related nightmare). Partly because it was too quiet. Usually, during the first half hour after lights out, the faint hum of camper chatter buzzed in the bunkroom since no one was quite ready to sleep. But tonight seemed different—maybe everyone was worn out from all of the exercise. Jerry finally dozed off a little after midnight. He was startled awake thirty minutes later.

Shff . . . shff . . . shff.

What was that? Still in a little bit of a mental fog, Jerry wasn't sure if he had actually heard something or whether he'd just been dreaming. And then he heard it again.

Shff . . . shff . . . shff.

Jerry blinked, trying to adjust his eyes to the dark room.

That was suddenly painfully bright.

The room exploded with what seemed like a thousand beams of light! One of those beams caught Jerry directly in the eyes. He instinctively squinted and raised his hands to cover his eyes. Luckily. Because . . .

WHAM!

Jerry's hands prevented him from being hit squarely in the nose by the projectile—though it did catch him on the left nostril.

"Owwww!" He immediately buried his face in his pillow as more objects pelted him on the head and back. He could hear the plaintive cries of a few of his other cabinmates as well. Obviously he wasn't the only target. Jerry felt a trickle of liquid travel from his nostril to his upper lip and feared his nose was bleeding. He touched his tongue to his upper lip.

Hmmm, my blood tastes like . . . like tomato juice. Jerry groped on his bunk bed for one of the projectiles that had glanced off of his head, confirming his suspicion. But this tomato felt *. . . Yuck, this is rotten! What is going on?!*

It was then that Jerry realized *nothing* was going on. The pelting had stopped. Other than some muttered curse words coming from other bunks, the cabin was quiet.

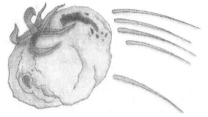

And pitch black again. Then lights began shining here and there, and Jerry feared another attack. But when Louie G whispered, "JP, you OK?," Jerry realized the coast was clear, and the beams of light now were his cabinmates' flashlights.

"Yeah, I'm OK. I'm covered in rotten tomato juice, but other than a few bruises, I'm fine."

Jerry pulled his own flashlight out from under his bed to survey the damage. The whole room was stirring now. Rotten, fleshy tomatoes were strewn all over the cabin, but there was a notable concentration of them by Jerry's bunk. Two oversized unripe green tomatoes sat on his sheets. Gingerly rubbing his head, Jerry wished he had been hit by more of the squishy, rotten ones. He'd take messy over painful any day. Though speaking of the former, other campers were cleaning tomato debris off of their pajamas and sheets, and the cabin as a whole was an utter mess.

"*The girls!*" Louie G slapped Jerry on the shoulder and sprinted towards the center kitchen and over to the girls' section of the cabin, his flashlight illuminating the way. Jerry was close behind.

The girls hadn't fared much better. Clearly the perpetrators had gone for maximum impact with minimum effort—and succeeded.

Mari's flashlight caught the boys in the face. "From the looks of you two, I'm guessing the same thing happened on your side."

"Yeah, and Jerry took the worst of it. You should see his bunk bed. It looks like he was trying to make tomato sauce in his sleep. Nothing like a little penne with red sauce," joked Louie G, pointing to Jerry's head. The bandana Jerry wore at night to keep his pasta hair under wraps was covered with tomato chunks and seeds. Jerry glared at Louie G.

"Too soon?" Louis G asked wryly. "I'll take that as a yes . . . not funny," Louie G conceded before pulling an imaginary zipper across his lips.

"Who do you think did this to us—and why?" Jerry barked angrily.

"Seriously, Jerry?" Mari asked. "I thought you would have been the first to guess. Let's see . . . what got thrown at us tonight? And what enemies have you made this summer?" Mari got even more sarcastic when she was tired—and it was one o'clock in the morning.

Of course! The Tomato Kitchen! This cabin raid had undoubtedly been orchestrated by Robert DeJourno and his Tomato cabinmates, especially his Mufia cousins, Lumina Foyle and Cello Feigni. Jerry ripped the bandana off of his head and threw it on the floor in disgust. "It's the middle of *la notte*, we have class in seven hours, an EFF match tomorrow night, and a cabin that's going to take hours to clean up. *Grrrrrr!!!!*" Tears welled up in Jerry's eyes. But instead of allowing the floodgates to open, he parted his quivering lips and took a deep breath, his frustrations somewhat subsiding.

Louie G's chuckle broke any remaining tension. "It's all good Jerry. Hey, this is part of the fun of camp! OK, it doesn't seem fun right now, but we get to spend the rest of the day . . . and what little is left of our night . . . dreaming about how we're going to get them back. *Payback!*" he said, slamming his fist repeatedly into his open palm. "And we'll have fun doing it. I mean, think about it for a second. Tomato Kitchen probably won't get much sleep tonight, either, and it probably took them a while to coordinate all this. Sure, they're in their cabin having a good laugh right now, but they'll be just as tired as us in the morning." He grinned maliciously. "Our prank will be better—and we'll be smart enough to plan in a way that we don't lose any sleep."

Jerry nodded his head and smiled. Louie G was right. This tomato-throwing episode was probably par for camp pranks—though it did seem pretty mean-spirited. Throwing rotten tomatoes was one thing. But hurling hard, unripe ones at point-blank range at people's heads? That wouldn't have even been allowed on the EFF field. But it didn't mean that Mayon-daise Kitchen's prank back had to be as violent.

The wheels in Jerry's sleep-deprived brain were already churning. The retaliatory prank was going to have to be reeeeally good.

The Mayon-daise cabin was finally all cleaned up by three in the morning. Jerry's four hours of rest consisted of deep, pillow-drooling sleep, the kind of sleep so deep that you either have crazy, mind-blowing dreams that linger on into consciousness or you wake up having no idea what you dreamed or even *if* you dreamed.

Awake thanks to his persistent alarm clock, Jerry had trouble rousing everyone else to make it to breakfast on time—and since the kitchens were deducted points toward The Toque for tardiness at meals, he wanted to avoid a repeat of the lake debacle. In the dining hall, the Tomato campers scattered around the room looked just as tired as the Mayon-daise ones except they all wore smug smiles.

Over breakfast, Jerry, Louie G, Mari and handful of other Mayon-daise campers discussed strategies for preventing future attacks. "We could hire an armed guard," Nigel A. Dawson suggested, a not-so-surprising comment from probably the richest kid at cooking camp. His parents were basically royalty in England.

"Um . . . that's one thought. Anyone else?" Louie G had no patience for Nigel.

"There's no lock on our cabin door, but I think right before lights out, we should string a bunch of empty aluminum cans to the doorknob. It's kind of a primitive alarm system, but it should work," said Mari, between mouthfuls of fruit-filled breakfast crepes.

"Great idea. No one should be leaving the cabin after lights out, so anyone coming in will be caught." Louie G yawned and stretched his arms high above his head. "I guess we should all sleep with our flashlights too. I think that ambush would have been a lot less successful if we'd had lights to use on them. Blinding us definitely worked in Tomato's favor." Louie G spoke as if the previous night's raid was part of some greater camp competition for best kitchen, as if winning The Toque wasn't enough.

"I've got two extra industrial flashlights, a motion-sensitive lamp at my bedside, a chargeable Taser, plus my iPhone has a built-in flashli--"

"Nigel, eat your crepes."

"But Lou--"

"Crepes, Nigel."

Mari cleared her throat to change the subject. "So what are we going to do to them?" she asked.

Mari's question caught Louie G by surprise. "Didn't figure you to be the vengeful type, Mari."

Mari shot Louie G the death stare. ""This bruise on my cheek hurts like the dickens. The girl who launched the tomato that hit me in the face throws like a professional cricket player!"

"Hurts like the what? Professional who? Sometimes I forget we're growing up on different continents Mari," Louie G lamented, shaking his head in disbelief.

"But how did you know it was a girl?" asked Jerry.

"I was actually awake just before the raid started because I was just about to go to the toilet. Just as I was sitting up, I was blinded by a bright light, followed by a tomato that hit me squarely in the jaw—followed by giggling. I got up and ran straight for the giggling and gave a swift kick—I made pretty good contact. I'm pretty sure my attacker was a girl; whoever it was cried like one."

The boys stared in awe, mouths agape. Mari was feisty for sure. And her feistiness probably saved the girls' dorm from taking as much damage as the boys'. Jerry and Louie G swapped a look that said, "Don't tick her off!"

Then Jerry hunched closer to his two friends. "Well, I do have one idea about how to get back at Tomato Kitchen . . ."

With Nigel concentrating on his crepes, Jerry whispered his idea to Louie G and Mari, who approved enthusiastically. "Let's work out the details over the course of the morning," Jerry added.

So instead of paying attention during the morning classes, the three exchanged surreptitious notes and finalized their plan right before lunch. Good thing they had something to focus on; the other Mayon-daise campers in the classroom kept nodding off—and getting in trouble for it.

"Guys, for this to work, we need to execute the plan *now*, while everyone's at lunch," stressed Jerry.

"But if all three of us aren't there, someone is bound to notice. Especially if *you're* not there, Jerry. So how about Mari and I slip out—and maybe our vacant seats at the dining table can be filled by a couple of your many admirers." Louie G gave Jerry a playful jab to the ribs.

Jerry conceded that Louie G was right on the money—he was too conspicuous, pasta hair and all, to go missing—though it irked him to no end not to be able to put his own plan into motion. And at lunch when Louie G and Mari didn't sit in their usual spots flanking Jerry, the seats were quickly filled by Rita Grodita and Christiana Latte.

"Hi, Jerry, are these seats taken?"

"No, Christiana, they're free," said a weakly smiling Jerry, with all the earnestness he could muster, still annoyed by her attempt to touch his hair the previous day.

"Oh, please, call me Ana. For real. That's what my friends call me," she pined in her most syrupy voice.

Jerry spent most of lunch not listening to the girl chatter, instead thinking and hoping that the Mayon-daise prank was going as planned. Word had gotten out about what had happened to Mayon-daise Kitchen during the night, and Jerry wasn't really interested in reliving it, so he didn't say much. But he didn't completely ignore the girls: as promised, he mentioned Louie G's name to Christiana, playing up Louie G's athleticism and mentioning where he'd be on the EFF field later that night. When Christiana excused herself to go to the bathroom, Rita took the opportunity to profusely apologize to Jerry about the attempted hair-touching.

"I *so* sorry, Herry. It was rude of Christiana to do that, and I yell at her later about it. Please forgive me for putting jou in an awkward situation."

"Apology accepted, Rita," said Jerry, his mind elsewhere as he looked past her, keeping an eye on the situation. Jerry was trying to fulfill his role as "lookout." If anybody from Tomato Kitchen left the dining hall before Mari or Louie G returned, he was to do anything in his power to stop them. Jerry dreaded having to confront a Tomato Kitchen member today, especially since they were likely to gloat about the raid.

Jerry was half listening to Rita saying something about the delicious lunch sauce when he spotted Robert DeJourno getting up from his chair and sauntering towards the exit.

Oh, boy, this is just great, Jerry thought. *God must have a sense of humor because this is the LAST person I want to talk to today.* Jerry guessed DeJourno had been the one pelting him in the head with tomatoes only a few hours earlier.

"Um . . . I need to run to the restroom," Jerry mumbled, excusing himself to Rita while rising to his feet. His legs felt heavy as he hurried to cut DeJourno off, and Jerry's sluggish brain furiously tried to come up with a reason to talk to his adversary, wishing he had thought of something before the moment was actually upon him.

Robert was five feet from the Eaditt Hall door when Jerry came sprinting over, blocking his path.

"*Ciao,* Robert."

A weary-looking Robert DeJourno, holding a yellow folder in his left hand, stopped dead in his tracks.

Well, at least I've slowed him down, Jerry thought.

"Hi," DeJourno abruptly answered, hurriedly trying to conceal the folder behind his back. He seemed genuinely surprised that Jerry was talking to him—and genuinely nervous. "Whaddya want? Oh, by the way—" he paused to yawn "—you've got some tomato sauce on your face," he added, tapping the corner of his mouth. He then doubled over laughing.

It was obvious that he had been waiting all day to use that joke on Jerry, who managed a half-hearted chuckle to play along.

DeJourno's demeanor abruptly turned serious again. "If you've got something to say, go ahead and say it. Otherwise, get outta my way!"

Jerry noticed a thick elastic bandage wrapped around Robert's right elbow. Determined to keep the conversation going and stall for time, Jerry offered, "Did you sprain your elbow or something?"

"Nah, this is just a minor thing I had to go see the nurse for this morning. I never realized that pickin' green tomatoes in the garden could be *sooooo* strenuous." He exaggeratedly clutched his right arm to his side, barely getting out his last few words before erupting in rip-roaring, thigh-slapping laughter. Again. Subtlety was clearly not DeJourno's strong suit. Neither was humility.

"Well, I've been thinking about the Mufia," Jerry announced, knowing this would get DeJourno's attention and end the mockery.

"*Really?!* Wanna finally join?" DeJourno's voice and attitude were suddenly earnest and eager—almost too eager.

Why does he care so much about me joining the Mufia? Jerry was dying to figure out why.

"Ummm"—Jerry scrambled—"I sort of wanted some more information. Do you have weekly meetings?"

"Yeah, every Friday night. And then we try to do something fun on the weekends. We're gonna sneak off campus to watch some American movies at the theater in town this Saturday. The stupid Sauciers are always trying to do the same stuff we do. Copycats."

"That sounds fun," Jerry deadpanned.

"So are you gonna join or not?"

"I, uh, actually, I think not." Despite his best efforts, Jerry had run out of things to say. Making conversation with Robert was about as useful as interacting with an empty vending machine. No matter how much you spent . . . you'd still walk away empty-handed.

"Then why are you wastin' my time askin' me questions about the club?" DeJouorno raised his arm menacingly, the yellow folder now poised inches from Jerry's nose. "I oughta—"

"You oughta head back to your seat, Robert. I think your momma wants you," Louie G said mockingly. He and Mari had reappeared just in the nick of time.

Jerry gave a sigh of relief at having been saved (at least temporarily) from another DeJourno beatdown. Although he might not be so lucky where Chef Pei Lei was concerned. She was briskly walking directly toward the four campers, appearing surprisingly intimidating for such a tiny woman.

"CAN I BE OF SERVICE TO THE FOUR OF YOU? DID YOU FORGET WHERE TO SIT?" Chef Lei was about as gentle as a meat tenderizer.

Louie G answered for the group, "Oh, no ma'am, we just had something to take care of." He paused to flash Jerry a covert wink. "*We*"—pointing to himself, Jerry, and Mari—"were just heading back to our seats. Don't know where Tomato boy was headed."

DeJourno's face turned red . . . cherry tomato red.

Louie G might just be the only boy here at camp bold enough to stand up to Robert DeJourno, Jerry told himself. He was glad his new pal was on the good guys' side. Jerry, Mari and Louie G nonchalantly walked back to their seats as DeJourno attempted to explain himself to Chef Pei Lei. Jerry noticed that Robert was still shielding that folder behind his back. *What was he up to?*

The thought immediately left Jerry's brain as the trio got back to their seats, which Rita and Christiana had apparently vacated when Jerry took off. Fortunately none of the instructors seemed to have noticed Jerry, Louie G, and Mari's absence. As the three friends sat down, Mari gave Jerry the good news.

"Mission successful, Jerry. We'll see tonight if the Ketchup Kitchen is able to *mustard* up their courage."

(An inside joke you'll shortly understand. . . .)

Chapter 19

Trick or treat, revenge is sweet, who's got tangy, stinky, feet?

The EFF matches would again take place after sunset, though by dinnertime the Mayon-daise team was already dragging a little, their sleep deficit beginning to take its toll. By eight o'clock, most of the kitchens had gathered at the Field of Greens for the announcement of the night's matchups. Tomato Kitchen was notably absent. (Who wouldn't notice that the team with the posh uniforms was missing?) Brock Lee pronounced the pairings. "Velouté will be playing against Béchamel, and Mayon-daise will be facing Espagnole. We will start the games in five minutes."

Louie G had been right! Jerry hoped Rita wouldn't be playing. She'd been training with the Mayon-daise squad for the last week, and it was possible that she'd earned a spot on the Espagnole team now that she had picked up some skills and appeared lighter on her feet. Jerry wasn't sure what would be more awkward: dodging food Rita threw at him on the field while he competed against her kitchen or dodging kisses she blew at him from the sidelines. He was going to need to clarify their relationship status soon.

Two minutes later the Tomato Kitchen team finally showed up, gingerly jogging, though Robert DeJourno was lagging ten yards behind the rest of the team, and Lumina Foyle was a few steps behind *him*, noticeably limping. Their uniform tops were snazzy as usual, but in place of their matching tomato-red socks, the Tomato EFF team wore white ankle socks.

When Robert DeJourno finally arrived on the sidelines, noticeably tired and out of breath, Brock Lee delivered the news that his team wasn't playing that week and had a bye. "Take your seat in the stands with the other spectators."

Robert's face fell, registering disappointment at having rushed out to play, only to be told to sit and wait for the next round of games. The Tomato team took their seats in the stands and, for the most part, remained relatively quiet. From their baggy eyes to their grim faces, none of them seemed to be in a talking mood. Which was surprising, considering they'd been gloating about their tomato prank ALL day.

Cello Feigni sat in an empty space next to Rita Grodita. Rita, not one to be shy, remarked loudly, "Someting smells stinky."

A few of her Espagnole cabinmates began to echo her observation. Still, no one from the Tomato EFF team said a word, sitting with rather uncomfortable looks on their faces. A few giggles erupted from May-on-daise campers as Rita repeated herself, even louder this time.

Soon many of the Espagnole, Velouté, and Béchamel campers were sniffing audibly, determined to locate the source of the odor. Rita was leaning down in the stands, smelling right and left. Cello Feigni attempted to tuck her legs under the bleacher seat when Rita brazenly announced, "I don't know how to tell jou this, Cello, but jour feet esmell like mixed condiments. Like, hmm, I think mustard plus mayonnaise. And jours do too, Lumina. . . ."

The Mayon-daise Kitchen campers, who had been in on the prank, could hold in their laughter no longer. The Gagasol brothers did their quirky twin tandem-laugh thing, their shoulders undulating up and down in unison. Even the usually reserved Nigel Dawson seemed to let down his guard, desperately trying to catch his breath between hearty guffaws. And just like that, the Mayon-daise Kitchen exhaustion and frustration seemed to melt away. (As the old saying goes, laughter is the best medicine. Mustard flavored in this case.)

Word quickly spread through the bleachers that when the Tomato EFF team had begun to dress for tonight's EFF match a half hour ear-lier, they found that their crimson socks and black cleats had been filled with—exactly as Rita had surmised—mayonnaise and mus-tard. Most of them had already slipped their feet into their team socks, immersing their toes in the  smelly, gooey substance. Even the ones warned about the socks hadn't anticipated their *shoes* being filled with condiments as well. They couldn't replace their shoes, so all they could do was wear white socks instead of the red ones and deal with wearing gooshy shoes.

When Jerry initially shared his inspired prank with his best pals, Louie G declared that in his humble, unbiased opinion, this shenan-igan was on par with some of the best Halloween pranks he'd ever seen. Better than egging or toilet-paper wrapping someone's house. Plus the condiment jokes were bountiful.

He now yelled out, "Good thing Tomato Kitchen's not playing to-night. They might have trouble playing ketchup—I mean, *catch up!*"

Several campers asked the Tomato EFFers if they had any Grey

Poupon, prompting Jerry, Mari and Louie G to exchange discreet fist-bumps. Their prank had worked perfectly! Robert DeJourno's face matched the color of his jersey. Jerry could almost see steam coming out of his ears, cartoon-style.

The old janitor/referee seated in the tall beach chair finally got everyone's focus by shouting into his megaphone, "Attention! It is time for the games to begin! Attention! To repeat what my colleague just told you, tonight the competing kitchens will be Velouté against Béchamel and Mayon-daise versus Espagnole."

Velouté and Béchamel played the first match, with Velouté winning handily, exposing the Béchamel team as clearly being at a disadvantage for not having played in Week One. When it was their turn to play, the Mayon-daise squad found that this Week Two match was more contested than their first match but not by much. The confidence boost from their successful prank provided the extra energy that the sleep-deprived team desperately needed.

This week was the vegetable round. Half-eaten corncobs, broccoli stumps, and browning lettuce heads were only a sampling of the leftover projectiles the kitchen staff had dredged up. Luckily Jerry had made the entire team work on target practice over the weekend, focusing on accuracy, not force of throw. Their aim was still fairly lousy, but Mayon-daise won handily 1,200 to 200 (it helped that Louie G was a formidable Pharaoh). Jerry stole the Espagnole's egg twice in the game, once in each half. He and Mari had been practicing at least thirty minutes a day; Jerry had them run drills while balancing the egg: zigzagging around cones, hopping on one leg, crawling on their bellies. In between classes, other Sphinxes-in-the-making were seen practicing by carrying eggs on ladles down the hallways. A common prank was to try to make them drop the egg by startling them—which had the unfortunate consequence of keeping the cleaning staff fairly busy. Those faculty members not cognizant of the EFF games would stare at the egg-carrying students, puzzled at what they saw as a strange, not-pertinent-to-cooking behavior.

Thankfully, Rita did *not* play for the Espagnole team that night. Jerry had actually looked for her in the stands during halftime—and she struck him as being a little sad, like she wished she was playing. She wasn't as demonstrative in her cheering for Jerry this game, out of respect for her team, it seemed. Though she did stand up and clap gleefully for a full twenty seconds after Jerry recovered the egg in the first half, notwithstanding the glowering stares from her cabinmates.

After the games were over, the afterglow remained for the May-on-daise Kitchen, who, despite their exhaustion, were high on life for having successfully bested their rivals 2 to 0 in EFF matches. And then reality came back in the form of Robert DeJourno, who confronted Jerry and the Mayon-daise team as they walked off the playing field.

Flanked by a limping Lumina Foyle and a glaring Cello Feigni, De-Journo sarcastically slow clapped when he was within a few feet of Jerry. "Cute prank. Didn't think you had the guts to fight back. But you have no idea what you just started. This means war. We're lookin' forward to destroyin' you . . . on the EFF field. Good thing we had a bye this week. Otherwise it would have been bye-bye Jerry Pasta. You had betta watch your back from here on out, Pasta."

As DeJourno and his cronies walked away in a huff, Louie G yelled after them, "Send us the laundry bill!"

Mari also couldn't help herself. "Hey, Lumina, what does it feel like to be a bruised Tomato?!" The large black-and-blue discoloration on Lumina's left shin readily identified her as Mari's attacker from the previous night—the bruise being the result of Mari's retaliatory kick.

Lumina stopped short, turned, and spat in Mari's direction, making a very unladylike gesture with her right hand. Then she hobbled away to catch up to her cohorts.

"I think we've antagonized them enough for one day," Jerry wisely cautioned. "Let's head back to the cabin to celebrate with everyone."

At lights out later that night, Jerry felt the kind of tired that was satisfying after a long, successful day. He smiled to himself as he replayed something Louie G had said earlier: "Grownups say that revenge is a dish best served cold.' I say that revenge is a dish best served with mustard and mayo."

Jerry fell asleep with a smile on his face, thinking, *Eat it up, Ketchup Kitchen. There's more where that came from!*

Chapter 20

Study Buddies

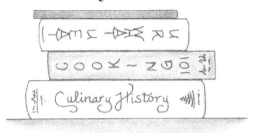

Thursday and Friday came and went, and as Week Two drew to a close, Jerry put his EFF duties on the backburner and poured himself into his studies. "Culinary History" actually proved to be quite fascinating—though Jerry mused that this meant the old janitor he met the first day of class was right: understanding culinary history would open up a world of cooking Jerry didn't realize existed. *Why had things changed so much now, in the present?* The concepts Jerry was learning would change his cooking forever.

One of Jerry's new heroes from the past was Antonin Carême, the great-great-grandfather of school founder Karim de la Carême. Antonin came from humble beginnings; abandoned as a baby by his poor parents during the French Revolution, he went on to become one of the most celebrated chefs in history, credited with classifying the mother sauces and creating the toque, the chef's hat and the inspiration behind the school's top award. Antonin once made an entire year's worth of food for French nobility using only fresh herbs and seasonal vegetables—making a different dish every day!

This bit of history made "Community Gardening" class all the more meaningful for Jerry. Antonin's cooking credibility made Jerry even more excited about reading his great-great-grandson's textbook; *Sauce for the Saucier* was brilliant. Karim de la Carême began the book by delving into the history of sauces; subsequent chapters taught how to make each of the five mother sauces, including secondary or "small" sauces, derivatives (spin-offs) of the mother sauces. (To clarify, small sauces are what most of us are used to eating when we go to restaurants where a sauce or gravy is served with the meal.) At the end of each major chapter, Karim de la Carême always left the tagline, "It's in your BONES! Be Original, Not an Everyday Saucier!"

I've heard something like that recently, Jerry mused, *though I don't remember when or where.*

Jerry was learning so much from the book that he began sharing some of the tips with Mari and Louie G since it was clear that they weren't learning half as much in Chef Beurre's Sauce class. The sauces Beurre had them creating so far were bland, boring, and—oddly—nothing like the sauces being served with meals in the dining hall in the UMZOW sauce boats donated by Carême. Jerry recognized a significant disconnect. *How could Chef Beurre, the Sauce instructor, create such masterpieces here in the dining hall but teach such disappointment in the classroom?* At that moment, Jerry made up his mind. He would have to go to the source: he would sneak into the main kitchen and watch Chef Beurre make the sauce. Why sneak? Well, he had tried the direct approach, asking Chef Beurre to let him watch, but Beurre quickly vetoed that idea.

"The kitchen ees off limits to campers, Pasta. Besides, you have every opportunity to watch me cook in class. Pay closer attention, and you will see how it is done—and done correctly!" Jerry—who couldn't understand why Beurre had been so standoffish—weighed the risks. This wasn't like sneaking to the lake, though he could still get kicked out if he got caught. But he simply needed to know.

Maybe an indirect approach would be better. Over the course of the first two weeks of camp, Jerry had noticed a growing number of campers, French campers in particular, spending more and more time following Chef Beurre around. They sat near him at the dining table, stayed late after class to kiss up to him, and generally did anything they could do to get into his good graces. Jerry surmised they were The Sauciers who Louie G had bumped into the first week..

On Saturday afternoon, Jerry found a few of the club members gathered in the empty Sauce classroom working on, of course, sauces. The smell in the smoke-filled room was terrible; it was a mix between sweaty feet omelette and burnt-hair bacon. Clearly, sauce making wasn't going so well for the "Saucy Posse," as Louie G had playfully named them.

Jerry, right hand protectively hovering over his upper lip, timidly entered the room. "Hi . . . uh . . . what kind of sauce are you making?"

A pale girl wearing a blue blouse and a stained apron approached him. Jerry recognized her as Julia Enfant, a thirteen-year-old Parisian. She was a good foot taller than Jerry, possibly the tallest girl at camp, and she towered over him as she shrilly announced, "Well, if it isn't the great Jerry Pasta! What are you doing here? Don't you belong to our rivals, The Mufia?" Her English was very good, with a gentle French accent. There was nothing gentle about her tone, however.

"Oh, no . . . *no!* I turned them down." Jerry watched the tension drain from her face.

"So you are here to join The Sauciers? *Marveilleux!* Marvelous!"she exclaimed, fairly bounding up and down.

Jerry quickly tried to bring her back to earth. "Actually, Julia, I was . . . I was hoping just to watch your group and learn how you make sauces. I mean, you all spend the most time with Chef Beurre, and I'm sure you have fallen in love with the dining hall sauces as much as I have, so surely you have tried to duplicate them."

Though some of her enthusiasm drained away, she was apparently convinced of Jerry's earnest interest. "Yes, we love the sauces served in the special sauceboats. And, yes, we spend many afternoons like this trying to replicate them. One of the cleaning staff unlocks this room for us so we can practice. Even Chef Beurre has come to help us on occasion—but the sauces never taste quite right— *Oh, la la!*" She suddenly slapped her forehead in reaction to a curl of smoke wafting towards them.

Jerry was dumbfounded. "So you mean even with Chef Beurre's help you haven't been able to make sauces as tasty as what he serves in the dining hall?"

"No, *pas du tout*. Not in the least. But we keep trying. It is actually kind of embarrassing. How can we call ourselves 'The Sauciers' if we can't make great sauces?" She looked around as if making sure no one could overhear, then whispered, "*Zut alors*, the elderly cleaning man who lets us in this room has given us better tips than Beurre."

Jerry spent the next thirty minutes schmoozing with The Sauciers, one of whom was Christiana Latte, who he thought was American and not French. Turns out, she explained, that she was a little bit of everything—French, Norwegian, German, Italian. She grew up in Suffolk, Virginia, and her last name was Italian but sounded French enough for the club's liking (Snooty? Maybe a little bit. The Sauciers had a clear preference toward French campers.). Ana loved being part of the club and really fit right in: she *was* a little snobby. But more importantly to the club, she *loved* the dining hall sauce.

The Sauciers were actually a nicer club than Jerry had expected (despite their pushiness with Louie G) and much friendlier than The Mufia. Jerry declined their repeated invitations to join but promised to share with them anything he learned about making sauces. He even showed them some of the basics he had learned from reading *Sauce for the Saucier;* they were in awe. Jerry's reputation as a pretty good chef preceded him, and The Sauciers were willing to learn from him, even if he *was* only eleven and didn't want to join their club. (Truthfully, Jerry didn't understand what the big deal was: everything he had taught them was from a book right off of the shelf in their classroom!)

One of the simple recipes that Jerry showed them was for making béchamel sauce, which can be put on eggs, fish, vegetables, or chicken. (Note: this isn't the healthiest recipe in the world, but the sauce is delish!)

SAUCE BÉCHAMEL

To make a white sauce such as béchamel, you must first begin making what's called a roux—a thickening agent made up of flour and butter. Once you've learned to make a basic béchamel sauce, you can create a host of secondary sauces just by adding other ingredients such as herbs and spices and cheeses.

INGREDIENTS AND SUPPLIES

Ingredients for the Basic White Stock
2 cups 1-percent milk
¼ teaspoon salt

Ingredients for the Roux
2 tablespoons butter
3 tablespoons flour

Supplies
2 small saucepans
Wire whisk
Wooden spatula

DIRECTIONS

1. In one small saucepan, bring the milk and salt to a boil, being careful that the milk doesn't boil over. Remove from heat.
2. While the milk is heating, make the roux in the second saucepan by melting the butter over low heat. Then slowly blend in the flour, one tablespoon at a time, until the flour and butter form a frothy white mixture (about 2 minutes). Use your wire whisk to mix everything evenly.
3. Remove from heat.

You've just made roux!

Now make the Béchamel. . . .

DIRECTIONS

1. Add the white stock to the roux, and beat vigorously with a whisk. It will look like a bunch of little crumbs in milk, but keep whisking until most of the "crumbs" are dissolved.
2. Heat this mixture on high, stirring with the whisk until it boils. Let it boil for 1 minute, but keep stirring continuously!
3. Remove the mixture from the heat, adding salt and white pepper to taste

You've just made Béchamel sauce!

(It can be refrigerated for up to a week or freeze it for later use.)

With this basic sauce you can make a delicious secondary sauce like Mornay sauce (great with vegetables, pasta, eggs, chicken) by simply adding these ingredients:

1/4 to 1/2 cup grated Swiss cheese or a combination of Swiss and Parmesan
Pinch of nutmeg
Salt and pepper

DIRECTIONS

1. Bring your Béchamel sauce to a boil.
2. Remove the saucepan from the heat, and then add the cheese, stirring until it is well blended with the sauce
3. Add the nutmeg and salt and pepper to taste.

Following his cooking tutorial on Béchamel sauce, Jerry almost ran over the old janitor on his way out of the Sauce classroom; the janitor was in what Jerry now thought of as the old man's usual position: on his knees, buffing the floor. Pausing for a moment to appreciate that announcing the EFF games must be a treat for the janitor compared to scrubbing and waxing floors, Jerry apologized for having to walk on the already-waxed area and then darted off, eager to share his Sauciers encounter with Mari and Louie G. Louie G's ears perked up when Jerry mentioned Ana Latte was a club member—Louie G suddenly wanted to be re-invited to join The Sauciers—but mostly Mari and Louie G were as surprised as Jerry about the club members' lack of sauce-making know-how.

Jerry shared with his buddies some of what he had learned from *Sauce for the Saucier*, including what he had shown The Sauciers that afternoon. The three spent some time in the cooking classrooms experimenting both with what Jerry taught them and what they had learned in class during the prior week.

Then Mari demonstrated how to make a soft, leavened, Indian flatbread called naan. Success took many tries, and some of the failed attempts were reinvented as mini-Frisbees. She also taught the boys about Indian spices and then showed them how to make samosas, a delicious, deep-fried triangular wedge filled with potatoes and vegetables. Mari and Jerry finally had a proper discussion of paneer, with Mari teaching him a few tricks about how to make one of her favorite dishes.

Mari Nera's
SAAG PANEER

You may need to go to an Indian grocery store that sells special spices or to the "ethnic" section of your regular grocery store for some of the ingredients in this recipe—but it will be worth the trip! Paneer is a kind of soft cheese that you can buy at most Indian grocery stores, but if it isn't available, I've included a substitute that tastes pretty good. And saag is spinach, which is used frequently in Indian dishes.

Feeds 4 to 6
Preparation time: 10 minutes
Cooking time: 30 to 40 minutes

INGREDIENTS AND SUPPLIES
Ingredients
¼ teaspoon ground turmeric

½ teaspoon garam masala

½ teaspoon ground cumin

½ teaspoon ground coriander

⅛ teaspoon red chili powder

½ teaspoon salt

1 cup paneer (can substitute queso fresco)

2 tablespoons vegetable oil

1 medium-sized onion, peeled and coarsely chopped

1 package sliced mushrooms

2 ½ teaspoons ginger-garlic paste

¼ cup tomato sauce, canned

¼ cup cream of mushroom soup, undiluted

1 package chopped frozen spinach, thawed

½ cup water

3 tablespoons heavy cream

Supplies

Small mixing bowl

Medium-sized saucepan

DIRECTIONS

1. In the mixing bowl, blend together the turmeric, garam masala, cumin, chili powder, coriander, and salt. Set aside.

2. Cube the paneer into bite-sized chunks and set aside.

3. In the saucepan, heat the vegetable oil on medium. Add the onion and mushrooms, and fry until the onions are golden-brown in color, about 5 minutes. Stir in the ginger-garlic paste, and sauté for 1 minute. Add the tomato sauce and mushroom soup, and cook for 2 more minutes.

4. Combine the spices into the mixture, and sauté for another 30 seconds. Then stir in the spinach, and cook for about 3 minutes, stirring constantly. Add the water, and cook uncovered on low heat for about 20 minutes. When the mixture starts to dry out, add a bit more water (no more than ¼ cup at a time).

5. Blend in the paneer (or queso fresco substitution), and sauté for 5 minutes. Stir gently if necessary.

6. Stir in the heavy cream while still in the saucepan, and serve hot with rice, naan, or chapati—another kind of flatbread! (You can often buy naan or chapati
   in the international section of your grocery store or at an Asian food market.)

Not to be outdone, Louie G shared some Ghanaian cooking secrets. Many Ghanaian recipes are onion and tomato based, and multiple meats are often combined in the same soup or stew to enhance flavor. Timing is also key, as Louie G quoted his mom saying, "Stew that brews overnight is better than hasty tasting."

"Your mother sounds like a professional chef, Louie G," Mari quipped.

"Well, she *is* a professional . . . a medical professional. She's a pediatrician. Both of my parents are doctors."

Jerry's jaw dropped. "You must be rich!" Jerry had a handful of friends who had a doctor parent—but not both parents!

Louie G shrugged. "Everybody assumes we're rich, which isn't true. I'm not saying that we're poor by any means, but my parents have worked very hard—neither of them was well off growing up. They trained at the medical school in Accra, Ghana's capital."

"But why not stay in Ghana? Doctors probably command tremendous respect and wield a great deal of power there," Mari noted.

"True, but not that simple, Mari. When my parents were just a young couple, the country was full of political unrest—crazy dictators and such—so they bolted for America to start a new life. A safe life. Respect and power was probably the last thing on their minds. And it wasn't easy leaving family behind. I have a gazillion uncles, aunts, and cousins who still live in Ghana. A lot of my parents' money goes back to support those family members."

"You ever wish you'd grown up in Ghana? I've always wondered what it would have been like to grow up in America instead of Italy."

"You know, Jerry, I wish I could visit Ghana more. I miss my aunts, my cousins. Skype just doesn't cut it, you know? But I love my life in America—and I get to meld my Ghanaian heritage with my American experience, which has given my upbringing a unique flavor! My parents are very supportive of my chef aspirations—though I know they wouldn't mind if I made 'doctoring' a backup career choice."

Jerry was encouraged by his friends' honesty and openness, and he did his best to reciprocate. He had never really talked candidly to other people about what it felt like having pasta hair or being a cooking celebrity at such a young age. He felt a little sheepish telling them about his family's financial struggles and how becoming a Master Chef was the path to a better life for them. His thoughts briefly wandered off, as he contemplated the monetary reward for winning The Toque for best cooking kitchen. *Is it shallow to be so money focused?* he asked himself.

After sharing details about their personal lives, the three friends realized that they had even more in common than they'd previously thought, especially their love of family and love of cooking. They also knew they had much to learn from each other and were eager to do so.

Talking about his future goals—none of which included saving the world—with people he could trust made Jerry feel so much better, so much more confident. Though he couldn't help but wonder why his parents had never talked to him about Della Morta's prophecy and if *they* thought Jerry's pasta hair was a sign of destiny. He made up his mind to write his parents before the end of camp to at least begin this rather difficult conversation—and hopefully get some answers.

Chapter 21

Something Fishy

Jerry's responsibilities as Mayon-daise Kitchen chef continued to grow, and doing so kicked his already impressive cooking skills up several notches. Plus by practicing with Mari and Louie G, he had added to his repertoire. He had organized about nine or ten cabin meals with great success by the end of the second week. This Sunday night's dinner was a big event, marking the halfway mark of camp. Jerry—with Louie's help in gathering the ingredients before he went off to practice some EFF drills—had decided to prepare a typical Ghanaian stew, whose aroma and flavor were unlike anything he had ever experienced before.

Louie G's
CORNED BEEF STEW

Serve this stew over white or brown rice or butternut squash (recipe not included).

Feeds 6 to 8
Preparation time: 5 minutes
Cooking time: 35 to 45 minutes
INGREDIENTS AND SUPPLIES

Ingredients
¼ cup vegetable oil
2 medium-sized onions, diced
2 fresh tomatoes, diced or a 14.5 ounce can diced tomatoes
½ can cream of mushroom soup (optional)

1 tablespoon seasoning salt (or to taste) and/or 1 beef, chicken, or shrimp bouillon cube

15 ounce can tomato sauce

12 ounce can corned beef (Note: Louie G's mom did not have a lot of fresh beef growing up in Ghana, so canned beef was a common source of protein. Give it a shot. It's a tasty recipe! An option is to substitute in 1 lb of cooked beef brisket, cut into tiny pieces.)

1 tablespoon curry powder

1 cup frozen mixed vegetables—usually corn, carrots, peas (optional)

3 eggs

Dash of onion powder

Supplies
Medium-sized saucepan (4 quart or larger)

DIRECTIONS
1. In the saucepan, heat the vegetable oil, and fry the onions over medium heat until they turn translucent, just starting to brown.
2. Stir in the diced tomatoes, mushroom soup, seasoning salt, and bouillon cube, and cook for 10 minutes.
3. Add the tomato sauce to the mixture, and cook for another 5 minutes.
4. Stir in the corned beef, leaving the meat in chunks
5. Cook uncovered on low to medium heat for 10 minutes, stirring occasionally, so excess water from the diced tomatoes can evaporate.
6. Add in the mixed vegetables if desired
7. Crack the eggs on top of stew (do not break yolks!), and sprinkle each egg with a dash of onion powder. Do not stir!
8. Cover the pan and cook over low heat for 10 minutes.
9. Serve and eat!

As Louie G's mom recommended, Jerry made the meal the night

before, giving the stew time to "steep" or "brew," allowing the flavors to percolate throughout the dish. He sampled the stew Sunday morning, then caught up with Louie G as the older boy was heading outside.

"It's brilliant, Louie G! I think the campers are going to love it tonight."

"You've got skills, Pasta; you're a quick learner for an eleven-year-old."

Jerry was so pleased that he didn't even mind Louie G's jab about Jerry's age.

The boys met up with Mari midday for lunch, after which the three spent half of their afternoon completing assignments and the other half enjoying the perfect weather. First they worked on a few EFF maneuvers that Louie G wanted to try out, and then Mari convinced the boys to join her on an hour-long hillside hike. While they hiked, most of the conversation centered around Mari's ongoing investigation into Moldy Coeur's dealings.

"From everything I've looked into, I think Moldy Coeur is trying to extend his fast food empire beyond just Italy. Look at what he's already done in India. I think America may be next."

"What evidence do you have?" Louie G inquired as he pulled himself over a large rock.

"I admit, it's not hard evidence. But I found a few recent Internet articles about Moldy Coeur meeting with America's First Lady, Ella Bomma. As you probably know, she's committed to fighting childhood obesity, and as part of her anti-obesity campaign, she's putting together a task force made up of chefs from around the world to improve healthy food options."

"Well, that hardly seems sinister, Mari," grunted Jerry as he struggled to climb the same rock Louie G had just vaulted.

"But that's exactly why we should be suspicious! Why would fat, fast-food-loving Moldy Coeur want to join an anti-obesity taskforce? Doesn't something seem fishy about that?"

Jerry had to agree that it didn't add up. He found himself in somewhat of a conundrum. *If I begin to care about Moldy Coeur's dealings, I might have to start taking that stupid prophecy seriously. But if I ignore the evidence, does Moldy Coeur win? And what can I do about it, anyway?*

As if Mari read his mind, she said, "It might seem that there's nothing we can do about it now, but I think we should look for ways to get that man as far away from Pesto's as possible. And then expose him for who he really is."

It sounded mutinous. Getting rid of one of the school's largest donors? How could the school survive without Coeur's money? The trio debated this challenge as they continued their ascent, though they agreed to begin thinking of ways to stand up to Moldy Coeur. Jerry briefly thought about telling his friends about the old news article written by Moldy Coeur that he'd found stuck in the 1993 yearbook, but he failed to see its relevance to the current conversation and decided against sharing.

When they reached the summit of Mount Pomona, they enjoyed a stunning ocean view. Yet again Jerry appreciated the fact that Presto Pesto's gave them the freedom to explore when they weren't in class.

They relaxed on the summit for a while, devouring the snacks that Mari had thoughtfully packed for them. But a glance at his watch confirmed to Jerry that it was time to head back for dinner preparations.

Thanks to his having cooked the meal the night before, "dinner preparations" meant merely supervising the heating and serving of the stew. One nice thing about being in charge: he didn't have to dish out the food or clean up. But being the thoughtful kid he was, he waited until everyone else had been served before stepping up for his own plateful. Paul Gagasol served the rice onto plates before handing them to Marco, who heaped on generous helpings of the warm stew.

Jerry sat down and was about to dig in when he paused, looking carefully at the contents of his plate. The food *looked* amazing, the colorful mix of meat and veggies glistening under the shine of the hanging kitchen lights. Bringing his nose closer to the plate's rim, he inhaled deeply, then abruptly yelled, "*Stop!!!*"

Everyone froze, forks pausing in midair, and stared at Jerry.

"Someone tampered with the stew. It . . . it . . . it smells fishy!"

Almost on cue, Manny Cotti, who had gotten his plate first and was nearly finished eating, threw up his entire meal. Seven of the other campers who had finished significant portions of their meal began throwing up as well. Jerry ran to the stove, found his ladle, and stirred to the bottom of the pot. He gasped as he pulled out what appeared to be a puffy spotted fish, scales and all, now partially cooked because it had been simmering in the stew for a little while—but had clearly been put into the stewpot raw. Jerry had never seen a fish like it; it looked like it had swallowed a balloon!

He was livid—his delicious meal had been sabotaged!

The sick campers were helped to the infirmary for medical assessment by the on-call nurse, Nurse Laplant, who immediately informed the faculty about the food poisoning. A formal investigation was promptly opened. Chef Jo Moi-Erreur, the camp librarian assigned to the case, arrived at the Mayon-daise Kitchen within twenty minutes of the incident. Chef Moi-Erreur sported a steel-rimmed monocle and a brown tweed jacket over a pressed shirt and blood-orange bowtie, topped off by a checkered deerstalker hat. Jerry wondered if perhaps the chef fancied himself Sherlock Holmes under the circumstances. Moi-Erreur was accompanied by a familiar face: the seemingly omnipresent old janitor—who in all probability was there to mop up the awful mess this incident had created. Chef Moi-Erreur, who appeared way too excited under the nasty circumstances, began asking Jerry questions about the poisoned meal in a thick French accent.

"Everyone loves a good mystery, *non?* You say your meal was sabotaged. Where ees this evidence?"

Jerry pointed to the fish, now lying on a ceramic plate on the dining table. "There's the fish I pulled out of the stew with my ladle. It was virtually raw. I don't even think it'd been washed or skinned. It's a strange-looking thing. Looks almost inflated. Here, let me show you. . . ."

Moi-Erreur reached out to pick up the plate. But instead of picking it up, his hands clumsily knocked the plate off of the counter. The plate landed on the floor with a loud crash, breaking into five large shards. The large fish lay limply in the middle of the floor. Jerry reached for the fish but had his hand slapped away by the janitor.

"*Owww!*" Jerry yelped, rubbing the back of his right hand.

The old janitor had a stern but protective look on his face. He shook his head disapprovingly.

"Aha, *le poisson* (pronounced *pwa-sohn*)," said the chef, staring at the fish on the floor with his arms folded, acting as if nothing had happened.

Jerry looked from the broken plate shards to the fish to Moi-Erreur. "Are you referring to the fish, sir?"

"Ah, *oui,* it seems as if the poison was the *poisson,*" confirmed Chef Moi-Erreur, grinning broadly at his pun and adjusting his monocle.

Jerry repeated himself. "Do you mean the poison was the fish?"

"Your French is not bad, *Monsieur Pasta,*" replied Moi-Erreur, smiling at Jerry. "'Poisson' does indeed mean 'fish' in French. Hence this is *poisson* poison, is it not?"

Chef Moi-Erreur giggled again at his own play on words. Jerry was not amused. Moi-Erreur continued his investigation by looking through the cupboards and refrigerator, examining the pots and pans, inter-viewing Mayon-daise campers, and looking for any other clues as to how the fish ended up in the stew. In the process, Moi-Erreur knocked four pots off the wall, broke two more plates, and spilled a gallon of milk onto the kitchen floor. The janitor faithfully cleaned up each mess, one by one, and Jerry now wondered if perhaps the old janitor wasn't there to clean up after the sick campers but rather to mop up after the re-markably clumsy Moi-Erreur. Finally the old man donned gloves before picking up the dead fish, wrapping it securely in several garbage bags.

Twenty minutes later, the "investigation" was complete—though it seemed as if the inspector chef had made more trouble than he'd come to fix. Jerry dreaded showing up at the dining hall the next day, knowing that he would be held responsible for the fishy meal and expecting all eyes would be trained on him. But it appeared at least any further sab-otage could be thwarted; Mari had brought a tiny video camera with her to camp, with the intention of capturing some memorable cooking moments to share with her parents. Now, though, she would hide the camera in the kitchen to monitor for future intruders.

"We'll turn the camera on after we make our next meal. If someone tries this again, we can catch the perpetrator in the act," Mari promised.

Jerry could only hope that the person responsible would be stupid enough to try the stunt again—and the thought of catching that person red-handed temporarily helped him forget how angry he was. While he didn't know who had committed the crime, he certainly had his suspi-cions. And the list of suspects was very short.

Chapter 22

League of Her Own

Jerry rushed through breakfast, eager to get to Monday's classes and focus on what he thought he did best: cook. Though his hope to just go on about his business didn't transpire. It was hard to ignore the dining hall whispers about the "ghost that haunted the Mayon-daise cabin last night." Worse, Jerry's skills would be called into question. When the public address system came on as Jerry polished off his bowl of cereal, Ward Moldy Coeur's voice crackled sharply through the speakers:

"As many of you have heard, there was a poor outcome at one of our cabin kitchens. We ask all of the kitchen head chefs to be extremely careful when preparing meals. Ensure that your meat and seafood are fresh and THOROUGHLY cooked. We wish to avoid future incidents like this. When campers get food poisoning, it reflects poorly on the chef involved—and more importantly, on the school."

Jerry felt as if his ears were on fire! He knew Moldy Coeur's word choice was deliberate and intentionally insulting. The shot to Jerry's cooking reputation hurt; his reputation was really all he had—other than crazy pasta hair that made kids laugh and adults irrational. *Is this how Papa felt after his accidents?* he wondered. He slunk out of Eaditt Hall after breakfast, avoiding all eye contact.

Jerry didn't remember a single word from Culinary History class. He was still fuming at lunchtime despite Louie G and Mari's attempts to console him. "We'll catch the culprit Jerry, we will," they assured him.

Jerry was a few minutes late to Sauce class because he'd wanted to get some fresh air and clear his head. Now, as he approached the classroom door, there was the elderly janitor again. *This guy really is everywhere! Does he sleep?! And where?* In fact, Jerry seemed to always notice this old man hanging around Sauce class (maybe it was just the old janitor's schedule?), cleaning the glass door, mopping or waxing the floor right outside, and sometimes even coming into the classroom to take out the trash while Chef Beurre was lecturing. Surprisingly, Chef Beurre didn't seem to mind.

His curiosity getting the better of him, Jerry waited a few minutes after class for the other students to disperse and then ventured to the teacher's desk to ask Beurre about the strange old man.

"Oh, zat's just Bones. He's worked at Presto Pesto's for as long as I can remember. Janitorial work mostly. Between you and me, I've seen better floor-cleaning skills, but we keep him around because he ees useful from time to time."

Bones. Jerry was glad to finally have a name—albeit a nickname—to associate with the man. *Calling him "the old janitor" felt a bit cold and impersonal, even a bit disrespectful.*

Leaving the classroom, he thought about what he had learned in Sauce class. *Oh, yeah . . . nothing.* The tomato sauce that Chef Beurre had them make in their classroom ICSs looked and tasted like Pepto Bismol. *Maybe it* was *Pepto Bismol. . . .*

Jerry made up his mind that tonight would be the night he would sneak into the kitchen before dinner to observe Beurre in action making one of his sauce masterpieces. When he told Mari and Louie G of his plans, they begged to come with him to see for themselves, but he convinced them that just one of them would be less conspicuous than all three.

Dinner was to be served at 6:00 as usual, so Jerry estimated that if he was in the kitchen by 5:20, he wouldn't miss the sauce being prepared. He had come up with a plan to get into the kitchen that he hoped would work. The swinging door was clearly labeled NO CAMPERS ALLOWED, and since Jerry knew his short stature would identify him quickly, he figured to take height out of the equation. He took a page out of Bones the janitor's book. At 5:15, armed with a bucket of warm water and a sponge and wearing a hooded sweatshirt, Jerry got down on his hands and knees and began to scrub the floor in front of the kitchen door as if he was part of the janitorial staff.

Good thing his hair was bowtie pasta today—nice and tidy, easy to hide under a hood.

His heart rate doubled when Chef Beurre walked right toward him! Cringing, Jerry braced for . . . *nothing?*

Beurre had completely ignored him, pushing open the kitchen door without missing a step. The disguise had worked! Knowing that Beurre would be making the sauce soon, Jerry inched closer and closer to the door. While pondering how he would actually get *into* the kitchen, the door abruptly opened again, and one of the kitchen staff ushered him in to continue his cleaning.

I'm in! Jerry rejoiced internally.

He made his way to a corner of the kitchen that gave him a perfect view of the stove yet effectively hid him from sight. Beurre had just begun. For the next fifteen minutes, Jerry felt like he was stuck in yet another boring Sauce class. Beurre made the Velouté sauce exactly the way he had made it last week in class. Predictable. Lackluster. Beurre tasted it, made a resigned face, and then walked out of the kitchen.

Was that really it? Jerry shook his head in disbelief. Had he zoned out and missed some of the cooking steps?

Just then, a cloaked figure wearing an oversized black beret atop long straw-colored hair seemed to materialize in a far corner of the kitchen. The figure was holding a broom, sweeping trash along the way. Strangely, Jerry hadn't noticed anyone come through the kitchen door. He himself began making his way toward the exit, making an uninspired wet mess as he went. Then out of the corner of his eye, Jerry saw the floor sweeper stop by the stove. The cloaked figure, head bowed just enough to conceal her face—at least Jerry assumed it was a woman, given the length of the hair—rested the broom shaft against the edge of the stove. But in a flash, the mystery sweeper was moving effortlessly around the pot of sauce—tasting, smelling, adding dashes of this and that, turning the flame down, then up again. The woman paused, then started up again reinvigorated, her long, straw-colored hair swishing playfully back and forth from under the beret. It all happened so quickly, Jerry could barely catch his breath.

Meatballs!

It was almost as if his *Sauce for the Saucier* textbook had come alive! This was sauce making at its finest! The cloaked intruder didn't seem to notice Jerry at all—or if she had, she paid no attention to him.

After about ten minutes, the mysterious sauce maker, with a confident swagger, seemed satisfied with her creation, or rather her transformation since the credit for the sauce's creation would surely go to Chef Beurre. Jerry got the definite impression that this wasn't the first time this mysterious saucier had been in the kitchen or had doctored a sauce. When the stranger reached for her broom, Jerry scuttled out of the kitchen to avoid being caught—and eager to share his discovery with his friends. On the way back to the cabin, he pondered who it could be under that cloak. *One of the female chefs, perhaps Mary Donna or Pei Lei? Or could it actually be a* man *with long blond hair? Who* was *this mystery saucier?*

Mari and Louie G had a difficult time believing Jerry's wild story. Could it even be possible? But as Jerry recounted the story to them a second time over dinner, they had no trouble believing that the Velouté sauce hadn't been made by Chef Beurre—they knew as much from being students in his sauce class.

Louie G observed, "Why didn't you just ask the mystery woman who she was, Jerry? Wearing a big black cloak and a beret that covered her face? She was clearly trying to hide her identity as much as you. Y'all were basically partners in crime; you might as well have introduced yourselves!"

Jerry scratched his chin. "I guess I didn't think of that. I think I was too much in shock. And what if I'd scared her away? What if she decided to stop doctoring the sauces? Our meals would be terrible for the next two weeks!"

Mari grinned. "Good point, Jerry. Maybe it's best you didn't confront 'Doctor Sauce.' No need to ruin two weeks' worth of meals. Do you think Beurre knows she exists? He can't really believe that his sauce magically turns from boring to tantalizing when it leaves the kitchen. And what now?"

To Jerry, it was obvious what to do now. He was going to keep observing "Doctor Sauce" (the moniker stuck). For the next two weeks, Jerry planned to sneak into the kitchen regularly before lunch and dinner to catch a glimpse of Doctor Sauce at work and learn as much as he could from her. He would continue to use his janitor disguise, and he promised to teach his friends everything he learned—which made Mari and Louie G feel included in the enterprise and made Jerry look like he wasn't trying to hoard all the fun himself.

And from what Jerry learned after just three days of stealthy observation—the precision and originality that went into making each sauce—it was clear that the good "doctor" was a culinary genius. Jerry took all the mental notes his brain could hold, sprinting back to the cabin to share them with his partners-in-crime, down to the last detail. To help him remember, he would crack open his Karim de la Carême *Sauce for the Saucier* textbook and annotate it with everything he was learning (alongside notes he had *already* written in the textbook). But it was waaaaay different seeing the cooking in action than reading about it. So Jerry, Louie G, and Mari did what every good chef should do: they took everything they had learned and put it into action. Weekend evenings were spent experimenting at the ICSs in Apley Court classrooms, working on mother and secondary sauces, until the three of them felt extremely proficient.

All this time spent mimicking Doctor Sauce didn't take away from Jerry's EFF responsibilities thanks to advantageous scheduling. The Mayon-daise squad received a much-needed bye after their second game. Jerry wisely spent the time working on tactics with Louie G, getting the team in better physical shape and throwing awkwardly shaped nonfood objects like stuffed animals to simulate throwing misshapen, molding food items. (Jerry had tactfully collected the stuffed animals

EFF TEAM	STANDINGS
Bechamel	0 - 1
Espagnole	0 - 2
Mayon-daise	2 - 0
Tomato	1 - 0
Veloute	1 - 1

from male and female campers who swore him to both secrecy and the safe return of their beloved stuffed pets in one piece, of course).

Rita continued to practice with the Mayon-daise squad. And to her great pride, she was looking *and* feeling fitter every day! Other campers were taking notice, especially the boys. Many of them stopped calling her "GORdita," and she was just 'Rita' for a change, which was nice.

So in the middle of Week Three, Rita was finally invited to join her team on the EFF pitch, substituting in for Patty Kapunan. Jerry tried to congratulate Rita before the game but had a hard time getting close enough to her. She was surrounded by a crowd of gawking boys, so Jerry settled for a long-distance wave and smile and walked back to the bleachers sulking.

"Looking a little sad there, loverboy. What's wrong? Not enough Rita to go around anymore, eh?"

Mari played big sister to Louie G's annoying big brother. "Oh, stop, Louie G. Jerry, Rita still likes you."

"She does?"

"Of course! She talks about you all the time. Maybe you need to tell her you like her too."

Jerry was blushing. *Ewwww! I can't believe I'm even having this conversation*, he thought to himself. *She* is *kind* and *smart* and *pretty, and I do* like her. . . .

Big brother jumped back in. "Jerry, Mari's right. If you like Rita, you've just got to tell her. And show her. Stake your claim. The other boys will back off—that is, if she chooses you."

It occurred to Jerry that maybe Rita would choose an older boy, especially since Jerry really hadn't given her a ton of special attention or expressed how he felt about her. Still, he had been her friend over the last few weeks when others had not. *Yes, Louie G is right. I need to tell her.*

Jerry settled in to watch the game. The Mayon-daise squad was particularly grateful that this was their bye round because the other kitchens had moved on to the dairy portion of the food pyramid—which meant water balloons filled with old yogurt and expired milk, plus moldy chunks of cheese. Mari would have refused to take the field! They were messy games, and Jerry and Louie G used the opportunity to scout the competition.

The first match between Tomato Kitchen and Béchamel Kitchen was a slaughter, in Tomato's favor. Tomato Kitchen made EFF matches feel like scenes from a gladiatorial engagement: they showed no mercy, and someone usually ended up bloodied. But Jerry was eagerly awaiting the Espagnole-Velouté match. Rita was easy to spot on the field once the match started. She was an Espagnole Jackal, attacking the Velouté Pharaoh with a ferocious combination of power and skill. Louie G turned to Jerry and said in a mixture of admiration and surprise, "She learned all that just from practicing with us?!"

This was the best the Espagnole team had ever looked, after getting bludgeoned in their first two games by Tomato and Mayon-daise. Rita was the difference maker. By the end of the match Jerry was hoarse—he'd been cheering loudly every time Rita made a great play. Whenever Rita heard Jerry's voice, she would look at the sidelines, beaming. At the end of the match, the Espagnole team crowded around Rita, chanting her name and patting her on the back. Rita broke through the ranks of her teammates and ran straight to Jerry. He hoarsely managed a "Congratulations!" before being smothered with kisses all over his forehead and cheeks.

"Thank jou, thank jou, thank jou, Herry Pasta! Because of jou I deed so very well today! I no could have done it without jou!"

The last kiss was a big wet one. *Right. On. The. Lips.*

Louie G was right . . . the other boys backed away.

Rita had chosen.

Plat Principal

(the Main Course)

Chapter 23

Fun, to be Fair

Cloud Nine is a place few eleven-year-old boys can claim they have ever truly reached. Playing a visually stunning and engrossing Xbox or Playstation game, scoring a game-winning basket or homerun or touchdown in a ballgame, having front-row tickets to see your favorite band play, cooking a great meal (for foodies like Jerry Pasta): these moments all come pretty close. But nothing quite takes you to Cloud Nine like being loved by a girl, even for a cooking nerd. So the next few days leading up to the weekend were awesome for Jerry. Sure, there were some awkward moments. The handholding. The occasional public kiss. The sitting together in the dining hall (and as for the latter, the perk of Jerry's love life for Louie G meant finally sitting beside Rita's cute friend Ana Latte; unfortunately this left Mari as the odd man—or, in this case, girl—out). But Jerry played matters wisely this time. He was still in Mayon-daise Kitchen, and Rita was still part of Espagnole—which meant they were still competing for The Toque award given to the summer's best kitchen. And Mari was still one of Jerry's closest friends—and she kept herself occupied by continuing her Moldy Coeur investigation. Plus there were still Doctor Sauce cooking skills to learn and interkitchen cooking competitions to win.

Which brings us to the end of Week Three.

That Friday at dinner, the faculty announced a Saturday "Skills Fair," a carnival-type extravaganza to include cooking contests, non-cooking games, a "surprise" competition to end the day and lots of carnival fare. All of this was free for the students, organized by the faculty but also supported by locals from the nearby towns who were paid by the school to provide entertainment and food. The dining hall was abuzz with excitement.

Imagine the Skills Fair as something like your State Fair minus the rides. Then subtract all parental supervision but add in Master Chef booth designers. Hold the booth fees but keep the competitive flair that a fair environment seems to breed. Are you getting the picture? You could freely wander from booth to booth, selecting the cooking—or, for that matter, noncooking—activity you wanted to participate in: pancake flipping, vegetable cutting, define that cooking term, name that spice, cooking spelling bee, you name it! The purpose of the fair was two-fold. One goal was to teach campers basic and advanced cooking skills. Some of the skills taught were ones the campers already had but were often rudimentary or needed polishing. The other goal was to have fun competing, adding points towards a kitchen's Toque total by winning tickets at each cooking booth. The most successful individual ticket winners would be entered into the "surprise competition" at the end of the fair—a clever means of encouraging camper participation.

None of the campers slept much that night, too excited about the next day's activities. On past Saturdays they had slept in, which was a nice treat, but no one had any interest in sleeping late on *this* Saturday. Jerry still managed to convince the EFF team to go for a quick two-mile jog before breakfast, which Jerry kept simple for the Mayon-daise campers with a recipe his parents had taught him. Why fill up on breakfast when the rest of the day was going to be spent stuffing their faces with carnival food?

Jerry Pasta's
FRUIGURT FLAKES

Feeds 1

Preparation time: 2 minutes

INGREDIENTS AND SUPPLIES

Ingredients

½ to1 cup vanilla or plain low-fat yogurt

½ to 1 cup cereal–your favorite but preferably something with flakes and
   healthy (examples: cornflakes, Special K, Raisin Bran, Basic 4, Cheerios,
   granola)

½ to 1 cup fresh fruit (blueberries, strawberries, blackberries, bananas, pine
   apple, apples, and grapes are good choices)

Supplies

1 large cereal bowl

DIRECTIONS

1. Scoop the yogurt into a cereal bowl (not too full; you can always add more).
2. Stir in your favorite cereal. Then mix in the fresh fruit.
3. Eat !!!

Around 11 o'clock the campers made their way to the where the carnival had been set up. The pavilion area had been transformed: a variety of booths had been erected all around the grass surrounding the pavilion, making the area nearly unrecognizable. There was a dunking booth (Jerry and other campers were elated to see Chef Beurre in the dunking chair), a petting zoo (many of the campers had yet to really interact with the live versions of the animals they were learning to prepare in the kitchen), and many other typical fair activities. A group of young musicians was warming up on the pavilion itself, the band members looking not much older than the campers. *Probably a group from the local high school*, Jerry speculated. The cooking-skills booths utilized ICSs, so they were set up closer to the pavilion, which had electrical outlets.

It was a bit of organized chaos at first, most campers not really having a plan of what to do but going toward what looked like the most fun. Many hit the food booths first, following their stomachs. Many of the older boys gravitated to the noncooking games of skill—or was it chance?—like ring toss, hit the bottle pyramid with the baseball, and of course the dunking machine. Chef Beurre, his face devoid of a smile, sat in the dunking seat of honor wearing a turquoise Speedo and a pink T-shirt that read, WETTER IS BETTER (is that mental picture sufficiently scarring?!). Jerry could almost hear Beurre's thick French accent in his head, reading the shirt's tagline. He imagined Beurre sitting on a giant ladle, perched over a large vat of chicken stock. *An appropriate fate for a cowardly sauce chef.*

Jerry and Mari headed toward the pavilion while Louie G sprinted to the dunking booth to join a line of nine other campers. He yelled over his shoulder, "Can't wait to see Beurre ... *brrrrrr.* Ha! You've got to admit that's funny!" Grinning, he picked up his pace to get in line.

"Doesn't Louie G know that we won't earn any tickets toward The Toque at the noncooking booths?" Jerry asked, with some annoyance in his voice.

Mari giggled. "By the look on Louie G's face, I think winning The Toque is the last thing on his mind, Jerry. To each his own. Let's go have some fun!"

It didn't take long for Rita to track down Jerry in the crowd of campers, and the three began to make the rounds of the cooking booths. Far from minding Rita's presence, Mari actually liked her, having gotten to know her better from all the time she and Jerry were spending together.

On the way to the booths, Mari steered Jerry and Rita clear of the petting zoo, not jazzed about the idea of seeing the food she was to prepare prance around in a fenced area.

"A lot of my relatives are vegetarians for religious reasons, and I prefer not to play with my food before cooking it."

"But in Mexico, sometimes I pick out the cheeken for dinner, help my mother pluck it. And then I help her prepare it for the meal. And though I play with the cheeken sometimes, I very thankful to the cheeken for feeding my family. I think that make me a better chef—because I respect the animal that I prepare to eat."

Jerry could see Rita's point—it was a good one. There was something to be said for appreciating the animal that was destined for your stomach, providing you sustenance, energy, brain power. *Food for thought,* Jerry said to himself, *literally. How could you waste food if you personally knew the animal that had been cooked?* It actually made the prepared dish seem more meaningful in a sense.

He was still contemplating that notion when they checked out the first cooking station. . . .

Knife Proficiency

The knives booth was run by Brock Lee, the martial artist turned kitchen chef (and head EFF referee by night), which was no surprise to anyone who was aware of his life story prior to being hired at Pesto's. At the booth, Lee taught campers how to properly select and hold a knife as well as safety guidelines for preventing fingers from becoming a part of the meal.

"You must respect the blade edge," Lee explained. "It does not respect you and will take from you without asking," his voice *and* face as serious as you would expect from a kung-fu master.

Campers took turns experimenting with different knives: serrated bread knives, butcher hatchets, and steak knives. Meat—from the kitchen staff, not the meal ingredient—was on hand to help demonstrate the proper technique for cutting up beef and chicken.

The actual knife competition consisted of cutting vegetables and fruits in a timed fashion. Brock Lee did a demonstration of his skills first, twirling tomatoes and onions in the air and finely slicing them before they even hit the cutting board. Many of the female onlookers—faculty, staff, and campers alike—ooohed and ahhhed more over Brock Lee's rippling biceps exposed by his sleeveless T-shirt than his amazing cutting skills.

Jerry wasn't the best at handling a knife. He stood back and watched Mari, Rita, and many of the other kids excel at the cutting task. *Maybe it's the size of my hands*, he thought. The older campers just seemed a bit more confident, more coordinated, with knives. Jerry placed the few tickets he had earned in his pocket, then urged his friends to try a different booth.

Pancake flip

This booth combined skills *and* eating. The skill was pancake flipping, and if you did it properly, your pancakes were your reward! There were multiple topping options, among them fresh fruit, maple syrup, chocolate shavings, whipped cream, and powdered sugar.

Potatoes (of the kitchen staff and EFF referee) was running this booth. He winked at Jerry as the three friends approached the booth. The rules for pancake flipping were fairly straightforward.

Potatoes instructed, "OK, ya'll . . . first, you gotta start with a good lightweight nonstick skillet. Always use a little bit o' butter to grease up the pan so your pancakes don't stick. And pick a skillet that ain't too big. You want the heat to distribute evenly, and if you're gonna flip the pancake without a spatula, a lightweight skillet is key. The trick to flipping a pancake without a spatula is it's all in the wrist."

Potatoes deftly demonstrated the technique, then slid the cooked pancake onto a plate for the campers to see.

"See? Perfection. The other trick to a perfect pancake is knowing when to flip it. Anybody have any idears?"

Campers shouted out various guesses, like smelling for doneness and counting to twenty. Finally Jerry timidly spoke up.

"Watch the edges, and wait until bubbles appear and pop?"

"Right on, Jerry. When you see a bunch of bubbles popping in your poured batter, it's time to flip!" Potatoes then turned on six of the ICS burners, and began teaching the campers how to control the heat underneath the skillet. "Not too hot, not too cold. Medium does it!"

They spent a few minutes doing spatula flips before graduating to skillet-only flips. Jerry was struggling with the skillet flips mostly because the skillet he had picked felt like it weighed as much as he did; even grabbing it with two hands was arduous. Everyone else seemed to be flipping OK—though not with expert ease by any means since some of the pancakes ended up splattered on the ground, and one landed on Potatoes' back, which he was not too pleased about. Rita seemed to be a natural at this booth, but as she pointed out, she'd been essentially doing this motion for years, flipping tortillas with her grandmother back in Mexico. Her combination of strength and skill even forced a compliment out of Potatoes. And despite Jerry's knowledge of when to flip a pancake, he didn't do so great during the competition portion of the booth. Potatoes even slipped in a jab that Jerry might need to hit the weight room to bulk up his skillet-flipping muscles. *Ouch.* Jerry took comfort in the fact that at least he could make a perfect pancake with a spatula; he'd get better with the skillet flip once his hands got a little bigger and his arms got a little stronger.

Name-that-Spice-or-Herb Cooking Bee

Finally, a booth that takes the physical completely out of the equation, Jerry mused appreciatively. He had a lot of fun with this one. Blindfolded—like the cheese-tasting competition at the start of camp—campers had to guess the herb or spice they were sampling. Sometimes the spice was sprinkled on a plain wafer for tasting. Other times campers had to simply recognize the spice or herb by smell. They were also permitted to touch the leaves (rosemary was easy to identify, whereas cilantro could be mistaken for parsley if campers were unfamiliar with the scent). Once identified, the camper could then spell the herb or spice name for extra tickets! Mari rocked this competition—she was somewhat of a spice nerd.

By now, Louie G had dunked Beurre a total of four times and had made his way triumphantly back to his friends. After (most appropriately) calling Mari a "Spice Girl," and then having to explain that the Spice Girls were a once popular girl band from the UK, which did *not* make her laugh, Louie G joined in the spice-naming competition. Thyme, tarragon, chervil, fennel, basil, saffron, chives. They each had a distinct smell and taste. And as good as he was at cheeses, Jerry knew he had so much more to learn in the herb/spice department—though Community Gardening class had certainly helped a lot. He also remembered reading in *Sauce for the Saucier* that herbs were perfect as "a complement" to a dish, "never to dominate the flavor." Jerry was eager to see if he could turn his simple sauces into tastier offerings by what he'd learned at this booth.

"Who cares about spelling 'marjoram' or 'turmeric' or 'thyme'? Spelling the names wrong doesn't change how they taste once they're in your skillet or saucepan," ranted Louie G as he walked away from the booth. "Last I checked, *time* is something that passes and a *sage* is a very wise man—like me." Louie G placed his palms together and bowed reverently, the wry smile on his face betraying admiration of his own cleverness.

"Have you been smoking . . . dill weed? You clearly need a greater appreciation of herbs and spices, Louie G. By the way, I do offer private lessons," Mari added tartly as she sashayed out of the booth, smiling superiorly.

"Ouch! Who put habañeros in your undies?!" Louie G crossed his arms, looking shocked. "I think I'll pass on the spice lessons, thanks. . . ."

Now That's Saucy!

Powered by a portable generator, six ICSs had been arranged on the pavilion. The contest was straightforward: Chef La Gasse, the chef in charge, would reach into a hat and pull out the name of a sauce, which participants then had five to ten minutes to prepare. Bones, the janitor, was helping facilitate the cleanup of the ICSs following each sauce venture. Chef Beurre was notably absent, likely still in the process of being dunked repeatedly by gleeful campers.

This was by *far* Jerry's favorite booth. With all the time he'd spent covertly observing Doctor Sauce, Jerry had picked up a few tips, to put it mildly. He easily made the white sauces, Velouté and béchamel, cruised through the brown Espagnole sauce, and then nailed the tomato sauce—he was half-Italian, after all, and had been making tomato sauce practically his entire life. The real fun at the sauce booth began when Chef La Gasse started pulling secondary sauces out of the hat. After the first couple, Chef La Gasse shot a perplexed glance at Bones and whispered, in earshot of Jerry, "*Mon Dieu!* I don't remember putting zees in zee hat. Must have gotten in here by accident. Hmmm. Well, zees will be a *real* test. . . ." Jerry was unfazed. He continued to impress, cooking the secondary sauces with ease. Reading *Sauce for the Saucier* was definitely paying off for him!

Jerry surveyed the booth to see how other campers were faring and made eye contact with Bones. He'd never noticed how hunched over Bones was, having really only ever seen him scrubbing floors or sitting in a tall beach chair on the EFF sidelines.

Bones gave Jerry two big thumbs up. "You are getting pretty good at making sauces," he said quietly as the competition wrapped up.

The two had seen each other quite a bit over the course of the summer but had not really had a conversation since Week One.

"Yeah, I guess I am, thank you. Been doing a lot of reading, I've got this great book . . . and I've been practicing a lot too."

"That's excellent, Jerry. With cooking, you can't forget to rely on your instincts. Remember, it's in your b—"

CRASH!!!!!!!!

Louie G had knocked over a bowl of the béchamel sauce he had just prepared, spilling it all over. "Son of a . . . *chef!!*" he cried.

Jerry stifled a laugh and turned back to Bones to finish their conversation. Bones just smiled the same smile he'd flashed when Jerry had spotted the old man through the window while sipping the anonymously prepared vegetable soup after their canoe debacle. And before Jerry could ask the janitor to finish his thought, Bones hurried over to help Louie G clean up his ICS. *Pretty nice old guy. A lot nicer than some of our teachers, for sure,* Jerry told himself. Jerry turned back to his own ICS and dipped a finger into the hollandaise sauce he had just made. It felt good to find a booth where he actually excelled at something.

Crack Egg, No Shell!

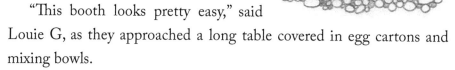

"This booth looks pretty easy," said Louie G, as they approached a long table covered in egg cartons and mixing bowls.

He was about to eat his words. Almost literally.

The concept of egg delicateness was demonstrated by engaging pairs of campers in a simple egg-toss activity. Jerry paired up with Rita, leaving Mari and Louie G as egg-toss partners. Mari and Louie G were still annoyed with each other as evidenced by the increasing force of their egg tosses. The game ended poorly for Louie G when Mari purposely launched the egg extra high in the air. Louie G's competitiveness (and Pharaoh EFF reflexes) kicked in, but he was completely inexperienced at the art of catching eggs cleanly. The egg burst through his hands, leaving his face slimed with viscous egg white and gooey bright yellow yoke! Mari put little effort into suppressing her giggles. Meanwhile, Rita and Jerry displayed excellent harmony: she threw the eggs in such a way that he was able to efficiently catch them all, even as the distance between them increased. Their performance earned their respective kitchens lots of points.

The egg toss was followed by a competition to crack and open three eggs in ten seconds. Though Chef Pei Lei's brief demonstration made it look easy, the campers who participated soon found this was easier to watch than do. Some utilized the one-handed crack-and-open technique: cracking the egg on a hard surface and then using the same hand to pry it open. Others resorted to the two-handed, multi-tap technique. (If you didn't crack the egg hard enough using the one-handed technique, you ended up using this second technique as a cover up.) Or you could use a blunt object like a fork or knife edge to crack the egg open. (*"NO REAL CHEF USE THIS METHOD!"* barked Pei Lei impatiently.) Once the egg was cracked, contestants had to release the contents without breaking the yoke—at the same time keeping the tiny shards of shell out of the contents.

No doubt you're getting the drift as to why this wasn't "pretty easy" despite Louie G's assertion. In fact, trying to make up for the (actual *and* metaphorical) egg on his face earlier Louie G managed to draw Pei Lei's ire by trying the one-handed technique *with an egg in each hand* to save time. He ended up breaking both yolks, leaving lots of shells in the bowl, and getting his hands VERY gooey.

For those campers who served as Sphinxes for their EFF teams, participation in this booth amounted to heresy. Their only job—the job they'd been practicing in the hallways and during their free time all summer—was to *prevent* eggs from cracking. So participating in this activity essentially cracked their psyches along with the eggs! (Try telling a serious basketball player to use her brand-new leather indoor ball as a backyard soccer ball. Better yet, tell a tennis player to use his $200 racquet to hit baseballs over a fence. You feel me?)

Jerry had no problem cracking eggs, either emotionally or physically. Eggs were one of his favorite dishes, and he'd cracked hundreds in his lifetime. He handled this competition like a champ, even earning a rare compliment from Chef Pei Lei.

"You crack egg very nice, Jerry Pasta," she began sweetly, before dramatically pausing for a full three seconds. "BUT YOU NO MAKE WHITE RICE SO NICE!"

OK, so it was a backhanded compliment, but Jerry was willing to take the good with the bad.

(For anyone concerned about the enormous waste of eggs, a sign posted at the rear of the booth informed fairgoers that the shells would be strained out and the eggs used for tomorrow's breakfast).

Whisk, Whisk, Whisk

The fair organizers smartly set up this booth right next to the egg booth; the cracked eggs had the shells strained out and were then used in this whisking competition. Many of the campers were familiar with whisking, though before attending Pesto's some of them only used a fork rather than a regulation whisk that looks kind of like a meatless drumstick made of wire.

So after the proper whisking technique was demonstrated, campers competed at whisking as fast as possible and as cleanly as possible. How was spillage determined? Everyone had a large sheet of fresh white paper placed under his/her bowl, making it obvious when sloshing had occurred. This was not Jerry's favorite booth. The task required a bit of coordination and hand speed. And though Jerry had both of these skills, he was somewhat notorious at home for being a messy chef. His parents were always reminding him to clean up after he cooked because he left the kitchen looking like a bear had rummaged through the pantry and refrigerator. And then that same bear smeared food on all the counters and stovetop. "But at least the kitchen smells good," Jerry would contend with a sheepish grin.

This whisking contest helped these memories of home resurface and took some of the drudgery out of the task. Jerry actually felt himself getting better as he worked, though he took note that this was something he really needed to practice.

The tickets were totaled at the end of the day, right before dinner. The top six ticket winners—who would participate in the "surprise" competition—were announced by Moldy Coeur, dressed in a black turtleneck and cobalt green slacks. Jerry got a serious case of déjà vu, remembering registration day. He hoped against an encore. Coeur methodically called out five names, each camper taking a place to Coeur's left. No one from Mayon-daise Kitchen had been called. Jerry wasn't holding his breath—he really hadn't done all that well in the competitions. *If anyone from Mayon-daise makes it, it'll be Mari,* Jerry guessed. She'd done pretty well at the spice/cooking-bee booth. Everyone waited in breathless anticipation for the final name.

Moldy Coeur paused dramatically, wiped the sweat from his brow with a black handkerchief, and then broke into a devious grin. "And the final camper selected for the surprise competition is . . . Mario Bitali!"

As before, a collective cheer came from the Mufia and Tomato Kitchen ranks when one of their own was selected. Or rather, *another* of their own. Robert DeJourno and Cello Feigni had already been named to the top six. *Come to think of it,* Jerry thought, *the Mufia looked to be having more fun at the nonskills booths.* He hadn't really seen a single one of them spend more than a minute or two at a skills booth. *How could so many of them have made it into the finals? Maybe it's no coincidence that Moldy Coeur, the Mufia sponsor, is reading off the names?* If any of Jerry's thoughts had made it to his mouth, he would have been accused of being a whiner, a sore loser. So though he suspected foul play, he kept his mouth shut.

So did everyone else. Initially. But the brief silence from the crowd was soon followed by angry grumbling, and those near Jerry turned and stared at him. Soon *everyone* was looking at him, as if they had expected *him* to be in the final competition.

Am I the only one NOT surprised that I wasn't selected?

"Some chosen one *you* are," whispered someone within earshot.

Jerry looked around at the members of his kitchen, hoping to get some support—but all he saw were disappointed faces. *You too, May-on-daise?! You can't possibly expect me to win everything!* Jerry yelled in his head, indignant at the response of his cabin mates.

"Mario Bitali!" Moldy Coeur repeated, and his voice made Jerry snap his head back to the front.

The first five finalists stood idly at Coeur's side. No Mario.

"Mario Bitali!"

This time, a slow-moving figure pushed through the crowd to the stage.

It was Mario.

Mario stumbled onto the pavilion, nearly bumping into Moldy Coeur. "I am here, Ward Coeur. *Mi scusi*, I was in the bathro—"

Midsentence, Mario vomited directly onto Moldy Coeur's black leather shoes. It looked like Mario had consumed an unpalatable combination of Italian sausage, chocolate gelato, and blue cotton candy. His face was a shade greener than Moldy Coeur's pants and eyes, which were alive with rage. Coeur jumped back in disgust, shaking his feet vigorously.

Suddenly Jaime (pronounced "Hi-me) Olivière, a Spanish camper in Béchamel Kitchen and one of the final six, lost his lunch as well. Groans of *"Ewwww!"* barely drowned out the retching sounds on the stage. It was like Mario and Jaime were competing to see who could puke the most. Mario was winning. In the sea of now-queasy young onlookers, Béchamel camper Paoladinho looked like she was going to vomit too, her face ashen, legs trembling; instead she placed the back of her right hand on her forehead. And fainted.

Moldy Coeur barked at the kitchen staff members to get the sick campers off of the stage and clean up the toxic mess. The faculty then briefly conferred, and Al Dente emerged with the group's decision.

"It appears we have lost-ah two of the campers for the surprise-ah competition. So we have decided to include the next-ah two highest ticket winners." Al Dente looked down at his notepad, scanning the list. "They are Marirajah Nera and"—Dente's face broke into a genuinely pleased (unlike Moldy Coeur's a few minutes earlier) smile— "and Jerry Pasta!"

Chapter 24

Mad Skillz Set or Killer Skillet?

"*Andiamo,* Jerry! Represent us well," yelled out Manny Cotti, who had fully recovered from the fish poisoning and was standing in a group with other Mayon-daise campers.

Jerry could see how his inclusion in the contest had energized his cabinmates. But talk about pressure to perform! Jerry wasn't sure whether to be excited or disappointed. *Is this destiny, with some higher power at work, or just dumb luck? Somebody out there was sure to see this as fitting in with some cosmic plan that ends with me saving the world. I wonder if every cosmic plan involves uncontrollable vomiting. If so, God definitely has a sense of humor,* Jerry pondered.

Al Dente motioned for the crowd to quiet so he could announce the details of the surprise competition.

"The surprise competition is a spin-off of *Iron Chef,* a very popular culinary game show-ah pitting chefs against each other. Our version also blends in another popular TV show-ah, *Dancing with the Stars.* I guess-ah you could call our version 'Cooking with the Stars.' We the faculty are the stars, and each of you will be paired with-ah one of us in a cooking competition. The wards and remaining faculty will serve as judges for flavor and taste-ah. You, the audience, will vote on flair and originality! The judges will-ah be blindfolded during the cooking and tasting portion of the contest. So it is very important that you, the audience, pay-ah attention!"

The contestants took their places at the same six ICSs used at the "Now That's Saucy" booth.

Jerry gave Mari a good luck pat on the back, then took his position near an ICS to wait for his pairing assignment. He crossed his fingers, hoping it wouldn't be an angry, dripping Chef Beurre. His prayers were answered. Sort of. Chef Jo Moi-Erreur skipped toward Jerry jubilantly.

"*Eh, voila! L'étoile est née!* The Star is born! I yam of course referring to myself," Moi-Erreur clarified, blowing into his fingers and then delicately brushing imaginary dust off of his shoulders. He then proceeded to knock a bottle of olive oil off the ICS counter (thankfully, it was plastic). Without missing a beat, Moi-Erreur picked up the bottle, fumbling it for several seconds, then asked, "Are you ready to cook, Jeremiah Pasta?"

"*Oui*, Monsieur, I am ..." said Jerry, voice rising, his phrasing more a question than a confident statement. Jerry was already preparing himself for a complete disaster.

"I can't wait to see what dish they choose for us to create. Hopefully something *excitant!*" Moi-Erreur clapped his hands rapidly, barely able to contain his excitement. Jerry saw Mari was paired up with Chef Pei Lei. Mari flashed Jerry a nervous glance and waved. *I'd be nervous too if I was Mari ... wait, I am nervous!*

A large fishbowl filled with tiny notecards was brought front and center for all to see. Ward Moldy Coeur reached a pudgy hand into the bottom, stirred up the cards, and selected the one that would serve as the basis for everyone's dish.

"Contestants, you are to create a simple boneless-chicken dish, for which you have thirty minutes to prepare with your faculty partner. You may begin."

Jerry respectfully turned to Jo Moi-Erreur; it would have been rude to *not* ask the faculty "star" for input. "Any ideas, Monsieur?" Jerry wasn't holding his breath. He knew only two things about Chef Moi-Erreur: one, he was more librarian than true cooking instructor, and two, he saw himself as a culinary Sherlock Holmes, as evidenced by his performance after the poisoning. Jerry wasn't expecting great epicurean advice from someone who was more bookworm than chef.

Oh, and there was a third thing: Moi-Erreur was a complete klutz. Jerry positioned himself strategically between Chef Moi-Erreur and the cutting knives, raising his odds of surviving the experience unscathed.

Chef Moi-Erreur cleared his throat and began to share his ideas.

(It's to be noted that anytime someone answers your question with a question of their own, you should be very concerned. Jerry was appropriately worried.)

"Jeremiah, have I ever told you the history of poultry in French cooking? Have you heard of *poule au pot*[*]? Or coq au vin[Ψ]? In the 1800s, Antonin Carême prepared meals for Napoleon and . . ."

Meatballs!

Moi-Erreur's voice faded away as Jerry heard what he needed to hear from the bumbling chef and began to focus on the meal at hand. For all of his ramblings, Moi-Erreur had given Jerry a risky, but possibly winning, idea.

While Moi-Erreur continued to talk, Jerry rummaged through the cabinet. A bottle of red wine, some balsamic vinegar . . . the faculty had asked for flair, and Jerry was going to give it to them. Jerry uncovered the three boneless chicken thighs on his countertop. He applied a liberal amount of salt and pepper, and then placed them in a greased saucepan, browning them for four minutes on each side. Grabbing the unopened wine bottle, Jerry attempted to put the wine opener to use. No success. The cork was tough to spear through—Jerry just didn't seem to have the strength (a recurrent theme for the day). He tapped Chef Moi-Erruer (who was still rambling) on the shoulder.

". . . and that's why it's called coq au vin, Jerry. Did you have a question?"

"Could you open this bottle for me, Monsieur?" *With flair, please?* Given Moi-Erreur's penchant for disaster, Jerry was secretly hoping for an entertaining bottle-opening show.

---

[*] pronounced pool-oh-poe

[Ψ] pronounced kōk-ō-van

Moi-Erreur grabbed the bottle of red wine from Jerry's hands. "Why, of course. A 2005 Merlot. A decent choice—but a white wine goes better with chicken, my dear boy." Moi-Erruer plunged the corkscrew in and began turning it clockwise. But he too struggled, finding the cork incredibly difficult to remove. His monocle clumsily fell away from his eye as his face turned redder with every rotation, sweat pouring down his forehead. Moi-Erreur repeatedly tried to talk Jerry out of using this particular wine while trying to open the bottle. "Perhaps a 2001 Chardonnay . . . *pfffff* . . . or a 2004 Riesling?" he grunted.

Jerry pressed on with his cooking, trying to ignore Moi-Erreur and hoping the crowd was not. And while he hoped they were getting a kick out of the chef's antics, Jerry *did* need the bottle opened eventually to complete his recipe.

After two full minutes of struggling, Moi-Erreur anchored the bottle between his legs and tried wrestling the cork from side to side. It actually *looked* like he was wrestling, Moi-Erreur only requiring flamboyant tights and a mask to complete the scene.

Moi-Erreur finally had the bottle in a full nelson when the cork came bursting out with a loud POP!

The distinguished chef-librarian fell squarely on his bottom, the wine bottle still between his legs. The cork flew toward the judges' table, striking a blindfolded Ward Moldy Coeur between the eyes, causing him to yelp. Meanwhile, the red wine bubbled out onto Moi-Erreur's beige khakis, with Jerry there just in time to secure the bottle before all the wine spilled out. The crowd burst into rambunctious laughter and cheers. *This was exactly the show I was hoping for!* Jerry thought as he calmly walked back to his ICS. Jerry flamboyantly poured the wine and balsamic vinegar into his simmering saucepan, one bottle in each hand. The campers roared in approval at the eleven-year-old boy with the guts to cook a meal with alcohol in front of all the teachers! Jerry had seen his dad do this before (with less flair). He knew that most of the alcohol would boil away and there'd be no worries that the food could get anyone drunk, even if they ate the entire dish and all the drippings. But the flavor would be *awesome*.

After allowing the dish to cook for fifteen minutes covered, Jerry removed it from the heat and placed it on a platter, garnishing the chicken with parsley and serving it with oven-baked asparagus he had made while the chicken was cooking.

Amidst a din of cheers, Jerry pivoted and began walking—almost strutting—toward the judges' table. He had gotten no more than five steps away from his ICS when the cheers turned to "Ohhhs!" accompanied by looks of concern and fingers anxiously pointed in his direction.

"Jerry, get down!" he heard Louis G shout.

Jerry's knees buckled; at the same time, he felt himself being tackled to the ground. Remarkably, as he hit the ground chest first, arms outstretched, he somehow managed to hold the plate level, keeping the braised chicken on the plate and off the lawn.

An earth-shattering *BOOM!* rocked the pavilion, followed by an intense blast of heat. A few ashen objects, including the charred remnants of the skillet he had just used, whizzed past Jerry's head, followed by billowy smoke.

The smell of gasoline was overwhelming. Slightly disoriented, coughing, Jerry struggled out of the grasp of the person who had tackled him and staggered to his feet. Though a bit shaky, he raised his arms high above his head in an effort to keep the cooked chicken out of the smoke. As he walked out of the smoke, he was greeted with a chorus of cheers even louder than the first!

(Mari and Rita later told him that he had looked like a superhero emerging from the wreckage of an accident, face stained with soot, having saved the damsel in distress—the chicken in this case—from certain demise. Girls are *sooooo* dramatic.)

"You OK, JP?"

Jerry immediately recognized the voice behind him as Louie G's and realized it was his friend who had tackled him to safety.

"Yeah, I . . . I guess so. Thanks for the warning—and the follow through. What happened?"

Louie G's white T-shirt was covered in soot, but he too was otherwise uninjured. Though he was coughing repeatedly. "When you started walking away from your ICS, the bottom of the stove started to smoke . . . a lot . . . and fast. Actually, that janitor"—he paused to cough at length—"Bones was actually the one who got *my* attention. You should thank *him*." Louie G paused again to fiercely cough for a good five seconds. "I knew there was a propane tank underneath the ICS stove, so the safest thing was to get you to the ground as quickly as possible. . . . I've had enough experience with backyard cookouts to know that propane tanks can be wickedly dangerous. Though come to think of it, it smells really gassy out here, like a lawnmower when the carburetor's flooded. I thought propane was an odorless gas . . . Anyway, I'm glad the chicken survived too. What is it?" Louie G pointed to the plate of perfectly seared chicken.

"Braised balsamic chicken cooked in red wine. Something Chef Moi-Erreur said sparked a recollection of a recipe I read about in *Sauce for the Saucier*, so I just kind of ran with the idea. I was trying for fireworks, but didn't really have *this* kind in mind." Jerry jerked a thumb over his shoulder at the charred remains of the ICS. "And once again you saved my life. I owe you doubly, counting the canoe episode."

"No worries, Jerry. Just go turn in"—another coughing fit interrupted him—"turn it that braised chicken and win something for our kitchen," Louie G finished breathlessly. He had his hands propped on his thighs, head bowed, gasping for air. Then he took a few tenuous steps away and turned his back on Jerry. Reaching into his pocket, he took something out and brought it to his face.

Jerry couldn't quite make out what the object was. He was about to ask Louie G what was going on, but his friend quickly shoved the object back into his pocket and turned to face Jerry, a look of relief on his face.

"I'm good, JP. Go turn in that chicken!"

But Jerry was still trying to figure out what the mystery object in Louie G's pocket was. Maybe a chapstick? His lips looked a little shinier. Jerry had seen Louie G do this before—though he couldn't see why moist lips were important after rescuing a friend from an explosion. Or for that matter before morning jogs or right after an EFF match. *Unless*—

A loud *WHOOSH!* interrupted Jerry midthought, bringing him back to the moment at hand. Fire-extinguisher-wielding kitchen staff smothered the remaining flames. Bones was already setting up a perimeter around the destroyed ICS to prevent curious campers from getting too close.

Jerry gingerly carried his platter to the judging table, growing bolder with each step, amazed by even his own standards that his body—much less his meal!—had survived the fiery blast. The faculty judges had briefly removed their blindfolds after hearing the loud explosion but were once again blindfolded to avoid being biased towards specific campers. Lucky for Jerry, Moldy Coeur had no clue as to who or what had struck him in the face minutes ago.

The judges took fifteen minutes to appraise the various submissions.

The remaining faculty then tabulated the crowd votes on originality and flair.

Jerry scored fairly high with the judges for taste. But he blew away the competition in the flair department. The wine-opening combined with the explosive finish gave him the clear victory. The reward for Jerry's performance was announced by Al Dente.

"Aside from a major point-ah boost for your kitchen, for outstanding cooking, you are given the privilege of planning next week's meals, through Thursday. You will have every kitchen staff-ah member at your disposal. This is one of the highest honors bestowed on a first-year camper. Of course you can get-ah help from-ah your fellow kitchenmates in planning your menu. The kitchen will-ah execute the details of your menu—you personally won't have-ah to do any of the cooking. Bravo!"

Jerry Pasta's
BALSAMIC BRAISED CHICKEN

Feeds 3 or 4

Preparation time: 5 to 10 minutes

Cooking time: 30 to 45 minutes

INGREDIENTS AND SUPPLIES

Ingredients

1/3 cup all-purpose flour

Salt and freshly ground pepper to taste (about a teaspoon of each)

3 boneless chicken breasts or thighs

3 tablespoons extra-virgin olive oil

1 yellow onion, thinly sliced

8 ounces (1 small package) white button mushrooms, quartered

2 cups white or red wine

¼ cup balsamic vinegar

3 garlic cloves, crushed or 1 teaspoon garlic powder

3 fresh thyme sprigs

1 bay leaf

Supplies

Large mixing bowl

Large saucepan with cover

DIRECTIONS

1. In a large bowl, combine the flour, salt, and pepper. Add the chicken, and toss to coat evenly.

2. In a large saucepan (preferably one that can fit all three chicken breasts side by side), warm the olive oil to medium-high heat. Add the coated chicken, and brown on both sides, 3 to 4 minutes per side. Transfer the browned chicken to a plate, and set aside.

3. Add the onion and mushrooms to the pan and cook, stirring occasionally, until golden, about 5 minutes. Remove the pan from the heat and pour in the wine and balsamic vinegar. Return the pan to the heat, raise the heat to high, and bring to a boil.

4. Return the chicken to the pan, and add the garlic, thyme, and bay leaf. Return to a boil; then cover, and reduce heat to low. Cook for at least 15 to 25 minutes, or until the chicken is very tender and thoroughly cooked. (Poke it with a knife to see if it is soft and white on the inside; if the meat is still pink, continue cooking.) Sample and season with additional salt and pepper if needed, remove the bay leaf, and serve immediately.

Winning the competition meant Jerry got a photo-op with the judges, one of whom was Moldy Coeur, who pulled Jerry aside for a select photograph of just the two of them.

"Jerry Pasta—a much better chef than a prior Pesto's graduate from your family," Moldy whispered into Jerry's ear as the photographer staged the photo.

The words stung Jerry to the core, but he held his tongue, refusing to give Ward Coeur the satisfaction of knowing he had hurt him.

But Moldavi Coeur wasn't finished. "Hopefully we'll have edible meals to eat this week. I heard you serve a nice fish dish. Blackened, perhaps?" he sniped, cruelly referencing both the fish poisoning and the explosion, while solicitously dusting soot and silt off of Jerry's shoulder with his black handkerchief. The photographer's camera snapped repeatedly, likely capturing the scowl darkening Jerry's face.

But Jerry finally retaliated, saying tartly, "I *do* make a nice blackened fish, as a matter of fact. Though oddly it starts out green. But I just add some black dye—you wouldn't happen to have any black dye I could borrow, would you?"

That got Coeur's attention. He was still standing behind Jerry, his hands on Jerry's shoulders, but Jerry felt one of the hands leave his shoulder, and he turned to see Moldy Coeur nervously running a hand through his jet-black hair.

He probably thinks no one knows the true color of his hair. I hope he just had a flashback of his yearbook photo, Jerry laughed to himself.

"And a sharp wit as well, Jerry Pasta. Another advantage you have over your father. You must get your talents from your mother's side of the family." Coeur's tone abruptly became threatening. "Be careful how you address me; I am a very powerful man. If you're as smart as you seem, you'll make sure you're on the right team at the end of the day—and you won't bite the hand that feeds you." He gave a firm squeeze of Jerry's shoulders as both hands were back in place.

And to be sure, the irony was not lost on Jerry; the boy with pasta hair had just bullied back the school benefactor with moldy hair. Touché, one might say. Or if you're keeping score, Jerry Pasta 1, Moldy Coeur 0. (Well, maybe it was still a draw since Moldy had zinged Jerry pretty bad over the fish poisoning in front of the entire camp.)

"Say *formaggio!*" The photographer snapped one last photo before Moldy Coeur stormed off, claiming to be late for an appointment. Jerry watched him leave, thinking, *On the right team? Bite the hand that feeds me? What could Coeur have meant by that?*

Unperturbed, Jerry remained ecstatic about his latest win. What an opportunity! He'd been quietly taking notes all summer about all the things he thought needed to be changed at the camp cafeteria. Fewer fatty foods. Smaller portion sizes. Greater emphasis on herbs and spices for aroma and flavor. Jerry was going to make sure all these changes were made—and he was going to make it a point to play to Doctor Sauce's strengths by having some great sauce dishes on the menu.

As Jerry returned from his photo-op to join the larger group, Louie G began loudly cheering, "Braise the roof! Pasta rules! Braise the roof! Pasta rules!" Many of the Mayon-daise campers seemed unfamiliar with the American origins of Louie G's cheer—but that didn't stop them from joining in, first timidly, then boldly. Jerry mimicked his admirers and pushed up on what he imagined to be a blazing, low-hanging roof dangling above his pasta hair.

This was going to be an awesome last week of camp.

Chapter 25

League of His Own

So Jerry eagerly stepped into his role as meal coordinator the very next day (Sunday) as Week Four, the last week of camp, began. He secretly hoped that this new job would make it easier for him to have access to the kitchen to observe Doctor Sauce in action. But he quickly learned, to his disappointment, that most of his "coordinating" was done outside the kitchen. He *still* wasn't allowed in.

Sunday's dinner meal was Jerry's "love song" to Rita. At least that's what Louie G was calling it—and the look on Rita's face corroborated that assessment. She couldn't stop beaming at Jerry from where she sat with her kitchenmates across the room.

"If this meal doesn't earn you some extra lovin', Jerry, I don't know what will," said Louie G, swallowing an extra-large mouthful of the Mexican-themed dish. "But I have to hand it to you. You're the only person in this world who's ever gotten me to eat 'salad' as my main course. First pasta salad, then this. What is this world coming to?" he asked rhetorically.

"Hopefully not to an end, if Jerry has anything to say about it," Mari affirmed.

Her reference to the Della Morta prophecy was not lost on Jerry. *No, Mari, the world is not coming to an end—and I'm pretty sure my cooking has little to do with that,* Jerry thought to himself. He was just glad that Mari and Louie G were finally on speaking terms again—the joyous celebration after the fair had led to forgiveness of any name-calling and egg-on-the-face transgressions.

Even Jerry was impressed with the kitchen staff's reproduction of his salad recipe. Jerry could taste Doctor Sauce's thumbprint on the meat and the homemade salsa. *A little adobo, some fresh cilantro . . . Well done, Dr. Sauce, I knew you'd pull through,* thought Jerry, silently thanking his mentor.

Jerry Pasta's

TACO SALAD

Feeds 4

Preparation time: 5 to 10 minutes

Cooking time: 10 minutes

INGREDIENTS AND SUPPLIES

Ingredients

1 tablespoon vegetable oil

1 large onion, diced

1 pound ground turkey or beef

Seasoning salt

Black pepper

1 tablespoon adobo seasoning (or curry powder)

3 large tomatoes, chopped

1 ripe avocado, chopped (Note: to test ripeness, the fruit should feel slightly soft when lightly pressed)

5 sprigs fresh cilantro

1 red or green bell pepper (optional)

1 to 2 jalapeños, thinly sliced (optional)

Salsa (optional)

1 head lettuce, chopped

1 bag yellow corn tortilla chips, crushed

1 can black beans, drained and rinsed

2 cups shredded cheese, preferably "Mexican blend" (Monterey Jack, cheddar, asadero, and queso quesadilla)

Light Catalina salad dressing (or dressing of your choice)

<u>Supplies</u>

Large skillet

Medium-sized bowl

DIRECTIONS

1. Coat a large skillet with the vegetable oil, then add the onions, , sautéing them over medium heat. As the onions begin to turn translucent (but not brown), add the ground meat.

2. Add the seasoning salt and pepper to taste (generally no more than 1 table spoon of seasoning salt and 2 teaspoons of black pepper per pound of meat). Stir in the adobo seasoning. Blend thoroughly until the spices are evenly distributed.

3. Stir the meat every 30 seconds. The meat should brown after 7 to 8 minutes. Reduce the heat to low, and cover for 2 minutes. Then remove the skillet from the heat.

4. In a medium-sized bowl, combined the tomatoes and avocado. If you wish to add the bell pepper and/or the jalapeno pepper, do so now. Then add the cilantro and a pinch of salt. Blend well with a fork. The mixture will be mushy. You can substitute salsa for the vegetables, but this version tastes fresher and is a little less spicy—especially without the jalapeños!

5. In individual serving bowls, layer portions of the remaining ingredients however you want. Some people put the lettuce in the bottom of the bowl first, then crushed tortilla chips, then beans, then the meat mixture, then cheese, then the avocado-tomato mix (or salsa).

6. Sprinkle each serving lightly with salad dressing. Go easy on the dressing; the salad already has plenty of flavor!

Rita caught up with Jerry after dinner as he walked back to the cabin with Louie G and Mari and told him how much she loved the meal. It gave her a little taste of home, something she had missed for the three weeks they'd been a camp. Her sustained bone-crushing hug and follow-up sloppy smooch was a clear expression of her gratitude. Standing directly behind Rita during the embrace, Louie G gave a blushing Jerry a wink and two thumbs up.

Monday's lunch was pork tenderloin with an Espagnole secondary peppery brown sauce called *Sauce Diable*. Paul and Marco Gagasol raved about the meal at length, simultaneously arguing over whether their mother's version was as good as Jerry's. To which Marco remarked, "Mamá is *not* going to be happy with you for that opinion, Paul." For dinner, Jerry came up with a penne and pesto dish—great colors, great taste. He even offered a demonstration in the Mayon-daise Kitchen before dinner, showing the campers how easy pesto sauce was to make.

Jerry Pasta's
PESTO SAUCE

Feeds 4 to 6

Preparation time: 10-15 minutes

INGREDIENTS AND SUPPLIES
Ingredients
1 ½ cups chopped walnuts or (as an option) roasted pine nuts

3 cups fresh basil leaves

2 to 3 cloves garlic, peeled

¼ cup grated Parmesan cheese

¼ cup grated Romano cheese (optional)

3/4 cup olive oil

1 teaspoon salt

Pepper to taste

½ teaspoon grated lemon zest (optional)

Supplies

Baking tray

Medium-sized skillet

Food processor or blender

DIRECTIONS

Preheat the oven to 350 degrees.

To roast the nuts, lay them out on a baking tray and bake for 15 minutes.
   Optionally, place them in a skillet over medium heat, shaking the skillet
   frequently to ensure even browning (no more than 7 to10 minutes).

In a food processor or blender, mix the roasted nuts with the basil leaves,
   garlic, and cheese until well blended. Slowly pour in the oil while intermit
   tently pulsing. Add the salt and pepper, and pulse again. The texture should
   be a thick puree.

Top any cooked pasta with this sauce for a tasty meal.

The faculty was impressed with the meals Jerry planned. They were healthy. They were tasty. And the portion sizes were just right—though some campers (and instructors) complained about not having enough. But for the most part, everyone loved Jerry's cooking. And whatever Doctor Sauce was adding to Jerry's sauces in the kitchen was PHE-NOMENAL. It was like she kicked it up another notch. Jerry's good meals became great!

After class each day, Jerry spent time cooking with Louie G, Mari, and The Sauciers, who had accepted Jerry as somewhat of an hon-orary member without him having officially joined. The Sauciers were spending less time with their club sponsor, Chef Beurre, and more time with their new hero, Jerry Pasta, who continued sharing all of Doctor Sauce's tricks with the group—though only Louie G and Mari knew of Jerry's continued covert excursions into the kitchen. Jerry's copy of

Karim de la Carême's *Sauce for the Saucier* was quite the workout; it was fraying at the edges, the pages stained with every mother sauce in the book. And just like his EFF workouts and games had toned his body this summer, Jerry's diligent reading and cooking were reaping dividends in his much-improved sauce making!

And in just three short days of eating healthier meals, some of the campers had started to trim down. Even Chefs Beurre and La Gasse had shed some pounds (which is to say they could fit into their dining hall chairs without groaning). The teaching faculty took notice. After Tuesday's dinner, Al Dente announced that the camp planned to permanently implement some of Jerry's culinary adaptations, specifically serving smaller portions and having salad or fruit with every meal. Plus instead of sodas and sugary drinks offered at every meal, water, low-fat milk, and flavored seltzers were served. This was, to be honest, the least popular of what was dubbed "The Pasta Rules" or "The Jerry Effect" on meals at Pesto's.

The beginning of Week Four was highlighted by Mayon-daise's third EFF match on Monday night.

EFF TEAM	STANDINGS
Bechamel	0 - 2
Espagnole	1 - 2
Mayon-daise	2 - 0
Tomato	2 - 0
Veloute	1 - 2

Only two food groups were left: meat and beans, fruits. Jerry was kind of hoping for fruits when they arrived on the field that day. Their opponent, the Béchamel Kitchen, had lost miserably to the Tomato Kitchen only a few days before. Robert DeJourno and his Mufia-thugs-turned-EFF-players had done what no one had done yet in the season: force a Pharaoh to surrender after pelting the Béchamel Pharaoh multiple times in the head. Though Tomato racked up a number of penalty points, the referees noticed the infractions too late (Tomato Jackals "accidently" threw food items at the referees at opportune times, forcing them to duck and dodge, their attention focused on self-preservation and not the deliberate penalties). The victimized Béchamel Pharaoh succumbed early in the second half, stunning everyone in attendance, referees included. DeJourno and his friends ridiculed the Béchamel team as they walked off the Field of Greens in disgrace.

As Jerry had expected, a new Pharaoh was playing for Béchamel for today's match. Louie G decided to go with a "shock and awe" strategy—something Mayon-daise hadn't used yet because of the previously poor exercise tolerance of the squad. But now that almost everyone was in good shape, Louie G was eager to "unleash the beast," in his words. Plus he assumed that the new Béchamel Pharaoh would have fresh memories of what happened to the previous one and be less than courageous.

The food pyramid gods had decided it would be a Meat and Beans fight day. Did Referee Meat have a little glint of mischief in his eyes, a little spring in his step? Jerry watched carefully as the kitchen staff laid out partially cut ham hocks, ox tails (tiny, rounded bones without jagged edges), and tiny bags of rotten unused beans.

Before the game started, Louie G taught the squad a new cheer he'd been working on. "The cheer is pretty simple. Remember the whole 5-2-1-0 healthy living thing? And how they based our team structure off that? You know, 5 Jackals, 2 Sphinxes, 1 Pharaoh and an egg? So, the cheer goes '5-2-1-0 (say *oh* not *zero*), Mayon-daise let's go, let's go!'"

And maybe, Jerry mulled as he repeated the cheer in his head a few times, *we* are *living healthy.* Thanks to his inspiration, the campers were now having five servings of fruits and vegetables a day, and The Pasta Rules had basically eliminated sugary drinks from the campers' diets. Plus they were certainly watching fewer than two hours of TV and video gaming a day—he doubted there was even a TV anywhere at camp. Factor in EFF practices, games, sports, and morning jogs, and the May-on-daise squad, at least, was getting well over one hour of exercise a day.

Learning Louie G's new cheer was the hardest part of the match because the match itself wasn't much of a contest. The well-rested and physically fit Mayon-daise squad literally ran circles around the Béchamel team. The constant-movement strategy quickly wore out the Béchamel Jackals and Sphinxes. Their Sphinxes could barely keep up with resurrections, as Louie G had instructed the Mayon-daise defense Jackals to lure their attackers as close to the Pharaoh's circle before mummifying them, making resurrection and attacking a time-consuming and exhausting process. According to the rulebook, once unmummified, an attacking Jackal had to return to his own side of the field before resuming play. In the end, Mari retrieved the egg in the first half (with Jerry as an escort), and the Béchamel Pharaoh surrendered from sheer exhaustion from being hit—not that any of the Mayon-daise lobs were illegal. The final score was 1,400 to 0, one of the most lopsided wins the whole summer.

Mayon-daise stayed to watch Tomato defeat Velouté (the only kitchen that didn't get a bye all summer). It was clear that Mayon-daise and Tomato Kitchens were headed for a final showdown in a couple of days to determine the EFF champion. The threats began during the post-game period, with Robert DeJourno launching the first volley.

"Hey, Pasta, you might wanna call your mudda to pick you up from camp a few days early. Not sure she wants to get smooshed ravioli all over her car seats. Oh, wait, it won't matter. It'll just ruin your booster seat!"

His Mufia sidekicks laughed hysterically as Mari and Louie G pulled Jerry away, admonishing him to ignore the boorish behavior. The three had just begun to distance themselves when a voice yelled, "Heads up, Pasta!"

Jerry instinctively dropped his right shoulder and began torquing his body clockwise. His right hand was split seconds ahead of the rest of his body, already reaching into the left side of his waistband to grab his ladle. Jerry spotted a white blur streaking toward his head, whistling as it buzzed by. But his right hand was already in place, level with his chin. His right arm braced for impact as he deftly caught the object in his ladle, allowing the momentum of both his spinning body and the object to carry him balletically in a complete circle. His excellent balance left him crouched in an attacking position: head up, arms out to his sides. He now stood facing the person who had thrown the object from ten yards away.

It was Lumina Foyle. She was frozen in a jaw-dropped stare, as was almost everyone else behind her. Jerry straightened up, not sure what was so shocking until he followed Lumina's eyes to his right hand. In Jerry's ladle rested the captured egg from the Tomato-Velouté match.

And it wasn't even cracked.

Chapter 26

Caught!

The legend of Jerry Pasta grew even larger after Lumina Foyle's egg attack. Now designated "The Catch," the story had been told and retold dozens of times before twenty-four hours had even elapsed, with some of the embellishments quite audacious. Like Jerry catching the egg bare-handed, eyes closed. Or that three eggs had been thrown: two caught with his "magic" ladle, one with his mouth! Louie G had even coined a new term for when he made cooking blunders, referencing the foiled attempt to egg Jerry in the back of the head. "If I hadn't *Foyled* that recipe, this food might actually taste decent," he'd joke. If only Lumina knew.

Jerry tried not to get caught up in the hype. He needed to learn so much more about cooking before camp ended in just days, and he didn't want unwanted attention to be a distraction. Not to mention, with all eyes on him, it was harder for Jerry to sneak away for his Doctor Sauce "lessons." But he had found a way, often having Mari and Louie G run interference for him so he could sneak into the kitchen. His disguises had become more elaborate: he'd found some discarded janitor's clothes in a hallway closet that he'd slip on over his own clothes.

Midway into that last week of camp (and after some sixteen or seventeen times of sneaking into the kitchen), it dawned on Jerry that he still hadn't caught even a glimpse of Doctor Sauce's face. He wasn't sure it mattered. Except that he really wanted to personally thank the individual who had—albeit inadvertently—taught him so much about making sauces. But identifying himself might scare Doctor Sauce away, which would effectively end this learning opportunity. And admittedly, he thoroughly enjoyed the "private lessons" and didn't want to ruin a good thing. A few times, Jerry felt sure that Doctor Sauce *knew* he was present and "performed," if you will, for his benefit.

So Tuesday's private lesson wasn't much different from any of the others, only that in the back of Jerry's mind he was thinking about Friday's dinner: the last of the kitchen meals that he was required to prepare. The two meals he cooked after the "poissoning" incident had gone on without a hitch. But something about this being the last cabin-made meal made Jerry uneasy. He was focusing extra hard during tonight's sauce lesson, which helped him temporarily forget about his meal anxiety. In fact, he was focusing so hard on Doctor Sauce that for about three seconds, Jerry thought he saw something he hadn't noticed before. *Those hands stirring the pot—where have I seen them before?*

As Doctor Sauce put the finishing touches on her creation, Jerry scooted out of the kitchen on his knees faster than usual, perturbed by what he thought he had seen. Imagine his surprise when he crawled right into the feet of Robert DeJourno!

"Jerry Pasta. Sneakin' around in the kitchen. Pretendin' to be a janitor. Kind of suits you, Pasta," DeJourno mocked, looking down at Jerry with disdain. His white shirt was soaked in sweat, his bowtie akimbo. And, as usual, he was a little out of breath.

Exhausted from spying on me? This kid needs to lay off the donuts. And what's with always dressing to impress? In the middle of summer?

Jerry stood up. "Are you spying on me, Robert?"

"Maybe. Sorta. Let's just say for the last few days, I noticed you sneaking around, so I had you tailed. Lumina and Cello have done well. I decided to follow you myself today. Nice disguise, by the way. I guess no one notices a midget with pasta bangs moppin' the floor? Ha, ha, ha." He paused to catch his breath. "I followed you into the kitchen and hid behind those bags of barley—didn't wear some stupid disguise like you. You seem awfully interested in the gal putting stuff into the sauce.

I've never seen 'er before. I better go tell Chef Beurre that somebody's tampering with his food—but I'm sure that's what you were rushin' to do, right?"

Jerry resented the fact that this Mufia clown had been tracking him. Worse, that he threatened to ruin a good thing. "No, you idiot! That 'gal putting stuff into the sauce,' as you put it, is probably one of the best sauciers ever!" Jerry yelled. "She's been making Chef Beurre's sauces infinitely better. Haven't you noticed how good the sauces served with our meals are?"

"Who cares about the sauces?" DeJourno said flippantly. "And who's to say that I won't turn you in for sneaking into the kitchen? But your secret could be safe—though I'd need you to do something for me. Don't play in Wednesday night's EFF match against us. Fake an injury. Oh . . . and join the Mufia. I don't know why our sponsor wants you, but he asked me to give you one last chance."

Jerry looked at Robert like he was crazy—like *he* was the one with pasta hair. That set DeJourno off.

"Do you know who I am, Pasta?" DeJourno spat venomously. "Have you ever heard of my family? We're pureblood Italians, like you. We run the largest frozen Italian food business in America. You could be a part of that great legacy by joining the Mufia. We're not *asking* you to become one of us, Pasta; consider our offer a 'mandatory suggestion.' Don't make the same mistake twice. Or three times. Or however many times it's been, I forget."

Jerry glared defiantly at his nemesis, and as he glared he couldn't help but imagine a knife with a dull blade (DeJourno's tongue) and a fat handle (the rest of DeJourno's body) standing in front of him. Robert DeJourno was not the sharpest tool in the shed—or the kitchen for that matter. But even dull knives can draw blood sometimes if they rub *juuust* hard enough.

"I will *never* join the Mufia. I'd rather choose real friends than belong to your exclusive club! Where you're from doesn't determine how good you can be at something. Pureblood? Hardly! My dad's family is from Italy, but my mom's great-grandparents are from somewhere in Africa. And my best friends here are Ghanaian-American and Indian. A great chef can come from any country and can be any nationality."

DeJourno's chubby face reddened until he looked like his name-sake kitchen—perhaps a large beefsteak variety. "Then you leave me no choice but to turn you in," he snarled.

Jerry merely shrugged. "You'd be stupid to turn me in, Robert. How would you prove it? Besides, you're just as guilty as me—you snuck into the kitchen today too, didn't you? You can tell your 'sponsor' that I'm not interested—never will be. He's wasting his time, and you're wasting mine. This conversation is over."

Jerry turned and walked away, his face splitting into a broad smile, proud of how he had stood up for his principles and spoken his mind. And he didn't even get beaten up for it! Plus Jerry felt like he finally understood the bigger picture as to why Robert DeJourno was so intent on Jerry joining the Mufia: it's what Moldy Coeur wanted. And why did Coeur want Jerry so bad? Jerry only had one guess. It was the old saying: *Keep your friends close and your enemies closer.*

DeJourno shouted ominous parting words that echoed the halls as Jerry turned the corner. "This *conversation* may be over, Pasta—but it'll never be over between me and you!"

At dinner that night, Al Dente announced the date of the final cooking competition. Three days from now . . . Friday night! For the grand finale, each kitchen would select a representative to cook dinner for the faculty. Over the course of the summer, the various kitchens had been awarded points for small competitions, cooking performance in class, and overall grades. And, of course, points had been deducted for naughty behavior, tardiness, and yes, lousy cooking. Based on the current point totals, all the kitchens were locked in a virtual tie! This final competition would determine the winner of The Toque—the chef's hat bestowing not only the title of best kitchen but also awarding the winners a fifty percent fee reduction for the next year's camp.

Al Dente explained why the ultimate competition was mostly an individual one.

"After a summer's worth of learning, we hope you have all taken the time to learn-ah from both your teachers and from-ah each other. As a kitchen, you should be able to select-ah the camper among you who best-ah represents the ideals of cooking that we are trying to instill in-ah you: integrity, perseverance, originality, precision. Two other campers from-ah the kitchen will-ah be allowed to assist-ah the selected chef in cooking the meal."

As dinner was served, Jerry's eyes locked onto the UMZOW sauce boat as it was brought to the table, which turned out to be a divine Sauce Béarnaise that paired perfectly with the flank steak. Flavors of white wine, shallots, and fresh tarragon tickled his palate. Jerry feared his earlier sneak peek at Doctor Sauce's sauce had been his last.

After dinner, as the three best friends walked back to their cabin, Louie G remarked, "Wow, Doctor Sauce really outdid herself today. That sauce was *sick!*"

Mari looked confused. "I don't understand. The sauce was ill?"

Louie G grinned. " 'Sick' is something we say back home when something is awesome or cool," he clarified. "So, yeah, Doctor Sauce's sauce was sick. Try saying *that* five times fast."

But Jerry couldn't say anything at all. He felt sick himself—and not in a good way—knowing he had to tell his friends that their sauce lessons had come to a screeching halt.

The three friends briefly talked about the final cooking competition, and—no surprise—Mari and Louie promised to cast their votes for Jerry as the one to represent Mayon-daise Kitchen. He thanked them for their support, then told them about his run-in with Robert De-Journo and his concern for repercussions.

"Yes, it's way too dangerous to sneak in again, now that that Mufia thug knows everything," Mari lamented. "What a shame. I was hoping we could learn still more from Doctor Sauce—and thank the good doctor personally at the end of camp."

"Well, looking on the bright side, we have learned a lot, haven't we?" Louie G noted.

Jerry and Mari nodded in agreement.

"So no moping! Let's make sure we apply everything we've learned to winning The Toque! Mari and I hereby volunteer as your kitchen assistants!"

Jerry grinned, then informed them, "In the world of professional cooking, you would be known as my sous* chefs."

"Sous chefs, eh? So if we cook poorly, I can tell the judges, 'Hey, sous me!'" Louie G quipped.

"Can we *sue* you for making awful jokes?"

"Admit it. You love me, Mari Nera. You do. Who else can turn that frown upside down?"

"Anyone who can figure out how to shut you up," she teased. "Goodnight, boys."

---

* pronounced *soo*

264

Chapter 27

The Impossible Snatch

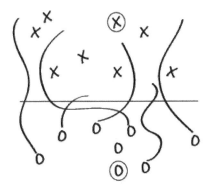

Wednesday night's EFF match came quickly. The Mayon-daise team looked tiny compared to the Tomato squad, but their plan was to use speed and smarts to their advantage. General Louie G would have the team ready. He'd filled notebooks with diagrams of prior Tomato strategies and appropriate countermaneuvers. He had even projected starting positions, noting that Robert DeJourno would probably be a Jackal and Cello Feigni, the Pharaoh.

It seemed as if DeJourno liked the role of defending Jackal for several reasons: it required less running, it gave him a good position from which he could call the shots, and it didn't involve getting pelted with rotted food. Cello had been Pharaoh from Week One, and with her powerful, chiseled frame (like her namesake instrument), she had gotten quite adept at both dodging and catching food thrown her way. Everyone seeing her and DeJourno together often wondered how they could have descended from the same protoplasm. (Maybe upbringing had made the difference. Cello's parents had clearly taught her moderation at the dinner table whereas her cousin's parents clearly had not; anyone could see that from watching DeJourno pilfer food from other's plates in the dining hall.)

The usual referees were already at the field, making preparations for the all-important match. Meat and Potatoes were laying out the fruit: green tomatoes—giving Jerry a bad case of déjà vu, having already had several servings of them recently—overripe tomatoes, and heavily bruised plums and peaches. There were going to be some sore campers the next day, judging by the projectiles. Bones prepared the scoreboard, while Brock Lee made sure the field lines were clearly marked with fresh paint. The two other referees took their places on opposite ends of the field.

With the stage set, the team captains met with Brock Lee in the middle of the field. "I want to see a good clean game, gentlemen," Lee said. "Winner takes all. Only one team of these teams will be etched into Pesto's EFF record books forever. Shake hands, and let's get started."

Jerry Pasta and Robert DeJourno shook hands, then quickly turned to walk back to their end lines. Jerry wasn't one for big speeches, but he pumped up the team by citing respect, teamwork, and determination. "So whether we win or lose, we have every right to hold our heads up. We play fair and refuse to stoop to the level of our opponents."

Louis G added, "No head hunting, no cheap fouls. Mayon-daise does it right! So bring it in!"

The players made a circle, linking arms shoulder to shoulder. In unison, they lightly bounced on their toes, whispering their team chant. The second chant was louder and the bounce firmer. By the third recitation, their volume was a yell, and the bounce was now a bound: "5-2-1-0, Mayon-daise, let's go, let's go!" The players, still linked shoulder to shoulder, were nearly jumping out of their shoes. Finally breaking off, the team exchanged high-fives and fist bumps, psyched and ready to play. Jerry was grateful for Louie G's leadership and feared that his friend would get hurt in today's game—Tomato would be playing for keeps, and as good as Louie G was, he was sure to take some direct hits, even some head shots.

"Be careful out there, Louie G," Jerry cautioned as they took their positions.

He just laughed. "You sound like my mom, Jerry. Like I tell her all the time, 'Careful is my middle name.' Don't worry about me. Just get that egg!"

Ten minutes into the game, Jerry didn't think he'd seen his team ever play worse. Louie G was dodging for his life but still taking an occasional hit. One particular Lumina Foyle rotten-peach rocket nailed him in the left eye. Though a foul was immediately called and points docked, the onslaught continued. To make matters worse, Jerry and Mari were having major difficulty getting the egg safely over the mid-line. They'd found it after about five minutes, but DeJourno had assigned two Jackals—Sean O'Connor and Jude Russell Sprautz—whose sole purpose was to disrupt Jerry's and Mari's every move. Jerry had elected to pick up the egg instead of Mari, the gentleman in him wanting to absorb the brunt of the food punishment—which turned out to be a smart call. The Tomato Jackals threw so hard, Jerry honestly thought he would drop the egg—he seriously doubted they would have made any concessions toward Mari for being a girl—so he slunk down into a low crouch that slowed his progress considerably. It also made his top half a choice target, and despite warnings and penalties from the referees, Tomato Jackals made him pay. Robert DeJourno even left his position of defense to take some nasty potshots at Jerry. The only spot of good news was that meant the Mayon-daise Jackals were able to get some hits on Cello Feigni.

But the halftime whistle blew abruptly when Jerry was only 10 yards from midfield, the Tomato egg in tow. "We award 500 points to the Tomato squad for successful retrieval of the Mayon-daise egg. Current score Tomato 750, Mayon-daise, 300.

They were a mere 250 points from losing! Louie G had been so preoccupied dodging projectiles, he hadn't seen until too late that Tomato Sphinx Mario Bitali had located the Mayon-daise egg, and by the time Louie G alerted his Jackals, Bitali was nearly at midfield.

The entire Mayon-daise squad appeared shell-shocked and utterly defeated during halftime. Slumped shoulders. Bowed heads. No one making eye contact.

Jerry tried to rally his squad.

"We're going to win this game, but we have to believe in ourselves. Sometimes all it takes is a little bit of belief. Guinness, keep up the good defense! Susie and Brad, keep being aggressive! So let's run harder, throw harder, and make Tomato squad wish they'd never shown up today! Let's make this a real fight!" He then looked directly at Louie G. "My friend, you've been single-handedly keeping us in this game with, as you would say, your mad skills. Keep dodging, catching, and buying me some time. I *will* steal their egg and end this if you just give me a little time."

Louie G—his left eye almost swollen shut from the Lumina Foyle foul—grabbed Jerry by the arm and pulled him close. "You sound like me, Jerry Pasta. And I love it! I'll give you all the time in the world to find that egg. My Jackals will score you a few hits too. Let's do this!"

The second half started with a bang. The Mayon-daise Jackals came out with intensity and scored two quick hits on Cello Feigni. Even Sushimi Sashimi, not the most talkative girl, taunted Cello after a green tomato she launched glanced off of Cello's defending left hand, bending her pinkie back and causing Cello to yelp in pain. "Hey, Cello, did'ja break a string?" Sushimi mocked. With the littlest person on the team talking big, everyone else on the Mayon-daise squad played even harder.

In fact, Tomato had seemingly become overconfident. Apparently believing the end was near with the score so lopsided—and tiring from their remorseless offense—they wanted to end the game quickly and sent four Jackals to attack Louie G, with only DeJourno staying back in defense. But despite their determined efforts, Louie G was still dodging everything—and doing so with only one good eye. And the emphasis on attacking the Mayon-daise Pharaoh left Jerry and Mari free to roam the field looking for Tomato's egg. Mari quickly found it in the back right corner of Tomato's field, picked it up without getting even Jerry's attention, and surged toward midfield, showing off her speed and balance.

Robert DeJourno was frenetically trying to keep the Mayon-daise Jackals away from Pharaoh Feigni, but he was focused enough to see Mari booking up the sideline. *"Jackals, she has the egg! Make the wall!"* he screamed.

The attacking Jackals abandoned their assault on Louie G and raced toward Mari, forming a loose wall directly in front of her. Jerry, who had paralleled Mari on the left side of the field, looking for Tomato's egg, knew there was no way he would reach Mari in time to block any throws aimed her way. And a ladle-to-ladle transfer would be too time consuming and risky. According to the scoreboard, Tomato had in fact gotten three hits on Louie G—for some reason the refs weren't calling the obvious penalties— and the score was now Tomato 900, Mayon-daise 500.

Jerry didn't know how much longer Mari could withstand the Tomato Jackal onslaught without dropping the egg. He could think of only one thing to do.

First sprinting up the left sideline, he then cut diagonally to the middle of the field. Mari was holding up well but taking a lot of damage. She was now crawling with her back toward midfield, the egg safely and delicately balanced on her ladle. When Jerry was almost near midfield, he turned and yelled at Mari, "Show me your cricket swing, Mari! Show me your cricket swing *NOW!*"

No one either on the playing field or in the stands other than Louie G knew what Jerry was talking about. In fact, Louie G's immediate reaction was to yell, *"No, Jerry, that's insane!"*

But was it?

It so happened that one afternoon Mari had shown Jerry and Louie

G how cricket—practically the most popular sport in India since the bat-and-ball game was introduced by British colonizers in the mid-18th century—was played. And the only reason Louie G had paid any attention to Mari's explanation of cricket is that she invoked the holy grail of American sports, saying, "Cricket is sort of like baseball—but with more scoring and no gloves." That had gotten Louie G's attention. So now, when Mari stood up, tilted her head back and cocked her arm, Jerry and Louie G knew exactly what was coming.

The Tomato egg launched from Mari's ladle and quickly peaked at forty feet in the air, creating a perfect arc along the way. It was the kind of heroic act that in the movies would be the cue for an intensely dramatic musical piece, a chorus of mournful violas, delicate arpeggios on a piano's high keys, the kind that would have everyone in the audience rapt at such daring. On this playing field, though, it was suddenly deathly quiet as everyone turned to watch the egg in flight, including all five referees.

The egg's destination was all that mattered now. In the bright floodlights of the field, Jerry, face upturned to follow the precious egg's flight pattern, fought the shadows and broke into a full sprint.
Mari's toss had been long enough to cross midfield, but the egg was angled toward the far sideline. Jerry wasn't even sure if it would land in-bounds. But there was no turning back. It was make or break—literally. His cap flew off of his head as he gathered speed. Thank God his hair was rotini tonight—not nearly long enough to obstruct his vision. With eight powerful strides, Jerry closed the distance; in fact, he had intentionally overrun the egg. Reaching his right hand behind and above his head, he swept the ladle gracefully toward the egg, rapidly dropping his right arm at the moment of impact with the ladle, the momentum of his run carrying him forward, the swing of his arm torquing his body

clockwise and downwards into a knees-first slide. From afar he looked like a giant top or a Whirling Dervish, spinning with both arms out. The crowd released a collective gasp. Jerry caught a momentary glimpse of Rita sitting in the bleachers, her hands gripping her head like a vise, a look of panic on her face.

When Jerry finally stopped spinning, he was twelve inches from the right sideline, his body having blazed a path of mud and trampled grass six feet long. His right hand was trembling. It felt weightless.

Jerry only then realized that his eyes had been tightly closed since coming to a halt. They flew open.

The egg was still there.

Brock Lee dashed to the spot where Jerry was kneeling and removed the egg from the ladle. Meat and Potatoes were close behind. They examined the egg for what seemed like an eternity but was actually only about ten seconds. Brock Lee raised his hands and signaled to Bones in his tall chair. The old man raised the megaphone to his lips.

"The egg is intact! Game over! Mayon-daise 1,000, Tomato 900!"

The crowd erupted. Everyone in the stands, save the Tomato Kitchen campers, rushed the field. Louie G, his left eye now completely swollen shut, had already lifted Jerry onto his shoulders and was carrying him around the field for a victory lap.

Amid the din of cheers, Louie G yelled up to Jerry, "If what you did earlier this week was 'The Catch,' I'm calling this one 'The

271

Snatch.' Wow! Talk about snatching victory from—" he had a sudden coughing fit—"from the jaws of defeat! You're a hero, Jerry Pasta"—another coughing fit interrupted his words—"you're a hero!"

Suddenly Jerry felt himself begin to fall, landing on the grass in a partial handstand, his feet hitting the ground a second later. He looked over at Louie G, who had collapsed into a heap onto the field. Louie G was no longer smiling; his mouth was a grimace of distress, and he was gasping for air.

Mari was quickly at his side. "What's wrong, Louie G?"

Louie G continued to struggle to breathe, his eyes widening in panic.

He tried desperately to get his words out, but he wasn't able to utter a single syllable without lapsing into a coughing spasm. He weakly raised his arm and pointed to the center of the EFF field. Nodding, Jerry dashed to the Pharaoh's circle on the Mayon-daise half of the field, leaving the rest of the Mayon-daise EFF squad and his kitchenmates staring after him looking perplexed. Fifty yards away, the referees finally noticed that something was wrong, turning their attention to the commotion surrounding Louie G.

Jerry reached the Pharaoh's stool that Louie G had occupied minutes before and got down on all fours, intently searching the ground, as if he was looking for the egg again.

"Jerry, the game is over! Vhat in the vorld are you doing?!" yelled Brad Vurst, who was on his knees at Louie G's side.

Abruptly Jerry was up again, sprinting back to the group with something clutched tightly in his right hand.

It wasn't an egg.

Reaching Louie G's side, Jerry slid to his knees (almost dramatically as he had minutes ago) and grabbed his friend's right hand, thrusting the object into his palm.

"Hurry! Use it!" Jerry yelled, more of a command than a suggestion.

Louie G uncapped the orange object Jerry had handed him and raised it to his mouth. He licked his lips and took two long breaths, his chest rising dramatically with each one. Within about sixty seconds, Louie G's breathing had slowed. His eyes were more relaxed. His grip looked stronger as he clutched the object in his hand with more confidence. The referees had now joined the crowd of spectators, asking what was going on.

Louie G looked up at Jerry, smiled, and said, "Thanks JP . . . I guess we're even now on the whole life-saving thing—but how did you know about my inhaler?

Jerry shrugged. "It all finally made sense."

A few minutes later, the school nurse arrived to help Louie G to the infirmary where she determined that aside from a fast pulse and a bit of shallow breathing, Louie G was going to be OK. But he would need to stay in the infirmary overnight just to be sure. (Fortunately the school nurse was aware of the EFF matches, and since occasional injuries required her assistance, all involved were thankful that she wasn't kept in the dark concerning this "secret" camp activity.)

Louie G protested, "But I feel a lot better, ma'am. Seriously. I'll be fine." But Nurse Laplant was insistent: Louie G was to spend the night at the infirmary so she could check his vital signs (breathing, heart rate) over the next twelve hours. "Can I at least go celebrate with my crew for a few minutes?" pleaded Louie G.

He was already looking a lot better. His breathing was a bit more relaxed, and he was able to talk in complete sentences now. Finally the nurse acquiesced on the condition that he not overdo his celebrating and return to the infirmary ASAP.

"Yes, ma'am, I promise to take it easy and come back here to sleep," Louie G told her, already heading out of the infirmary with Jerry and Mari at his side.

"You gave us quite a scare," Jerry said.

Mari just nodded quietly and forced a smile, feeling guilty about her comment last night about shutting Louie G up.

"Yeah, sorry about that. But how did you figure out that the inhaler was what I needed?"

"I've seen you reach into your pocket a ton of times here at camp. But you always had your back turned to the rest of us, so I couldn't see what you were doing. But after you saved me from the ICS explosion, I started putting two and two together. You always reached into your pocket before or after exercise or running. And, c'mon, Louie G—you don't think kids in Italy have asthma too? I've got three cousins with it."

Louie G gave Jerry a sheepish smile. "Yeah, I guess it was kind of dumb of me to pretend nothing was wrong." Then his smile blossomed into a wide grin. "I guess I don't like to think that I'm anything but perfect!"

When the three friends returned to the Field of Greens, the referees were ready for the formal presentation of the EFF championship. It was obvious by the looks on their faces that they had never seen anything quite like "The Snatch" before. No one had ever won the Golden Pyramid on a play like that. Not to mention, this was the first time Tomato Kitchen hadn't hoisted the Golden Pyramid in ten years! (Indeed, a lot of the kitchen staff more than doubled their betting money that night— Jerry's food was safe from any unwanted . . . extras.) Jerry gladly accepted the trophy for Mayon-daise Kitchen (a 14-inch-tall plastic gold pyramid) and held it high above his head for all to see.

In the shadows off in the distance, a hulking cloaked figure stood watching everything unfold. Furious, he slammed one pale-fisted hand into the open palm of the other. This was nothing to celebrate.

Last Suppers

It was tough to contain the exhilaration at Thursday's breakfast. Everyone wanted to talk about the one thing they couldn't talk about in front of the faculty. The faculty, in turn, sensed a palpable excitement in the dining hall that morning, but most wrote it off as end-of-camp anticipation and the final cooking competition. But those ex-Pesto-students-turned-faculty knew exactly why the room was abuzz; a few of them might have even watched the game from the shadows and cheered silently as the usually dominant (and obnoxious) Tomato Kitchen lost!

During the EFF celebration in the cabin the previous night, the Mayon-daise campers had unanimously voted Jerry to be their representative for the final cooking competition. Jerry kept his promise to select Mari and Louie G to be his assistants, a choice also met with enthusiasm by the rest of the cabin, and the trio looked forward to representing the Mayon-daise Kitchen.

As he'd assured the nurse, Louie G returned to the infirmary after the night's celebration, and Jerry assumed his pal would be at breakfast the next morning—but Louie G's usual seat beside Jerry remained empty. Jerry figured that the nurse was just being cautious and was keeping him in the infirmary a bit longer to make sure Louie G didn't overexert himself after his severe asthma attack the night before.

The Mayon-daise campers had spent a good portion of that Wednesday evening deliberating what recipe to prepare for the competition, with all of them providing input but ultimately leaving the final decision to Jerry. It was also up to Jerry to choose what dish to prepare for Mayon-daise Kitchen as their final meal at camp on Friday night. Jerry decided on something simple but filling: grilled cheese sandwiches with tomato soup. But he chose it for another reason: it was pure comfort food to him, the kind of meal that made him feel like he was home again. All of the campers felt reasonably homesick at this point, and Jerry wanted them to have that "home" feeling as one of their final Pesto's memories. Something to make them want to come back the next summer and do it all over again. It was the one American meal that Jerry's mom made for him often; Jerry loved the way she made it, but he never tried to make it himself, as if it was some "sacred" Mamma recipe.

Moreover, grilled cheese and tomato soup was the perfect tribute meal to honor the ailing Louie G. In fact, Jerry had practiced making grilled cheese sandwiches with Louie G as part of his "Americanization" process because as Louie G explained, "It's an American classic, JP! What's more American than white bread and American cheese?"

But for the cabin meal, Jerry wanted this "American classic" to have some variety. So he had many different breads available—pumpernickel, rye, whole wheat, multigrain, sourdough, to name a few—as well as a variety of cheeses, including cheddar, provolone, Swiss, Gouda, Havarti, Colby Jack, and, of course, American. If there was one thing Jerry had learned this summer above all else it was that even simple recipes could become gourmet meals purely through great execution—and originality.

Most of Thursday was an "educational day" for the campers to study and prepare for their final exams. To Jerry's surprise and concern, still no Louie G! At the conclusion of classes, Jerry and Mari went by the infirmary and asked if they could peek in on their friend. They were politely told that Louie G was still in recovery and was not in good shape for visitors. Jerry peered around Nurse Laplant, and managed to catch a glimpse of Louie G through the thick-paned glass—and it looked like his friend was wearing an oxygen mask, a thick mist swirling around his head. Louie G's body shuddered in sync with each hacking cough. Trying to keep their alarm in check, Jerry and Mari left the infirmary hopeful that after rest and medical attention, their friend would be his usual self tomorrow.

Back at the cabin, Jerry planned his final meal and finished studying. But at lights out, instead of feeling relaxed and confident, Jerry barely slept, a gnawing feeling brewing inside of him. He finally managed to drift off to sleep, but it was hardly restful. He found himself jogging in that night's dream (or, rather, *nightmare*) on the Field of Greens! He was running circles around something lying in the middle of the field. The "something" was Louie G! And Louie G was lying on a patch of the greenest grass imaginable. Suddenly the green patch of grass he was lying on began to turn to black, as if some toxic mold was taking over, sapping the life out of the grass. Then the mold began enveloping Louie G's body so that Jerry couldn't see where his friend began and the black mold ended. Jerry started profusely sweating—he still couldn't stop running circles around Louie G's body, and he didn't know how to save his friend. And as the sweat beaded on Jerry's skin, his skin began to burn. He was sweating boiling water! Jerry finally managed to stop running and tried to cool himself down by taking off his shirt and fanning himself with his hands, but the boiling sweat continued to pour out of him, and his skin continued to scald. Jerry felt himself passing out in his dream from the searing pain . . . he prayed for it to stop. . . .

"Ouch!!!"

Jerry awoke with a start, finding himself facedown on dusty cabin floor, his nose aching. *Nice. A swell start to the last day of camp! All I need today is a red nose to go with my pasta hair. I can already hear them singing, Jerry, the red-nosed pasta-haired kid, had a very shiny nose . . .' Thank GOD I was on the bottom bunk.*

Jerry rubbed his nose gingerly, hoping that when he was home sleeping in his own bed tomorrow night, the nightmares would end. But who was he kidding? These dreams had been going on for too long. Already lying on his stomach on the floor, he reached under his bunk and pulled out his running shoes to go for his usual morning jog. Of any day, this was definitely one to go for a long, mind-clearing jaunt.

Friday was officially the last day of school, which meant final exams! But as Jerry discovered, and as the teachers had promised, not much studying was required if effort had been put in over the past four weeks.

Exams were done by noon and grades posted an hour later on the Apley Court main bulletin board. Jerry and Mari passed with flying colors. They wondered if Louie G's exams were administered to him in the infirmary, or if he'd have to make them up later.

Friday's lunch was delicious, partly because of relief that exams were over and partly because the lamb dish was served with a splendid Velouté sauce, smooth and velvety. This brought joy to Jerry and Mari because it clued them in that Doctor Sauce was still working her kitchen magic, and that Robert DeJourno had not followed through with his threat to expose her. At the same time, their feelings were bittersweet since Louie G was notably absent. His jovial mood usually kept everyone in good spirits. So while the day seemed to be building up to a climax for Jerry (final cabin dinner followed by the final cooking competition), it just wouldn't be the same without his pal.

That Friday afternoon, Jerry prepared the tomato soup for his kitchen's evening meal. Then he went to the main kitchen to ask the head chef for extra toasters so that multiple grilled cheese sandwiches could be made simultaneously. The head chef obliged Jerry, but it took twenty minutes (with Bones's help) to gather the extra toasters and another twenty minutes to slowly cart them back to the cabin. Jerry arrived to find most of the campers outside enjoying the beautiful summer weather. Mari was proudly teaching them how to play cricket, which they were eager to learn so they could possibly recreate "The Snatch."

A few campers busied themselves in the bunkrooms, already packing their bags. Jerry enlisted a couple of them, along with some of those who'd been playing outside and followed him in, to give him a hand getting the toasters off the cart. He instructed them to begin toasting bread while he stood at the large stove greasing up skillets to make the sandwiches. Lefsa Stovon had already begun warming the soup, which Brad Vurst took advantage of by ladling out a bowlful that he slowly sipped.

"*Das* soup is *gut,* Jerry!" Brad told him enthusiastically.

"Glad you're enjoying it," Jerry replied. "Make sure to save some to dip your grilled cheese sandwich into. That's the American way. It's to die for."

Jerry Pasta's

GRILLED-CHEESE SANDWICH AND HOMEMADE TOMATO SOUP

Soup: Feeds 4 to 6

Sandwiches: Feeds as many as you make!

Soup Preparation time: 5 to 30 minutes (depending on canned versus fresh)

Sandwich Preparation time: 5 to 7 minutes.

INGREDIENTS AND SUPPLIES: SOUP

Ingredients

2 tablespoons olive oil

1 medium onion, coarsely chopped

3 pounds ripe tomatoes, peeled and chopped with
   juices or 3 cans of diced tomatoes

¾ teaspoon salt

¼ teaspoon ground black pepper

1/8 cup chopped fresh rosemary

¼ cup heavy cream or milk (optional)

1 can tomato soup (optional)

Supplies
Large saucepan
Blender

INGREDIENTS AND SUPPLIES: SANDWICH

Ingredients
2 slices of multigrain bread (or bread of your choice)
Pat of butter
Unsalted margarine or cooking spray
1 slice American or cheddar cheese (or cheese of your choice)

Supplies
Toaster
Skillet
Spatula

DIRECTIONS

1. Coat a large saucepan with the olive oil, and sauté the chopped onions until tender and transparent but not browned. Add tomatoes (fresh or diced), and simmer on medium-low heat for about 25 minutes, stirring occasionally. Carefully pour the thick soup into a blender, and puree until smooth. Return the soup to the pot, and stir in salt, pepper, and rosemary to taste. Add cream or milk if creamier soup desired. (Alternatively, you can make tomato soup from a can, but fresh soup is much healthier and tastier!)
2. Lightly toast two slices of bread. Then lightly butter one side of each slice.
3. Place your preferred cheese between the bread slices, buttered side facing out.
4. Lightly grease a skillet with margarine or cooking spray, and heat the skillet to low-medium. Place sandwich in the skillet, and cover with a saucepan

lid. This will help to melt the cheese. When the bread is nicely browned, use a spatula to flip over the sandwich, and brown the other side. The cheese should be melted after a few minutes.

5. Dip into your soup for added flavor!

When the first grilled-cheese sandwich was done, Jerry, grateful for the earlier compliment, personally carried it over to Brad. As he placed the plate on the table, he noticed Brad's face looked . . . pale, almost pea green.

"You feeling OK, Brad?"

Before Brad could respond, Jerry was racing back to the stove where Lefsa was about to dip in with a soup ladle. Shoving Lefsa away from the pot, he grabbed a large slotted spoon and plunged it deep into the soup pot. What came up made Jerry's stomach churn.

Another raw fish. But this time it was *headless!*

Thirty minutes later, after getting Brad to the infirmary, faculty arrived to inspect the scene again with a repeat performance by Chef Moi-Erreur, accompanied by Bones; Moi-Erreur only managed to break two plates this time. Bones disposed of the poisoned soup and carted off the headless fish. Fuming, Jerry focused on finishing the grilled cheese

sandwiches so that at least everyone had something to eat immediately. He then scoured the pot and made a fresh batch of tomato soup—and despite the chaos and the latest attempt at sabotage, everyone enjoyed the meal. There were even a few jokes cracked about the fisherman that Jerry must have angered in a former life. Jerry pretended to be amused, but in truth his confidence was shaken. On the eve of

the big competition, his kitchen had been compromised. *Again!* He was furious.

Mari suddenly stood at the head of the dining table and clanked loudly on her drinking glass with her spoon.

Uh-oh, Jerry said to himself, *Mari looks like she's about to pull a Louie G.*

Clearing her throat (which somehow added to the importance of her announcement), Mari said, "Fellow campers, we've just enjoyed a wonderful farewell dinner here at Presto Pesto's, thanks to Jerry Pasta. When we got here, none of us knew each other. I would venture to guess that some of us did not even know how to cook. Some of us came to camp because our parents wanted us to be here. But after four weeks, I think we can all agree that we *belong* here. We have learned a lot. And we are incredibly lucky to have a great kitchen head chef like Jerry. Sure, he's young, and, yes, his hair makes me laugh. But you cannot say the same about his cooking. He cooks better than most of our parents and even some our teachers; his cooking is nothing to laugh at." She paused and winked at Jerry, adding, "Though, Jerry, if I had one piece of advice, it'd be that most people remove the scales and cook a fish before serving it to others.'"

Jerry laughed loudly along with everyone else. Mari had just done what Jerry thought only Louie G could have pulled off: made him laugh in the middle of a frustrating moment.

"So everyone raise a glass. Here's to Jerry Pasta! Whether he wins tonight or not, he's still our chef and friend with the crazy hair!"

Everyone cheered, glasses raised. Jerry felt the weight of the world lifted off of his shoulders. It felt good to be loved. And it felt great to have good friends.

Amidst the cheers, someone yelled out, "So what are you dishing up for the faculty tonight, Pasta?"

Mari joked, "Might I recommend tomato-soaked filet of fish? It's ready to be served."

Jerry shook his head, chuckling. "Well, if you guys really want to know, it's going to be something ordinary but with a twist. A bit like our meal tonight. It'll reflect what I've learned from cooking with and for all of you this summer."

"Well, what is it?" several campers asked simultaneously.

"Let's just say . . . I'll give all of you the recipe if I win the competition!"

More cheers followed, and Jerry went to gather his cooking utensils and supplies. Opening his satchel, he reached in to make sure his ladle was where he usually packed it. But it wasn't.

Jerry frantically checked the counters and cabinets with no success. He walked to his bunk bed and pulled the sheets back, hoping the heirloom ladle had simply fallen out of his bag by accident. And there it was. Or at least the handle of it.

It had been speared deep in the mouth of the missing—and extremely foul-smelling—fish head.

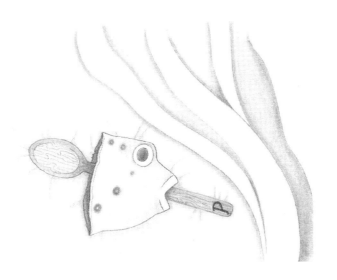

Chapter 29

Betrayed?

Clearly, someone was trying to rattle Jerry before the final competition. But now Jerry was even more determined. He left his ladle handle jammed in the fish's mouth as a reminder that despite everything that had happened at camp, there was nothing magical about his ladle. His *bacchetta magica* was just going to have to sit this one out. Cooking utensils didn't make the meal; the chef did. That was a principle his dad had drilled into him during dozens of cooking lessons over the last several years—they'd cooked masterpieces together using the oldest and dingiest of pots, pans, and utensils.

Focused (and a little pressed for time), Jerry made his way to the main dining hall. In Eaditt Hall, five ICSs had been arranged in the middle of the room, allowing all of the other campers to observe the various chefs at work. Six instructors were seated at a long table at the head of the room, Chefs Beurre, La Gasse, and Moi-Erreur among them. Several of the wards were also in attendance. It goes without saying that Moldy Coeur was present. Jerry and Mari took their places at the ICS assigned to Mayon-daise Kitchen, the only kitchen with just a two-person team. Unsurprisingly, Robert DeJourno, Lumina Foyle, and Cello Feigni represented the Tomato Kitchen at another ICS. When everyone was settled, Al Dente stood to make his announcement.

"We now commence-ah the final cooking competition of the summer. Each chef-ah and team members will have thirty minutes to prepare a complete dinner entrée to be served to the six-ah faculty judges. It is a privilege for you to be cooking for these esteemed experts. I reiterate that since all of the kitchens are currently separated by only a few points-ah, the winner's kitchen will-ah be awarded The Toque, the highest achievement a kitchen can win-ah during the summer. Chefs will-ah be judged as they were in previous competitions. I believe we are ready to begin-ah, but Ward Moldy Coeur would like-ah to make a brief announcement."

Jerry and Mari glanced at each other, expecting to be annoyed by whatever came out of Moldy Coeur's mouth. Coeur's presence was like a dark cloud on a sun-shiney day: expect rain.

"Campers, I was supposed to be catering a meal for the Italian national football team today, but I was called to the school to attend to a grave matter. It is with great satisfaction but regret that I announce that we have found the person responsible for poisoning the Mayon-daise Kitchen not once but twice."

Gasps filled the room. Jerry and Mari exchanged mystified looks.

"We of course had assumed that it was that kitchen's head chef who was responsible for the poorly cooked food, but one of our fine students, Robert DeJourno, has brought some new evidence to light. Thanks to his tip, this individual was caught in the main kitchen before another meal could be poisoned."

"Ooohs" and "ahhhs" echoed across the hall. Paoladinho fainted. Again. Jerry gulped, having a bad feeling about what was about to transpire.

"Bring the offender to the front of the hall for all to see," Moldy demanded.

Jerry cringed as the cloaked, beret-wearing figure was wrestled in front of the main table. *Doctor Sauce?!?!?!?!*

"Raise your face for the campers to see!" barked Moldy Coeur.

The cloaked figure stood erect and defiantly removed "her" beret, and a blond wig fell to the floor in the process. Jerry gasped. The gray-haired figure before them was hardly a stranger.

It was Bones!

But *how?!* The same Bones who had washed his ICS and devoured his leftover breakfast eggs? The same Bones who had hovered outside the Sauce classroom? The Bones who was sideline referee during the EFF matches? The janitor who'd given thoughtful cooking advice, brought Jerry and his friends warm soup (Jerry had guessed that had been a Bones act of kindness), and cleaned up messes he didn't create, without complaint? And since DeJourno claimed to have caught him in the main kitchen, and Bones was wearing the same cloak, beret, and blond hair as Doctor Sauce, it was apparent that Bones actually *was* Doctor Sauce! Mari stood beside Jerry in disbelief. It was like being told Santa Claus was really the next-door neighbor you'd known your whole life.

Even Moldy Coeur stared at Bones, an odd mixture of disgust and disbelief playing on his face. Coeur quickly refocused his (and everyone else's) attention. "The Mayon-daise meals were poisoned by a blow-fish, or puffer fish, whose skin and organs contain some of the world's deadliest toxin. It is fortunate that no students were killed! Thankfully Brad Vurst appears to have ingested very little of the poisoned soup and should make a full recovery." He now aimed his wrath at the janitor. "As someone employed at this school for decades, Monsieur Bones, I think you owe the faculty, the wards, and the students an apology for this heinous violation of our trust before you are locked away in jail for a very long time."

Bones looked around the room. His face bore a pained expression, but behind the expression was a kind of peace.

"I have never poisoned anyone in this school—at least not intentionally," Bones began in a light French accent.

Jerry was only half listening, trying to remember where he had read about blowfish toxin....

"I love this school and have, as you pointed out, worked here for decades. I would never betray Pesto's. I care only about the campers." He now addressed those campers. "The only thing I want you all to remember, especially those of you cooking tonight, is that cooking is in your bones. Be original, not—"

Moldy Coeur cut him off midsentence. "That's enough! Hold him securely until the police arrive to remove him from the premises and cart him off to jail where he belongs."

The room erupted in chaos. Some campers cursed at the old janitor for his misdeeds, and a few even threw cooking utensils at Bones as he was escorted to the back of the room. As Jerry watched the proud old man being hauled away unceremoniously, he didn't believe for a second that Bones had been the poisoner. But he definitely *did* believe that he was, in fact, Doctor Sauce.

"Campers!" Al Dente bellowed, trying to restore order. "It is time for the cooking competition to begin-ah. I am-ah setting the timer *now-ah*. Good luck-ah!"

With little time to dwell on what had just happened, Jerry and Mari sprang into action, Jerry instructing her to slice onions and tomatoes while he readied the other ingredients. Twenty minutes later the sauce was finished. Tasting it with a borrowed ladle, Jerry pronounced it *perfetto*. He then transferred the finished sauce into the sauceboat that had been provided—one of the UMZOW ones used at all the meals.

It was time to cook the pasta. The water was just about at a boil, and Jerry called over his shoulder, "Mari, would you mind getting the pasta from the cupboard while I clean up this sauce spill?"

"Sure thing, JP."

Jerry spun around at the familiar voice. "Louie G! When did you get back?!" Jerry raised his hands to receive his buddy's high fives. Mari surprised Louie G with a quick hug.

"Just a few seconds ago. I didn't think Nurse Laplant was ever going to let me leave. I had to prove to her I knew how to use my inhaler properly . . . with a spacer." Louie G reached into the baggy lower pocket of his cargo shorts and pulled out a long cylindrical plastic tube. "This attaches to my inhaler, like this, and then I take my puffs. It does make a big difference." He shrugged. "I use one at home most of the time. My parents are going to be pretty upset with me when they find out I came to camp *without* my spacer. But in my defense it turns out that was only half the problem. Nurse Laplant said my inhaler expired *three years ago!* So in fact I've been giving myself old medicine for most of the time I've been at camp. But that doesn't make any sense because my mom picked up a new prescription for me the day I left for camp! Nurse Laplant looked through her charts but couldn't find my medical record to verify any of this . . . but, hey, why are we talking about this now? We've got to get that pasta cooked and into a serving bowl!"

"Right you are, Louie G!"

"Um, Jerry, we have a problem," Mari said solemnly, nodding at the open ICS cupboard that usually contained the grains and starches.

Jerry's jaw dropped.

"There's no pasta in this cupboard," Mari said, stating the obvious.

"When have these cupboards NOT contained pasta?" Louie G said.

Mari looked stricken. "Jerry, what can we do?!"

Jerry was incredulous. *How could this have happened?* He looked over at the Tomato Kitchen ICS. Robert DeJourno stood with his arms folded across his chest, his chin lifted triumphantly, his face plastered with a spiteful smirk. On his ICS countertop was a boatload of fresh packages of pasta.

"Dang, I'm getting sick of that guy screwing with us! I should go over there and—"

"No, Louie G," said Jerry, holding his friend back. "I've got a better idea . . . give me your Alabama cap. Now!"

Louie G looked at Jerry like he was nuts.

"I don't have time to explain, I've got to run to the bathroom. Mari, hand me those cooking shears, a large mixing bowl, and a towel," Jerry barked.

Louie G handed Jerry his cap. "OK, here's my cap. You've got a million of 'em back in the cabin, I'm not sure why you didn't wear one of your own today. But if my cap comes back cut up in pieces, I'm gonna—"

"Relax Louie G, your cap is safe."

With a conspiratorial wink, Jerry gathered the supplies and raced toward the boys' bathroom. Some of the staff were whispering to each other, undoubtedly wondering why Jerry would be using the bathroom at such a critical juncture in the competition—especially with those supplies in hand.

Five more minutes elapsed, which meant the competition had less than five minutes left. All of a sudden, the bathroom door burst open, and Jerry came sprinting out, Louie G's cap on his head and a towel-covered bowl cradled in his arms. Practically screeching to a halt in front of the Mayon-daise ICS, he asked, "Did you miss me? How do I look?"

"Great wardrobe change, Jerry," Louie G deadpanned, clearly failing to see the humor in the moment.

"This is no time for joking, boys, we only have two minutes left!" Mari squealed.

"Well, that should be plenty of time to rinse this and serve it onto plates," said Jerry, handing her the covered bowl.

Mari removed the towel. Her eyes widened in amazement. Behind her, Louie G gasped.

"Dude! Where'd you get this cooked pasta from?! Was there a secret stash behind the soap dispenser or something?

"Just get it washed *pronto!* We've got a competition to win!" Jerry shot back, his eyes twinkling with excitement.

"Time's up!" Al Dente yelled about forty-five seconds later.

Jerry and the four other chef contestants were asked to bring one serving of their entrée to a faculty member at the judging table. Jerry carried a plate of pasta in one hand and the sauceboat in the other, still somewhat in disbelief that he'd been able to pull of this meal—especially the pasta part. He placed the plate in front of Al Dente and took a step back.

"This is a bold choice for the final competition. Your pasta and sauce will need to be exceptional to win," Al told Jerry.

Jerry slowly poured the sauce, trying not to spill. And then a wave of sadness hit him. Sadness because the UMZOW sauceboat reminded him that Doctor Sauce, a.k.a. Bones, was being arrested for a crime he likely didn't commit. Sadness because Moldy Coeur's accusation was the ultimate low blow: once Robert DeJourno had told Coeur about Jerry's daily observation of Doctor Sauce (after Jerry's final rejection of the Mufia), Coeur must have known that having Jerry's hero arrested would crush the boy's spirit. *If this is true, Moldy Coeur is even more evil than I thought. He's willing to hurt someone else just to get to me.* But sadness also because if the accusation *was* true, Bones had tried to poison Jerry and his kitchen. *Is he working for Moldy Coeur? Bones had been present after each poisoning incident*, Jerry thought to himself. *But then why would he slap my hand away from the poisonous fish? That doesn't make any sense.* Luckily no one had died from food poisoning.

And the ultimate sadness: fewer than forty-eight hours previously, Jerry's best friend had almost died from an asthma attack. *Would any of this be important if I had lost my friend two days ago?* The thought suddenly struck him that if Moldy Coeur didn't care who got hurt in pursuit of his goal, maybe Louie G's inhaler problems hadn't been an accident!

Jerry fought to keep his emotions in check. *Maybe this is what it feels like to be depressed, feeling overwhelmed by circumstances around you with nothing making sense,* Jerry reflected, his eyes tearing up despite his efforts to remain calm. To distract himself, he stared intently at the sauceboat as he poured so as to not spill onto the sparkling white tablecloth.

As he tipped the sauceboat to pour so that it was almost vertical . . .

Meatballs! The answer has been right in front of me all along!

UMZOW. That wasn't the name of the sauceboat manufacturer as most everyone thought—or just random letters as some others thought.

Jerry almost laughed out loud.

When tilted vertically the letters read . . .

Jerry finished pouring and started walking back to the ICS, sauce-boat in hand. His head was swimming, his thoughts in a fog. *Doctor Sauce, Bones, the sauceboats . . .*

The faculty had begun sampling the meals, passing the plates amongst themselves, nodding in approval. Jerry meandered back to his ICS, where Mari and Louie G were cleaning up. Their mood was somber—Mari had updated Louie G on Bones, who couldn't believe Bones was a bad guy. Jerry, still lost in thought, couldn't lighten the mood the way his American friend could. And even though he'd made

Mamma smile plenty of times during her most depressed moments, and even encouraged Papa during his jobless days, he just couldn't come up with the words to tell his friends, to tell himself.

Until the fog finally cleared.

The sun poked through.

And a lightbulb went off in Jerry's head.

Gazing at the sauceboat one more time, Jerry's eureka moment came when he suddenly remembered his dad's words to him the day he was dropped off at camp: *Cooking is in your bones. Be original, not an everyday chef.*

Immediately, Jerry confidently strode back to the judges' table and announced, as loudly as he could, "Bones can't be the poisoner! He's actually a brilliant saucier!"

Al Dente and Moldy Coeur simultaneously sprang to their feet, faces rife with confusion.

"But that's not why you can't arrest him. You can't arrest him because . . . because you'd be arresting one of the school's founders, Karim de la Carême."

Revelations

Suffice it to say, everyone was in shock. Food fell out of agape faculty mouths. Many of the students snickered derisively. And Robert DeJourno took the opportunity to yell, "Jerry Pasta's finally lost his meatballs!"

Mari and Louie G were about the only ones who didn't immediately think that the anxiety of winning the cooking competition had taken its toll on Jerry's sanity, and they quickly stood supportively at Jerry's side, though even they peered at him skeptically.

"You better have some proof to back up an outlandish claim like that, Pasta," Moldy Coeur growled. Al Dente seemed to be at a complete loss for words.

Jerry didn't hesitate. "I can prove it. But I need access to the basement."

The faculty began whispering among themselves. Mari and Louie G sidled up closer to Jerry.

"Jerry, you know this is culinary suicide. You may be mowing grass for the rest of your life," Louie G warned. "But I believe in you, nonetheless. Once a friend, always a friend."

"I believe in you too, Jerry," Mari added, "and I'll stick by you. But this had better be good, or my mum and dad may permanently ground me if I get kicked out of camp for backing you up."

Jerry looked at his friends and knew they were right. He was taking a huge risk. If he was wrong, he was flushing his Master Chef dreams down the toilet. *And then what would happen to my family? Maybe Papa will never get his job back, the Pasta name permanently smeared because of my failure. And how low could Mamma's depression go? Would she have to be put in the special hospital again?*

But Jerry needed to focus on the challenge he had set up not just for himself but for Mari and Louie G, who also had aspirations and a lot on the line. They had put themselves out on a limb for him in the name of friendship. It was nice not needing to tell Mari and Louie G to trust him—a mark of true friendship. But he did need their help.

Jerry whispered into Mari's ear. She nodded as he spoke and then took off running. He then turned to Louie G, who listened carefully and did likewise. Jerry then faced the faculty and wards, who appeared to have finished an impromptu meeting of their own. Al Dente, acting as the spokesperson, said, "Jerry, what you have alleged tonight-ah is both-ah improbable and ludicrous. Everyone knows-ah that Karim de la Carême died-ah nearly twenty years ago. Yet you claim he stands-ah here before us in the person of-ah the . . . *janitor*. OK, we will allow-ah you to state your evidence; if the initial claims are sufficiently compelling, we will grant-ah your basement access."

Moldy Coeur futilely tried to object, but Jerry boldly began to present his case.

He cleared his throat. "Esteemed instructors, I apologize that my first bit of evidence comes from breaking the rules. You see, I am in awe of the sauces served here at camp. And no disrespect to Chef Beurre, but the sauces served at meals are not the same ones that he taught us to make in class." Chef Beurre's face went pale, a shade lighter than the color of Béchamel sauce. "I needed to see Chef Beurre in action to understand why the sauces were so different—so I confess to sneaking into the kitchen every night for two weeks. What I found was a person

I named Doctor Sauce—who is actually Bones, our janitor—doctoring each and every sauce as if he was a master saucier. Believe me, I am as surprised as the rest of you to find that he is the one responsible for the delectable dinner sauces."

A quiet murmur rumbled amongst the stunned adults who sat before Jerry.

Moldy Coeur interrupted, shaking his head and waving his hands in the air like a traffic cop. "Even if this ridiculous story is true, Pasta, how does this make the janitor the great Karim de la Carême?"

Jerry countered with his own question. "When did Karim de la Carême die? And I mean *exactly* when? And what were the circumstances?" Jerry was a little scared of what the answer would be. From what little he had gleamed from American TV court dramas, this next bit of "evidence" would be considered pure speculation.

The teaching faculty conferred briefly. When Al Dente spoke, his rosy cheeks were redder than usual. "The exact year was 1993. Chef de la Carême retired from teaching Sauces that same year, on the eleventh of January, and he moved back-ah to his country home in Provence, France. Just three days after he retired, Pesto's received word-ah that Carême had died unexpectedly on January fourteenth. The next day the school received delivery of a casket, stating that it contained the remains of Chef de la Carême, and the casket was to be immediately taken to the basement, where it was-ah to be placed beside Presto Pesto's remains." Al paused. "I remember it well-ah. I was still a student. There was a little ceremony, and the casket was indeed placed beside Presto Pesto's coffin. We respected the great chef's request-ah." Al Dente shook his head. "But I still don't see how this-ah relates to Bones."

Jerry responded, "That is what I intend to show you. May I ask, is there an official records keeper here? Because I believe I can prove that Karim de la Carême never actually left the school. I believe the records will show that the person we know as Bones was hired by himself—that is, by Karim de la Carême—not coincidentally around the time of his supposed death!"

At this point, Jerry was sure he was correct. Maybe it was just saying it out loud that gave him such confidence. He was also buying Mari and Louie G some time to complete the tasks he had given them. Moldy Coeur took advantage of the lull to pull Jerry aside and issue a clear threat.

"I warned you about playing for the right team, Jerry Pasta. Don't assume that the money that paid for your camp fees will be there next summer."

The all too familiar sinking feeling hit Jerry's stomach again. *Moldy Coeur was my anonymous donor?!* So he was only there at camp because Coeur, who he now knew to be his enemy, had paid his way. But suddenly Jerry wasn't the least bit surprised. Now Coeur's "Bite the hand that feeds you" comment made complete sense! *What better way to ensure my demise than to bring me to the camp that he personally funds? Nothing that has happened this summer was an accident . . .*

Jerry wrestled his arm from Moldy Coeur's grip. As he glared at him resentfully, Jerry thought how Coeur had grown so much more grotesque looking since his 1993 yearbook photo.

"I'm not so sure the 'right' team and 'your' team are the same thing, Ward Coeur. But thanks for the free ride this summer. I'll be back on my *own* terms next year." Jerry had no idea where all his confidence was coming from, but he hoped it wouldn't run out anytime soon. So he drew on his most dependable recipe for success: he closed his eyes, said a quick prayer, and took a deep cleansing breath. When he reopened his eyes,  he felt older, more mature, as if he'd aged a year in just those few seconds.

It didn't take long for an official records book to be brought to the faculty table. Jerry giddily bounced up and down on his tippy-toes in anticipation. The thick, black, leather-bound book contained all the hires since the school's inception. Jerry did worry whether Karim de la Carême was actually hired under the nickname "Bones."

The suspense didn't last long. Looking over Al Dente's shoulder, Moldy Coeur had a triumphant glint in his eyes.

Al Dente stuttered. "Um-ah, well, um-ah, yes, it appears that on January 15, 1993, Chef de la Carême made a hire. Here is the record:"

Date: January 15, 1993.
Employee: Les Os.
Contract signed and approved by Karim de la Carême.

Moldy Coeur wore a smug smile. "So there you have it Pasta. A hiring, yes, but I'm sorry, no one named Bones."

But it was Jerry's turn to hit back. "*Au contraire, Monsieur Coeur.* I would think that with a French last name, you of all people would be the first person to catch on. Look again."

Moldy Coeur peered at the page again. The color immediately drained from his face.

Jerry continued. "Not only is it odd that Karim de la Carême would hire someone on January fifteenth, 1993, *the day after he died,* but the name is rather obvious. Les Os? Anyone care to translate that from French?"

Chef/Librarian/Inspector Jo Moi-Erreur was the first to yell, "Bones! '*Les Os*' is French for 'bones'! Oh, la, la!"

Jerry beamed. "I think it's time to go to the basement to complete my case."

The room was abuzz with excitement. Bones stood quietly against the back wall, looking down at his feet, avoiding eye contact with everyone. Jerry didn't want to make eye contact with him either, not until all the evidence was revealed. The instructors, wards, and Jerry headed out of the main hall to the basement. Al Dente privately had words with Jerry before proceeding any farther.

"The entrance to the basement is in the main kitchen. This-ah was done for-ah convenience purposes because-ah the basement was the original location of large freezers for food-ah storage, so it made sense that the entrance was in the kitchen. The basement is used very seldom now. I know why-ah you want us to go down there, Jerry. You have made quite the case, and as one of the senior staff, I have convinced the others—some against their wishes—to indulge you. If it wasn't for the stellar, win-  ning meal you prepared tonight-ah, we would likely be calling your parents to come pick-ah you up-ah immediately. I hope you do not make me regret-ah my decision." Al Dente winked before turning to walk to the front of the group.

It took a few seconds before Jerry registered what Al had just let slip: *he had won the competition!* Being told he had made the winning sauce was just the confidence boost Jerry needed as he followed the faculty to the main kitchen. *That means we won The Toque! And I won't need anyone's financial generosity to get back to camp next summer!*

Jerry struggled to refocus on the matter at hand as they trooped to the back of the main kitchen and stopped before a large oak door. Jerry thought to himself, *So this is why I never saw Bones enter the kitchen to doctor the sauce. He was already in the kitchen!*

With Al Dente leading the way, the group descended down a wide staircase that opened up into a long hallway. About twenty yards down the hallway they reached a dimly lit room on the left.

Chef Beurre was the first to nervously comment. "It ees bizarre for zere to be a light on in zat room. Isn't zat zeh Founders' Room?"

"Yes, it is-ah," Al replied. "I assume that's where you want us to go-ah, Jerry?"

Jerry nodded, but before he could open the door, Moldy Coeur headed off the group and spun around, his long black cloak twirling as he stopped at the front of the Founders' Room. "I cannot allow this desecration to continue," he snarled. "Why are we allowing this boy to goad us into committing this atrocity? Let the Founders rest in peace!"

Al Dente held up a hand. "Ward Moldy Coeur, the Founders simply wished to be buried with the school-ah. This room was created so that they—and any faculty member who loved the school as the founders did-ah— could be buried here to be a part of the school-ah forever. So there is no desecration being done here, only respect-ah. So please-ah remove yourself from-ah the doorway."

The power struggle between the head of the school and largest money donor tilted in favor of Al Dente when the faculty animatedly voiced their agreement with the administrator, some out of a sense of faculty loyalty, some from pure curiosity. Al Dente pushed past Moldy Coeur, and the other instructors followed. Jerry was right behind them.

The light in the Founders' Room seemed to emanate from the room's center. For being in the basement, the room was well ventilated and not as dusty as Jerry had expected. Sitting in the light were two large rectangular boxes situated about twenty feet apart.

"This first-ah casket is that of Presto Pesto, born 1910, deceased 1980," Al Dente noted. But Jerry had already continued to the second casket. Behind him, he heard a gasp.

"Is that casket open?" one of the group asked. As they crowded around the coffin, someone turned on an overhead light. The collective gasp seemed to suck all the air out the room.

It wasn't just an open casket. It was a virtual bedroom!

It contained a custom-made mattress, with fresh sheets and pillows. A tiny nightstand was wedged in beside the mattress, holding a clock and an open laptop—the dim light source. Pages of printed text were strewn on the floor around the "bed."

"OK, OK, voila, c'est moi, vraiment."

Everyone turned to the voice. Saddled between two kitchen staff, the cloaked defendant, no longer hunched over, confidently rose to stand at his full height. "I am indeed Karim de la Carême," he announced, pulling off his fake beard and mustache. "You have revealed my true identity, Jerry Pasta. But how did you do it? I have been hidden for nearly eighteen years."

Dessert

Just Des(s)ert

The faculty was beyond words—though Al Dente grinned broadly as did Jerry. Chef Beurre shivered as if he'd just emerged from another dunking booth—this one freezing cold—and chefs Moi-Erreur, Jardin, and Lei looked as if they had seen a ghost. Chef La Gasse inelegantly broke the silence by . . . breaking wind. That certainly broke the tension, eliciting a few chuckles from the group.

Jerry had been saving his choicest words, like a lawyer making closing remarks.

"It was just like you said so often in your book, Chef de la Carême. 'It's in your BONES!' Which I hadn't realized was an acronym, standing for: Be Original, Not an Everyday Saucier.' My dad said virtually those exact words to me when he dropped me off at camp. When he was a student here, he must have read the same book that I've been reading for the last four weeks.

"And after sneaking into the kitchen for the last two weeks, I was convinced that an incredible saucier like Doctor Sauce must have read Carême's book too. It wasn't until I was pouring my sauce tonight that I noticed the markings on the sauceboat spelled BONES when tilted up. Knowing that Karim de la Carême had donated these boats to the school, I began putting two and two together. When I thought through my dad's words and then your tagline, it all clicked. I figured the word 'bones' had special meaning for you, so you chose it as your alias."

Jerry swelled with pride when he saw Carême's face light up at that deduction. He continued. "I found a newspaper article about how you were forced out and placed on probation. I'm not sure why you made everyone think you had died, but you must have loved the school so much that you didn't want to leave, so faking your death was your only way back in. You hired yourself so you could stay close to the place you loved. Forgive me, Monsieur, but how old are you?"

Karim was smiling back at Jerry. "Would you believe I am ninety-five years old? You are one smart chef, young man. But let me say that your disguises and hiding ability are terrible. I did enjoy performing for you in the kitchen these past weeks."

Jerry blushed.

Karim continued his explanation. "I decided to leave the school in 1993 because I had overseen a horrible event. During the Christmas holidays I had cooked an amazing feast for a reunion weekend for faculty and alumni. But something went terribly wrong. Almost everyone got food poisoning except me—I ate while I was cooking and was unscathed. I was disgraced and frustrated. So the wards and trustees forced me out. Were they wrong? I thought that at seventy-seven years old, maybe enough was enough. But I *knew* I hadn't poisoned that meal. I had been framed! I also knew that whoever framed me wanted me far away from the school . . . but I couldn't let that happen.

"So I faked my death and hired myself as an employee. I shipped myself this cozy casket and have been living partially in the basement, partially in the Sauce classroom for the past decades. You always see me by the Sauce classroom because I use the faculty washroom just outside the class and keep a nice supply of clothes in the wardrobe there. So there you have it. I never wanted to leave—and so I didn't. But thank you, clever boy, for finding me out. Maybe now I can officially retire."

"Never mind retirement!" an angry voice interjected. "You may be going to jail—or worse—for violating your probation and serving up more poisoned food. Poisoning children is punishable by death!" Moldy Coeur's voice was filled with malice. Flanked by two armed police guards, Coeur gestured at Carême.

"Not so fast!" Jerry shouted. "I'm not done yet!" He pointed in Coeur's direction, and the ward whipped around to find Mari and Louie G standing behind him with their arms crossed, faces scowling. Clearly they had heard everything and were about to add their own two cents.

Mari was the first to speak. Holding up her tiny video camera, she announced, "I have irrefutable evidence that will completely exonerate Chef de la Carême because it shows who actually twice poisoned the food in Mayon-daise Kitchen. We hid this camera after the first poisoning occurred, and fortunately we had the camera rolling today." Making a *tsk-tsk* sound, she declared in a sing-song voice, "The Mufia club has been *very* naughty, I'm afraid."

The faculty gathered around Mari and watched on the tiny video camera screen, their faces twisting in disgust at the image.

"Furthermore, based on the details of your court case Chef Carême, your probation actually ended years ago. You're a free man!"

Jerry looked at Mari with utter surprise. "How do you know so much about the legal details of his case?"

Mari gave Jerry that know-it-all look she had given him so many times during the summer. "Jerry, seriously, is there anything related to cooking that I haven't known gory details about this summer? I'm a cooking nerd; how could I not know the history of one of our school's cooking legends?" Mari flashed Carême her most syrupy smile and batted her eyes. He winked back.

It was Louie G's turn, and he held up Jerry's satchel. "Here's the bag you asked me to bring, Jerry."

"Thanks, Louie G." Jerry pulled out his *Sauce for the Saucier* textbook and turned to the copyright page, eyes scanning it. Looking up, he grinned. "Just as I had suspected." He nodded at Bones. "You've been busy down here, Chef de la Carême. The first time I opened your book in class, I noticed it was the second edition, and the copyright date was 2001. Yet you were listed as the editor! If my math is correct, that's eight years after your supposed death. Now, I know books are sometimes published after the author dies, but rarely are they *edited* by the deceased author! Which likely means that you've been busy writing in your free time. And something else . . . your hands! I thought the hands used in the book photo looked familiar. It wasn't until I had all the facts in place that I realized I had seen those same hands on Doctor Sauce one day in the kitchen, but it was such a quick glance, I couldn't be sure."

"Right again, Jerry. You certainly have the observational skills to become a Master Chef someday," remarked an impressed Carême, looking down at his scarred hands. "Every great chef has some memorable battle scars."

Jerry could have sworn Carême stole a glance at Jerry's head.

The old chef rubbed the backs of his hands, as if they were somehow flint to spark his memory, and continued. "I published my first edition of *Sauce for the Saucier* in 1990 when I was still the Sauce instructor. That very next year, after the food-poisoning incident and my faked death, I immersed myself in cooking and writing between my janitorial duties. I surreptitiously perfected my art of sauce making upstairs and put the results on paper down here in the basement. My textbook, both first and second editions, was a way of giving back to the students. And my dabbling in sauces for their meals was another." He shook his head. "The Sauce teachers hired since my departure have been an absolute embarrassment. . . ."

Chef Beurre seemed to have melted (like butter) into the back of the room, as if trying to become invisible.

"But I am still writing. Since I purchased this laptop I have been much tidier. I am working on a companion book to my first; I was going to release it under the pseudonym 'Les Os' because obviously authoring a new book under the name Karim de la Carême—even if I had pretended that the work was discovered after my death—would have raised too much suspicion. But I guess I *can* use my real name now, thanks to you, Jeremiah Pasta. And Marirajah Nera. And Kwabena Louis Gyan." That he knew their full names gave the three a real sense of pride. (Being on a first name—heck, full name—basis with the school founder? Not bad, not bad at all.)

The police officers flanking Carême timidly stepped away from him, taking their hands off their holsters. Moldy Coeur's face was as white as whipped cream. He might as well have had a real pie thrown in his face to hide the apparent emotional crisis he was experiencing. Karim de la Carême, on the other hand, appeared overwhelmed with positive emotion, wiping away tears of joy with his food-stained sleeves.

"I had completely lost track of time! I am . . . I am actually free! Thank you, children, thank you!"

The old man clasped the hands of the trio of campers one by one. They, in turn, fought back their own tears—even Louie G, who was not prone to emotional displays.

Jerry then turned to the faculty and wards. "So I guess that clears up everything. Chef de la Carême is innocent of these current charges, and we know who the poisoner is. Can you indulge me with one request, Chef de la Carême? Will you put off retirement to stay at the school and continue to teach us? And maybe make sauce every once in a while?"

Karim de la Carême gripped Jerry by the shoulders, beaming. "It would be my honor. But I would like to have the approval of the teaching faculty."

The instructors in the basement room gave Carême a rousing round of applause, most looking completely awe-struck, truth be told. They were in the presence of a cooking legend! One thought long dead! The wards and trustees who were present (Moldy Coeur now notably absent) also gave their assent, albeit more discreetly, murmuring and nodding approvingly. Jerry duly noted that Carême hadn't asked for *their* approval.

Carême raised an eyebrow. "Come to think of it . . . I suppose technically this is still my school so I could hire myself *again* to resume my role as Sauce instructor. But the support of the faculty is greatly appreciated."

Unwilling to make direct eye contact with Chef Beurre, Karim spoke in his general direction.

"Chef Beurre, you are fired. You were never one of my favorite pupils, you rarely paid attention in class, and you don't even encourage your students to read my book! You weren't always a terrible saucier, but you've gotten lazier over the years. I'm sure you always knew someone was tampering with your kitchen sauces—how could you not?—hence your insecurity with the students. I've long noticed the campers avoiding the dinner sauces, no doubt based on their experiences in your class. Never once have you made a great sauce—yet every time you tasted "your" sauce at mealtimes . . . Tell me, did you believe some miraculous transformation occurred from the stovetop to the table? No miracles, Jo-Guy Beurre—just great cooking from a true saucier. But  I'd also like to thank you. If your sauces weren't so terrible, I wouldn't have stayed around so long."

Jerry couldn't help but giggle.

"And, Jerry. Perhaps Della Morta wasn't as crazy as I always thought she was when she taught here decades ago. In fact, I've been following your story for years and knew you would eventually end up at Pesto's. Perhaps you *are* the chosen one she spoke of. If so, the future of cuisine looks quite bright. After everything I've seen of you these past four weeks, you are quite a catch."

Carême's knowing wink put the finishing touch on an amazing day for Jerry.

He would treasure the famed chef's words for years. *But seriously,* Jerry thought, *is there anyone who* doesn't *care about this prophecy besides me?*

The drama was finally over. Jerry, Mari, and Louie G made their way back through the basement corridor and up the stairwell that led to the main kitchen. As they walked through the kitchen, Jerry abruptly slowed down. His stomach was growling. It occurred to him that he hadn't eaten any of the grilled cheese or tomato soup he'd made for his cabinmates earlier. He was hungry!

"Something wrong, Jerry?" asked Mari.

"Yeah, I'm starving. I wonder if there're any snacks in the fridge," he asked mischievously. He had just exposed the school janitor as actually being the school founder, a scenario that could have ended embarrassingly for Presto Pesto's had Carême actually been arrested, so he figured he was totally entitled to a little scouting expedition. (If Jerry had the *cojones* to raid the off-limits main kitchen fridge, by gosh he was certainly within his rights!)

Jerry sauntered over to the industrial-sized fridge and pulled open the large double doors simultaneously, which required his full body weight. Leaning back, Jerry perused the shelves.

"Well, guys, there's some mozzarella, some yogurt, rack of lamb . . . not really in the mood for lamb though. Olives, fresh trout, grapes . . . I'm sort of in the mood for dessert, something sweet . . ."

"Pssssssttt ... *Pssssst!*" Louie G was desperately trying to get Jerry's attention, but Jerry couldn't hear Louie G's voice *or* the steps approaching over the loud hum of the refrigerator's cooling system.

"Looking for something, Monsieur Pasta?" Jerry craned his head back and looked up. Karim de la Carême was looking back at him. Jerry turned around quickly, almost losing his balance, his right hand trying to close the door as he spun around. But the door didn't budge. Carême's outstretched right arm was holding it open.

"Might I suggest you check the back of the bottom shelf? I usually leave a little late-night snack for myself in a blue container. Consider it a small token of my appreciation for you three. *Bon appétit et bonsoir!*"

Carême walked back to the door leading to the basement. Jerry glanced at Mari and Louie G; their eyes were as wide as his. Looking back into the refrigerator, Jerry quickly spotted the blue Tupperware container behind a quart container of plain yogurt. As Jerry opened the cover, Louie G and Mari sidled up behind him, trying to identify the contents.

Louie G was the first to venture a guess. "It smells sweet, guys, but to be perfectly honest, it looks like maggots swimming in milk."

"EWWW! That's just great Louie G. However hungry Jerry was before, he's surely lost his appetite now," chided Mari.

But Jerry was already dipping his finger into Carême's offering, bringing a dollop of the substance to his mouth.

Mari and Louie G stared at Jerry, waiting for a reaction. They got one: His eyes fluttered dreamily, his lips smacked contentedly.

"Hmmmm . . . one of the greatest snacks ever. I think he makes it better than my mom," said Jerry.

"Geez, Jerry Pasta, don't keep us in suspense! What is that stuff?!" Louie G. demanded.

"Tapioca. And I refuse to leave camp without getting this recipe!"

KARIM DE LA CARÈME'S
TAPIOCA DELIGHT

Feeds 2 to 3 (Makes three 1-cup servings)

Preparation time: 5 to 7 minutes
Cooking time: 10 to 15 minutes

INGREDIENTS AND SUPPLIES

Ingredients

3 tablespoons precooked tapioca pearls (buy at any grocery store)

2 ¾ cups 1-percent or low-fat milk

⅓ cup sugar

1 egg, well beaten

1 teaspoon vanilla

Supplies

Medium-sized saucepan

DIRECTIONS

1. In a medium-sized saucepan, mix the tapioca, milk, sugar, and egg. Let stand for 5 minutes.
2. Cook over medium heat, stirring constantly until fully boiling.
3. Remove from the heat, and stir in the vanilla. Cool the mixture for 20 minutes.
4. Stir again and serve warm or refrigerate and serve chilled.

Chapter 32

Shave the Last Dance

After the dramatic reveal that Karim de la Carême was not only very much alive but had been masquerading as the school janitor, the official announcement of Jerry's win—and hence Mayon-daise's Toque victory—was made.

The kitchen celebrated wildly, hooting loudly, and high fiving each other. For the second time in forty-eight hours a jubilant Jerry was hoisted onto Louie G's shoulders, and with the entire cabin following, the two, made a victory lap around Eaditt Hall accompanied by chants of, "Braise the roof!" and "Pasta rules!"

"I promise my asthma is under control, so I won't drop you this time JP," Louie G said with a wink and a smile.

Jerry thought to himself how his good friend—and Mari too—had carried him quite a bit this summer . . . and not just literally.

As Jerry navigated the room from his lofty perch, he noticed that campers from the other kitchens were politely clapping but unable to mask their disappointment. Robert DeJourno stood stoically with crossed arms and furrowed brow next to Cello Feigni. Jerry figured that his sworn enemy had issues other than The To

If nothing else, he surely was thinking about what fate awaited Lumina Foyle. She had been brusquely ushered away by the police before The Toque winner announcement. Jerry was glad that the girl who had poisoned his friends with raw fish would finally get her just deserts—though her cousin was not going to forget Jerry's role in Lumina's fall from grace anytime soon; now it was personal.

Karim de la Carême was formally presented to the rest of the campers and exonerated of having played any role in the poisoning. Initially, most of the campers awkwardly gawked at the man they previously knew as a janitor; eventually, they were all eager to meet the co-founder of the school, many of them offering apologies for hallway slights and sloppy spills they'd made. Carême graciously accepted their apologies, even autographing a few of the campers' cookbooks. Jerry watched from a distance, happy to see that everyone would soon get to know the great saucier that he'd had the privilege to observe.

When the Mayon-daise campers returned to their cabin, everyone wanted to hear every last detail of the "basement story" again and again—especially the look on Chef Beurre's face when he was fired. At eight o'clock, a voice on the intercom announced that lights out would be extended to eleven, and an end-of-camp celebration would be held at the pavilion.

It was the last night of camp! Jerry had almost forgotten, what with everything that had happened. The kitchens made their way down to the pavilion, which had been transformed into a dance hall. A mirror ball hung from the vaulted ceiling, and an Italian DJ was already blaring music, mostly American, from the bank of equipment he had set up. Miley Cyrus's voice greeted campers as they reached the dance floor, as did the smell of beer and cigarettes. Some of the campers were obviously taking advantage of the dark lighting and minimal faculty supervision to engage in naughty behavior. *Tsk, tsk.*

"This is pretty cool, guys. I could get used to this camp thing," quipped Louie G, as he broke into "the robot." Some of the other campers had started dancing as well (not nearly as well as Louie G), and most were just standing in place with cups in their hands. Louie G's energy was contagious, and soon at least fifty campers were wiggling their arms, legs, butts, and hips (doesn't seem right to call it "dancing"). Jerry wasn't much of a dancer, so he made a beeline to the snack table.

Louie G moonwalked over to Jerry and asked, "You see Christiana anywhere? I have *got* to dance with that girl before the night is over."

Jerry looked up from his plate and scanned the crowd. He pointed out Christiana, who was huddled with a few of her friends on the far side of the dance floor.

"Thanks, Jerry! If I see Rita, I'll send her over."

Jerry knew Louie G wouldn't have to do that. Rita would find him all by herself. She always did. Almost on cue, Rita Grodita appeared virtually out of thin air, grabbing Jerry by the hands and twirling him in a circle. She was wearing a long flowery skirt with a bright-red blouse. She'd even put on a little makeup, though she didn't need it. To Jerry she was beautiful just the way she was.

"You were amazeen tonigh'! I am so proud of jou!" She gave him a sweet, prolonged hug. Jerry braced himself for a kiss that never came— and he was surprised to feel a twinge of disappointment. He was starting to enjoy this whole boyfriend-girlfriend thing. The pavilion was fairly dark now except for a strobe light that had come on. Rita put her hands on Jerry's shoulders. Jerry did his best to move as she moved him, and to keep his eyes on her *face* as she towered over him. They danced for several minutes, and as awkward as he felt, Jerry was actually having fun. Louie G had made his way back to Jerry with Christiana Latte draped on his arm. Jerry continued to clumsily dance, with Louie G admonishing him with cries of, "Go, Jerry, go Jerry, it's your birthday, it's your birthday. . ."

Wait a minute! It is my birthday! Jerry suddenly realized. *It's actually my birthday! June 28th!* In all the excitement, he had forgotten that too! He shouted back at his friend, "Yes, it is my birthday, Louie G! Woo-hoo!"

It took Louie G a few minutes to understand what Jerry was telling him over the loud music. When he finally understood that it was Jerry's actual birthday, he gave his friend a huge bear hug and lifted him off of his feet.

"Happy birthday, JP! What a day to celebrate! This is like your own private birthday party, with all of your camp friends and your girlfriend here to wish you a happy one! If only we had cake.... Wait here! I'll be right back!"

Louie G returned two minutes later with a slice of pound cake that he'd snagged from the refreshments table. Jerry appreciated his friend's gesture and happily accepted the candleless cake. Louie G, Mari, Rita, and Christiana gathered around Jerry and sang the *Happy Birthday* song—in three different languages simultaneously—at the top of their lungs.

I'm finally twelve years old! Jerry told himself. Yes, that still leaves me almost a year younger than all the other kids ... but that doesn't matter. My friends treat me as an equal.

Jerry bowed graciously as they finished singing and then hurriedly ate his slice of pound cake. Not exactly your typical birthday cake—but what *had* been typical about this summer?

Louie G excused himself to get a glass of lemonade and Rita followed to get one for Jerry to wash down his somewhat dry cake. As Rita walked away, Alicia Keys' voice belted out in a hip-hop beat, "New York ... where dreams are made of ... there's nothing you can't do!" Smiling, Jerry looked up at the mirrorball, catching numerous miniature versions of himself still wearing Louie G's red Alabama cap. Despite the locale being Monterubianno, Italy, and not, say, New York, at least for tonight, Jerry did feel like he was on top of the world....

Until he unexpectedly found himself upside down, being dangled by his legs, head inches from the floor. He suddenly felt a sharp pain in his chest, followed by the sensation of all the air rushing out of his lungs. Jerry couldn't even muster a scream. *So that's what a tennis shoe in the solar plexus feels like.* Jerry struggled to see his attackers' faces, but he didn't really have to. He could tell one of them by his smell—Robert DeJourno's signature scent of cheese and perspiration mixed together was unmistakable.

Jerry braced himself for another blow as DeJourno got his retribution for everything he felt Jerry was responsible for, including getting his cousin exposed as the poisoner. DeJourno was about to make good on his promise to send Jerry home as smushed ravioli.

But the next blow never came. Jerry vaguely heard two grunts, and then he crashed to the dance floor, face first. Though dazed, Jerry heard what sounded like a girl yelling. Then something splattered onto the floor immediately next to Jerry's face.

It looked like tomato sauce.

Shifting around, Jerry looked up in time just to see Robert DeJourno holding his nose, backing away from Rita Grodita's raised fist. Before he blacked out, Jerry could only think that this was his second close shave in just a few hours. And that he had just been saved by his feisty older girlfriend. Well, wasn't *that* the icing on the birthday cake. . . .

Chapter 33

One Last Bite

Jerry was relieved that most of the talk after the dance was about Robert DeJourno's broken nose, not Rita's rescue of him, which would have been embarrassing. (And anyone with half a brain knew that the normally gentle Rita would only be this aggressive defending her *hombre,* her "man" for those of you not up on your Spanish.) Still, Jerry couldn't be mad at Rita; she'd probably saved his life—or at least his head and ribs. As it was, he would have to wear a shirt around his mother for several weeks until the bruise healed so he wouldn't have to explain how he'd gotten the large colorful injury to the middle of his chest. If he claimed a cooking accident, like being whacked in the chest with an iron skillet, his mom would never let him come back because camp "wasn't safe for such young children." On the other hand, if she knew the truth . . . well, Jerry would be picking olives at his uncle's farm for the next several summers. Nonetheless, Jerry was determined to add some muscle to his frame before next summer so that he could stand up for himself—not to mention wield that ridiculously heavy wrought-iron pot in Sauce class.

Louie G loudly lamented missing the fight. In his inimitable way, he ran through a short list of all the things he would have done to Robert DeJourno and Cello Feigni had he been there. "And when I was done with them, I'd just snap my fingers and Robert would immediately go make me a sandwich. I'd yell 'jump,' and Cello would simply ask, 'How high?' 'cause that's how I roll!" Before Mari could bring him back to earth, Louie G added, "I know, I'm just showing off—but I wouldn't have to if you hadn't bought tickets to the gun show!" He flexed his biceps, posed like a bodybuilder, and grunted. For what felt like the one hundredth time that summer, Mari responded to Louie G's posturing in her usual way: derisively rolling her eyes.

It was almost time for lights out, and the campers packed their bags in preparation for going home in the morning. As Louie G was stuffing the last of his cooking supplies into his duffel bag, Jerry came over and held out his hand.

"It's been a great summer. Thanks for your friendship."

"And thanks for yours, Jerry," Louie G, gripping Jerry's outstretched hand. "Ready to do it again next year? Hey, maybe during the year you could take a trip to the United States, visit me on my turf. Though I guess it's your turf too, isn't it?"

"I would love that. I do have family there. But it's expensive to fly."

"Hey, it's worth every penny, Jerry. And just think about how much you've saved your parents next summer by winning The Toque! Also, you haven't lived until you've tried Southern barbecue ribs, baked beans, and homemade potato salad."

Jerry groaned. "Just promise me you won't gain thirty pounds between now and when I come to visit you," he ribbed.

"Pasta, I've learned my lesson about moderation in eating. Maybe I'll teach my friends back at home a thing or two. I might even keep running every morning, now that you've gotten me into the routine. And every time I drink sweet tea—or should I say, every time I *think* about drinking sweet tea—I'll curse you under my breath and get a glass of water instead." He became serious for a rare change. "So I guess this is, how do you say it, *a river durkey?*"

Jerry chuckled. "I think you mean *arrivederci*—but close enough. Save your official good-bye for tomorrow morning."

The two shook hands.

Mari had finished packing and came to say her good-byes.

"I'll teach you how to make tandoori chicken next summer, Jerry. Try to stay out of trouble in the meantime."

"Sure thing, Mari," Jerry promised. "And try not to shut down all the fast food restaurants in India or how will you find time to work on your cricket swing?"

The two embraced. As Jerry turned back to his suitcase, Louie G cleared his throat to get Jerry and Mari's attention.

"Hey, JP, as much as I like you, you're not leaving camp with my Alabama cap." He cocked an eyebrow. "And you're definitely not leaving without explaining to Mari and me where the heck you got the pasta for the competition meal. I mean, I know you didn't hide cooked pasta in a bathroom stall . . . did you?"

Jerry laughed. With a flourish, he removed his cap—and his friends let out a collective gasp.

Jerry was bald.

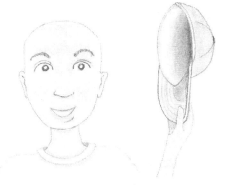

And it was more than apparent where the pasta had come from.

"Wow! I've heard of people winning by the skin of their teeth, which makes absolutely no sense to me. Teeth with skin must come after your adult teeth fall out when you're old. Come to think of it, gums are kind of like teeth with skin," Louie G's imagination carrying him away . . . just a bit. "But winning by a hair? A little too literal for my liking. Tell me you tasted it first, Jerry," cracked Louie G, his face cringing.

"It's multigrain, apparently. And who cares how it tasted to me—the faculty loved it, didn't they? We've got The Toque to prove it!"

Jerry tossed the red cap to Louie G, who caught it in both hands and turned it over a few times, admiring it lovingly. He put his face into the cap and inhaled deeply. Then almost immediately he threw it back to an astonished Jerry, who caught it against his chest.

"It's yours now. You've made incredible memories with that hat. Besides, I can find another one when I get home. Maybe I'll make you a true 'Bama fan someday. Roll Tide, Jerry Pasta!"

Jerry placed the crimson cap on his head, a wave of gratefulness peacefully washing over him. Going with the flow like he had all summer, Jerry responded in kind.

"Roll Tide, Louie G."

The kitchenmates gathered together one last time the next morning, exchanging hugs, email addresses and phone numbers. Before they made their way to the pavilion, where the summer began, Jerry had one last thing to say to his new friends.

"Thank you everyone for your support. I'll miss all of you and hope to see you next summer. We can hold our heads high—we're kitchen champions until someone takes The Toque away from us! And the Golden Pyramid proves we food fight better than anyone else. You all have given me so much. I believe though, that's there's one thing I still owe you."

The Mayon-daise campers looked at each other, unsure of the unpaid debt Jerry spoke of.

And with that, Jerry gave them his award-winning spaghetti and sauce recipe.

Jerry Pasta's WINNING RECIPE
SPAGHETTI AND SAUCE
INGREDIENTS AND SUPPLIES

Ingredients

2 medium-sized onions, diced

¼ cup vegetable oil

1 pound ground beef or ground turkey

1 polish or turkey sausage, sliced

1 small package fresh mushrooms, sliced (optional)

1 tablespoon seasoning salt (or to taste)

½ clove garlic, minced or 2 teaspoons garlic powder

1 tablespoon curry powder

½ to 1 tablespoon Italian herb mixture of rosemary, thyme, oregano, sage

2 fresh tomatoes, diced or 14.5 ounce can diced tomatoes

½ can cream of mushroom soup, undiluted (optional)

28 ounce can tomato puree (or 28 ounce can of tomato sauce)

1 box multigrain or whole-wheat spaghetti (or other pasta of your choice)

Supplies
Large (6 quart or more) saucepan

DIRECTIONS
1. In a large saucepan over medium heat, sauté the onions in the vegetable oil until the onions appear transparent/glassy but not browned.
2. Add the ground meat, the sausage, and the mushrooms. Then stir in the salt, garlic, curry powder, and herb mixture. Cook until the ground meat is browned, stirring occasionally, leaving large meat chunks.
3. If desired, drain up to 1/2 cup of fat from the pan using a spoon or measuring cup.
4 Add the tomatoes (and optional cream of mushroom soup if desired). Cook uncovered over medium heat for 10 minutes to allow excess water to evaporate.
5. Add the tomato puree, and simmer over medium heat for 20 minutes.
6. Meanwhile, heat 3 quarts of water to a boil. Add the pasta and cook according to package directions until al dente or desired firmness. Drain.
7. Serve the sauce over the pasta. Enjoy!

Rita stopped by the Mayon-daise cabin to say her good-byes. Naturally, Jerry's bunk was her last stop. "*Hasta la vista*, Herry Pasta.* Jou have taught me so much this sommer. I've changed so much thanks to

---
*   Hasta la vista is Spanish for "until we meet again" or simply "see ya later"

jou. I will miss jou." As she gave him one last hug, she whispered in his ear. "Never stop believing in jourself, Herry Pasta. Maybe jou no save the world this sommer, but jou save *me*. And I am very grateful. I see jou next sommer, yes?" Jerry pulled back from Rita, but not completely. What he was about to do, he'd only seen in the movies. He held Rita's face in his hands and looked directly into her eyes. Then he closed his own, stood on his tiptoes, and moved in for a kiss.

Smooooch!

The kiss felt amazing! But something else felt just a little funny. Jerry opened his eyes. Having regrown overnight, a solitary squiggle of angel pasta hair had slipped out from under Jerry's new Alabama cap and wedged itself between the lovers' lips.

Rita's mouth broke into a wide smile. "This is the first time I touch jour hair all summer. I love jou and jour pasta hair. It deserve that kiss!"

Jerry could not argue with her at all.

"There's just one thing, Rita."

"Yes, Herry?"

Jerry winced.

"Uh, yeah . . . It's just a small request."

"What, Herry? I listening."

"Could you pretend . . . pretend my name is spelled with a *y*?

"But jour name is spelled with a *y*. J-E-R-R-Y. Jou know this."

"I mean at the front. A *Y* instead of a *J* at the front."

"*Y*-E-R-R-Y? But that spells Jerry."

"Exactly."

Jerry kissed her again before she could respond, the kiss lasting a full six seconds. Rita's eyes widened midkiss when she finally understood.

She kissed him back with

mucho gusto.

Most of the campers were picked up by their parents by noon on Saturday. Some of those who had international departures would be leaving on red-eye flights later in the day. Jerry called his parents and told them to come later because Pesto's had made a special request of him: make his winning spaghetti recipe for the entire faculty's lunch on Saturday. It was a way to honor Jerry for all he had accomplished that summer—plus an opportunity for him to cook for his new hero, Karim de la Carême.

This time Jerry didn't have to worry about ingredients, especially the pasta. He was given enough multigrain angel hair pasta to feed a small army. Everything he needed was provided to him as he prepared his spaghetti sauce—including assistants! With the sauce simmering and the pasta boiling, Jerry ducked out of the kitchen to make sure that the tables were set and the teaching faculty ready to eat. There was nothing like having food ready without mouths to feed. He returned to the kitchen about a minute later to check on the pasta.

He was about six feet away from the stove when the pot erupted, spraying boiling water and pasta everywhere. The noise was ear-splitting, a cross between a mechanic's shop and a busy fire station. As if he was back on the Field of Greens, Jerry dove to his right in the nick of time, hiding behind a rack of freshly baked bread, as scalding pasta and water splashed chaotically and smoke filled the kitchen.

The assistants came running in when they heard the commotion. Al Dente and Karim de la Carême were close behind them. "What happened in here, Jerry?"

"I don't know, sir! The pot of pasta just suddenly exploded . . . I don't know—"

Jerry suddenly felt lightheaded, like he'd been drugged. His head was spinning. *Am I dreaming?* Someone was laying him on the floor, a cold towel placed on his forehead. As his senses cleared, Jerry realized he'd been hyperventilating. His breathing was now more even.

Al Dente knelt at his side. "Jerry, one of the kitchen staff-ah found remnants of what looked like firecrackers in-ah your pot. Someone does not want you to succeed. Tread-ah carefully, my boy, tread-ah carefully. I promise to do my best to keep-ah you safe while you are here at Pesto's. I made that promise to your father, and I intend-ah to keep it."

Another pot of pasta was cooked, and Jerry's meal with the faculty was a huge success. Karim de la Carême gave him two thumbs up, like he'd done at the Sauce booth at the Skills fair, but he also pulled him aside for a private conversation.

"You are no everyday saucier, Jerry Pasta. You are the future of cooking, and this old chef is honored to have made your acquaintance. I have been waiting for you for quite some time. During my . . . let's call it my sabbatical, I had eighteen years to reflect on my legacy at Pesto's. It was depressing to watch the school I created slowly be taken over by powerful private interests; the wards and trustees use their money to manipulate the school in ways I never imagined. When Presto and I first formed the directorial board of wards and trustees, we were simply hoping to make the school more financially secure, sustainable for future generations. Instead, the board has used their influence to affect almost every aspect of the day-to-day running of the school. It's more a business than a school. Year-long formal cooking training became four-week summer camp; the board figured we could charge almost as much money for far less teaching time. I'm no longer confident that our graduating Master Chefs are learning how to cook *the right way*."

Carême paused, gathering his thoughts. He looked to be fighting back tears. "Now that I am back, I hope that with the help of dedicated faculty and students like you, we can begin the process of restoring Italian cuisine, with Pesto's as the cooking utensil."

Hairy didn't know what to say. Was Carême saying he believed the prophecy too? *When are people going to realize that I'm just an elev-*

en-year-old—now twelve, I guess—boy with weird hair?

Carême continued. "Moldy Coeur is dangerous. You no doubt see the parallels between what happened to me almost twenty years ago and what has happened to you this summer. He is playing for keeps, Jerry. I did my best to keep an eye on you this summer, like Al asked me to, but Coeur is getting too powerful, he has too much influence."

Jerry was in shock. "Wait . . . *what?* Al Dente asked you to watch over me? Are you saying he knew . . . he knew who you were all along?"

"It's a little more complicated than that, and it's probably for your own safety that you don't know the details. Just know this: You must believe in yourself. Right now, you are filled with doubt, so much like your father—another great chef—was. But you must learn to believe."

Jerry was stunned into silence.

Jerry's parents arrived a few hours later. Toni and Olive were overjoyed to see their son and proud beyond words for the awards he'd won—though Jerry held back on telling them about the scholarship money that accompanied The Toque. And he knew not to mention the Golden Pyramid, at least not in front of his mother, who actually seemed to be doing very well. *She's either just happy to see me or she's actually been taking her medicine. Maybe both?*

During the ride home, Jerry answered his parents' many questions—What was your favorite experience? How many new friends did you make? Do you want to return next year if we can afford it?—as best he could without causing them any concern, but he made sure to leave out any stories with even a remote hint of danger. He didn't want to alarm them, after all. They would never let him return to camp if they thought his life was in any danger.

Karim de la Carême's words about Toni Pasta being a great chef but one filled with doubt echoed in Jerry's head, and his final near-death encounter continued to claw at his insides. *What did Carême mean by what he said about Papa? And what lasting enemies have I made this summer? Was Moldy Coeur behind every bad thing that happened—the poisonings, the exploding ICS during the Skills Fair, Louie G's asthma attack, the pot of pasta that nearly killed me an hour ago?* Maybe camp wasn't as safe as he'd thought—his parents were right to be anxious.

Jerry struggled to see the bigger picture that Carême had alluded to earlier. Did some of the faculty and wards feel upstaged by a peculiar eleven- (now twelve-) year-old boy who had singlehandedly saved the school's reputation? Pesto's would have been the laughingstock of the culinary world had Bones been arrested and his identity later revealed as Karim de la Carême, especially if the evidence of the true poisoner had never come to light. The school might have been closed down permanently for endangering children. *I guess they should be thanking me,* he told himself.

Jerry dreamily gazed out the car window. *Next summer I will be older, wiser, stronger, and more prepared to face new challenges.* He wasn't going to spend the intervening year thinking about silly prophecies or evil people trying to hurt him. And he wasn't ready to believe that in some fantasy world, he was special because he was the "chosen one."

Yeah, maybe he *was* special. Maybe it was his cooking. Maybe it was his weird hair. He thought wryly how his hair had proven to be quite the asset at camp, something Jerry would have never expected since for so long it had been a source of ridicule and embarrassment. Recently, his hair had begun to represent all the grand expectations people had for him, which made him even more resentful of the pasta locks. Jerry wanted to be special not because people thought he was *supposed* to be, but because he actually *was*. He didn't want to be an extraordinary chef because of the expectations of some magical prophecy; he wanted to be extraordinary because he expected it of himself—Chef de la Carême's book and four weeks of camp had taught him that. *Be original, not an everyday twelve-year-old.*

Jerry knew he would need to stay focused on reality. And the reality he had learned this summer was that cooking wasn't magic. But learning and experiencing the art of cooking could certainly be a magical experience.

"You failed me. Miserably, I might add."

"Sorry."

"You should be sorry! Actually, you should say 'sorry' to Jerry Pasta because by this time next summer he will wish he was dead." The festering man smiled wickedly. "I have not shown the full reach of my power by any means—and at least I know the boy will be back next summer, at half price."

"So . . . uh . . . do I still get a reward? Somethin' for all my troubles?"

"Foolish boy. Perhaps you could have not gotten humiliated by an eleven-year-old runt all summer! Your reward is that you get another chance *next* summer to prove your worth to me by finishing the job I gave you. You are lucky that your parents and I are such close business partners. Otherwise you'd be home flipping burgers next summer.

"And I think I would avoid surgery. The crooked nose makes you look fierce—you're more grizzly bear and less panda now."

A plane buzzed overhead. The man pulled something out of his pocket.

"You want a reward? Here's a coupon for a free milkshake at Fasta Pasta. There's one at Terminal B . . . ."

Epilogue

So there you have it. Just the beginning of Jerry Pasta's saucy tale (sorry about all the hugging and smooching—just reporting the facts). Jerry saved "food" in more ways than one. He saved one of the great sauce makers of all-time in Karim de la Carême, thereby saving our meals at Pesto's. Heck, he saved the entire school, which by the transitive property (something I learned in Algebra class last week), he saved your meals too. How, you ask? By saving culinary school, Jerry saved the pipeline of great food that begins at culinary school and ends up on your plate. No culinary school equals no Wolfgang Puck or Gordon Ramsay or Emeril recipes for you to enjoy at dinner next week. These great chefs get their food into your kitchen and local restaurants every day via the person that cooks for you (Mom? Dad? A neighborhood chef?) and you don't even know it most of the time. You really think yo' mama came up with redeye mole chili, balsamic glazed chicken with grilled radicchio, or apple-smoked bacon, white cheddar potato omelettes all by herself? Think again.

And if you think *I'm* forgetting something, you're wrong: Jerry saved my life at camp, and I'm forever grateful.

But Jerry's war with Moldy Coeur and his followers (henceforth called "The AntiPasta") had only begun. Moldy Coeur was willing to hurt people Jerry loved (Doctor Sauce/Bones/Carême's near arrest, blowfish poisonings), but how far would Coeur go?

And you're probably wondering what I really think about all this. Do I think Jerry is the hero in the Morta prophecy? Maybe. But does it really matter what I think? Jerry needs to believe the prophecy for any of this to matter: he believes, we win. He doesn't, we lose. It's that simple. Heroes have to believe in themselves; isn't that what the whole summer was about, anyway?

And you've probably guessed who I am, your willing narrator: Pharaoh extraordinaire, Jerry Pasta confidante, handsome chef from the Southside, the rammer jammer yellow hammer from Alabammer. But don't tell Jerry I wrote this, OK? And I know you're ready for more, but please: be patient. Allow this one to settle. This was just the first five-course meal; there are many more to come.

About the Author

A graduate of Harvard College and the Yale School of Medicine, Kwabena "Bobo" Blankson is a pediatrician with subspecialty training in Adolescent Medicine. He has over 13 years of military experience. Dr. Bobo has published in peer-reviewed journals on adolescent health-care utilization, obesity and energy-drink consumption and has been featured on NYTimes.com, HuffingtonPost.com, CNN.com, Time.com, Forbes.com, CBSnews.com and more. He is passionate about teen and young adult health, and in 2015 he joined Girls to Women Health and Wellness, a medical practice in Dallas, to help launch Young Men's Health and Wellness. He is also a medical consultant with GoodThink, a positive psychology consulting firm. His hobbies include sports, music, video gaming, reading, and obviously cooking. Dr. Bobo lives in Dallas with his wife and three daughters.

www.doctorbobo.org   www.thesauciersbones.com

Made in the USA
Middletown, DE
05 November 2015